I0671237

A LUCKY SHOT

A NOVEL

A BLUEBIRD SKY
BOOK 2

ELLORY DOUGLAS

A LUCKY SHOT

a novel

*for everyone who needs to make themselves a priority
and everyone who needs to ignore his text*

or wouldn't mind unlocking a new kink

To a billion stars across a billion galaxies.
In every version of every universe.
I will follow you anywhere.

Dr. Donovan Rykoff, *Sirius Darker*

PROLOGUE

SHE WOULDN'T BE HERE IF SHE COULD JUST IGNORE HIS TEXT.

She could be movie marathoning with Libby, wearing comfy pants, and indifferent to the frizz level of her hair.

Instead, Cassidy St. Claire was praying her back would forgive her for wearing shoes without arch support.

But ignoring him was her weakness. An Achilles heel swapped for some other body part, defenseless against his charms.

No. Not charms.

Wiles.

She peeked over the top of her menu at the man smoldering beside her. It wasn't her fault a corner of his mouth ticked up in a way that turned any smile cheeky. Or that the man knew how to dress to show off his athletic body. Or how his faint accent rolled over her ears like auditory catnip.

Tonight, his dark eyes had cruised over every inch of her curves when he met her in the lobby of the exclusive restaurant, and his brilliant grin sent a flutter straight to the silky seam of her black underwear.

"Hey, gorgeous. You ready for some fun tonight?" His whisper in her ear sent a cascade of goosebumps down her neck.

Catnip.

Fine. She had a lot of weaknesses where Nick was concerned. Including remembering that approximately half the women in a two-kilometer radius were susceptible to the same wiles she was.

He'd flirted with the coat check girl, who batted her lashes at him. He'd left the hostess giggling like a schoolgirl chatting up her crush. Even the server, whose job was to act interested in the hopes of a good tip, lingered at their table longer than necessary.

Cass was a fifth wheel on her own double date.

The couple across from her traded doe-eyed glances, fingertips trailing over each other. Cass picked at the edges of her salad and peeked at her date's hands, firmly on his side of the table. Hands that had explored her entire body, but fingers that never interlaced with hers. She swallowed her envy along with a ripened tomato and stared out the picture windows.

"The tarte tatin looks delicious." Jill bit her lip. "But so does the lemon cheesecake."

"Get them both and I'll eat what you don't," Alex said, and whatever Jill whispered into his ear shook his shoulders.

Nick blinded the server with his thousand-watt smile. "What's the most delicious thing I could eat here?"

"Oh, um, everything you see would be delicious," she flustered out, then pointed at the menu and added in a low voice, "but this will melt in your mouth." She turned an awkward glance at Cass. "What would you like, miss?"

To be wrapped up in the tablecloth and defenestrated? Forty floors to the pavement below would give her enough time to rethink every one of her life choices that led to opening his text that night.

Cass folded the menu. "I'd like what she's having, please."

The gilded bathroom looked like it should have its own cover charge, and Cass stepped up to the rows of deep copper sinks. The ridiculous riot of curls she'd tried to tame refused to behave. She adjusted a willful strand and applied a fresh layer of her signature Ruby Woo.

Bold lipstick equalled big confidence. She needed it.

"You two are just the cutest," Cass said. "I've never met Alex before, but Nick talks about him all the time. I don't know what he was so worried about."

Jill stilled, avoiding Cass's eyes in the mirror. "Oh?"

"I just mean," Cass continued, trying to extract her foot from her mouth, "he gets a little twitchy where Alex is concerned. They've been friends a long time. But I think he warmed up to you quickly."

"Right." Jill made a doubtful noise in her throat. "So, you and Nick have been together for a while?"

Did a year of an on-again, off-again situationship count? Cass managed what she hoped was a genuine smile and shrugged a shoulder. "We can't seem to figure each other out."

That was one way of putting it.

Jill's fair brows drew together. It didn't take an empath to pick out the concern in the storm of emotion that crossed her face. "Well, I hope you figure out what's best for you."

All that time not-exactly together, it seemed more unlikely by the minute.

Jill fiddled with her lip gloss a moment and added, "That textiles exhibit you mentioned sounds fun. Maybe I could tag along?"

The exhibit Cass had raved about while Nick ignored her to snag Alex's focus away from his date. Jill had listened with rapt attention.

A genuine bubble of excitement inflated Cass's chest for the first time in hours. "Absolutely, but it's only here for a few days, and it's selling out fast, and be warned I'll talk your ear off, and there's a whole bondage section that I need to check out for an upcoming erotic Shakespeare production I'm working on." Cass stopped to draw breath and lowered her waving hands. "I'll send you a text, if you're still interested?"

"Erotic Shakespeare production?" Jill choked on a laugh. "I can't wait."

Her new friend floated across the restaurant to her boyfriend, leaving Cass to find her date for round two of their night.

Dancing. Which used to be her favourite. He wouldn't try to merengue with her. Or maybe he would. It was highly unlikely he planned to bring her to the type of place where it would be on the playlist anyway.

Cass hitched up the corners of her mouth and slid beside her maybe-dancing partner at the restaurant's front. His eyes scanned from Alex, to Jill, and back to Alex, watching as his friend wrapped his new girlfriend in an embrace.

"I've never seen him hand over his balls so fast."

Something tilted under Cass's ribs. Is that what he called open affection? The hope of getting similar attention vanished with the last of her energy.

Nick turned on the smile that usually made Cass giggle like she'd downed a glass of champagne. The smile was directed at the tittering attendant, who nearly prostrated herself over the counter.

Nick's a flirty guy. He's like this with everyone. Cass pretended she didn't see the attendant slip something in his pocket.

The club bounced with bodies and heat. It was the last thing she'd have chosen to do. The music pulsed, the crowd vibed, and her feet protested after a long day on set, even with the painkiller she took before dinner. Cass dug her thumbs into the small of her back and waited for the bartender to pour the vodka and sodas.

This was still a date, and that was something. Dinner, dancing, a chance to dress up. The hour she'd agonized in front of her closet hadn't been for nothing. The plunging neckline of her French navy-blue jumpsuit earned an appreciative double take from the bartender, and although she couldn't wear the heels she'd bought to go with it anymore, the gold Mary Janes looked gorgeous.

Not as gorgeous as the woman currently trailing her fingers up Nick's arm. She was tall and blonde and everything Cass wasn't. And she looked like she was about to crawl into his pants.

The condensation from the drinks dripped over her fingers as she held her breath, waiting for Nick's response. Would he brush her hand away? Or would he lean in and whisper in the woman's ear, like he'd done with Cass only hours ago?

Why would she wait to find out something that shouldn't be a guess.

She tipped one vodka and soda into her mouth, chased it with the second, and escaped without a backwards glance.

At 12:37 a.m. on a Saturday morning in the back of an Uber, Cassidy St. Claire decided she'd had enough of Nicholas Martin. For good this time.

Probably.

Meanwhile, down a back alley in Vancouver's West End

GOD, HE HATED NIGHT SHOOTS.

Josh Graham pulled the collar of his jacket tighter around his neck in a futile attempt to ward off the unseasonable chill and glowered at the crew like they had ordered the rain to personally piss him off. He raked the dark strands out of his bloodshot eyes. Any effort into styling his hair sixteen hours ago was long undone by now.

The black night ejected tepid sheets of rain over the set, seeping through the tents and permeating every layer he wore. Water smoked off the lights, glare reflecting off every surface and, even from up here, he could see the actors squinting into the downpour when they should be wide-eyed in awe. How the director could see the blocking through the downpour was a mystery. Even if he could see it, the shot was a loss. Unsalvageable, even in post. Not like they had a budget to fix anything.

Of course it was raining. The entire week had called for clear skies and balmy temperatures. Then this. The shoot should have ended hours ago. If they didn't call it a night soon, they'd be on the hook for union breaks, too. Not like anyone would want to eat right now. The stench of garbage from the back alley coated the inside of his nose in an oily sheen. Breathing through his mouth didn't help.

Still.

They had finally nailed the tracking shots. Got the B-roll for the exteriors. And he'd convinced the director to go ahead with the shoots, using the rain instead of the golden hour glow they'd planned on. The lead actress's close ups, her teeth bared to the sky and mascara artfully streaking down her cheeks in inky rivers with the light spangling through the rain behind her? It would be the money shot in every trailer.

Come to think of it, it had been a pretty good fucking day. No number of soaked toes or botched takes or repositioning of lights could hinder the fact that they made magic.

Plus, he had promised Isabella he'd text her if they wrapped the shoot by midnight. If his feet were soaked, at least his dick could get wet tonight, too.

Fucking call it already.

As predicted, after another fizzled take, the director gave the crew the long-overdue permission to wrap for the night to a round of weak cheers.

Half past midnight. Isabella would forgive him.

Josh whipped out his phone to scroll through his contacts, but Emily's name popped up before Isabella.

Emily (Hanson or Harris idk) blonde, 5'7", 8/10 head, spanking. Not his preferred kink, but as long as she didn't want to escalate, he could play.

He twisted his lips in thought. Isabella had a killer ass, but Emily was a professional cheerleader.

hey beautiful. wyd?

You, hopefully <3

Excellent.

CHAPTER ONE

CASS

If she'd forgotten her phone again, she was sewing a new pocket into every pair of her pants so she'd have no excuse not to have it attached to her body.

Cass rooted in her bag, shoving gum wrappers and receipts to the side. She could almost visualize herself grabbing it before leaving set that morning ... or was that yesterday? She dropped her eyes from the lights where she waited for the red to turn green and rooted deeper.

It's not like she needed her phone at this exact moment. Brunch was always the same time, the same place, and up until the last couple of years, the same five people. She wasn't expecting an urgent text, but still. It could happen. Her friends wouldn't be wondering where she was yet. Fifteen minutes late was almost early for her.

But her sister might call. Or her brother. Or the head of costume on the TV show Cass was working on, wondering where the design portfolios were stashed. Which were probably on the floor of the wardrobe closet. With her phone on top of them.

Shoot, or maybe she left it at her sister's place after babysitting last night?

She blew a loose curl out of her eye. Maybe there was a scrunchie in there, too. Her fingers closed around the case, and she breathed a sigh of relief.

Now, where did that leave the design portfolios? It didn't matter, she could head back after brunch and find it. Unless it was at home.

Double shoot.

A car horn blared behind her, and her eyes popped up to the now green light. It couldn't have been more than a two second delay, but she still mouthed *Sorry!* into the rearview mirror as she lurched her truck forward. The finger in reply answered her.

"Dick!" Libby yelled out the truck's passenger window. Her best friend sank back, unperturbed, wedging her toolbox between her feet. "It's barely noon. How hot can his date be?"

"It was my fault. What if he's late to his daughter's birthday party or something?"

"His inability to plan does not make an emergency on your part."

Cass passed her phone to Libby without taking her eyes from the road. "Did Terry say we need to come back to set later this afternoon?"

Libby tapped in Cass's passcode from memory and scrolled. Her face scrunched. "Nope, but it looks like Raina can't make it again."

A familiar disappointment settled behind Cass's breastbone. This was the third brunch in a row Raina had blown off. "Why?"

"Her husband is sick, and she needs to stay with the kids."

Last time she bailed, she had needed to bring her daughter to a Mommy and Me ballet class. The time before that had been an emergency trip to the craft store to make party favours for her son's birthday after her husband had done the unthinkable and bought Superman plates instead of Spiderman.

But kids ranked over friends. Every time.

"Of course. Understandable," Cass said softly, and pulled up in front of the diner. At least now she'd avoid another of

Raina's lectures about Cass and Libby getting back into the dating pool. The shallow, toxic dating pool. At least she assumed it still was.

Chatter and the clinking of cutlery poured through the diner's front door, sending the familiar scent of sausages and hash browns wafting over her. While the staff had rotated through a hundred university students slinging greasy breakfasts between classes, the yellow paint and black-and-white tiled floors hadn't changed since before she could tie her shoes.

Cass waved at the line chef through the pass-through window, who smiled back. They'd gone on a couple dates a few years ago, but Cass broke it off when he insisted he wasn't looking for anything serious. Awkwardly running into him with his new girlfriend a few months later proved he was fine with something serious. Just not with her.

He still slipped extra slices of bacon on her plate as a gesture of goodwill.

More bacon instead of lame dates watching him play acoustic guitar? A decent trade, honestly. Besides, it stopped being weird seeing him several situationships ago.

Jill sat solo at their usual booth and sprang up to greet her and Libby with a crushing hug. Cass slid across the red plastic bench, worn smooth by the butts of a thousand families before them, Libby crashing in after her in a storm of faded turquoise hair.

Cass picked strands of Libby's hair out of her mouth and didn't bother asking where the other girls were. They would all be variations of the same excuse. Kids, significant others, work.

At least ever since Jill joined their circle, the only brunch date she'd missed was when she'd been out of town. Even if it meant she came straight from the shelter with cat hair still on her clothes.

Cass would take a cat hair-covered friend over an absent friend any day.

Their server circled by their table seconds later for their

orders, and Cass turned to her friend who was always pretty, but today glowed like she had swallowed the sun.

"So, is it just us today?" Jill was shredding her napkin into ribbons, and from the way she was jackhammering in her seat, Cass knew her friend's foot was bobbing in triple time under the table.

"Yep!" Cass forced a cheerful smile. "We could probably start booking a smaller booth—"

"Alex proposed yesterday!" Jill blurted out.

Cass let out a whoop and jumped around to the other side of the booth. "Congratulations!"

"Tell us all about it! Leave out no detail," Libby said, sliding in from the other side and smooshed their beaming friend between them.

Jill described a day of coffee in bed that started hours earlier than Cass could fathom, a monster hike that made her tired just listening to it, and a blushing allusion to some frisky hands along the summit that ... actually, that last part sounded pretty good.

A couple of years with only her vibrator for company was getting stale.

"... and then I was screaming *yes!* at the top of my lungs before Alex could even get the words out," Jill finished with a breathless laugh.

If there was a better proposal for her friend, Cass couldn't think of it.

"Lemme see the ring," Cass said, making grabby motions with her hands.

Jill flushed but held out her left hand to show off a modest antique ring, and Cass swallowed a sudden wistfulness that threaded her stomach.

Another friend moving on to marriage, and likely motherhood, turning her attention to the new chapter in her life.

At least my first emotion was joy for her, and not sadness at losing another friend.

"I'm so happy for you," Cass said, and any remaining heaviness faded with her friend's shining eyes. "Any dates planned yet?"

"Alex would get married this afternoon if he had it his way, but we don't know where we're going to have it, let alone when."

Libby took a swig of her coffee. "Just elope and skip all the annoying details. Family drama? Trying to decide on what colour of tablecloth? No, thanks."

"As tempting as eloping sounds, we have people we want to be there with us."

Already turning into *we* instead of *me*. Cass hitched her smile up her cheeks. "I'm sure you already have a wedding planning app downloaded."

A blush crept up her friend's neck. "Three of them. But if I have to delete another push notification threatening wedding annihilation if I don't decide on save-the-date invitation fonts eighteen months in advance, I'll just cave to Alex and use APA standard formatting."

Libby snorted. "Ah, engineers are so romantic."

"In his own way," Jill said, grinning into her pancakes.

From her friend's smile, it sounded like Jill's boyfriend—wait, make that fiancé—was the right kind of romantic for her. No surprise, really. One crook of her finger and the man would break an ankle running to her. If Jill wanted a unicorn to officiate their ceremony, Alex would find a way.

Cass swallowed a bite of her French toast. "I'm just glad you still came to brunch today. You'll probably be too busy soon, planning everything."

"I wouldn't miss spending time with you two," Jill said, tsking.

Lots of friends had said that before. But then girlfriends stepped out of the single scene, trading weekend trips for wedding planning. Sunday mimosas for management positions.

New jobs that meant longer hours. Kids at soccer practice instead of new art exhibits. That was how it went.

Cass gave a weak smile and hoped this time would be different. "Good," she said.

"It's been forty seconds of wedding planning talk and it's already stressing me out," Jill said, fanning her face. "New topic. You guys seem tired. Rough morning on set?"

Libby wobbled her head, and Cass shrugged. Yesterday had gone long. Again. Then Terry, the show's production coordinator, had called her that morning to solve an emergency wardrobe issue on her day off. Granted, no one else could fix the ripped costumes with her speed or skill.

But it was the same the week before, and the one before that. Until there was a year and a half of back-to-back films and TV shows without a vacation under her belt.

Cass yawned just thinking about it.

"So, it wasn't a date keeping you out last night?" Jill asked.

Dating in your thirties? That was the opposite of stress relief. Besides, she was busy. With work. And her friends.

It had nothing to do with a certain someone ghosting her and bruising every part of her already fragile ego. She was getting enough questions from her mom.

"That's the last thing I need," she said.

"But it would be nice to get laid again," Libby said. Her dry spell was even longer than Cass's.

"You have men falling all over you, Elizabeth. You can say yes every once in a while."

"Or at least have some fun," Jill replied, pulling back her ashy blonde hair into a low ponytail before diving into her pancakes. "You two have been going at a thousand miles an hour for as long as I've known you."

Cass shrugged. "You met me at a busy point in my life."

"A year and a half is longer than a bit. And not all dates end in flames."

The last date she'd been on ended in a pathetic fizzle, complete with slinking away without saying goodbye.

But the night hadn't been a total loss. The night Cass had finally declared she was swearing off Nick Martin for real, she met one of the best friends she'd made in her life. While Nick had collected numbers from women all night, Cass had finagled a woman's number, too, and Jill had been welcomed into the fold of friends like she had been there since elementary school.

Libby brushed off the hint. "Don't talk about the Flames. They suck."

"That may be, but you both still deserve a break," Jill said.

Enter the champion of work-life balance. Cass jutted out her chin. "We do deserve some fun. I'm ordering extra whipped cream."

"Whipped cream just leads to yeast infections," Libby said.

"Ew! I had different plans for the whipped cream."

"For once, whipped cream is not the answer. I know exactly how to fix this." Jill sat straighter, her eyes sparkling. "We've been talking about going on a girls' weekend forever. Just the three of us."

It would have been the five of them. But Raina hadn't left her kids for more than a couple hours, like her husband was a third child she needed to supervise, and Phoebe was on an open-ended honeymoon and had given no indication of when she was coming home.

Two more friends becoming mere acquaintances.

"Vegas or Vancouver? I bet I can find cheap flights," Jill continued, cutting into her thoughts. Her phone was already in her hands, scrolling deals.

A weekend getaway would be amazing. Candlelit bubble baths were all well and good, but this relaxation called for a bit more than that. Plus, even for an indoor cat like herself, it had been a long, snowy winter, and a change of scenery could be the ticket.

"Think Alex will let you out of his sight for three whole days?" Cass asked to gauge if Jill's interest was sincere.

"Alex doesn't *let* me do anything. Besides, I like it when he gets a chance to miss me."

"Love it," Libby said. "Next weekend?"

Jill looked horrified. "I was thinking later this summer would be a perfect amount of time to plan a spontaneous weekend."

"It's March. Six months from now is not spontaneous. Anyway, I hate Vegas. I vote for Vancouver," Libby wheedled. "C'mon. We've been talking about having a girls' weekend for a year."

Cass lit up. "There's a new indie film fest in the West End next month, and I bet there's a fun run Sunday morning for Jill while Libs and I sleep in."

"Next month?" Jill said and paused her scroll of the flight list.

"We can look for a race with a cute shirt," Libby pressed, and Cass snickered.

Movies for them, and a race for Jill. Maybe a spa visit for the three of them? It sounded perfect.

Jill looked both nauseated and determined. "Okay, one month from now. Let's do this," she said, and tipped her head back down to her phone. "Ha, flight sale." Jill flashed her screen with a triumphant grin.

A pleasant surge rolled through Cass. This trip had been hypothetical for almost a year. She didn't think it would happen.

Cass beamed. "When are the flights?"

The weekend unfolded, exactly as Jill had planned. Spa treatments leached every ounce of tension out of them, even though Libby complained the seaweed wrap made her feel more like a sushi roll rather than detoxified. A tasting menu at dinner, that Cass thought was more of a social media influencer's dream than a foodie's dream. Then a 10k race in the morning for Jill, complete with a cute shirt.

Even though everything was perfect, Cass didn't think Jill would talk to either her or Libby ever again.

The theatre had seen better days. Generations of feet had worn the lobby's blue-and-green patterned carpets threadbare, and the scent of fake butter and stale popcorn suffused the poorly circulated air. Cass had to squint through most of the film, the projector's bulb on its last legs, and had sunk deep into a seat that had lost its springs two prime ministers ago. But none of that mattered.

The film played out with a creeping dread that crawled up the back of her neck and down her throat. Negative space layered a cold eeriness, each minute shifting the meaning of the scene before. Her blood pressure had spiked a dozen times, and her fingers were still getting circulation back from Jill gripping them. Cass had gasped out loud at the end. Not from a jump scare, but from the lack of oxygen as she held her breath, waiting for the characters to break out of the futile prison of their own making.

It had riveted her from opening credits to curtain close.

"That was brilliant. The use of shadow? Silence? The waiting?" Cass gushed to her friends as they spilled out of the theatre and into the lobby. She pressed the back of her freezing fingers to her flushed cheeks. "What did you think?"

"That was terrible," Jill answered, still shaking and sounding queasy. "I hate you both. Forever."

"You love us. And if you need an extra boost of energy at the race tomorrow, you can just think about the ending," Libby said, grinning.

"That is not helpful!" Jill squeaked. "I have to pee."

Cass gave Jill a reassuring squeeze, then pulled Libby into a triple hug. "I'll wait here and find our next movie, and I promise nothing scary enough to give you nightmares."

"Won't be a problem. I'm not sleeping for the next six months."

Libby supported Jill to the washrooms, where there was more light and therefore less terrifying, and Cass turned her attention back to the programme.

Oblivion was hands down the best indie film she'd seen in the last few years, even with its rough spots. If it had been playing again, she would have jumped into the next screening, but it had been a lot to get scaredy-cat Jill to see the horror film in the first place, and Libby wanted to see a rom-com.

No romances to be had, comedic or otherwise, but if they left now, they could hit a dark comedy. The reviews were mixed, but she'd worked with the guy who had done the sound design.

Actually, the dark comedy wouldn't be comforting enough, and Cass searched the list for the sci-fi she knew was playing in a couple hours.

"Not a bad line up this year."

The voice of raw silk spoke from just above her shoulder. Her eyelids fluttered shut to let it sink in. She almost wanted to break into song, so sure that his smooth low tones would complement her clear soprano. When none came, she turned to follow the words, and her own stopped.

Eyes like green ice narrowed down at her through fine black lashes. His thick black hair shagged in unruly waves around his face, with cheekbones sharp enough to cut diamonds. An old long-sleeved concert tee clung to his crossed arms, and distressed jeans hugged his long legs, all faded, all black, and showing off his sinuous frame. A climber's body. No, with how he moved with a casual grace, a dancer's body. Panther-like, purposeful. Like he knew exactly how he took up space, with that half-scowl, half-smile looking nothing short of trouble. Or a good time.

Or both.

She blinked twice and cleared her throat. "It's looking really good."

CHAPTER TWO

JOSH

HE LEANED INTO THE CORNER, WATCHING SHELL-SHOCKED attendees exit the theatre. A few people looked pale, but that could just as easily be the tail end of a cloudy winter as lingering fear. He was too far away to hear anything, but it didn't matter. No one was talking.

Was that good? Or bad? Fuck.

The last stragglers left the theatre. A grinning, teal-haired woman with dark roots and tatted arms supported a shaky blonde who looked seconds away from throwing up.

He repressed a smirk. Blondie had picked up on the film's mood.

Josh turned his head back to his phone to scroll his messages. Replied to Stephen with thumbs up. Declined an invite to drinks that night. Left a few women on read.

Still hadn't seen the message he was looking for. Whatever. He wasn't expecting a response today.

The two women turned down the hallway to reveal a short woman studying the flimsy paper programme taped to the theatre entrance with her back turned to him.

Hello, fun size.

His eyes lingered on her thick thighs and round ass, before

sweeping up over the boisterous chestnut curls that dusted the tops of her sloped shoulders. She rubbed her hands over her upper arms as she scanned the lobby like she could feel his eyes on her, and when she turned in his direction, he drew up from his calculated slouch.

Excitement flushed her cheeks, her chest rising and falling as she drew quick breaths, her clothes sliding over her curves like a caress. He wondered if those fantastic tits looked as good naked as they did under that shirt.

If he kept creeping in the dark like an asshole, he'd never find out.

Josh left the shadows to stand behind her. She looked even more touchable up close. One more step forward and her hair would tickle the underside of his chin. Too close. That would invade her space. He stepped back, crossing his arms as he leaned against the wall beside her.

"Not a bad line up this year," he said, and she spun to face him. Her hazel eyes widened slightly as her gaze took a lingering path down his body and up to his face.

Good. They were on the same page.

Her long, dark lashes fluttered as she cleared her throat. "It's looking really good."

A spark of goosebumps erupted over his arms. Well, shit. Her voice was as sweet as she looked. That mouth looked like it tasted just as sweet.

He nodded his head to the marquee, his mop of shaggy hair flopping into his eyes, and he shook it back with an irritated toss. "Just got out of *Oblivion*?"

"What? Oh!" She blew out her breath in a rush, as if remembering she had just exited a film. "What a ride! Nothing happened, but everything happened? Watching them fall apart? I mean," she waved her hand, "the costume design needed a stronger presence, but the claustrophobia? And everyone tried so hard to do the right thing, but it didn't matter? I wanted to see a clear resolution for the ending, but watching it coming?" She shook herself with a light shiver. "Incredible."

Whoa. She saw it. Themes, intent, everything. In one viewing. Josh twisted his mouth in a crooked line to stifle the smile threatening to break through. "I don't know. There were continuity errors, bad lighting in the beginning."

"Sure, and they could have cut a few minutes, but I know the novel the film was based on. The director nailed it," she said, dismissing his arguments. "They distilled that rambling story into a cohesive narrative. I bet it's one of those movies that just gets better every time you see it. I'd see it again right now, but my friend is never going to forgive me for making her see it just once. My palms are still sweaty." She lowered her waving hands and shook her head with a sheepish grin. "I'm gushing. But wow. That director is going places."

He ran his hands through his hair, as if he could shove away her praise. "He has some work to do," he said.

"I didn't say it was perfect." Her smile spread even farther across her rosy cheeks, stirring a long dormant feeling somewhere in his torso.

"It's an amateur film fest. Everyone has work to do. This director just needs a team. I like this one even more than ..." she continued, rambling other films from this year's lineup and last year's, listing off their strengths and weaknesses. Some of which he agreed with. Others that were, in his opinion, blasphemous. But still, informed.

What the hell. His dick could wait. "What are you seeing next?"

"I've got a few on my list I'd like to see, but I'm open to suggestions. My friends should be—"

"—right here."

The friends were back. Blondie wedged herself between him and Fun Size, shooting her a look that asked *do you want to talk to this guy, or do you need a rescue?*

Josh took half a step back. He didn't need to get in the way of a friends' night out, even if he wanted to take her back to his place and find out what that mouth could do.

Worst-case scenario, he could get her number and meet up with her another time. A few offers sat unread in his messages that he could turn his attention to for a hookup tonight.

None of them interested him, though.

"We were just about to decide on what to see next," he said, and his target shot him a smile that lit up her face.

Sweet holy hell, she was cute. Cute, and still nameless. If tonight went well, he'd need to figure that out. Her number had to go in his phone under something.

A broad smile spread across the face of the tall woman with teal hair. "That is a *fantastic* idea. You two should have fun with that. Jill and I would *love* to join you but we were just saying we wanted to go back to the hotel for a SpongeBob marathon, weren't we?"

Hotel? Friends from out of town? Or were they all? One more reason to make sure he spent time with her tonight.

"We are?" The friend named Jill blinked at her. "What about Cass?"

Ah. Fun Size had a name.

"Cass probably wants to see another thriller and you don't look like you're up for another one," the friend replied, and Jill quailed.

Well, *Oblivion* wasn't for everyone.

"Ted Lasso looks more your speed right now," Cass suggested, giving her friends a side eye that Josh read as *yes I want to talk to this guy and would you please stop cockblocking me*?

Tall and teal nodded, tugging at her friend's arm. "Plus, you have a race in the morning. Don't you need to eat pasta or something?"

If he could have given her a high-five, he would have.

"Oh. *Oh!* Right! Pasta and SpongeBob! My favourites," Jill said, adding under her breath as the tall one dragged her away, "Turn on Find My Friends. Text me every hour."

This friend deserved a high-five, too. Partly for watching out for her friend's safety, partly for getting out of the way and letting said friend get laid. Hopefully.

Jill let the third friend pull her away, tossing glances over her shoulder and a thumbs up for good measure.

"Yes, mom," Cass called after them, and turned back to him. "One of my friends worked sound design on a dark comedy starting in half an hour. I've heard it's completely miserable. Interested?"

He let his gaze wander over her body. "Extremely interested. I'm Josh, by the way."

"I'm Cass … and you already know that." She tilted her head up to smile at him, and he felt that foreign tug in his torso again.

Yeah. This was exactly what he wanted tonight. "Let's laugh at people's misery."

A dollop of mayo squirted from the end of her hot dog and splattered the sidewalk an inch from her sneaker. The flat overcast sky did its best to grey the city, but the last of the cherry blossoms blushed a pink haze along every sidewalk and clogged the gutters. In the time they had entered and exited the film, the rain had tapered to a mizzle. Cass huddled next to him under the awning of a high-end clothing boutique with their half-eaten hot dogs in hand.

"I didn't like it." She pursed her lips in thought. "I need to tell Karl—he's the sound designer—I couldn't hear any dialogue over the street noise. That's not like him. Great premise and the actors were perfect deadpan, but the marketing push and what was on the screen were a complete mismatch. All comedy, no dark, no resolution."

"Disagree. I thought the ending was brilliant, but yeah, not enough misery to earn the dark. And you're right on the sound." It might as well have been filmed through a tin can. Not her friend's fault, though. That theatre had shit speakers. "So, what do you do?"

"I—" Cass's words died as a bus splashed a petal-saturated wave inches from her foot. Josh caught her waist to pull her back at the last second.

"Careful, now," he said, voice rustling the tendrils of hair by her ear. His hand splayed over her belly and down the curve of her hip. "Wouldn't want you to get all wet."

"I'm okay getting wet," she said, then stammered, "I just mean, my hotel is close, and I could get changed if I needed to."

So, she was from out of town, too. Disappointing, but one night with her would be better than nothing. Not to mention less complicated than adding someone to his rotation. And if he made her a little nervous, fine. She was cute as hell when she was nervous.

Her tongue darted out to the corner of her mouth and nodded down at his shirt. "So, are you a fan?" she squeaked out.

He glanced down at the tee he picked up at the concert his sister dragged him to when they'd been visiting family in Australia a decade ago. They'd gotten so high he'd made out with a stranger right beside his sister, who'd been too mesmerized by the light show to notice. While he never remembered to get the name of the concert hookup, he remembered every second of the show, and had seen him live half a dozen times since.

"I vibe," he said noncommittally. "You?"

"Yes, but not deep into the catalogue. I just know just a little of his last album, but I prefer his second. Some of the older stuff is a little psychedelic for me, and did you hear he's coming to Canada next year?" She stopped, cutting herself short with an awkward smile. "Sorry, I'm rambling," she blurted out. "Um, what do you do?"

"Hit on beautiful women outside of movie theatres." He swiped his thumb over her lip, clearing a small smear of mustard. A musical laugh erupted from her throat and warmth flooded his extremities. He had the sudden urge to be the funniest man in the city.

"That is a fantastic line," she said when her laughter had subsided. "Does it work for you a lot?"

First time he tried it, but he filed it away for future reference. "How long are you in town?" he asked instead.

"I'm just here for the weekend. Blow off a little steam." She finished her hot dog before pulling out her phone, and he snuck a glance at the text she sent to her friends from over her shoulder.

> Not dead. He smells really good

Well, she smelled amazing, too, but if he had it his way, that body might kill him tonight. He swallowed his chuckle, along with the last bite of his hot dog.

She slid her phone away, retrieving a pack of gum and offering him a piece. When he finally moved in to kiss her, fresh breath would be preferable. He held solid eye contact as he put the piece in his mouth, the spicy sweet bite of cinnamon flooding his mouth.

"What do you want to do now?" she asked in a breathy voice, her eyes still locked on his lips.

Right. Movies. She was in town for a film fest. And there were a few more he wanted to see. He wiped his fingers on a crumpled napkin and tossed it into the bin. "I had the last pick. Your turn."

"Horror? I couldn't get the girls to agree to another thriller."

"Are you telling me you're not like other girls?"

Whatever that could pass for an admonishing glare flashed across her cherubic features. "I'm exactly like other girls. Other girls are awesome. I like rosé and bubble baths and pampering. I just also happen to like horror movies and other ways of getting my heart rate up that don't involve motocross."

How could such a sweetheart put him in his place so decisively? It was like a superpower. Josh tipped his head back and laughed. "Fair," he said. "Other girls are awesome, too."

But this awesome girl—this awesome woman—was right in front of him. And after that little hint of other ways of getting her heart rate up, he was pretty sure she was steering the night in the same direction he wanted, too. But even if she was in town just for the night, they were having a different kind of fun right now. A kind of fun he hadn't had with another woman in a long time.

If he was wrong and their night didn't finish where he thought it would, he had backups.

He wrapped his arm around her waist and tugged her down the street. "Alright, beautiful. Let's get thrilled.

CHAPTER THREE

CASS

"See? Now that's how you resolve a story."

Cass's heart rate still hammered in her chest, but not from the film's ending.

Josh furrowed his brow at the blank screen. The arm that wasn't slung over the back of her chair rested on his knee, foot propped up on the empty armrest in front of him. He gestured with the arm around her shoulder, and she let him nudge her in a little closer.

"Disagree. Too tidy. Nothing left for interpretation. Plus, whoever was in charge of lighting needed a handler. I'm all for a good lens flare, but it's like he thought he was J.J. Abrams or some shit."

"Lens flares? Are you kidding? Amateur hour."

Josh parroted her earlier words back to her. "Amateur film fest. Everyone has work to do."

"Fine," she said with a grin. "I'll admit the reveal was pretty good."

"Pretty good? You were freaked out. You nearly cut off circulation with how tight you gripped my arm."

"And you're one to talk? Like you didn't grip my knee."

"Not why I gripped your knee." His scowl turned into a

smirk, revealing a devastating pair of dimples, and any hope of resisting him popped like a soap bubble.

"Um, excuse me?" a gawky teenager interrupted, fidgeting at the end of the row. "The film ended twenty minutes ago, and we need to finish cleaning up so we can let the next showing in."

Josh led her through the maze-like lobby, out a back door, and onto the steps of an unfamiliar street. Headlights and traffic signals reflected off every surface, tires making an electric sizzle on the wet asphalt as they rolled by. She stopped on the last step from the bottom to get her bearings, failing to orient herself in the darkness that had fallen over the city.

He leaned against the metal railing, one foot on the stair beside her to box her in. A few raindrops collected at the ends of his hair to drip down his cheekbones. Cass wanted to lick away the drops rolling down his neck.

"What do you want to do now?" she asked, mouth dry.

Josh looked at her appraisingly. "I think it's time to test the waters."

"Test the ... is that a movie?"

He closed the space between them, sending a wave of heat washing over her body. Standing on the last step put them almost at eye level, and he dropped his gaze to her mouth, his lips only inches from hers.

"What if I said I've wanted to kiss you since the moment I laid eyes on you?"

Oh. *Test the waters*. Waters she hadn't swum in a long time. The thrill winding its way up her spine bloomed into a smile, and she chanced looping her thumbs into his belt loops to draw him closer. "I'd say what took you so long."

"Had to finish arguing with you first," he said, eyelids half closing, and slid his hand up the nape of her neck.

His grip tightened in her hair, gently tugging her head back to open her lips, and he flicked his tongue along hers, the sharp spice of cinnamon sparking where they met. It was wild, breath taking. It wasn't nearly enough. She stood on her tiptoes, arching her body flush against him as she sucked his lower lip, and a short moan escaped the back of his throat.

The hand that wasn't cupping the back of her neck meandered to her hip and squeezed, a restrained urging of his pelvis into hers. A warm fuzziness stole over her as she pulled back to gauge his reaction.

He looked hungry, sly. He pulled her back, forcefully this time, and sparks flared at every point of contact. She slid her hands up his biceps, their solid warmth flexing under her fingers.

It had been years since she'd hooked up with someone she'd just met. She didn't want to bail on her friends—anymore than she already had—but Libby would be the first one to cheer her on, and Jill knew Cass's luck with men had been less than stellar.

And dang it, she was thirty-two freaking years old and trudging through the longest dry spell of her adult life. She could have a one-night stand with a hot guy in another city if she wanted to. If the pulse beating at several key points in her body was any indication, she wanted to.

No reason to hold back. They'd never see each other again. She could make him feel good for a couple of hours and let him make her feel good. Then she'd head home tomorrow with no strings attached and no expectations. Perfect.

Waters tested.

"I can't believe I'm going to say this, but I don't think I want to watch movies anymore."

"Where's your hotel?" he demanded, his voice snapping the surface of her skin to rapt attention.

For the first time, Cass wished she wasn't having a fun-times girls' sleepover weekend. "My friends will be there. Not up for an audience," she replied, fingers threading his hair. The thick waves slid through her fingers, and she wondered if she'd have her hands there if he was the kind of man to go down on her. "Your place?"

He appeared to think for a moment. "Okay, we'll have the place to ourselves."

"Roommate?"

"Something like that." He sucked on her lower lip, rooting in his jeans pocket for his phone with one hand and the other still bound up in her hair.

Oh, she loved a man who could multitask. "What if they come home?"

"I have walls," he said. "You can make all the noise you want, beautiful."

Cass could count on one hand how often she'd made out in the back of an Uber, but that hand was busy roaming under his shirt. Every inch of him was warm and smooth under her fingertips, and she could not wait to get his shirt off and lick the firmest abs she'd touched in a decade.

"I don't want to sound like a cliché, but I don't usually do this," she breathed.

He pulled his teeth back from where he'd been nibbling the skin below her ear. "Then I am a lucky man."

The Uber dropped them at the steps of a sleek Yaletown building. Not that she noticed much of the lobby or elevator. He dragged her to his front door and into a blast of warm air as they stumbled into his empty condo.

Cass shed her jacket. "Why's it so hot in here?"

"More comfortable when I take your clothes off."

Ah. Well, who better than a player to break her dry spell with? She followed him straight through the tiny living area into his bedroom. Spare and clean, just like him. A botanical mural painted in stylized negative decorated the dark walls. Blackout curtains pooled on the hardwood floor and the faint scent of sandalwood surrounded her. The glass lamp beside his bed threw off an amber glow, making him look like he was dipped in gold. He shucked his jacket and dove his hands back into her hair, tilting her face up to kiss her again.

"Can I get you anything?"

It would have sounded sincere if he hadn't been pinning her to the wall with his hard-on rocking against her stomach.

"Just you." She arched forward, the pulse between her legs seeking friction. He slid his hand down her neck, along the curve of her round shoulder, and stopped with a look of confusion.

"There are no straps to slide off, if that's what you're looking for."

"What is this?" he asked, dimples piercing his cheeks as he ran his hand over the material covering her ribs.

"Just some underthings."

His eyes blazed darker at her, and he inched his hand farther up. "I'm going to unwrap you like a fucking present," he rasped in her ear, "and it's going to take a while."

He could take all the time he wanted if he kept pouring his rich voice into her ear. This close, the vibrations made the tiny hairs on her neck stand up, marching down her chest until her nipples stood at attention, waiting for him to …

"Wait!" She hadn't texted a status update in hours. Libby would be fine, but Jill would be freaking out. "I need to let my friends know where I am," she said, pulling out her phone.

Sure enough, Jill had left a series of texts of increasing intensity, and Cass frantically hammered out a message into their group chat.

> sooo maybe don't wait up??

LIBBY

YOU WHORE!!!! GET THAT D!!

JILL

I'm so clueless it took me forever to realize you were trying to hook up!

I don't want to be a buzzkill but what's his name?

First and last?

The reminder yoinked her out of her daze for a half beat, and Cass peeked up at the gorgeous man dimming the room's lights. "Um, what's your last name? My friend is having a mom moment and wants some details."

"Graham. Scorpio sun, Leo moon. If she wants a different horoscope, I'm a Metal Horse," he said, and added with a sardonic smile, "No criminal record, and my credit score is excellent."

Cass stifled a giggle as she typed, then whipped her head up.

"I read your name on the programme! You directed *Oblivion*! Why didn't you say anything? It was so good! I loved it when—"

"Fuck me." He cut her off with a wild kiss that crushed the breath from her lungs. He pulled back and nipped at her lips, looking pained and gratified at the same time. "I can't believe I'm saying this, but I really don't want to talk about my movie right now. Tell your friends what they need to know and put your phone down."

A thrill swept through her at his command. "Yes, sir."

> Josh Graham and he's funny
>
> not a criminal

JILL

> Okay stay safe

> I have my phone beside me if you need us to come get you <3

LIBBY

> Bet you're glad you splurged for the waxing yesterday

Her friends were beautiful, perfect, predictable angels, and she was buying breakfast tomorrow. If she wasn't still tangled up in the bedsheets of Josh Graham with the excellent credit and compatible horoscope. Before she could kiss the screen, he took the phone out of her hands and put it in easy reach on the nightstand.

"God, you're so beautiful. I don't know where to start." One step, two steps, and he pressed her against the wall, pinning her with his mouth on hers, his knee parting her thighs. The musky scent of sandalwood and citrus surrounded her as he kissed where her pulse hammered at her throat. His hands flowed under her shirt and grazed her nipples over the satin bra cups.

A heady rush washed away the last of her control, and she breathed, "Oh no."

He released her instantly. "No? What is it, baby?"

Just that you're making me lose my mind and I haven't taken my clothes off yet. "Just a reflex," she gasped, tugging at the hem of his shirt he was holding down with his free hand. "Keep going."

"If you say 'no' I'm stopping. I don't play with consent."

"You've got it. It's yours. Just whatever you do, don't stop."

A look of pure hunger consumed his features, and he closed his hand over hers. "Are you saying you want me to keep going, even when you tell me to stop?"

One night. No reason to hold back. That was exactly what she was saying. She bit her lip and nodded. "Even when I tell you to stop."

"Where the hell did you come from?" he asked, almost to himself, and finally let her pull his shirt over his head.

Cass gasped. His long torso rippled with lean muscle, and he hissed out a breath as she ran her hands over the flat disks of his nipples. She pushed off the wall behind her to bring him closer again, and he teased her with a step back.

"Pick a safe word."

Creative, funny, *and* respectful, in the kinkiest way possible? Cass felt like she had manifested her ideal man in one mouth-watering package. A laugh burbled from her lips. "I've never had one of those."

"Boundaries now, play after. What if you say 'don't'?"

"I will say that at the exact wrong time," she said, his belt buckle jangling and leather strap cracking as she whipped it through the loops.

"I'm not touching you until we can communicate."

"I want you to touch me."

"I'd gag you, but I don't know you well enough," he murmured.

A spark shot through her nethers. Exploring a little light submission play with him? That sounded fun. Perhaps not their first time.

Only time.

"And then I wouldn't be able to say the safe word that we can't agree on. Maybe you just want to fight with me instead?" she said, batting his hands away long enough to pull her shirt over her head and pressing herself against his chest, where the swell of her boobs drew his eyes like a siren's song.

The bustier was an unholy union of a bondage-style corset and a French maid outfit. Royal blue lace panels held together by thin satiny straps criss-crossing in a complex latticework. It had taken her weeks to get the design right.

Josh sucked in a breath. "Christ, woman. Do you always dress like you're ready to slay dragons?"

The weeks she'd spent creating the art she was wearing had been worth it for this exact moment. Ego stroke, achieved.

"I like wearing beautiful things," she said. "Do you feel slain?"

"Fully slain," he said in a strangled voice, and his hands gravitated back to her breasts, thumbing her nipples in delicious circles, until he remembered he didn't have what he needed yet and snatched his hands back.

"I can take it off."

"Take it off. No, leave it on." His gaze fell to her boobs again, and he raked his hands through his hair. "You're killing me, beautiful."

"Does it hurt? I could kiss it better."

"Fuck, we need that safe word." He leaned in and brushed his lips over her neck. "How about 'potato'?"

A peal of laughter erupted from her throat, and she felt his lips turn into a smile on her neck. "The thought of carbs will just make me hotter."

"'Potato', it is."

"Okay," she said, still giggling, "if I say 'enough', I want you to stop."

"Let's practice. Enough with these clothes."

Cass turned around and placed her palms flat on the wall, presenting him with the hooks of her corset-like bra.

"Will you unwrap me like a present now?"

He released the hooks—*one, two, three, four, five, six, seven, eight, nine*—until the last hook gave way and the garment dropped to the floor. He slid his hands around her ribs to stroke her nipples into hardened peaks.

"Jesus Christ, is it my birthday?" he hissed under his breath, looking down over her shoulder where he palmed the weight of her breasts. "Your tits are spectacular."

Ask me about my spectacular tits! was going on her next cross-stitch project when she got home. She shivered as he teased her nipples and wiggled her hips against the hard ridge pressing into her butt. "I thought you were a Scorpio. You're not lying about our star sign compatibility, are you?"

"I would never." He tugged her pants over her thighs until they pooled at her feet, her underwear unveiled, peeks of skin showing through the satin and lace that matched her bustier.

"Fully fucking slain," he muttered. He gathered both her hands into one of his fists to pin her arms over her head, eyes darkening as they raked over her body. Down her forearm, biceps, the mound of her breast, and when he dipped his head to take the dark bud of her nipple between his teeth, she swallowed a whimper.

After a minute of noisy sucking, he rasped against her skin. "Tell me you don't want it gentle."

If that had ever been something she'd wanted in the past, her mind was fully changed.

"Not gentle," she gasped.

"Good girl." He nipped her; almost too hard. "Now, spread."

She stepped her feet apart, and he stroked a path over the fine satin, his touch sure and teasing. The sweet torture of his mouth on her breast and his fingers circling around her clit was driving her wild. The man hadn't even touched her bare skin, and she was already bucking into his hand.

A soft whimper escaped her throat. "Please."

"Please, what?"

Oh, screw it. He'd eaten up everything she'd done so far. Might as well go all in. She closed her eyes as she pushed her hips towards him. "Please make me come."

"Oh, beautiful, you have no idea how hard I'll make you come."

He pushed the lace of her panties aside, and Cass's knee ligaments turned to rubber. He stroked a path along her core, his eyes blazing as he curled a finger deep inside, her hands still pinned over her head.

"You want more?" Another finger joined the first, pulling out to trace teasing circles before sinking back in. So perfect, the tension building in layers. He dragged his teeth over her neck, his fingers sliding in her, catching every tremble, picking up speed, the heel of his palm a steady pressure against her clit. She writhed against his hand until she clenched around his fingers, whimpering against his mouth as her orgasm slammed into her. She tried to clamp her legs together, but his thigh wedged between hers kept her open to him. His fingers didn't slow, even after she came again, and her legs buckled.

"Enough!" she cried, and he finally pulled back with a satisfied grin. He released her wrists and dropped a delicate kiss between her breasts, snaking his arm around her waist to hold her upright. A warm, loose pleasure unfurled through her body, and she blinked herself back to the gorgeous man caging her against the wall, pushing her into the mural behind her.

I'm going to have a palm leaf imprint on my butt for a week, she thought with a giggle, and ran her hands down his torso, all taut, compact muscle stored like energy under his fevered skin.

"You did so good." His gaze bored into her, and he undid the buttons of his jeans one-handed. "Now, get on your knees."

Her heart stuttered in her lungs, and without thinking, she slid down the wall until her face was level with the bulge tenting the front of his black boxer briefs. Her knee would not be happy with her later, but she could ignore it for now. And ice it tomorrow.

She tugged at the front of his open jeans. "Off, please." For good measure, she pouted, just a bit.

He shed the jeans in a flash, his breathing growing shallow as she worked the band of his boxers over his narrow hips. His dick sprung free, and she wrapped her fingers around him. He strained, thick and hard, in her hand.

She knew what guys liked about her. Boobs, primarily—Josh had already called that one—but her cupid's bow lips and wide eyes made her look like some sweet thing come undone. She licked her lips and looked up at him through her lashes as she brought his free hand to the back of her head.

"What do you want me to do?"

Josh looked like he was about to detonate. "Open wide."

With a dainty flick of her tongue over the gleaming crown, she parted her lips and worked the length of him as far as she could. Her gaze held his until he hit the back of her throat, and he dropped his head with a groan.

The clean, musky scent of him was heady. His smooth skin slid over her tongue, his eyes glassy as he watched her take him. She wanted to touch him everywhere.

Her fingers fanned over the front of his thigh, wrapping around his hips and down the cleft of his ass, and she felt a thrum of pleasure when he gasped at her light touch. She brushed over the tight ring of muscle, gently tugging on his balls, her fingers playing with the soft skin between, and his thighs opened to give her better access.

Well, well, well. Looks like they both knew what they liked. She hummed in appreciation as she let her exploration continue.

"That's right, baby," he whispered. "Faster."

He was getting close. She could feel it, his glutes tightening and hips jerking. She let out a small noise of dissent from deep in her throat and slowed down, gripping the base of his cock, eyes watering.

Please don't come in my hair. She pulled back and asked a question she knew the answer to. "Do you want to come on my tits?" she asked sweetly.

"Fucking hell," he groaned in response, and she worked him with her hand for the last seconds, rubbing the head over her nipples until he spent himself, hot jets painting her cleavage. He sagged against the wall, forehead pressed to his arm and chest heaving as he caught his breath. "You are full of surprises," he gasped, hand still firmly in her curls as the last shudders rolled over his body.

Instead of ducking to the washroom for a towel, he pushed her back to his bed, and licked every drop he'd marked her with. Again, he trapped her hands over her head, his other hand teasing her clit, and when she was clean of him, sucked and bit the oversensitive rosy peaks of her nipples until she crashed under his hand again.

That was hot. Unexpectedly hot. All of it. This man, whose name she'd just learned, who she'd never see again, was blowing her mind. They moved in perfect tandem, like they'd danced together for years. No need to hold back. Every reason to let go and let the pleasure of the night guide them.

The length of their bodies pressed together, even as she tried to pull him closer, his taste musky on his tongue, and she felt him hardening against her again.

She had to give it to him. He had impressive stamina.

"I'm going to fuck you now."

He grabbed a condom from his bedside table, moving slowly, as if giving her time to demur. Cass nodded with drunken eyes and spread her legs farther. The condom was on in one swift motion, and he rolled onto his back, pulling her to straddle him, and immediately her knee resisted at the sharp angle.

"Not like this," she said, embarrassed to kill the mood, "but do you want me on my knees?" The mattress would be cushioned enough, and she turned around.

"Yes, but not now." He slid his arm around her hips, flipping her onto her back in one fluid motion. "I want to look at your beautiful face when I make you come on my cock."

Her stomach fluttered. He probably wanted to look at her spectacular tits, but it felt good to hear him say it, anyway. She wiggled lower and wrapped her thighs around his hips. He pushed into her with one thrust, and a sharp cry ripped from her throat. It was intense, almost painful. Enough to bring her to the edge in less than a minute.

"Stop, too much," she breathed into his ear.

He thrust into her harder in response. "I don't fucking think so."

Perfect.

He drove into her with punishing strokes. Hard and deep, the sound of their skin slapping filling the space around them. Tremors built in her core, and he wrapped his fingers around the back of her neck to force her gaze up. His hand worked between them, applying the perfect amount of pressure on her clit, and she tightened around him with a gasp.

"Fuck, yes. Come for me."

For the first time in her life, she was going to come on command. She obeyed, arching back and clenching around him as he drove her over the edge.

"Jesus, you're so fucking pretty when you come," he panted. "Hold on, baby."

She was spent, with no strength to hold anything, but she

wrapped her arms around him as he drove her into the mattress, his teeth on her neck as he came apart over her.

The tang of their sex hung heavy in the air. The only sounds were their racing breaths and the rustle of the sheets as the last spasms rolled through his body on top of her. He withdrew to his back, legs splayed and one arm shielding his eyes, skin golden and smooth and radiating with a light sheen of sweat and satisfaction.

Cass shifted to her side, trailing her fingers over the ridge of his hip. "You are really good at this," she said. "All of it. No notes, would recommend."

Josh burst out laughing, eyes hidden behind the crook of his elbow, teeth flashing in the dark. "Only glowing reviews on my end, too," he said when he got a hold of himself. "You are fucking fantastic. Every inch of you. Stay here."

She traced a circle on the sheet, the rest of the covers lost to the floor and crumpled around them, and watched his perfect ass cross the room. She felt heavy, liquid. Like she could curl up and fall asleep against his solid angles. He was funny and was as obsessed with movies as she was. He argued with her without condescending, even when they had disagreed, then took all control the minute she gave permission. They fit together so well. She couldn't remember a more perfect night.

He returned from the bathroom a moment later and handed her a warm washcloth, and reclined back on the bed, his hand trailing along her hips into the crease of her thigh.

He spread before her like a feast. She'd never seen someone so masculine before. Usually something broke the spell: curly eyelashes she'd kill for, or soft eyes. But everything about him was so aggressively male, all hard angles, and taut muscles. Even his smooth chest made it easier to count his abs and trace his defined pecs, his ribs a razor's edge beckoning for her fingertips. Fine, straight lashes closed over those icy green eyes. Firm, narrow mouth, edges curled slightly, that fit so well against the soft fullness of her own lips, but she pulled back from the urge to press her mouth to his again.

If he wasn't such an obvious player, she'd wish he lived in Calgary. And that was her problem. This was a hookup. A raging hot, explosive hookup. Nothing more. She was leaving town tomorrow.

They'd kissed when they first explored each other, but that, as he'd said, was testing the waters. Now it would cross a line into real intimacy. Casual and done. That was how this worked.

Her heart rate still raced, her skin rubbed raw, and if she had to guess, her hair was tousled into an outrageous mess. The sheet stuck to her skin as she lifted to her elbows, and she blew a strand out of her eyes with a grin. "I guess I should be going."

His eyelids peeled open, smile still in place. "Or you could stay. There's a great diner down the street for breakfast."

The offer sounded genuine, but that didn't mean anything. Besides, dealing with the awkwardness of morning breath, toilet noises, and the deeper intimacy of sharing a bed? So many chances to make the night less than perfect, and every minute she stayed was giving her heart a chance to build scenarios in her head that wouldn't amount to anything. Late nights watching movies, later mornings lazing in bed. Lingering kisses over light bondage …

She shook her head. The last thing she needed was another man she couldn't have taking up space in her thoughts.

"Want to shower first?" His eyes raked over her breasts, where traces of him lingered on her skin. "Think I might have missed a spot. I've got the fancy shit. I'll give you the best body scrub of your life."

The thought of him slicking soap over her nipples while he dragged his teeth over her neck and his cock hard in her hand sent a fresh rush of heat between her aching thighs. *Why am I saying no to this?*

Right. Player. Who knew the game, far better than she ever would. She steeled her resolve. "I really should get back."

"You got something on the stove or something?"

Cass giggled into her folded arms. "My friends and I have early morning plans," she said awkwardly—which was mostly true—then gave a genuine smile. "But this was really, really fantastic."

"It was fantastic a few times," he replied. He pulled on a pair of sweats and handed her phone to her, reciting his number. "Call me the next time you're in town. I know some theatres with less shitty light and sound we can check out. Maybe I'll be lucky enough to run into you again one day."

Being in two different cities, it didn't seem likely, but it was the polite thing to say. She kept her head down as she plugged his number into her phone. "Maybe you will."

She dressed quickly as she could without making it look like she was trying to escape. At the last second, she looked down to see the exposed seams of her inside-out underwear, and bit back another giggle.

"Ride's on its way. Silver Tesla," Josh said, closing the app. He walked her backwards until her butt hit the door frame. "Now, what could we do for the next five minutes?"

Take off all my clothes again so I can put my panties on right-side-out? And once her clothes were off, all bets would be, too. Cass tipped her head to the side to give him better access to the ear he was taking nips out of, and let her hands slide under the band of his sweatpants to explore the dimples at the base of his spine. Of course, he had sexy dimples everywhere, and she reluctantly withdrew her fingers before she let herself get carried away. "I'm going downstairs to pull myself together, so I don't grin like a fool the whole way back to the hotel."

His musk enveloped her one more time as he covered her mouth with a lingering kiss. "Text me when you get there," he whispered against her lips, "and call me if your plans change tomorrow."

Cass pulled back before her heart could override her brain

and she agreed to anything he lay out in front of her. Including himself. "Okay."

In the Uber, she did her best to ignore the fact that the driver was probably thinking Cass had been doing exactly what it looked like she'd been doing: her curls in wild disarray, her lips swollen and smiling, looking just a little wicked. Sated and undone and thinking about herself first, for once.

Look at me go!

Her room key hadn't pulled its usual trick of demagnetizing in her purse, and the hotel room door flashed green. The lock snicked open louder than it needed to, and the bedside light flicked on as Cass tiptoed into the room. Libby sprawled on the pull out couch in her usual dead-to-the-world slumber with her hair obscuring half her face. Jill was already leaning back from turning on the light, squinting at her through sleep-crusted eyes.

"I thought you'd be back in the morning. Is everything okay?"

Cass did a little scream into her hands. "If multiple orgasms with a smoking hot guy who is generous with his compliments is okay, then yeah, I'm okay."

"Hell, yeah," Libby yawned, rousing herself awake. "Didn't really deviate from your type, though, did you?"

"What do you mean, my type?"

"Hot, dark hair, and a where-did-my-panties-go smile?" Libby said. "Sound like anyone we know?"

Jill raised a wary eyebrow but said nothing.

"Everyone likes hot, and lots of people liked dark hair. And who could resist smiles like that?" *He* was the last person she wanted to think about. Not when she just had an amazing time with Josh, who paid attention to her instead of the other women around them. "Anyway," she continued, evading the dangerous territory, "that was fun. I'm a wreck, and I need to sleep."

"Oh no, you are not getting off that easy." Libby pressed on. "Did you get his number? Did he ask for yours?"

"Not sure if you noticed, but Sexy Dimples and I live in different cities."

"If he's into you, he'll make it work," Jill said, already turning off the bedside lamp.

"Thanks, Jillybean, but tonight was a one-time thing."

She'd had more than her fair share of booty calls within her own city limits, let alone plane hopping for them. In the bright lights of the hotel bathroom, the entire front of her body from neck to thighs glowed with a constellation of bite marks. She grinned as she pinned up her hair, and stepped under the lava-hot shower.

The last thing she wanted was to complicate a perfect hookup. It would be too easy to find an excuse to come back to Vancouver for a night that he might not be into. That would just hurt.

He hadn't said her name once since they exchanged names. He probably didn't remember it. And that was okay. The memory of the night would be enough.

She stepped out of the shower, wrapped herself in a plushy robe, and slid under the bed's crisp sheets with her phone in hand.

It was a risk. He'd have her number, too, but he may not use it.

> I'm all tucked in

Then, before she could change her mind, added,

> I'll be thinking of you the next time I touch myself xoxo

That was a given.

Thanks for the perfect night, Sexy Dimples. It had been perfect.

Stress? Relieved. Ego? Boosted. Best of all, it would stay in a tidy little bubble in another city, well away from temptation.

CHAPTER FOUR

JOSH

JOSH PARKED HIS BMW BESIDE THE SPOT THE DIRECTOR WOULD ROLL into two hours from now. An ear-popping yawn cracked his jaw as he yanked open the lot's back door. As first assistant director, it was a point of pride to be the first person on set every day. Even when he got less than four hours of sleep the night before.

Five weeks left of filming, and he needed every minute to make sure they wrapped on schedule. He'd make sure they did.

That's why he kept getting hired.

And since he wasn't having breakfast with Cass of the thick thighs and pouty lips, no reason not to be the first on set, as usual.

> Morning, beautiful
>
> Dreamed of you last night
>
> Here's the name of breakfast place I was telling you about in case you want to check it out

Sending good morning texts to a hookup, though? Asking her to spend the night? *That* was far from usual.

Not as unusual as a hookup wanting to take off right after. He couldn't blame her. When he hooked up, he preferred to sleep in his own bed, too. Even when his partners wanted him to stick around after. Occasionally he obliged. Had to if he wanted to keep them in rotation. But they knew the drill, and he'd be gone before they woke up.

It was far easier to leave than to kick someone out. Stephen still razzed him, months later, after one crazy ex had banged on his apartment door after midnight. It had been enough to make him swear off bringing women home.

At least until Cass. Didn't hurt that she was from out of town. Less likely to show up unannounced.

A surprise visit from her would be alright, though. Maybe she'd call him the next time she was in town.

The venti coffee still steaming in his hand would caffeinate him for a couple of hours. Enough time for everyone to trickle onto set. Josh rolled his shoulders under his snug black tee, making the white graphic of Stormtroopers doing *Saturday Night Fever*-style dance moves ripple over his chest. Digging his fingers into the knots at the base of his neck, he logged onto his laptop and let his email load.

Newest first. He read and filed his emails in batches, delegating, deleting, and firing back responses to a litany of names above him in the food chain. An hour later, the office door creaked open and the film's production coordinator slunk into the seat beside him, surrounded by a musty miasma.

Josh flared his nostrils. "Jesus. Did you sleep in a bar last night?"

Stephen scratched his armpit, sniffed his fingers, and grimaced. "Might as well have. Feels like I did," he replied. "Why didn't you wait for me this morning? We could've carpooled."

"And let you stink up my car? No fucking way." Delete, forward, flag for reply. Sixty emails after being out of the office for a day? Not bad. "Didn't hear you come in last night, anyway."

"You were busy, from the sounds of it."

"A gentleman never tells."

"What do you know about being a gentleman?" Stephen rubbed his hands over his beard, the unkept blonde ends making his chin look an inch longer, and shifted into work mode. "Think we'll get the shots we need today?"

Nothing short of an earthquake would prevent them from getting the shots today.

And that is not an invitation, he silently whispered to any powers that be. He flicked through the call sheets fresh off the printer. "Take a shower. You're disgusting."

"Can't. My landlord gives me shit when I use too much hot water."

"I'm not your landlord."

"Then what do I pay you rent for?"

"You don't, but if you did, it would all go to my water bill."

His attention was pulled from Stephen's bemused shrug with a new flash in his inbox. Fuck, a new email, just as he'd gotten through everything.

This one was different.

LookBACK Films. The script he sent months ago. Long enough for someone to have finally read it after following up with every contact he had. He ground his teeth together and braced himself to open the message.

Dear Mr. Graham, Thank you for your submission; however, we ...

Josh bit back an expletive. No need to read any further. He resisted the urge to delete it, instead filing it in the folder labelled *What Doesn't Kill You*. At least, he didn't think twenty rejections in half as many months would kill him.

Might not make him stronger, but it put him in good company.

Everyone got rejected. All the time. Josh Graham was used to rejection. His scripts, anyway. Back in college, he was one of the few people in his film and screen arts program who wanted to be behind the camera, unlike the actors who feigned camaraderie, then backstabbed each other later while they all vied for the same roles.

His friends tried to convince him he belonged in front of the camera. He had the looks for it. It was like his parents had thrown all their features in a bag, shook it up, and built their son with whatever they grabbed first. The thick black hair that looked good, no matter what he did with it, came from his mother. He also got her dimples, but the cheekbones and glacial green eyes came from his father. The lanky, sinuous torso came from his father as well, and while his father would die before being seen unclothed outside of a sauna, Josh's agent insisted shirtless photos be at the top of his portfolio. More than one modelling agency had tried to recruit him in the past decade, but he wanted to do more than stand around and look pretty.

Or look angry, if any of the feedback he got was any indication.

"You have this whole murderous supermodel thing going for you," his drama coach had said, fingers fluttering in a circle around his face. "You're a shoo-in for any villain roles."

If he wanted people to think he was an asshole, he'd keep doing what he was doing. So, yeah. The bullshit in front of the camera didn't interest him. He might make an exception for a reimagining of *Newsies* set as a nineties gangster film, but those roles didn't come around that often.

Unless …

He whipped out his phone. "Siri, take a note. Screenplay idea *Newsies* remake meets nineties mafia." After a beat, he added, "Upcoming actors who dance question mark."

At least the bullshit behind the camera was better than in front of it. Usually. A few of his screenplays for short films had been optioned, even if nothing had come of it yet. Executive producers were allergic to risk. *Oblivion*, the film he'd directed, sound-mixed, lit, and everything else, had taken him over a year to make, and he still hadn't thought it was ready. He'd never have entered it if Stephen hadn't berated him into submitting it.

And Cass had said she'd liked it, even without knowing he'd directed. She got it, got *him*, what he was trying to say.

That felt good. Really fucking good.

So, minor success on his shorter works. No bites on any of his feature length screenplays, though.

Yet, he reminded himself. One of these days, the self-gaslighting might turn into an actual positive thought.

Stephen rolled his chair over. "Hear Westy's in today?"

Of course Josh had heard. If anyone would know when the executive producer would be on set today, it'd be him. Melanie Westwood, latest trophy wife of the film mogul Darren Westwood, had been far more hands-on during production than anyone had expected. Everyone said she was just a purse to fund this movie. They'd groaned when she showed up and started making decisions. Weird, dark ideas, but then those cryptic, esoteric choices had launched tiny indie projects that were barely expected to break even into the deep black. While she hadn't bagged any major awards yet, it was only a matter of time.

After that, people had shut up about the decisions she made. Josh couldn't believe he was working with her.

"Yep. One o'clock." Which meant she'd be here anytime between two and seven tonight.

"Are you going to ask her about it?"

Josh nodded without looking up from his screen, tapping out his reply to the second assistant director's frantic notes. Because he was nothing if not a masochist. Maybe he could get into Emily's spanking kink after all.

Fuck. He'd promised Emily he'd call last night. Well, he hadn't thought of anyone other than Cass the minute he'd laid eyes on her. Emily would get over it. And if she didn't, they both had other people they could call when they needed to blow off steam.

Stephen clapped his hand on Josh's shoulder. "You got this."

At least one of them had confidence.

Besides a craft services mishap in which no gluten-free sandwiches arrived, causing the lead actor to have a kindergarten-level hissy fit, the day passed incident-free leaving him free to keep vigil for Mrs. Westwood's arrival.

Near the end of the dinner break, Stephen signalled from across the room and pointed at his cell phone.

Westy's in the house

Go time.

The grip team was still adjusting the lights for the next scene, so Josh made sure everyone was doing something useful and strode to the entrance she always used.

"Mrs. Westwood, here for the finale shots?" he asked and waved a PA over. "Can we get you anything? Sparkling water? Decaf latte?"

A palanquin to carry you to the director?

She motioned for him to join her brisk pace, heels clicking on the concrete floors. She handed her knee-length jacket to the scurrying PA without breaking stride. "It's Melanie, Josh. Mrs. Westwood is my mother-in-law." She scanned the set through narrowed eyes. "Where's Brynne?"

Hiding from everyone on set. "In her trailer. Visualizing."

Casting Brynne Sparo had been one of Melanie's many conditions in bankrolling the tiny film. She was nowhere near the most famous actor he'd worked with, but her diva act put any A-lister to shame. Her breakout role in a historical drama last year had everyone predicting she'd be the next "It" girl. Melanie believed it, and was willing to bet the literal box office that everyone was right. From everything he'd seen, Josh was inclined to agree.

Act the diva, indeed.

"I want to see her when the scene is over."

"Of course, although it might take a while." It wasn't a complicated shot, but who knows how many dozens of takes the director wanted? So that meant they'd have time. Now was as good a time as any. Josh ground his molars and pushed ahead.

"Melanie." Nope, first name was still weird. " I wondered if you'd had a chance to look at the script that I sent through last month. Several actors have been making noise about doing grittier films and horror—"

"Horror isn't our brand. We're not LookBACK."

Fuck. Horror was having a moment and he wanted to ride the wave. The script was good. At least, he'd thought it was. Over a dozen studios disagreed though, and now Melanie, too. That dream was rapidly disappearing in the rearview. Maybe his script was a garbage heap, after all.

"Understood, thanks for looking—"

"But," she continued, "I heard you're working on an adaptation of *Sirius Darker*? I didn't know you had an interest in sci-fi."

He froze. How would she have heard he was writing that? No one knew what he was working on.

Except for Stephen. That sneaky little shit had been hounding him for months to finish that screenplay. Last time Josh opened the file, he'd stared at the screen for an hour before closing it without writing a word.

"*Sirius Darker* was the book that made me a fan of the genre," he said, trying to weigh how much of his enthusiasm he should show. "I've read it a few times."

Fifty times, but who was counting? No need to tell her he'd cosplayed the lead character at San Diego Comic-Con for the last three years. Or moderated a fan subreddit. Or posted fan art when he was in high school.

She tilted her head up to drill him with her gaze. "Is it a faithful adaptation?"

"Yes," he said, then added, "with gender-flipped main characters." The genre didn't need another female main character getting fridged. The dude could go on ice for once.

"Gender flipped isn't exactly faithful."

"The core of the story is the same."

"That'll piss off the fanboys."

"Something always does." He bit his tongue, ordering himself not to offer to flip back the gender roles. *Keep your fucking mouth shut.*

"Alright," she said finally. "I want it by Friday. I'll read it on the weekend."

Josh swallowed a bubble of panic. Sci-fi was not having a moment. The book was too niche. The *Sirius Darker* fandom had the worst kind of gatekeepers, testing arcane trivia to see if newcomers were worthy enough to be a fan. He'd picked away at the script since university. It was as much a fanfic as a passion project, half done, with no plans on ever sending it out for spec. Getting it done for the weekend? It would be nearly impossible.

He'd do anything to make it happen.

"Absolutely Mrs. W—I mean Melanie. It'll be in your inbox on Friday."

Because so what if he already worked fourteen-hour days? Friday was all the way at the other end of the week. Sleep was for assholes, anyway.

A tidy little pile of coke would've come in handy right about now.

"You look like shit, bro."

"Fuck you, too." The fuzz clouding Josh's brain made him feel like he was thinking through wool, and a sheen of nausea coated his intestines. He'd gutted his way through fifteen pages, a pot of coffee, and a packet of instant ramen noodles every night for the last week while Stephen crept in and out of the condo like a shadow. But his completed script had hit Melanie's inbox at a quarter to midnight that Friday, as promised.

He didn't even consider scrolling through his contacts to unwind, falling into bed, alone, minutes after hitting send and sleeping a decadent six hours before getting back onto set. He barely remembered getting through the day.

"You could have saved us from your sparkling personality until you actually needed to be here," Stephen said. "Seriously, go sleep in the trailer. I'll call you when we need you."

Josh nursed his third Americano of the Sunday afternoon—to the mutual displeasure of his blood pressure and stomach lining —and peered at the call sheets through gritty eyes. The crew wouldn't miss him for an hour. It was a sign of how under slept he was that he considered Stephen's offer. He was about to head towards the trailer's relative quiet when his phone buzzed in his pocket and his already skyrocketing blood pressure jumped a few more points.

Only three contacts were selected to break the Do Not Disturb notification ban on his phone: His mother, who never called during the day when she might be with clients; Melanie, who called whenever the hell she felt like it; and Vivian, who only called at the most presciently inconvenient times. He hit accept without bothering to check the caller ID.

If Melanie was calling him already, the script was either really good or he'd really fucked up.

Didn't matter. The script was a draft. Draft-lite. It was an uninsulated house without windows level of draftiness. If she didn't like it, he could revise. Honestly, he knew it had been shit when he'd sent it to her. He shouldn't have told her he could do it in a week. He should scrap it and start from scratch. He could—

She didn't even give him a chance to say hi. "You said it was faithful."

His blood turned to ice. It hadn't been *un*faithful. The message was the same. Locations, settings. Even half the line readings. Just not the eighties space race backdrop. Or the melodrama.

Did she want the melodrama? Fuck.

"Mrs. Westwood, I've—"

"People will lose their shit if we film it like this, and I don't know how many times I have to remind you to call me Melanie."

"Melanie, if you have notes, I can get to work on revisions."

"Absolutely not. It's genius."

Josh stood in stunned silence. Melanie was many things. Prone to hyperbole was not one of them.

She liked it.

Be cool. Josh kept his face neutral, like at any moment it would turn into a FaceTime call. "You thinking of optioning it?"

"No. I want it in production. Now. We have some negotiating to do, of course, so now's the time to tell me if there is anything I need to know about. People you've talked to about this. Anything before I can get moving."

If Stephen could hear what Melanie was saying, he'd be screaming, *say it!*

He fixed his gaze on the wall in front of him and commanded his lungs to draw breath. He'd never let himself dream about what this could mean. A million things he wanted raced through his mind. Producer credit. Reversion rights if they didn't end up making the movie. Points on the back end if they did. A say in casting …

"I want to direct."

A long silence played out on the other end. "Josh," Melanie's cautious tone came through, "this is a big deal. I have someone in mind."

His stomach roiled. If there was one thing he hated, it was negotiating.

"Melanie," he said in a voice far more confident than he felt, "I know this story better than anyone. I know what it looks like, sounds like. I know what it fucking smells like. I can bring life to this like no one else. And I know what needs to change, and another director might miss it. Casual racism. Gender stereo-types that"—*Fit your husband's generation and not ours*, he thought, but said—"modern audiences won't respond well to."

Good. Hit her in the target demographics.

He plowed ahead. "If you go with someone else, they'll turn this into a blockbuster and ruin it. The fans will revolt over that more than a female lead, and you'll lose the investment."

That was it. Time to let her think. He gripped his biceps so hard his hand ached.

"I saw *Oblivion*."

Josh ground his teeth together and said nothing.

Melanie sucked air through her teeth. "Why do you think it wasn't the breakout film of the festival?"

A wrenching gripped his stomach. She was right, of course. He couldn't even handle a short film with a four-figure budget, let alone a major motion picture. He'd be way over his head.

Then Cass's words from the previous week floated to the front of his brain. *The director saw the true essence of the story. They just need a team.* She saw his work and believed in him.

"It didn't break out because I needed help," Josh said. "With a continuity coordinator, a decent electrical and grip team, and the rest of the crew, we've got this. Let me put together the design team and I'll show you."

A noisy exhalation buzzed the earpiece. "Fine. You're directing, but I'm putting together the design team, and I'm going to be breathing down your neck the whole time. Now …"

The rest of her words blended together as he collapsed into his chair, listening numbly as she listed off casting ideas, locations, and a budget that pumped a dose of adrenaline straight into his veins.

Sweet holy hell.

He was directing *Sirius Darker*.

The week hammering through the script meant nothing else had been done. His condo reeked of closed windows and unwashed laundry. He dropped his keys on the slim entryway table and surveyed the piles of dirty dishes. He'd take care of it, but not now. Tonight, he'd let himself relax. Stephen texted he'd be out that night, so he had the place to himself. Catch a new documentary on Netflix. Maybe order in.

Or better yet …

He dropped onto his couch and scrolled his contacts. He still owed Emily a text, but he hadn't seen Jessica in forever. Or maybe Aubrey had broken up with her boyfriend.

His brow wrinkled. Did he even like Aubrey?

Switching to his messages, he swiped down to the last message Cass had sent.

> I'll be thinking of you the next time I touch myself xoxo

Had she done it yet? Slide her fingers over her clit with his name on her lips?

His dick pulsed. Jesus, just thinking about her made him hard. It wasn't too late. He could drop her a line. He lowered the fly of his jeans and stroked himself over his boxer briefs.

> Hey beautiful, wyd

> I'm not lucky enough you're back in town, am I?

He closed his eyes and dropped his head back, firming his grip and giving himself a slow pump. The way she'd cupped his balls with a gentle tug when she'd taken him deep in her mouth, teasing him, edging him until he'd had to hold himself back from fucking her face into the wall behind her. How she'd rubbed his cock on her nipples as he came, then those panting whimpers as he licked her clean, her pussy tight and wet around his fingers.

Fuck, she'd taken everything he'd given her. Beyond hot. The phone buzzed beside him on the couch.

Oh hey Sexy Dimples :)

Not in town, but if I was, you'd definitely be
getting lucky

I'm just getting out of the shower

Sexy Dimples, hey? He liked that. And it sounded like he caught her at a good time, even if she was just saying that. She was probably in an old tee shirt with her hair up in a towel. Bubbles flashed, and a minute later, his jaw dropped at the photo that popped up on his screen.

Oh, fuck yeah. She had a towel, alright, but that was it, and she wasn't doing much to hide behind it.

Cass sat on her bed, those wide hazel eyes looking into the camera, her skin flushed pink from the heat of the shower. Her hair hung in dripping ringlets, beads of water running over her sloped shoulders to where she held the towel over her tits, each droplet illuminated by the light diffused around her. Gone were the fiery red lips, now replaced with a dark blush that, if he remembered correctly, were the exact same colour as the tips of her breasts. She'd let the towel fall away from the rest of her body, so her soft belly and hip peeked from behind it, but tantalizingly still hidden. He wanted to reach through the photo and rip the towel off her.

If she was sending him a picture like that, she wanted to play.

Have you touched yourself yet?

I'm touching myself right now

Thinking about what you felt like inside me

Can you show me what I'm missing?

Oh hell, she wanted to *play*. He twitched against his grip, and pulled his cock free from his boxer briefs, already rock hard, and fisted his length.

Wait. Nothing sexy about straight up dick pics, even solicited ones. More subtle. He angled his leg to show the invitation of his open jeans, and what wasn't obscured by his hand hid in shadow. He fumbled with the phone to snap a picture and fired it off.

Ping. Another photo, her hand trapped between her thighs, a dust of dark hair visible between her fingers. She'd leaned forward, arms pressing those glorious tits together, her beautiful nipples looking like lollipops waiting to be sucked.

Fuck, that woman was nuclear. He hadn't been stroking himself for five minutes and he was going to come, but not without her. He fumbled for the FaceTime app, cursing when it went to voicemail.

Fine. Texting it was.

He stared at her photo with half-lidded eyes, imagining his lips teasing her rock-hard peaks. He hadn't gone down on her that night, like a fucking chump. When he saw her again—if he saw her again—he'd have his tongue on her before he said hello.

"Hey Siri," he groaned out, "text Cass Spectacular Tits."

> I want to know how sweet your pussy tastes

> Come for me baby

I'll tell you when

Will you think of my mouth on you?

Jesus. He slammed his eyes shut and shoved the thought aside, slowing his hand and thinking about mutual assents and the rainforest. Not that tongue down his length, how she'd managed to suck even with him deep in her throat, and the minutes later when he had come all over her and she'd taken his kiss like she was starving.

What would she look like now, reclined on her bed with her

legs spread? Did she pump her fingers inside? Rub her clit with one hand and pinch her nipples with the other? Did she have a favourite toy, one that she'd grip with her voluptuous thighs and shake to pieces when she came?

Fuck, he couldn't hold back much longer. He squeezed the base where his balls were tight against his body and swallowed hard.

Client negotiations. Billable hours. Legal liabilities.

God, thinking about her body was a liability.

> I came for you
>
> I think my neighbours heard me scream
> your name

> Show me your fingers. I want to see them wet

The photo came back, her eyes glassy and lips parted, fingers held up to the camera, glistening.

Oh fuck, she really had come. He rocked into his hand, imagining that little cry she'd let escape when she crested underneath him, the walls of her pussy gripping his cock as she came down from her orgasm, and he convulsed as he spilled himself onto his stomach so hard it hurt.

This woman could turn him on more than anyone he'd ever met, and she didn't even need to be in the same city. He looked down at the mess on his clothes and let out a lazy chuckle. He had to do laundry, anyway. This made it worth it.

> Now I need to take another shower :)

Damn, she was beautiful, her eyes sated and fingers soaked with her cum. Why the fuck hadn't he put his mouth on her to feel her come on his tongue? He squeezed the base of his cock once more, and a final shudder coursed through him. When he'd fucked her last week, she'd quivered around his cock so long he almost got hard again, seconds after coming twice already that night.

> Send me your last name and I'll book you on a flight tomorrow

Impulsive, maybe, but worth it.

And when they were finished in bed, he could bring her to that theatre he'd told her about. A new dark comedy was playing. She'd love it. Or maybe she'd hate it and they could argue about that one, too. The diner he'd suggested they go to for breakfast was down the street. Unless she was one of those weirdos who skipped breakfast. Maybe he'd find out.

A smiley face pinged his phone, then was dry for the rest of the night.

CHAPTER FIVE

CASS

Good morning, beautiful

I had an excellent sleep last night

> Lmao me too

> But I slept on wet hair and I look ridiculous this
> morning

Send pic

> Absolutely not

PING! A PHOTO LANDED IN HER MESSAGES. STEAM POURED OUT OF the open shower door to fog the mirror, obscuring his reflection. The towel, which must have roughed his damp hair, hung loosely in his other hand to just cover his interesting parts. Water beaded his chest and the stretch of hip she'd run her tongue over. A second photo followed, the fog wiped from the mirror, the towel a little lower, showing the dark hair at his base but still covering himself.

Please?

She caught her lower lip between her teeth and stretched her phone out to capture her hair, wild on her pillow, covers pulled up to her nose and eyes crinkled in laughter.

There. He asked for it.

> You look divine

> I need to see your bedhead in person. Come back to Van

> How's my beautiful girl this morning?

This morning's photo was cropped purposefully off centre; she was sure. He half hid behind the mug he sipped from, eyes narrowed over the rim.

> Need extra caffeine today

> Was up all night thinking about you again

Sure you were. Cass snorted as she walked down the sidewalk, iced coffee in hand with shades and a floppy sun hat, snapping her own photo to send back.

> That so? What's for breakfast

> Don't usually eat breakfast

> But I'd make an exception to eat it with you

> Or eat you

> I'm not picky

> You would, would you?

> I don't believe you

> You didn't when you had me in front of you

Ouch

I'm not kidding when I say I will fly your fine ass
down here and correct the error of my ways

Say the word

"What are you smiling at?" Libby half shouted.

The bar looked more like a middle-aged meat market than a hot spot for a production wrap party, but Terry, the film's production coordinator, had hired a killer DJ, and the restaurant had won awards for their sliders.

Cass looked over Libby's cocktail, some bizarre Caesar with a whole host of bar snacks precariously skewered into it, and turned her phone face down beside her rosé spritzer with a nervous grin. "So, ah, I've been texting with Sexy Dimples for a few weeks."

Libby perked up. "That dude from Vancouver? What happened to keeping that as a one-time thing, no contact, et cetera, et cetera?"

Right. She might have said that.

"He texted me, then all of a sudden I was telling him how good he felt that night and I'm sending him nudes."

Lots of guys had asked her for nudes. She'd never sent one. But her nipples had tightened when his message popped up on her screen, and at the memories of his hungry look when he'd uncovered her body that night, peeling off all her layers. The thought of that expression on his face again—of putting it there again—was too much to resist. It hadn't even crossed her mind *not* to let the towel drop and send him photos.

One of her getting out of the shower. Another with her fingers splayed around her breasts. Last night, she'd sent one with the waistband of her sleep shorts tugged down to the side. Then another one with her shorts pooled around her feet.

And not just nudes. Of her eating a bagel on the river pathway. Her eyes crossed at an art exhibit downtown. His appreciative replies to every text had warmed her to her toes.

"And now there are naked photos of you floating around. I thought you looked extra slutty today."

Cass slapped a hand over the grin that hadn't faded since the exchange that morning. "He doesn't seem like the type to share them, does he?"

"He might be. You don't know him."

A doubt clouded her stomach, and her smile dimmed. "What was I thinking?"

"You were thinking your kitty needed a little fun." Libby plucked a pickled asparagus out of her drink and snapped off the tip. "At least I know you're heading into vacation with a head start on being relaxed. But if you have FaceTime sex with this guy on the beach, I'm tossing you in the ocean."

"My data plan isn't good enough to support orgasms via international video calls."

But sex on the beach with Sexy Dimples? With her knees and elbows cushioned in the warm sand, and his hips slapping against her butt. Heck, it didn't need to be on the beach. She'd happily jump on a plane back to Vancouver for a weekend. Take him up on his offer to eat with her. Or her. A fresh shiver rolled over her collarbones, and she clamped down on the feeling working its way under her skin.

"To Cancun," Libby cheered, clicking her glass against Cass's, shedding a few flakes of batter from the deep-fried crab leg into her rosé, "and good riddance to this clusterfuck."

"To Cancun," agreed Cass with a grin, focussing on her friend and fishing out the batter sprinkles from her drink, "Although I'll miss everyone."

"Not like we won't see them on the next project."

But before the next project, she and Libby—no Jill for this getaway, too busy with a new promotion—would be on a plane for her first real vacation in years. Not a weekend away, not an unplanned break in filming because of bad weather, and not their usual hop-on-a-plane to bum around some new city until they crashed. The last time they'd slept in a hostel, Cass had woken up with a rash and all of Libby's underwear had been stolen.

So generic beach destination it was. The new cover-up and two-piece bathing suit she'd sewn especially for the trip were already packed in her bags at the door. Though packing had taken longer than she'd planned, thanks to last night's texting and sweetly spicy exchange that morning. His black hair mussed around his face, partly hidden behind another coffee, eyes narrowed in a flirty stare. The flutter in her chest picked up.

Crap. Here she was, obsessing over another unobtainable man, this one all the way in another province. She could barely afford rent, let alone regular plane tickets. And on the off-chance he was serious about flying her out, fantasizing about Josh would lead to pining at best and plane-hopping booty calls at worst.

This was how it always started. She'd fall hard while he was having fun, and she'd have to pretend she didn't care. Which never worked.

Before she could change her mind, she swiped the thread clear and blocked his number.

There. Temptation gone. No more thinking about Sexy Dimples or the way he made her pulse beat against her ribs and between her thighs. Time to focus on the future. A future that included a vacation with her best friend. Spa treatments. Sleeping in. Unlimited margaritas, seashell-dotted sand, and a bathtub-warm ocean. That was all that mattered.

But visions of sand between her pedicured toes and a margarita in her hand were shattered when Terry, whom she adored like a sibling and was the person who roped her into ninety percent of the projects she'd worked on in the last decade, had her in their sights from across the bar. And was coming her way.

"No," Cass said pre-emptively as Terry hopped onto the bar stool beside Libby, who scowled at them.

"Hello, my lovelies," they said with a broad smile. "Having fun tonight?"

"I'm not doing it."

"Me, either."

"Come on, now. You haven't even heard what it's about."

"Oops, sorry the guys are calling me over byeeee!" Libby jumped up, calling over her retreating shoulder as she disappeared into a crowd that had not been waving her over.

Traitor.

"So, as I was saying—"

"I'm busy."

"You don't even know when it is."

Cass tried to glower, and Terry cackled at her attempt.

"You'll want to hear about this," they said. "Trust me."

"I love you, but find someone else."

"You've been asked for by name."

That didn't mean anything. Everyone in the tight-knit Calgary film and television industry knew her name. Cass remained stoic and silent, but pleasure tiptoed over her ego.

"You'd be head of costume," Terry nudged in a sing-song voice. "And I know you like the hands-on stuff, so you could probably still get your mitts on wardrobe …"

Head of costume? It was likely some little indie thing that would be wrapped up in a month. Cass squinched her eyes shut. "No."

"It has a budget," they continued, "and pre-production meetings are starting next week."

"I'm literally out of the country next week," she hedged.

"So take a virtual meeting. You can be the asshole on the beach drinking mai tais, or whatever, while everyone else sweats in a boardroom. Not that you're an asshole, darling. You are my favourite person ever. And Libby, too."

The reason there was no rest for the wicked was because they kept getting more work. *When will I learn to say no?* Cass grimaced into her half-finished drink and sighed. Apparently, not today. "What's it about?"

"Ever heard of *Sirius Darker*?"

She shook her head, nonplussed.

Terry grinned. "Ever hear of Melanie Westwood?"

"I'm in Cancun for a week," Cass whined into her mochaccino. "And I wanted to do theatre this year."

But Melanie freaking Westwood had personally picked Cass for head of costume. No idea which TV show or film would have caught her eye, but it didn't matter. Terry said the director, whom she hadn't looked up yet, had pushed to bring in their own talent for the costume department, but had been overruled. Terry had stopped badgering her after she promised to think about it, so now she dealt with the indecision of a steady paycheque or something new. Leading costume on a show that wasn't either another Western, blood-stained tatters, or sourced exclusively from thrift stores would be completely new.

"She told the director my work was understated but forward thinking." Cass could hardly believe it. Not only did Melanie Westwood know who she was, but she asked for her by name. "But theatre!"

"This does sound like a great opportunity," Jill said. "But you've been talking about working with your friend in theatre all year. What's the movie?"

She could always count on Jill to enable her decisions, especially in work-life balance. Cass pulled out her phone and scrolled her inbox. "They said it was something serious. Serious armour, serious ardour ... it was really loud last night."

Jill's entire posture changed, eyes widening. "You don't mean *Sirius Darker*, do you?" she whispered.

"Yeah! That's it!"

"*Sirius Darker* is going to be a movie?" She seized Cass's forearm and shook her. "That's one of my favourite books! It's a dystopian love letter to humanity! It's a new modern classic!"

So, she'd heard of it? Funny. Terry said it was niche. "Nothing's confirmed yet, and you can't say anything to anyone."

"I won't, I swear," Jill said breathlessly. "I can't let you not do this. You have to do this."

Cass's face dropped. "What about work-life balance? Theatre?"

"You won't regret it. The story is incredible." Jill put her elbows on the café table. "How about this? I'll lend you my copy while you're on vacation. Read it, then make up your mind."

Cass could feel herself being talked into it. Theatre didn't pay well, anyway, and her friend had a solid backup costumer if Cass backed out. They wouldn't even miss her.

She sunk her head into her hands. "Fine. I'll read a hundred pages."

"And then you'll read the next four hundred pages. Trust me."

"I'm not even sure I want to even work on another movie right now," Cass said, sucking the foam off her drink. Then a thought occurred to her. There could be other benefits of joining the crew. "Plus, if I'm busy again, I won't have to answer any questions about why I'm still single."

"Cass," Jill said, softening, "not everyone is like him."

The swath of fizzled situationships begged to differ.

"Of course not!" Cass said. "But like you said, this is an amazing opportunity I can't pass up!"

And if it meant she'd be too busy to date for the foreseeable future, even better.

I'M MEETING MELANIE WESTWOOD TODAY!!!!!

I can't breathe!!!!

DAVIE

who

SUZIE

isn't that the chick who flashed her boobs on
Secret Celebrity Dancer a few years ago?

How her siblings still didn't know who Melanie Westwood was after the hours Cass had talked about her made no sense. Or it did make sense. If a topic didn't involve her sister's kids or her brother's dirt biking, they didn't pay much attention to anything Cass said.

Sure, Melanie had gotten the streaming company a fat fine for her striptease, but she'd also gotten noticed by Hollywood mogul Darrin Westwood, who was responsible for executive producing some of the biggest films every year. Nothing with awards show buzz, but the man knew how to make money. When he met Melanie, Mrs. Westwood Number Four was retired, and Melanie was promoted to Mrs. Westwood Number Five later that year. Overnight, she bank rolled her own passion projects, tiny little films that never would have been noticed.

She'd discovered Brynne Sparo, of all people.

And Melanie had asked for Cass by name. Cass squealed the entire time she scrolled her email.

The studio wanted her on the crew enough that they upgraded her vacation, with the caveat that she read the script on the beach. Staying at a five-star hotel instead of a three-star made for good bribery. Cass tucked the script into the pages of the brick Jill had lent her to read on the beach. Libby, having been hired on as the head electrician, declined the hard copy, instead downloading the audiobook so she didn't have to lug the thing around.

Packing the tome into her carry-on bags precluded the addition of an extra pair of shoes or another dress. At the last minute, she threw her sketchbook into her carry on, in case inspiration struck over daiquiris.

Sci-fi wasn't her jam, only ever getting through a few of Octavia E. Butler's books. But dang. She devoured *SD* (the small but rabid fanbase online referred to the book by its initials, she'd learned) by the third day of vacation and the screenplay right after. She could already picture the trauma on earth. The other-worldliness of the Travellers. The screenplay adaptation took the major story elements and distilled them into a shockingly tight script. Cass couldn't believe it worked, but it did.

The film had a real budget for costume, too. The last theatre production she'd worked on had given her six hundred dollars for the entire cast. And while the last TV show she'd costumed on had a budget, it was all tattered jeans and grimy shirts, and she had been a grunt on that crew, anyway. But a few of the smaller projects she had led herself, her design portfolio posted online? Her being handpicked for costume made sense.

Cass scooted her beach chair closer to the umbrella and balanced the laptop on her crossed legs. This was the one spot the glare off the pool wouldn't reflect off the screen, and there were little side tables with legs buried deep in the sand to hold her rotation of fruity drinks. She wrapped her hair back in a silk scarf, popped her earbuds in, and pulled her beach wrap around her shoulders.

Just because she was taking a meeting on the beach, didn't mean she wanted to flash a bunch of cleavage to the new creative team.

"The timing on this could not be worse," Libby grumbled, dragging her chair closer to Cass.

It was short; more of a meet-and-greet than an actual get down to work type meeting. The details had arrived in their inboxes while the plane was still in the air, then dropped to the bottom of their inboxes when they promised each other to ignore their computers for the sea, buffet, and the book, in that order, until the very last second.

The hotel Wi-Fi barely reached where they sat, so not flashing cleavage to the meeting was no longer an issue. She logged into the invite and typed into the meeting chat bar.

> Cass and Libby here. Bad reception. Will stay off video and on mute for now!

Not great for a meet-n-greet, but everyone knew they'd be on vacation. They could deal. Plus, the first time Melanie Westwood was seeing her wouldn't be with sunblock smeared cheeks or humidity hair.

Cass brushed sand from her feet as thumbnails of different crew popped up on the screen. And then nearly dropped her daiquiri.

Any other time, she would have squealed at Melanie Westwood occupying the corner of the screen, with Brynne Sparo beside her. Maybe she'd have spared a second glance for the handsome blond man with dreamy blue eyes she didn't recognize.

But a face with sharp features and glacial green eyes scowling through the screen froze her in place.

"What's up, babe?" Libby peered at her through her aviators. "You look like you've seen a ghost."

Not a ghost. Someone much more physical than that.

Was this a mistake? She grabbed her phone and plugged the name under the thumbnail on screen into IMDb.

No dimples on his impassive headshot, but his intense eyes and high cheekbones were present and accounted for. Hair shorter than what she ran her fingers through, but those were the same lips that had roamed down her body and set her skin on fire.

With her attention half on the video call as people chimed in, she checked his credits.

Confirmed. Director and cinematographer for *Sirius Darker*, pre-production. She frantically scrolled down to the biography section.

Josh Graham took a circuitous path to film, starting at the University of British Columbia in …

"Holy. Shit." Libby's eyes widened, falling back into her own chair.

Cass closed the app like it would make it untrue. Sure, the industry could get small pretty quick, but really?

The laugh started deep in her stomach, shaking her ribs and making her eyes stream until the people sitting beside her glared.

If this wasn't her luck, nothing was. Her first big gig—leading the department, no less—and she would be working with the man she'd had gloriously fantastic sex with mere weeks ago. The man she'd traded filthy texts with, flirted with, that had watched her beg for his dick on her knees.

The one she had planned never to see again.

Her special, perfect one-night she held like a treasured jewel, close to the warmth of her heart, was about to crash with the harsh light of reality.

Maybe he wouldn't recognize her. It was possible. Between the theatres and his condo, most of the time they had been together was in the dark.

Oh, who was she kidding? He could be scrolling one of the dozens of photos she'd sent him right now. He had her nudes on his phone, full frontal boobage with her fingers dripping wet after he'd made her come from a thousand kilometres away.

It was a cosmic balancing of the scales. Noticed by Melanie Westwood, but she had to work with the director she'd slept with.

And what was she going to do? Send him a text? What would she say?

Hey there, Sexy Dimples! Small world! Guess we can skip the usual icebreaker questions! Hope that incredible dick of yours is still awesome. Kisses!

"Libby?" she said, turning to her best and longest friend.

"I know." Libby looked as ashen as she felt.

"This is bananas. What—"

"I haven't seen him in years," Libby whispered. "What am I going to do?"

Who hadn't she seen in years that was an oh-my-god-I-know agreement? Cass opened and closed her mouth like a fish.

"It's fine," Libby continued. "That was a long time ago. He could have a girlfriend. Or be married. He probably doesn't think about me anymore, anyway. Besides. I've moved on. Totally over him. I'm a different person now. It's not like I didn't think it would happen one day, anyway."

A sinking dread pooled in her stomach. Libby's reaction could only mean one thing. Cass hadn't looked past a single name after Josh jumped out, and she scrolled through the rest of the agenda.

Stephen. On as first assistant director. Libby's long-time boyfriend, who left for Vancouver right after university without a second glance. No wonder Libby was freaking out.

Cass shoved her own concerns aside. She could spiral over Josh later. A one-night stand was nothing compared to a broken heart that still hadn't healed.

"It *will* be fine," Cass said, her eyes on the screen, where her perfect one-night stand twiddled a pen between his fingers. The same fingers that had plunged deep in her pussy as he licked his cum off her breasts.

Oh. Dear.

She squeezed her eyes shut. Spiral later. This was about Libby. "It will be better than fine. You are brilliant. You are capable. You are a smoke show. Who knows what could happen?"

"Hey, Libs," Stephen said to the black square he would have seen on his screen, an affectedly casual tone to his voice Cass hadn't heard before. "Been a while."

Libby pulled her gaze to Cass, eyes pleading. "We're going to need margs and nachos."

Cass squeezed her hand. "It'll be okay."

A private message landed in her chat. Karl, her old sound buddy.

> A few of the guys in lighting said they worked with the director on a shoot in Van where he was first AD, and he's a mofo. We're in for a ride on this one.

What if I've already ridden that one?

They had clicked instantly. They'd talked each other's ears off for hours before they dragged each other into bed. He'd texted her after, and almost every day since, just to say good morning. Until she blocked him, anyway.

Maybe he'd want to pick up where they'd left off. Who knew where things could lead?

Texting him now, after hiding behind a turned-off camera for an hour, would be the coward's way out. The in-person production meeting was scheduled for next month. She'd test the waters then.

Where he could turn her down in front of the entire creative crew if he wasn't interested.

Honestly, if she didn't have bad luck, she wouldn't have any luck at all.

Cass tipped her head to look up at the faded underside of the umbrella. "We are going to need all the margs and nachos."

CHAPTER SIX

JOSH

MELANIE HADN'T BEEN KIDDING ABOUT WANTING TO GET STARTED. Once production planning was moving, it *moved*. A month of meetings blurred by and the filming schedule came together. Summer for pre-production, and fall and winter for principal photography in Calgary.

Back when he didn't think Sirius Darker would ever get made, it had seemed like a good idea to write a winter script. A barren, icy landscape was the perfect backdrop for SD's bleakness. After googling Calgary winters, however, he regretted not adapting the movie's setting to the fucking tropics.

Life in Vancouver was easy to put on hold. No pets to care for, no plants to water. He notified insurance companies, cancelled grocery deliveries, and, after very little debate, parked his car in the safety of his parents' garage.

"Don't worry, angel. I'll be home before you know it," he'd whispered as he draped the custom protective cover over her. No way the Bimmer was coming to Calgary. The junker Stephen drove was pitted with hail dents and rust spots.

He had a few things to put in his storage locker to make room for the renter he'd lined up for his condo. One of Stephen's cousins had just broken up with her boyfriend and needed a place. Easy enough to help her out. Moving on after a breakup was a shitshow at the best of times. Plus, the cousin was far more responsible than Stephen was, and the roommate she'd brought with her was cute. Maybe he'd get her number when he got back. If the bedroom eyes the roommate had been giving him were any indication, that number would be in his phone the day he got back.

It was always nice to have a welcome home committee.

He sent a mass text to a group of friends to arrange a few get-togethers before he bounced from town. Then, a separate series of texts over the next few weeks, copied and pasted—no group text here—all saying a version of

> Hey beautiful. Heading out of town for a while

> Want to make sure I don't forget you while I'm away?

His incoming messages folder gushed with declarations of how much he'd be missed, followed by invitations to see him that night. Or the next. Or the week following. He had a busy month in more ways than one, ending with the woman whose bed he was currently trying to extract himself from.

"You're not going already, are you?" Emily cooed as he swung his legs off her bed. She stretched out, letting the sheet slide down and display her tits. "I'm going to miss you."

"I'll miss you, too, beautiful," he mumbled, scanning the floor for his pants. The sheets clung to the sweat on the back of his knees, and he pulled himself free of the cheap satin. He stood, pulling up his boxer briefs and eyeing the time on her phone propped up on her nightstand.

Just enough light from the streetlamps filtered through the rain-splashed windows to give him the impression of where his clothes lay in piles on the floor. The vanilla-scented candle she always insisted on lighting had burned to halfway, its cloying perfume threatening to drop a headache on him. Her shiny pink lipstick pristine and foundation were flawless. How her makeup remained perfect after everything was a mystery. But it's not like he'd kissed her mouth, and she didn't give head. Or move around enough to get sweaty.

Maybe it wasn't a mystery. The night was already fading from his memory.

Frankly, none of the last several nights had been memorable, but he couldn't muster up more than the barest enthusiasm for any of them.

His mind kept wandering back to Cass. Her smooth skin was like silk under his hand, the thick flesh of her thighs jiggling with his every thrust. How she bucked underneath him, her hair wild and her lipstick smeared across his face and dick. Her laugh that rang out when he teased her, letting her take his hand to pull him down the street to the next movie.

If half his thoughts were full of being with her, the other half was wrapped in why she'd stopped replying to his texts.

"I'm not gone forever. I'll call you when I'm back in town." He leaned over to brush his mouth over her jaw, thought better of it, and ran his hands through his dishevelled hair. Emily didn't love it when he left right away, but his flight was booked early the next morning, and he still needed to pack a carry-on. The majority of his stuff had been shipped ahead to the long-term rental waiting for him, but that didn't mean he wanted to go eighteen hours without a toothbrush.

"Maybe I can come out and visit you for a weekend," she said, walking her fingers up the plane of his hip to sneak under the hem of the shirt he'd pulled over his head.

"Probably not a good idea. I'll be too busy, Em," he said, wiggling out of reach and peering at the mess on the floor in a futile search for his pants.

Her hand froze mid-air. "Em?" she said, her voice turning icy.

Fuck. He mentally scrolled through the texts he sent that afternoon. "Sorry, beautiful, I know that," he lied smoothly. Who was it? Madelyn? No, Vanya! Almost a hundred percent sure it was Vanya. He scanned the room for a trinket or embossed photo frame with a name, or even an initial to tip him off. Ninety per cent sure it was Vanya.

Eighty percent sure.

"I'm just thinking about a note I need to send to a woman named Emily I work with before tomorrow morning. So rude of me to be thinking about that right now. But that's what I mean. I'm not going to have the attention to lavish on you that you deserve."

She apparently bought the line, and he breathed a sigh of relief as he spotted a notebook with a stylized "V" on the cover. Ninety-nine percent sure it was Vanya.

"You're right, I deserve all of you," probably Vanya pouted playfully, before turning more serious. "I've been thinking. I want to see more of you when you get back, not less. Promise to call me when you're in town?"

And that would be that. One more contact out of his list.

He'd been clear he was only looking for something casual. No time, no interest, and no appetite for anything serious. Vanya had been on board when they started hooking up last year after meeting at her friend's gallery opening—or was it hers?—and she'd invited him into her bed after the second drink. They'd met up five, maybe six times since, and always at her place.

Too bad she wanted to change the rules. He wouldn't lead her on, but he sure as hell wasn't breaking things off right after leaving her bed. Even he wasn't that much of a piece of shit. Usually.

He swiped his thumb along her jaw and let her press a kiss to his thumb tip. "I'll send you a text."

The parched air attacked his skin as soon as he stepped out of the arrivals gate. Back home the wind had heft, humidity. Here, every drop of moisture had evaporated the second he exited the plane.

"Why didn't anyone tell me we were shooting in a fucking desert?" he grumbled, stripping his jacket the moment he closed the door of the town car the studio sent.

Stephen ignored him, reciting the address to the driver with a series of preferred directions, and tugged at the wrinkles in his shirt. "We should get there with plenty of time. I promised Westy I'd call her and Brynne in when everyone arrived."

They still wanted to make an entrance, even if they weren't in the room. "We literally booked the call at their convenience. Westy's the one who wanted to start filming a winter movie in the summer."

"We're not shooting for months, although you never know when we might get surprise snow."

"You're shitting me."

"Nope." Stephen rolled up his sleeves and turned his face to bask in the sun pouring in through the open windows. "Man, it's good to be home."

"Home's a ninety-minute flight away. You could go back every once in a while and stop eating all my food."

"Nah. You'd miss me too much."

"Doubt it."

"You finally going to add me to your DND list?"

Josh hissed out a pained sigh. When—no, *if*—any emergencies happened during filming, Stephen would need full, immediate access to him. "Yes," he said grudgingly.

"Oh sweetheart, I love this new step in our relationship."

"Fuck off."

A series of chirps pinged Josh's phone as he flicked it off airplane mode, adding Stephen's contact info to his short emergency list. After a quick reply to his mom and swiping a few conversations with women into the trash without reading, a twinge of disappointment plucked at his ribs. Nothing. He didn't expect anything from Cass anymore. It had been weeks since she'd replied to his texts, his last one being

Heading out of town for a bit

You should call me sometime

If he found out she'd been in Van while he was away, he'd bust down a wall.

Or maybe not. He thought they'd had fun. Trading movie recs and spicy pics, more of the former than the latter. No more of her morning selfies with her giant fancy coffees and sweet smile. Or that one pic where she'd had her curls held back with a scarf like a fifties movie star. Too fucking cute.

For some reason, she'd ghosted. Who knew why. Maybe she got bored. Maybe she got a boyfriend.

Josh scowled at his phone one last time before shoving it in his pocket.

The town car zipped through the mid-morning traffic on unfamiliar streets. The city was still a black box. He'd been out once for a meeting, flying home the same evening. Seen photos of location checks, but not enough to get a feel for the place. He felt like he was going in blind.

It was a good fucking thing he trusted Stephen.

Between landing and the team-lead production meeting starting in an hour, there was no time to stop at their rental apartments. The car dropped them in front of what passed for a heritage building in the west. A brick building still shy of a hundred years old. The scaffolding affixed to the front showed renovations underway.

Great. Now they'd have to deal with construction noise during production meetings.

A perky young woman who introduced herself as Bex the PA, bounced out of the front doors to lead them to the meeting room, pointing out Josh's office and Melanie's corner suite as she led them down the hall. He glanced in as they passed by. He wouldn't argue for the bigger space, even if she'd rarely be here. There'd be other battles he'd need to fight.

He hadn't argued for much after he'd gotten what he wanted. The most important thing was that he was directing. He could work his way around everything else. Melanie got who she wanted for casting, because of course she did. Hiring Stephen as his first AD meant he didn't have his usual production coordinator. The entire grip and electrical department were based in Calgary. Location scouts, too, obviously. Plus, props and costume and everything else the storm of emails had covered in the weeks since he negotiated the deal to get him out here.

He and Melanie had spent enough time together hammering out every detail of the next several months that Josh knew what she wanted from makeup to set design. Hell, he could probably name her brand of tampons.

Of course, Melanie insisted Brynne have the lead role. Good thing he had gender-flipped the main characters. Brynne would never accept another arm-candy role, and she pulled enough star power that, save the most misogynistic "fans," movie goers would laud, or at least tolerate, the changes. He hoped.

Miraculously, film rights for the novel hadn't been secured, and the author had been so passive through initial negotiations that Josh had quietly asked her who her representation was. When she replied she didn't know she'd needed one, Josh sent her the names of a few contacts. Negotiations were rougher after that, but fuck if he would let someone get creamed from lack of savvy. Josh had combed through the contract for a day and a half after the studio's lawyers had their fingerprints on it and found a few loose ends to tie up before he'd given the go-ahead for the final sign off.

Dozens of people had their fingerprints on his baby before a second of film had been shot.

"Look at you, being a team player," Stephen said, beaming like a proud dad. Josh scowled in return.

Josh claimed a seat in the empty meeting room, facing the

door, ready to stare down anyone sauntering in after the scheduled start time. He scoured the agenda: twelve people, and not a single one was early for their first in-person meeting. A bunch of people he didn't know and therefore didn't trust, but Stephen knew Terry from when he worked here early in his career, and Josh trusted Stephen, so by proxy …

"Chill, dude," Stephen said, fidgeting with his pen and snatching glances at the door.

Josh grabbed the uncapped pen out of Stephen's hand before he was able to absently draw blue streaks through his beard. "Then show me what chill behaviour looks like."

Everyone thought that film was this loosey-goosey, artistic, temperamental shitshow that ran on whims and muses. Well, it kind of ran on muses. But it also ran on the hard work of dozens —if not hundreds—of people, all pulling together in one direction. And it worked better when the pulling all happened at the same time.

People bumped into the room, trading greetings and hugs as they took their seats, and when the door opened next, a lyrical laugh from down the hall pattered over his skin like a spring rain.

The sound washed over him. He knew lots of people with lots of laughs, but something about that pure voice tugged at his memory and sent an eruption of goosebumps over his torso as he tried to place it.

Just as the door was closing, it wrenched open with a gangly, balding man standing back to let a short, curvy woman in first, with a gorgeous mess of curls and the most kissable lips he'd ever seen.

Make that the most kissable lips he'd ever kissed.

Sweet holy hell. He glanced down at the names making up his design team, and the scowl melted from his face.

Cassidy St. Claire.

Cass was his head of costume.

Of course he'd looked up everyone on IMDb, but very few of

the crew had photos attached to their profiles. Melanie had over-ridden his longtime costume collaborator, so he'd poured over the long list of St. Claire's work and became slightly less pissy with the quality of her resume. Hell, he'd swapped emails with her on wardrobe direction for weeks, and she hadn't said a thing. Not like he would have connected the Cassidy St. Claire signing off on correspondence to the Cass Spectacular Tits saved in his phone.

He'd have blamed it on being busy, getting everything ready, but that was no reason not to know everything happening on set. He always knew everything on set, just not much about the women he slept with. And this woman was good luck. Not only had they had volcanic sex that night, but Melanie had asked him about his script the morning after they'd hooked up.

Definitely good luck. But terrible timing.

He'd have to listen to that laugh, smell her hair when she bent close, see those inviting curves that begged for his hands to run over them. Like she'd begged him to do that night. He rubbed a thumb over the angle of his jaw, the memory of where she'd run her tongue, and that sharp inhalation after he'd slid inside her. His dick twitched, and he shut down the train of thought.

He had one priority right now, and it wasn't chasing after a woman. Not even this one.

He dragged his gaze up to her face. Of all the things she looked—nervous, embarrassed, hesitant—surprised wasn't one of them as her eyes met his, then shifted, and her face lit up.

"Stephen!" Cass threw her arms around his friend, who scooped her in a bear hug that swept her feet off the ground.

The fuck? Something acidic flickered through his gut. Obviously not jealousy. He was just pissed that the meeting was delayed. That was it. They were starting in two minutes and Cass was busy squeezing the life out of his friend.

Stephen released her roughly with an *oof* and a broad grin. "Cassie! It's been way too long!"

Cassie? For fuck's sake.

"Ten years." Cass finally stepped back, shooting a glance at Josh, and her smile morphed from open to awkward. She dipped her head in greeting as she sat on the other side of the long table, a few chairs down. Far enough that they wouldn't be locking eyes every two seconds; close enough that it didn't look like she was avoiding him. She tucked a rogue curl behind her ear, resuming her conversation with the gangly man she'd walked in with and a pretty woman with teal hair he vaguely recognized.

Oh, shit. That was Cass's friend.

Small world.

Josh leaned over to Stephen and whispered behind his hand, "Our head of costume is the woman I told you about from the film fest."

Stephen tore his eyes from the woman with the teal hair. "What?"

"Cass and I have met," Josh said, loading the last word with as much weight as he could muster.

His friend closed his eyes. "Fucking hell, dude. Why am I not surprised?" He sighed. "Shit is about to get complicated."

"Thank you for that astute observation."

Josh pulled up Melanie and Brynne on the monitor, still back in Vancouver, and started the meeting. They went around the room, Josh giving the same benign nod at Cass's intro as he did the others as they made introductions, her friend Libby looking much paler and quieter than the feisty person he had met outside the theatre.

Storyboards and design elements were presented. They talked vision, about how they were going to turn the sci-fi epic with a trilogy's worth of pages into a single film that was *Arrival*-meets-*Contact*. With less than half the budget of either.

It was the largest budget he'd ever had, by an order of magnitude, but he still wanted fifteen million more dollars. Better yet, twenty-five million more.

And the team was strong. Lots of experience pulled from

Melanie's contacts, and the people who the union had insisted work on the project had solid portfolios. Cass included. Josh felt a slight unclenching until Cass spoke up.

"I saw the inspiration art Melanie shared, but this script is so character focused, I think we need a different look for costume." Cass pulled up a series of sketches and photos of cosplayers from conventions over the years.

And a link to fan art Josh had shared on an *SD* forum years ago. The digitized watercolours were attributed to dr-rykoff-xxx69—he cringed at his sixteen-year-old self for that embarrassing handle—and any moisture in his mouth evaporated. She couldn't have known the fan art was his. How did she find this, and where was she going with it? He held his breath as she continued.

"This is the kind of dedication these fans have. They love this story. The die-hards will be furious either way, but since we already switched to a female lead, I think we lean into her power, and strip away artifice. Plus," she continued, smiling at Terry as she pulled her mock-ups out of her design folder, "it'll save money."

Damn if it wasn't the exact look he had been too afraid to bring up with Melanie. Worried he'd already stuck his neck out enough getting the director role, he'd swallowed every creative idea she'd thrown his way.

But not Cass. It was like she had dumped out the contents of his brain and picked out all the rationale he couldn't put into words. And then levelled it up.

"Realism on Earth," Cass said, flipping through each design mock-up, "and dirty, near future sci-fi for interstellar travel."

Josh jumped to agree. "She's right. This isn't a space opera."
Or at least it shouldn't be.

Melanie narrowed her eyes as she studied the muted design specs in front of her, unmoving.

"Plus, fans will clamour to cosplay these two at all the Cons." Cass continued, "These costumes will be around for years. We can tap into the maker community and release DIY tutorials. It's built in buzz."

A gleam flared in Brynne's eyes, and she nodded once. Melanie glanced off screen. "Okay."

Josh released a pent-up breath. Holy shit. Melanie was on board with Cass's ideas.

Maybe she was bringing good luck here, too.

When the meeting wrapped, Cass lingered, fussing with her bag until the last person filtered out of the room. She stopped fiddling enough to stare up at the light fixtures.

"So, this is awkward," she said.

Maybe she had been telling the truth, that she didn't do that a lot. One-night stands. Swapping nudes. He'd run into hookups outside the bedroom more times than could realistically be left to chance and had navigated his share of fully clothed conversations after swapping orgasms.

Cass, apparently, had not. Her flushed cheeks and nervous tics hadn't subsided, though she was clearly trying to stay cool.

"Doesn't need to be awkward," he said. "We had a fantastic night—"

"We did." Cass perked up, wringing her hands. "You know, I was thinking—"

"—and we get to work together on a fantastic project. We had a great night, and I'm glad we had it. We're professionals. I don't see a problem working together."

"Oh." Her shoulders dropped and her face lost some of its glow. "Good. I thought it might be weird. Having seen each other naked and all." The spots of colour high on her cheeks deepened. "And that's how you make it weird."

A huff of laughter escaped his throat before he could shut it down. He'd missed that unfiltered personality. Something funny and disarming came out of her mouth at the most unexpected times.

"We're probably going to have a few weird moments, but we got along great then," he said, determined to put her at ease, "and who knows, it might help us work better together now."

"We really did. I hope we still do." She bobbed her head, her mass of curls bouncing alongside her round cheeks. "*Oblivion*. I looked it up when I got back. You did everything yourself."

He had. Every mistake was his. The continuity errors. The jilted performance he barely coaxed out of the lead actor. At least six minutes could have been cut. He crossed his arms. "It was a piece of shit."

"It was really good."

"The festival should never have accepted it."

"The vetting for that festival is stringent. You should be proud."

He pressed his lips into a thin line. He didn't need her sucking up, but her comment didn't have the usual sycophantic reek. And she had said she'd liked it months ago, even before she knew it was his project. "It needed a lot of work. It wasn't perfect. It needed—"

"It needed an editor, a budget, and good wardrobe, and now you have those."

That he did. Even today's meeting with the team was putting his fears at rest. He let a half-grin creep onto his mouth. "Careful, now I just have a budget for lens flare," he said wryly. "Might still be amateur hour here."

"I don't believe that for a second," she said, smiling. "Plus, I'll design such a gorgeous wardrobe you won't need to resort to gimmicks."

"Gimmicks? You offend me."

"I don't believe that, either. I think you like it when I tell you what I think."

His smile spread to match hers. Yeah, they'd work together just fine. "We'll see about that," he said. "Looking forward to working with you."

"Same." She closed her eyes and looked like she was psyching herself up. "Um, if you haven't already, I'd really appreciate it if you deleted our chat thread," she said in a quiet voice.

Josh didn't need to blush. Cass was going red enough for both of them. He couldn't blame her for not wanting intimate photos in the hands of someone she was working with. "Of course," he said gently. "Do you want to see me do it?"

"Thanks, but I don't need to watch. I trust you."

That felt good. Unearned, but good. He'd delete the thread later, when she wouldn't see herself saved as Cass Spectacular Tits in his contacts. Cass Head of Costume was more appropriate for a strictly working relationship, anyway. "I'll see you first thing tomorrow."

"Raya's useless here." Josh scowled down at the app and scrolled ... for nothing. He'd received an invite for the exclusive dating app years ago but had never used it. Never needed to. But here in Calgary, with no one he knew in town, he was still out of luck, and Raya's list of locals was so thin it was virtually non-existent.

For the best, really. Focussing on the production and all.

"Does poor Josh need to use Tinder like a peasant?" Stephen mocked, turning the car into the underground parking garage of the long-term rental Terry had secured for the out-of-towners. "Those fuckers better not have given us a shared wall. I don't want to listen to your—"

"Life changing lessons on how to please a woman?" Josh checked their apartment units. Nine-oh-eight and eight-oh-eight. Lucky numbers. He'd have to call his grandmother and let her know. "I'm right below you. Take off your fucking boots when you're home."

"If I wanted to be told how to live, I'd have moved back in with my parents while we were here."

The neighbourhood seemed fine enough. Just outside of the

city's tiny downtown, the fully furnished apartment was by far the nicest accommodations a studio had ever put him up in. Modern appliances he wouldn't use, with sleek chrome finish on everything. Grey walls and dark faux hardwoods, the spare furniture selected to coordinate without looking too matchy-matchy. The designer must have gotten a discount. The same set up could be seen through the windows of the neighbouring suites.

Stephen exited the elevator on Josh's floor, following him to his eighth-floor apartment.

"Aren't you going to, I don't know, go home?" Josh said, turning the key in the lock.

"Later." Stephen toed off his shoes and pushed past him. He dropped onto the rental's couch and kicked his socked feet up on the coffee table. "So, Cass, huh?"

Josh deposited his bags in the tidy bedroom and crashed on the other end of the couch. "Yep."

"And?"

"She stuck around after the meeting, and we talked. Didn't dance around it. We agreed we can leave it in the past and be strictly professional."

"Really? You talked about her for weeks after she left. I don't think you talked about anyone you'd hooked up with. Ever."

He didn't. Not usually.

But Cass was different. Funny as hell. Great taste in movies. Gorgeous and sweet.

And his head of costume. Fuck.

Josh rolled his shoulders under his tee shirt. "We had a good time. We hung out. Once. I'm keeping her at arm's length."

"Uh-huh. Well, you're pretty good at keeping people from getting too close. Maybe you didn't like her that much. You didn't bother to find out her last name or where she lived when you hooked up."

He tried. The offer to fly her out was genuine, but she didn't give it to him. Maybe she was the one who wanted to keep things casual. Josh shrugged it off.

Stephen kicked up to leave, but hesitated in the doorway. "Listen. I've known Cassie for a long time. She's a sweetheart. Don't mess around with her, okay?"

"I'll be too busy to even think about anything other than this movie."

"Good." Stephen stepped into his shoes without doing up the laces. "And about the film? Don't worry. I've got your back."

It wasn't home, but it was for now. He already missed his walls, bronze so dark they were almost black. The botanical mural he'd painted over the course of a year, with each fiddlehead fern and palm frond painstakingly placed. The expanse of wall in front of him was a blank canvas, waiting for something to fill it. The studio would lose the damage deposit, but that sounded like a *them* problem.

Josh chucked his phone onto his rental's couch and sunk back onto its tightly woven tweed, scrubbing a hand over his patchy stubble. He hadn't been lying earlier. He did think he and Cass would work well together. Even before they fell into bed, they'd had a good time. The most fun he'd had in ages, arguing about every detail about the films. If he hadn't wanted to put his hands on her so badly, he would have talked with her all night.

It had been a pleasant surprise to see her come through the door, even if she looked like she was seconds from dying from embarrassment.

Go figure. The one person he knew in town was the one person he couldn't hookup with. It might be nice to have a friend in town. Nice change from his usual relationship status. And they could argue about other things without landing up naked.

Lots of people in the industry mixed business with pleasure. Lead actors entering liaison, stunt coordinators falling for each other, the director screwing a production assistant. Or a handful of production assistants.

That wasn't his style. One poorly ended fuck buddy arrangement on set was enough. The only drama he wanted to be responsible for was on the other side of the camera, so not having a rotation of women here to dip his dick into was a blessing. He needed to focus. No room for mistakes. Melanie might not fire him from the project if he screwed this up, but she'd never work with him again.

More than that, *Sirius Darker* was too important to *him* to fuck it up.

No, his energy was needed on set, not trying to get laid. Especially not with someone he worked with, even if they'd sparked so hot they set the night on fire. Her round ass fitting perfectly in his hands, every curve softening against all his hard parts.

He willed himself not to take a final look at her gorgeous body when he pulled up their chat to delete the thread. For good measure, he cleared the cache, to remove temptation.

No rule against thinking about her, but he'd be too busy for anything other than pulling this movie together over the next several months.

Come to think of it, it was probably a good thing they had already slept together. Otherwise, he might be distracted wondering what it would be like to have her underneath him.

Good thing he got her out of his system already.

CHAPTER SEVEN

CASS

THE SCUFFED TWO-TOP TABLE IN THE MIDDLE OF THE CROWDED DINER
had enough real estate to let the two women spread out purses
and phones and still have room for their meals. Cass scooted to
the front of her seat, her toes just reaching the stool's crossbar.

"I can't believe I didn't make the connection. I think I saw
Stephen's name on the list and I just ..." Libby mimed the words
flitting out of her brain. She stabbed a sausage link rolling across
her plate. "Now Sexy Dimples shows up on our film set and gets
to walk around looking gorgeous in front of you?"

"We can't call him that anymore." Not now that she had to
see him all the time. It'd be just like her to drop that nickname in
the middle of a meeting. "And, technically, it's his film set."

"Aren't you worried about proximity effects?" Libby asked.
"All that untapped sexual tension building up?"

It hadn't been all that bad. They'd met so much over the last
month in pre-production, respectfully disagreed on a hundred
things, but everything was hammered out. Josh stayed in his
narrow, professional lane, never once making a comment about
their time together in front of anyone.

It was like their night together—and the weeks of flirty texts
that followed—had never happened at all.

"That sexual tension is tapped," Cass muttered, "and no fears about proximity. I work with good-looking people all day long."

"So, hotness isn't a factor. Then, what's the problem?"

"I mean …" Cass sighed. "I hadn't hit it off with anyone in so long. Since Nick, anyway. And Josh and I had a really good time. It was all safe and everything because he was out of town, and I could just be myself and we had this amazing night that I could fantasize about and let it be perfect."

"And now it's going to get messy and real."

Cass nodded miserably. And fine, maybe she was a little worried about proximity. Libby had been right. Men like Josh were more than her type. They were her weakness. All chemistry, then after some time, empty promises.

That was one of the reasons the out-of-town thing had worked so well. There was no chance to get to the point of empty promises.

She'd never been fastidious about keeping work and personal life separate, dating a few people she'd met on set. But never during production. And it's not like she and Josh had dated. They'd known each other for nine hours, which was spent silent in movies, arguing about the movies, then rolling around in bed. Or him pinning her against the wall. Or on the floor on the way to the bed.

Cass dropped her head into her hands. "He'd made it clear he had no interest in being anything other than being strictly professional. Plus, that was months ago. If he can forget, so can I."

"Can you though?"

"It's different this time."

There was no her and Josh to forget about. She could ignore him leaning over her sketches, the warmth radiating off his body and the scent of sandalwood and citrus wrapping around her. Watching his lithe fingers trace the storyboards, like they had traced the curve of her hip as they lay in bed in a post-sex-frenzied haze.

Cass shook herself. "Why are we talking about me and my nonexistent issues? I'm not the only one who needs to worry about proximity. Aren't you worried about working with Stephen?"

Libby sucked in her cheeks and stirred her coffee, the ice cubes clinking in the tall glass. "That was a long time ago. We were kids."

They'd been more like new adults than kids, but still, as far as amicable breakups went, Libby and Stephen hadn't spoken since he'd moved to Vancouver. From the way they'd been stealing glances at each other over lighting rigs, Cass figured she might not be the only one with sparks flying.

"Have you two talked yet?"

Libby shrugged, face blank. "What's there to talk about? He lives there. I live here. He's happy there, and I'm not leaving."

If Libby could see through Cass's inability to put a romantic encounter in the past, Cass knew Stephen leaving Libby was a wound that never healed.

"Let's make a pact," Cass said briskly. "We'll keep each other from getting into trouble until this thing wraps, then we'll grab Jill and try to convince Raina to go on another vacation."

"Okay. No trouble," Libby agreed. "Unless we really want it."

The mass email invite said the engagement party would be casual. Showing up two hours late wasn't the coolest move, but Cass had told Jill she and Libby might be late if their meetings ran long again. One week until filming, and Josh had been growing increasingly twitchy. He hadn't gone on any of the sociopathic rants Karl had warned her of yet, but from the sounds of it, those might be coming.

Voices and music poured through the front door of Jill and

Alex's bungalow as they let themselves into the party already in full swing. Libby dropped a couple bottles of wine on the kitchen counter, walking past people Cass vaguely recognized as players from Jill's softball team and a mix of guys from Alex's rugby team. A few people from Jill's work lounged around the dining room table with drinks in hand. Libby joined a group of kids running dizzy circles around the coffee table. After a hug with Rachel and Omar, Cass continued through the house until she found her friends on the back deck, cuddled on a single chair.

"Congratulations!" Cass said for the seventeenth time. She leaned in for a hug and kissed them both on the cheek, already wishing she had worn a lighter top for the early summer evening. "Any dates planned yet?"

"Tried to convince her we should do it this afternoon before everyone came over," Alex said, an easy grin on his face.

Jill landed an affectionate punch on his shoulder. "I want to plan something perfect for us."

"Whatever makes you happy," Alex said, beaming at her. "You becoming my wife is all I need."

They just looked so … at peace. A prickle worked its way up Cass's throat. To be a priority, to know her happiness was important to someone? That was the dream. "Whatever you two decide will be perfect."

Jill and Alex turned to greet another friend as Libby sauntered out with a grubby toddler perched on her hip, chubby fingers pulling at her hair.

"I just heard Dan and Marta have number two on the way. Poor woman is upstairs puking. Little Olivia is going to be a big sister already," she said, shifting the little girl to her other hip. She gave Cass a careful look. "That's exciting, right?"

So, Dan was having another baby. She was happy for him. Really. She and Dan only dated a while, and they hadn't been exclusive. Not like he'd wanted to be. He had never introduced her to his family, or any of his friends. Honestly, she'd met more of his friends since meeting Jill and coming along to parties where Alex and Dan played on the same rugby team.

That first meeting was weird, with Jill innocently introducing Cass to Marta and her squirming daughter, Dan coughing awkwardly beside her like he hadn't told Cass he didn't want anything serious for a long time. By Cass's admittedly lax math skills, that long time translated into a month before the things he wanted had changed.

Now, he had a beautiful girlfriend he was devoted to and a daughter he was wild for, with a second baby on the way.

Good for him.

It wasn't envy—she didn't want to be with someone who didn't want to be with her, and lord knew she didn't want to be saddled with two kids—but what was it about her that made men pull hard U-turns when it came to commitment?

Right. Her superpower.

Cass covered her wince with a tight smile. "Yeah, so exciting."

———

"I told you. Tyrant."

Karl tucked a boom mic under his arm, the crew shuffling around as Josh bellowed yet another set of conflicting instructions at the grips. Rehearsals that morning hadn't been enough, and Dawson James, the film's lead actor, was trying—and failing—to soak up the crossfire.

It was weird to see Josh like this. However briefly she'd known Josh the hookup, Josh the director was a completely different person. Then he had been charismatic, argumentative, and demanding; Josh the director was still argumentative and demanding, but the charisma was absent. And he was alienating his team before they'd even shot a minute of film.

She'd joked he liked it when she told him what she thought. No time like the present to test that theory.

"I'll talk to him."

Karl raised his brows. "Good luck."

Cass crept up, staying in Josh's sightline.

"So, how's it going?" she asked carefully.

He glared as he looked up from the sheets in front of him, but a look of recognition softened his face when he saw her. "Fine."

She crossed her arms. "Doesn't seem 'fine'."

"It is."

This was going great. She shifted back into his eyeline and tried again. "It's going so fine that people are calling you a tyrant."

"I'm not a tyrant," he said, affronted. "I'm particular."

"Two of the grips are having panic attacks in the back, and an extra just quit."

A flicker of guilt crossed under his scowl. "They're not giving me what I need."

"That's because they don't know what you need."

"But I said—"

"Three different things. In three different ways." She tried a smile to soften the blow. "You're blowing up at people for not keeping up with changes they don't know are coming, and you kept them three hours late last night."

The crew edged around the set, throwing nervous glances between her and Josh's thunderous expression. He eyed the crew and huffed through his nostrils.

"Are they really having panic attacks?"

"No, but they are freaking out that they're getting fired."

Josh ground his teeth. "No one is getting fired."

"You should tell them that. And maybe apologize?"

"I'll apologize," he said, like he was offering to donate a kidney to his high school bully.

"Maybe wait until you aren't scowling," Cass said, and when he narrowed his eyes at her, the hint of a dimple appeared in his cheek. Good. The snit was over. She pressed her lips together and smiled. "Everyone wants this to succeed.

We're all behind you. We just need you to work with us on this."

"Alright. Work with everyone," he grumbled, turned and shouted at the crew, "Everyone, take ten."

An audible sigh went up from the people around them, and Cass grinned as he gave her a look of begrudging acknowledgement. Not so much of a tyrant, after all. She checked the time on her phone. Shooting would wrap in two hours. She and the girls would head out after wrap to poetry night. The line up was strong. Maybe he would come. Not as a date. Only if he didn't have plans.

A not entirely unexpected flutter stirred her stomach. Cass shifted over, and hesitantly said, "I was thinking—"

A crash across the set snapped his head up. Josh tore his eyes away from her and the scowl took up residence on his face again. "Hold that thought," he said, and strode over to where Stephen and Karl argued in hushed tones.

Of course. He was the most in-demand person on set. She'd monopolized hours—days, really—of his time over the past months. Cass could have written a paper after all the research she did leading up to the design meetings. It had been time well spent. After everything, Melanie had agreed to dial back the outlandish vision they'd had for costuming Brynne as the harried-but-glamorous astrophysicist and Dawson as her long-time collaborator and sometimes lover. Josh had jumped to agree with Cass's designs.

Now that costume designs were signed off and in production, he wouldn't need to spend as much time with her. Other people on the crew needed him more. Priorities and all.

Cass backed away until she drew level to where Dawson and his dialect coach were running lines. With the way he'd stepped between Josh and the grips earlier, she was surprised he wasn't covered in scorch marks.

"What fire's burning his butt?" Dawson asked, running a hand over his sandy hair.

"*Fire*, not *far*," his coach enunciated. "And you're dropping your *ings* again."

"C'mon, you know I'm not method. I only need to talk like that when the cameras are on," he replied with a dimpled grin, and the dialect coach tittered. "But here. What fire's burning his butt?" he repeated, this time with all traces of his Tennessee drawl obscured behind a bland, mid-American accent, and the dialect coach hummed her approval.

"No fire. He's just a bit tense." Cass pasted on a smile and turned to the giant sweetheart towering over her. "I reminded him his crew wasn't comprised exclusively of mind readers."

"Cassidy, your voice is music enough to tame the savage beast," Dawson said, bending the quote. "He's lucky to have you here."

That's me. Making life easier for everyone. Cass shrugged. "I still don't know why they made you lose the accent," she said, straightening Dawson's rumpled lab coat.

Dawson code-switched seamlessly into his character's voice, posture changing from his easy lean against the props into a rigid stance. "Because Dr. Donovan Rykoff, NASA physicist, is from Washington state."

Cass shook her head. Early in theatre in high school and college, she had learned she'd never be a triple threat. Singing? A joy. Dancing? Her one true love.

Acting? Her inability to hide her emotions precluded her from ever having more than bit parts. In a high school production, she'd been relegated to the role of Tree Number Two and still managed to sob loud enough to drown out the lead actor's lines. Admittedly, he couldn't project his voice to the second row. But still.

"They could have moved the character to Tennessee," she pressed. "It's so charming."

Dawson relaxed back into himself and scuffed his shoe on the set's concrete floor. "Aw, shucks."

No one had ever aw-shucked her before. Bex melted into a

puddle of starry-eyed goo as she walked by, and Cass grinned at her. The accent *was* charming, and no doubt Dawson was a good-looking man. In a cute kind of way.

Not in a captivating way, with glacial eyes and a wicked smile. Not in a way that snared her attention whenever they were close enough to share oxygen. She turned to find Josh across the room, eyes locked on her even as he nodded to a grip, and the flutter under her skin surged back.

Maybe they didn't even need to share oxygen.

"Mrs. Westwood said it was distracting," he continued, breaking her out of her dangerous train of thought. "Besides, don't we all put on a face when we go out into the world?"

"Nope," Cass said, rubbing her hands over the goosebumps that flashed across her arms. "I'm an open book. If I started hiding things, I'd forget who knew what and get in trouble."

"That's awfully refreshing. I never really got used to how fake this industry is, you know? It's nice to meet someone who's honest."

"That's me. Refreshing and honest as a bar of soap." She shrugged sheepishly. "My mom used to wash my mouth out with soap if I ever cursed or lied. I still feel a little guilty when I see a bar of Irish Spring."

The corner of Dawson's mouth curled as he let out a gentle chuckle. "I promise I won't tell anyone if you let a cuss slip out."

Stephen beckoned Dawson to join a huddle, and Cass tore her gaze away from Josh, who was absorbed in a new conversation with Brynne. Both focused on the monitor in front of them, neither of them smiling, but it was just a matter of time until he turned those dimples on someone else. He'd given off player vibes the night they met in that theatre's lobby.

Who knew how many women were currently on the receiving end of those dimples.

"I'm going to start calling you the bomb squad," Libby said, brushing her hands on her jeans as she walked up. "Stephen said

Josh was a little temperamental, but you diffused that whole thing before anyone died."

"Dawson said I tamed the savage beast," she said, trying to force a laugh. She doubted anyone could tame Josh. "Did you check out the lineup for the poetry reading tonight?"

"Oh, about that." Libby's face etched with a mixture of guilt and anticipation. "An old band Stephen and I used to see is playing downtown. I asked him if he wanted to check it out. For old times' sake."

Cass narrowed her eyes at her best friend. "What happened to staying away?"

"It's no big deal," she stammered, watching Stephen huddled with Dawson. "You should come."

Poetry night had been a standing tradition for years. Cass's shoulders dropped.

No, she shouldn't come. She'd be in the way. Maybe Raina would show up this time. She was the one who'd started the poetry night tradition, after all.

"No. You two have a good time."

A group of girlfriends giggled their way past Cass out of the bookstore's narrow door into the crowded parking lot. She stepped aside to let a cozy couple bump by.

The entire audience at the poetry reading hadn't been couples and friend groups. It just felt like that.

She could be in a pitiful mood, but she wasn't. Definitely not. So, what if yet one more ex-boyfriend transformed into Mr. Commitment seconds after they'd ended things. Or if her oldest friend was lining herself up for another heartbreak and ditching her on the path to said heartbreak. Or that she couldn't even muster the courage to ask a man who was just a friend to spend time with her.

No pity here.

Cass climbed into her truck and pulled out her phone to reread Raina's text.

> Don't hate me but I have to bail

> The kids are exploding from both ends and I will spare you the gory details

> Won't miss next time, promise!

Yes, she would. Cass sighed. Time to go home. There was a comedy special she'd been meaning to watch on streaming. Or she could wallow in a dark comedy. Or maybe Pride and Prejudice again. She was about to turn the ignition when a text banner flashed across her phone's screen.

Her heart jumped into her throat and a breathy huff escaped her lips, and she glanced around as if the text was projected on her truck's windshield.

After a year and a half of radio silence? Immediate delete. Don't even bother reading it. You know what will happen.

Cass bit her lip as she opened the note.

> hey cass its been a while

Oh, absolutely not. No way. Even if he did make her toes curl and heart race whenever they were together. Or when she thought about him. Like now.

Too late. She'd opened the message, and he'd seen the read receipt. Maybe it was good he had. She could leave him on read. That would show him. He deserved it for ghosting her, and whatever mysterious falling out he'd had with Alex. Jill never gave details, and Cass never pressed her.

And why now? Maybe he wanted to pick things up. She'd sent him a couple texts, but he'd ignored them.

She had promised herself she was done with him. He'd strung her along like a glittery charm on a cheap bracelet for years. That road led to a wild orgasm and a lonely morning after, to showing up to dates with another girl there and not getting what she needed. She moved to flip her phone upside down when it buzzed again.

just got back in town

Be strong. Even if he had been out of town, he couldn't have sent a note to let her know he was leaving?

But he thought of her first? Cass felt her resolve shiver at the edges.

ive missed you

Something fizzed hot in her stomach. It wasn't like anyone else wanted her time. She rubbed a hand over her throat and squeezed.

Dammit.

CHAPTER EIGHT

JOSH

DAWSON'S MASSIVE FORM CURLED AROUND THE JAGGED TEAR IN THE ship's hull. Shards of metal pierced his torso, and a shuddering breath hissed out of his lungs as he used his remaining strength to close the airlock, sealing the room and his fate.

He knew the consequences. There was no coming back. Brynne swallowed silent sobs, her hand pressed against the thick glass separating them, but she held his gaze until his eyes fluttered closed for the last time.

Dawson was dead.

Or rather, Donovan Rykoff was dead. Again. He'd been dying all day. And it still wasn't right.

"Cut!"

His lead actors traded glances as they made their way over to the monitor, followed closely by Cass.

Brynne glared at him over crossed arms. "What was wrong with it this time?"

Nothing, other than the fact that I've seen you two show more emotion when catering was late.

"I'm still not getting what I need," he ground out.

"Which would be what, exactly?"

Josh slumped into his director's chair, elbows on his knees

and fingers tugging his hair like he could pull his thoughts straight through his skull. He could practically hear Cass say that wouldn't be helpful, and instead swore under his breath for the hundredth time that hour.

"You need them to look like they didn't just meet a month ago."

All three heads turned to Cass, who paused her adjustments on Dawson's costume.

She blinked between the three of them, shifting uncomfortably. "Our main characters have a long, complicated history. They've been rivals, colleagues, lovers—" the way that last word rolled off her tongue sent a jolt straight to his groin "—but you two don't know each other yet. My hunch is once you spend more time together, feel each other's rhythms, it'll flow out of you."

Josh sucked in a breath. That was it. That's what was missing.

Time. History. Trust. No one would mourn the loss of their future if they didn't have a past.

Cass just solved the problem that had plagued him for days.

Her instincts were incredible.

He studied her. She was always put together, but today her normally boisterous curls were more dishevelled than usual. Her blousy top had wrinkles, and he'd seen the pleather pants recently. Very recently. Something he couldn't put his finger on plucked at the corner of his brain.

Dawson's bloodied face broke out into a lopsided smile. "Well, shoot. That's a right neat way to put it. I think that's my block."

"I know it would help me," Brynne agreed. "Can we move this scene?"

If they filmed the scene later in production, they'd have months to build trust. But expenses would climb, and continuity would need a full review. Juggling the schedule now would cause a shitstorm.

Fuck.

"One day you're going to have permanent elevens creased into your brows." Cass reached over to smooth them out with her thumb, and a warm glow flowed over him as the tension left his body. She hummed in approval. "Don't worry. Stephen and Terry are magicians. They'll figure it out."

Josh exhaled sharply through his nose. Right. He didn't need to do it himself. His team had his back. He felt the corner of his mouth turn up. "Stephen will blow a gasket when he learns this is your idea."

Cass waved a hand. "Stephen loves me."

Like a sister? He bit down on the words before they escaped his mouth.

"Come on, you two," Cass nodded to Brynne and Dawson. "I'll get you out of those suits."

He tore his gaze away from her ass as she crossed the set. What the fuck was wrong with him today? None of the things on his to-do list included mentally undressing his costume designer. He motioned to a hovering Bex. "Tell Stephen and Terry I need them."

Most of the directors he'd worked with had been yellers. When he was a production assistant, they didn't know his name, and just snapped their fingers at him. When he was first assistant director, a lot of the yelling was for him to get someone to do something different, not something Josh had done wrong. The stories he'd heard from other sets, there was nothing but screaming, which, for whatever reason (money and egos—the reason was always money and egos) people put up with. But it was a lot easier to get things done when he wasn't being an asshole.

See? Not even barking orders at Bex anymore, thanks to Cass. Although that was still more of an order than a request. One day he might even say please.

"On it!" she chirped, and skipped off in search of his first AD and production coordinator.

It took less than thirty seconds to fill them in on the scheduling change.

"You're springing this on me *now*?" Stephen said. "Are you trying to kill me?"

"And deprive myself of the pleasure of your company?" Josh deadpanned. "Never."

"Impossible."

"Impossible is part of your job description."

"It's going to cost us."

"With the savings Cass has brought in on her design changes, the budget can handle the extra expense." Probably. Stephen hired Terry, and Josh trusted Stephen. And Cass trusted them both. "You can figure it out."

"Okay," Terry said doubtfully. They wiped a hand over their face as if to scrub off the pained expression and bent over to crunch numbers or count beans or wrangle whatever math needed to happen.

"She seems to have your number."

Josh broke off his stare from where Cass was busy unstrapping Dawson from his suit. "What?"

"Cass." Stephen flicked through various screens, not looking up. "She got you to figure out a problem without you yelling at anyone."

Almost no yelling. He'd still have to apologize to Brynne for biting her head off.

"Yeah," he muttered. "She did."

Terry looked up from their tablet. "We can do it, but we'll have to push the scene to mid-January. No cost overruns, but I have to book it now." Their finger hovered over a button, hoofing at the cement floors like a bull ready to break into the ring.

She was right again. Terry was a magician. "Do it."

Hell, that might even get them finished early. And he'd be back in Vancouver just after Christmas. The shoot would be over before he knew it.

If it wasn't for her, he still might have his head shoved up his ass. He might have gotten here by himself, but she'd saved him time and embarrassment. Still his good luck charm.

"Hey, Bex?" Josh snagged the PA as she walked by. "Can you tell Cass I need her?"

Now he was upgrading from orders to requests. Assholery, under control.

Cass avoided his eyes until she drew level with him, looking somewhere over his shoulder. "Bex said you needed something?"

"Yeah. I need to say thanks."

"For what?"

"The solution you conjured out of thin air that's probably going to save my ass? Terry and Stephen said they can make it work. Thanks."

"Oh, sure, no problem," she said, inching backwards.

Josh squinted at her. "Are you avoiding me?"

"No!" she stammered. "I'm just busy. With stuff."

Busy with stuff? Cass looked like she'd rather disappear behind the green screen than be having this conversation, and his stomach tightened as he realized why.

Blousy top, pleather pants? Platform loafers? That outfit looked more than familiar.

"You wore that yesterday."

Cass crossed her arms as if trying to hide the offending repeat clothes. "So?"

"I've never seen you wear the same thing twice."

"Why are you memorizing my outfits?"

He hitched up a smirk instead of the scowl that threatened to cross his features at the thought of her with someone else. Which she was free to do. "I make it a point to observe beautiful women."

She rolled her eyes, a spot of pink appearing high on her cheeks.

"Someone didn't go home last night." He leaned back in his chair, then grinned in triumph as she snapped her head up. That was as good an admission as anything. He continued, "Not a boyfriend, though. You'd have makeup and hair stuff and clothes at his place if it was serious." The thought was oddly comforting. "But not a one-night stand either, because you'd probably have left his place afterwards and gone straight home."

"I don't do one-night stands," she said, already looking like she wanted to take back her words.

He felt his smile deepen enough to pop his dimples.

Cass made a pitiful attempt at a glare, a comically incongruous look with her sweet features. "That was one time."

If that was true, he'd definitely been lucky that night. He splayed his hands between them. "No shade. So, a regular hookup? Friends with benefits?"

"Not exactly friends. And the benefits are pretty limited."

"Not a friend and no benefits? Sounds like a bad deal."

Cass's defensive demeanour wilted, and she slouched into the chair beside him, hands supporting her forehead. "Are we really doing this?" she asked in a pleading voice.

This wasn't the effervescent woman he knew. Kind of knew. All the confidence and cheer evaporated, leaving this timid, quiet stranger in her place. He sucked in his cheeks, appraising her. "We don't have to," he said, softening his teasing tone. "If you've had enough of this conversation, we can stop."

She fiddled with a strap on her boot and let out a resigned sigh. "There's a guy I used to see. Casually. He and I never really figured out what we were doing," she said in a low voice, then turned to him with a look of determination. "That's not true. I wanted to see if things could go further with us, and he didn't."

He'd been on the other side of that conversation, more than once. It sucked seeing the other side. "Ouch."

She looked more embarrassed than weepy about the whole thing. At least that was good. She gave a chagrined shrug. "At least he didn't lie about it. But I keep coming back for more like the glutton for punishment I am. Last night, I got a text out of the blue and I hopped on that dick like it was a free pony ride."

God, he loved that unfiltered sense of humour. Almost enough to distract him from thinking about her riding someone else's dick. She was an adult. She could ride any dick she wanted. He just didn't need to think about her riding anyone but him.

The memory of whispering filthy nothings against her creamy neck as he buried himself in her perfect pussy popped into his head. She had *begged* for him. He shifted uncomfortably on his chair as his blood flow headed south.

He wiped his face blank. "So, this fuckboy got under your skin and is leading you around by the cooch?"

"Sounds about right. Cassidy St. Claire falls for the cooch whisperer again."

"Again? Sounds like a pattern."

"At the risk of giving out TMI?" She pursed her lips. "I foster fuckboys."

If she didn't look so beat up, he'd laugh. "I think that's the first time I heard you swear. What does that mean?" he said, managing not to choke.

"Men stay with me until they find their forever homes. Libby says it's practically a public service."

"So, like, dudes go on to their OTP after dating you?"

"OTP?"

"One True Pairing. Like soul mates and shit. Jesus, it's like you don't even read fan fiction."

"My nerdery lies elsewhere."

The chair's fabric strained as he leaned back. "Do tell."

"Not telling. You'll laugh."

Josh pulled his phone out. "Hey Siri, take a note. Find out what Cass's nerdery is."

Cass smiled at her shoes.

Good. Smiling was an improvement. "Now, you were saying. Fostering fuckboys as a public service."

"My record is flawless," Cass said. She held out her fingers. "Liam got together with Therese while we were dating, now they've been together for five years. Rafael and Cindy are getting married next month. Dan and Marta are about to have their second kid."

"And you dated all these guys?"

"And others. Those are just some recent ones." Cass gave a rueful smile. "Every single one of them, players until they met me. Once a friend asked me to go out with this guy she had a crush on to see if he'd settle down after a couple dates with me."

The fuck? With friends like that ... Josh shook his head. "That's messed up."

"She was kidding, I think." She stared wistfully to where Libby and Stephen huddled. "I guarantee Nick will announce the future Mrs. Martin within the year. Two, tops."

A thought unsettled the edges of his brain. Stephen played his romances close to the chest, but surely, he would have said something if they'd had a history. "You and Stephen ever ..."

"Oh, god no. He and Libby go way back." Cass laughed. "Plus, Stephen's not my type."

Something unclenched and he let his lip curl. "How's he not your type?"

"I don't fall for guys who are nice to me, and when the guys I date do start being nice, they are nice for someone else. They put their energy into someone else."

"Ever think you just make them realize they want more?" asked Josh.

Cass winced and stared down at her hands.

"Oh, shit. That sounded really bad," Josh said hastily. "I didn't mean it like that."

"I'm not sure you're wrong, though." Rose blossomed on her cheeks again. "I'm just tired of it. And Nick, he's just the latest, and the worst. I need to get over him once and for all."

Josh couldn't help but think she was extremely cute when she was embarrassed, and she embarrassed herself a lot. But this wasn't the kind of embarrassment where she was having fun.

Cass gave him a put-upon look, but a small grin broke through. "Sorry, I don't usually throw pity parties like this."

He did. He was practically an event planner for pity parties. And he knew how to break out of them.

"There are way better people out there, and definitely better fuckboys."

"Haha," she said. "The last thing I need is to be under someone else's spell."

Again, she'd been under him. Those fantastic tits pressed into his chest, one shapely calf wrapped around his back, the other locked around the back of his thigh to urge him deeper. The way she'd cried out when she came, arms twined around his neck as he ... absolutely shouldn't be thinking about this right now.

Talk about getting someone out of your system.

He cleared his throat. "You need to meet people. A bunch of dates with a bunch of different men. A bunch of different women?" he finished with a question.

"Unfortunately, I'm only attracted to men, although being into women would just double my chances of getting ghosted. No one really wants this package."

"Package looks spectacular from where I'm sitting."

"Stop it."

"Are you on Raya?"

Cass scoffed. "Not all of us are big enough names to get an invite to that."

He hadn't gotten his invite through his name. The model he'd slept with added him because it was the only messaging platform she used. Easier to hookup when he was in LA. Not like he messaged her back after.

"Never mind, that's useless up here, anyway. Tinder? Bumble? That new one?"

She looked away, fiddling with the tail of her blouse. "I have a Tinder account. I haven't used it in a while," she hedged. "It's really out of date."

"We're in production here for months," he said, a plan forming. If he was in a self-imposed celibacy to focus on his movie during that time, at least he could get vicarious stories out of Cass, and maybe help her get over this schmuck. "Go on two dates a week. That's plenty of time to see what else is out there."

"That sounds exhausting!"

"You're not on set for fourteen-hour days. Ten, max," he said, waving a hand to dismiss her objections. "Do you want to get over this guy or what?"

She gave a pitiful grimace and nodded.

"Then great things require great effort."

"Aren't you being a little melodramatic?"

"Yes, but what's that got to do with it?"

She pressed her lush lips together, failing to hide her amusement. Good. She barely looked miserable-adjacent now. "Here's the catch," he said, pausing for dramatic effect. "No second dates."

Cass drew her eyebrows together. "Why not?"

"You need to see what's out there. It's like inoculation. Get exposed to a whole bunch of different guys so you can spot the players and become immune."

"That is the least appealing description of dating I have ever heard in my entire life," she said, swallowing a dry heave. "Besides, isn't that mean? Going out on one date and ghosting them?"

"No one said anything about ghosting. You can send them a text after thanking them for the nice time, but you didn't vibe. Good luck on your 'insert topic of conversation here' and move on." He spread his hands magnanimously. "Simple. "

"I'm starting to think you might be a bad source for dating advice."

"Dating advice? I'm your guy." Relationship advice? That was another story. "What do you have to lose? A few Thursday nights? Worst-case scenario, you get a bunch of free drinks and dinners."

"No. Worst-case scenario, I get murdered and dumped in the river."

A chill ran over his spine. Right. "Fine, text me in case you need a rescue. Plus, then I can make sure you're doing your homework."

"But then I have to shut all these guys down after one date? That sounds so cruel!" She looked genuinely worried to upset strangers she didn't even know yet. No wonder she got played.

"It'll be good practice. You need to learn to say no."

"Like I should say *no* to you right now?"

You don't mean it when you say no to me. His dick twitched again. Fucking hell. "I'm different."

"This might be the stupidest thing I've ever done in my life," she mumbled.

"If this is the stupidest thing you've ever done, then you need to live a little."

"Okay, what do I have to lose? Thursday nights and not my life." She brushed her hands down her bare arms and studied her fingers. "Could you maybe send me your contact info?"

He looked at her, nonplussed. "I know for a fact you have my number."

"I deleted it?" She squirmed in her seat.

"Oof. If I didn't know any better, I'd take it personally," he said wryly. Maybe she'd have an easier time with this whole 'see-them-once-and-ghost' thing than she let on. He swiped her phone out of her hands to plug in his info and paused. Might as well have fun with it.

Cass clicked her tongue and smiled. "Sexy Dimples? Really?

"What? Isn't that what you call me?" He scrolled his own phone until he reached Cass Head of Costume, and renamed it Lucky Charms. His fingers hovered over the keys for half a second, her comment about getting murdered and dumped in a river circulating his brain. Unlikely, but he added her to his Do Not Disturb exception list. Just in case.

"So, how exactly do we do this?" Cass asked. "I randomly swipe on dudes until one of them agrees to go out with me?"

Like it would be hard for her to find men to take her out. Only an idiot would swipe left on those lips. He frowned at her. "Thirty dates, thirty guys. No more than three texts each. If they haven't declared their intentions by then, or you don't like them enough to ask them, move on."

"Declared their intentions? You make it sound like they should be asking my father's permission for a betrothal," she laughed, shaking her head in resignation as she stashed her phone away. "Why am I letting you talk me into this?" she said, more to herself than him.

Because you're a good girl who does what she's told. His thoughts strayed to him directing her movements, her getting on her knees and looking up at him through those lush lashes. Her licking her lips before wrapping her fist around the base of his cock. That sweet mouth sucking him so well, asking him to cum on her tits, him tipping over the edge before he could growl *yes*.

The thought of someone else with her sent a feral rage searing through his chest.

"Also," he said, clearing his throat, "since you're not actually trying to meet anyone, no sex. No kissing. No second dates. No exceptions."

Cass tilted her head and narrowed her eyes. "Are you allowed to be ordering me around like this? That has to be against some union rules, right?"

"No exceptions."

"But what if—"

"No. Exceptions."

"—I really like a guy?"

"Fish in the sea and all that bullshit. Besides, if he really likes you, he'll be around when your homework is over."

"No second dates. No exceptions." Cass nodded and gave a helpless shrug. "What do I have to lose?"

CHAPTER NINE

CASS

"IT'S NOT A WALK OF SHAME IF YOU HAD A GOOD TIME," JILL SAID. She curled her legs under her in the nylon chair and leaned closer. "Who is he? Are you going to see him again?"

Cass, Libby, and their friend Rachel sat around the fire pit in Jill's backyard in the late summer evening, sipping a now warm rosé and fishing out the dregs of potato chips from the bottom of the bag.

"No one you'll see anytime soon," Cass replied, truthfully. Ish.

Omissions weren't lies.

"You should look happier if you've had orgasms," Libby said, stoking the fire. "Unless he was shitty in bed and you didn't have any."

"No, that wasn't an issue." It would have been easier if it had been. He had answered her "it was good to see you, want to grab coffee?" text she'd sent the next morning with a "I'll get back to you" hours later, then nothing else. She checked her phone again. Not like she'd reply if he'd finally said anything. "But I definitely won't see him again."

"If you like him and he makes you feel good, what's the problem?" Rachel asked.

How about a hundred problems, starting with he only calls when he wants to get laid and ending with I chase after him like a dog in heat, topping it off with a healthy dollop of he might have screwed over my friend's business.

Cass stayed silent and waited for the wine to make its way to Jill's tiny bladder, and Rachel followed her inside for more snacks. The moment the patio door closed behind them, Libby swivelled her head to Cass with narrowed eyes.

"You've been weird for days. What's going on?"

Dang. She wasn't getting out of this. Cass drew a fortifying breath.

"It was Nick," she spewed out in a rush.

There. Done. Like ripping off a guilty little Band-Aid.

Libby paused with her glass halfway to her mouth. "Pardon?"

"I slept with Nick." Cass sighed. "He's back in town."

"Oh, honey. No." Libby mirrored Cass's hunched posture and looked at her with imploring eyes. "Why do you do this to yourself?"

If she had the answer to that, she might be able to say no to him. She'd never been able to yet. Cass snuck a peek over her shoulder to make sure the coast was still clear. "Please don't tell Jill."

"Cass, don't put me in this position …"

"Please," she begged. "I swear that was the last time."

Libby raised her eyebrows with the disbelief of someone who had heard that line way too many times to believe it. Cass didn't blame her.

The patio doors swished open. Cass wiped the guilt from her face and gave Libby her *please don't say anything* look. Libby just shook her head in resignation.

"So, where were we?" Jill folded herself back into her chair and refilled her wine. "Mystery guy was a one-time thing."

Cass could feel Libby's stare drilling a hole in her back. "In the past."

"You seem to bring up Josh a fair bit," Rachel said, tossing another bag of chips onto the table. Her own new engagement ring flashed in the firelight.

First Jill. Now Rachel. These things always happened in threes. Someone had to be next.

"Actually," Cass said carefully, rippling with embarrassment, "Josh has a theory."

It sounded weirder every time she thought about it. She hadn't gone on a date, a real date, since Nick had taken her out with Jill and Alex almost two years ago. As much of a blow to her romantic self-esteem as that night had been, she wouldn't have traded it for anything. The friendship she'd grown to cherish with Jill, fitting her into her best friend circle with Libby, had been a joy. But she'd shied away from dating ever since.

Now, she was signing herself up for dozens of dates with the intent of *not* getting serious with any of them.

Rachel scoffed when Cass wrapped the spiel. "So this whole charade is to learn how to recognize fuckboys? You've been alive in this world for over thirty years and can't do that yet?"

"No. She has shit taste in men and wouldn't recognize a fuckboy if she fell face first onto his crotch," Libby said blithely.

Rachel snorted rosé out her nose and Cass shrugged weakly. Her track record was tough to deny.

"Wait. So your kinda boss, the one you slept with, the one you are obviously still hot for, is ordering you to go on a bunch of dates?" Jill gave a bemused smile. "That's the weirdest thing I've ever heard."

"That's what I tried to say," Libby grumbled.

"Why don't you just date him?" Jill said, scooting over as Alex dropped beside her with a beer in hand. "You two seem to get along pretty well."

Cass scoffed. "I'm not dating anyone on set. Workplace romance just leads to ..."

Alex pinched Jill's thigh. "Worked for me," he said, taking a smug pull from his beer, and Libby cackled.

"You're impossible," Jill said, blushing.

Well, not everyone is as lucky as you.

Cass was trying to get over someone, not dive into something new. Just have some fun. Who knew? Even with the no second date rule, if she liked someone, there was no reason she couldn't send them a chat when all this was done. She didn't *need* a partner. She *wanted* one. Someone to share her adventures with.

"Weird or not, I've, um, already got a few dates planned."

Libby shook her head. "Let the games begin."

Date 1

Alright beautiful, how'd it go?

His profile said he was my age but could have been my dad or def a young uncle

Prob tried to text me from a rotary phone

Hehe you got catfished. That sucks

Date 2

Cass, checking in

Who was tonight's tribute?

Tyler

Which should have been the first red flag

Every Tyler I've ever known has been juvenile

Literally or metaphorically? I don't condone cradle robbing

EW!

Date 3

> Is there any rule about having to stay for the whole thing?

Full permission to bail

Date 4

Report in

> Not sure if he's a general misogynist or just hates his ex with the literal fires of hell?

both?

Date 5

> How many more of these do I have to do?

Oh, beautiful

You barely started

"He talked about tropical fish for two hours! Without a break!"

Cass shouldn't have been surprised he didn't ask her any questions about herself. She'd felt lucky to get out with splitting the bill on overcooked burgers and a boredom-induced migraine. When he said his mom couldn't pick him up for an hour and asked if she could drive him home, her people-pleasing instincts overruled her self-preservation instincts and she drove to the out-of-the-way suburb well after dark.

Stupid.

Five dates in and their little experiment forcefully reminded her why she got off the apps in the first place: a sorry group of guys that could be categorized as Chads, Bads, and Wanna-Be-Dads. Not to mention the portfolio of pathetic dick pics that now polluted her DMs.

Besides her latest date with the tropical fish-o-phile, she had coffee with a guy who listed himself at thirty-five but was pushing fifty; beer with a guy who kept swiping other matches on his phone the whole time; lunch with a guy who talked about how much he missed and hated his ex; and one guy who was so mousy she couldn't remember either his name or what he looked like. At least she hadn't feared for her life.

"Ouch. Zero for five, then?" Josh grinned, his dimples on display. He laced his fingers behind his head, signature black graphic tee shirt snug over his lean torso. Lighting was still setting up for the next scene, with Libby's booming voice ordering the grips around, and the rest of the crew was making a serious dent in the craft services table.

"I've learned more about cleaning fish tanks than I ever thought possible. If I ever need to change careers, I could get a job at the zoo," Cass said. "I mean, I'm fine with weirdos. Just not a tropical fish obsessed type of weirdo."

"So, what is your type?"

Hot, dark-haired, and a where-did-my-panties-go smile.

If she could woman up, she'd say he was her type. Even if it didn't mean anything would happen between them anymore. But if she said that, it would lead to a series of jokes that would make him laugh as she blushed. And the last thing she needed was his smile wrapping around her like a trap. Those dimples had already lured her into bed once.

No, not lured. She'd tripped over her platform sneakers to jump in his bed.

"I think my type is the problem," she said finally.

He swept his eyes over her and appeared to come to a decision. "Hand it over."

"Hand what over?"

"Your phone. Unlock it."

"Why do I already not like where this is going?"

He held out his hand, curling his fingers in a give-it-here gesture. "Your first checkup. Need to see what you're swiping on."

This was going to be the most embarrassing experience of her life. Way worse than the time her leotard split up her backside during a competition, and she'd had to keep dancing for a full forty-five seconds in front of a panel of judges with her butt crack hanging out. It felt like she was about to show more of her ass right now.

"No." For good measure, she stuffed her phone into her cleavage and crossed her arms over her chest.

Josh's face opened into a dangerous smile, his dimples deep enough to swallow her whole. "Do you really think hiding your phone in your tits will stop me? I will gladly go in to retrieve it if you don't hand it over."

"You wouldn't! Not with everyone around?"

"Care to test what I'd do to you in public?"

Something deep in the recess of her lizard brain stood up and waved madly. The last thing she needed was his hands on her again, no matter how much she cared to test what he'd be willing to do to her in public. Instead, she fished it out, trying to hide her reddened cheeks. She swiped to the end of her phone's screens before dropping it into his open hand.

"I've never been so jealous of a phone in my life," he muttered. After a few seconds of scrolling, he looked up in dismay. "What the hell is this?" he asked, appalled. "This is your profile pic?"

"What's wrong with it?"

"There's another dude in it, for starters." A muscle ticked in his jaw. "Who is he?"

She leaned over his shoulder, getting a whiff of the heady sandalwood and citrus scent that clung to his warm skin. She shook her head and focussed on studying the screen. "Oh, that's Grady."

"Grady." He said the name like an epithet, and continued to scrutinize her photo. "Did you pull this photo from Instagram? You did! This is the Valencia filter! How old is this?"

"A few years." She shifted between her feet. "I liked my hair in that picture."

The sea air had done both wonders and nightmares for her hair. Libby had snapped the candid shot outside a shop on La Jolla beach years ago after a dance competition. Cass had turned at the last minute so her curls, still long at that time, bounced around her shoulder blades. Grady, her former dance partner, held her hand up to frame her. Sure, there were a few other people in the shot, but the palm trees had looked so pretty against the background of the setting sun.

The outfit was still one of her favourites. The second-hand vermillion fit-and-flare sundress swirled at her knees and gave serious vintage vibes. She'd altered the neckline to a sweetheart and added boning for shape to the bodice. It made her feel assertively feminine when she wore it. She could still wear heels back then, too, kicking up her foot to show off the three-inch rattan espadrilles.

Too bad half of her was hidden behind a mailbox in the photo. And her hair covered most of her face.

Okay, it was a bad picture.

"Men don't have patience for profiles like this," he said, frowning as he swiped through her photos. "I can't see any of you."

"Maybe I don't want to show off everything right away?"

He side-eyed her and scanned her bio. "'I like to have fun?'" Josh scoffed. "Everyone likes to have fun. What kind of fun? Crochet? Cliff diving? So vague."

"I like crochet, but that wasn't what I meant," she said, squirming.

"How about … I make all my own clothes, so I know how to take them off quickly?" he deadpanned, and pretended to type it in.

She looked at him, horrified, and made a half-hearted attempt to steal her phone back. "Don't you dare!"

"You're a gorgeous woman, and men are visual creatures. Let them see who you are," he said. "With that hair and those curves and those lips? It worked on me."

A wave of pleasure washed over her, but she whipped her head back and forth, checking who was in earshot. Seeing everyone otherwise occupied, she turned her widened eyes to him. "Josh!" she hissed through gritted teeth. "Keep it down!"

"All I'm saying is play to your strengths," he said, clearly relishing her discomfort. "We need to up the game. I'm in charge of your swiping, and I'm rewriting your bio."

"What if I don't like it?"

"I think I know more about what will appeal to men. At least, from the state of this," he said, wiggling her phone with the offending profile in front of her, "you don't."

His sexy dimples softened the landing of the teasing barb, and she turned her own wry grin to him. "Okay, but I can veto."

"Of course."

She wasn't the least bit convinced by the look on his face.

"And you need new pictures." He handed her back her phone. "Show me some good ones."

Cass swiped through her camera roll. And swiped. And swiped. Her nieces. Blurry stills from the last wrap party. Her modelling a new dress pattern she was drafting, the half-basted pieces floating around her. "Um, I could just take a selfie?"

"I used to have a couple of your selfies, but you made me delete those."

Before she'd deleted their texts, she'd pulled up the photos he'd sent her on more than a couple of occasions. When she was lying in bed, her vibrator between her thighs and imagining his thick length in her mouth and his hands in her hair. A flush crept farther up her cheeks, and it didn't feel like embarrassment.

He twisted his mouth and tapped his finger on his knee.

"There's a break in shooting on Wednesday and I'm only on set in the morning. We're doing a photo shoot that afternoon."

"A what?" She'd spent loads of time singing and dancing for audiences, but posing for Josh sparked a frisson of electricity through her. Plus, her time in front of audiences had been years ago. Back when she could still move how she wanted.

"Photos. Wednesday," he repeated. "And I'm pretty sure Stephen doesn't need you on set that afternoon, either."

She *wasn't* needed that day, and it was not like she had other plans. Her friends would be at their normal nine-to-fives. Her day was wide open. Nothing else to do. "Okay."

"Excellent, let's start now." He pulled her in close, and a just as he took the shot, closed his teeth around the shell of her ear. His breath was warm and minty on her neck, but she wiggled out of his grasp.

"There are people around!"

"You're saying you'd have no problem with me doing that if we were alone?"

She scrambled to look at the photo over his shoulder. His smile looked perfectly evil, her eyes wide, and mouth popped open in surprise.

"What happened to being professional?" she demanded through clenched teeth, looking to see if anyone had seen while trying to quell the flutter under her ribs.

"What? I bite everyone. Ask around," he said, setting the photo as his contact profile pic in her phone.

Maybe he did bite everyone. He'd sure bitten her. The nips he'd taken down her breasts and over her stomach stayed proof of their night together for days after. Heat flooded her with the memory, and a small streak of jealousy chased it.

Don't go down that road. You know where it leads. Cass smoothed a wrinkle in her blouse. "I'm not sure I need to hear about all the people you bite."

He paused for a moment, but ignored her comment, finally

handing her back her phone. "I haven't had a day off in a month. Pick a spot. Some place that captures who you are."

Why was she agreeing to this? Why was she agreeing to *any* of this? She looked down at the blurry photo and plain bio. Maybe it would help to have some updated photos, some help with the text. She hadn't had many matches, and the ones she'd had weren't great.

Come to think of it, why had she swiped right on any of those guys? She knew she was supposed to give people a chance, but yikes.

And a photo shoot sounded like fun. Maybe. A little.

She shook her head and closed her eyes, which was becoming her signature move in any conversation with him. "Okay, let's take some photos."

LIBBY

Any winners?

> Nope. 5 dates and 5 duds. One of the guys was at least 15 yrs older than he said. Thought he was going to ask for a seniors discount

LIBBY

Sugar daddy material?

> Haha no

> But Josh offered to help me update my profile. He's writing my bio and take some photos

JILL

That's so nice!

> Right? My friend at Danceworks is letting us do a quick shoot in their studio after hours

JILL

What are you wearing?

A lack of options wasn't her issue. She had racks of custom designed clothes she'd sewn to cast any mood that struck her fancy. She needed an outfit that said *date me, but only once.* Her hands skated over her dresses and stopped.

Not sure yet.

My black fit-and-flare dress and tights? Makes my boobs look good.

LIBBY

your boobs look good in everything :)

Thanks muffin

JILL

Is that all you two are doing?

Yep!

She glanced through her closet, undecided. Should she go sexy? Playful? Demure?

A man's opinion would be helpful right about now.

Cass worried the corner of her lower lip with her teeth. Nick would have texted back *everything looks good on you* if he was feeling generous, or a generic *fine* if he wasn't.

Well, no, that wasn't true. If he wasn't feeling generous, he wouldn't text back at all.

Josh said to put her profile in his hands. He might have an opinion.

Knowing Josh, he'd definitely have an opinion.

Before she could change her mind, she snapped a photo and hit send.

What do you think?

Put them on. Show me.

A tingle rolled over her chest. He hadn't seen these clothes on her before, so it made sense he'd want to see what they looked like on her and not on a hanger. It seemed so intimate, though. Inviting him into her bedroom, even by proxy. Especially after last time, sending photos back and forth as they jerked off together.

Not thinking about that. Right now, anyway.

She quickly cycled through the outfits, stripping and donning each of the options one after the other, sending Josh the pics one by one with the discard pile growing beside her in each subsequent shot, ending with the black dress.

> Knew you could take your clothes off fast
> for me

> Have you ever once turned your game off?

> Black dress, no tights and add that silk scarf
> you wore last week

The scarf was a favourite, picked up at a warehouse sale years ago, a perfect match to her favourite lipstick. She'd barely been around him the day she wore the floaty red scarf on set. She was surprised he'd remembered.

Even in the privacy of her bedroom, her cheeks warmed. Maybe she wasn't the only one who didn't filter. Well, two could play. She angled the shot to capture the assets Libby had complimented and added,

> You said to show off what I have

> Won't the scarf cover these? Someone once
> told me they were spectacular

> I'm not taking photos of you in the dress, just
> want to see them again in person

She choked on her laugh. She could practically see his dimples popping through the text banter.

> ??? You are the worst??

Kidding

When a guy uses a line like that on you, he wants to get in your bed

> Are you using a line on me, Josh Graham?

Aha. You recognized it

See? Inoculation works

> Ew!

Well, that's what happens when you ask for it, she thought, and shut the thread down with a grin. Throwing the black dress and scarf into her bag, she gave a last wistful glance at her curls mussed up from the rapid clothing changes.

So much for having a good hair picture on her Tinder profile.

Bring the crop top and jeans too

Huh. She didn't see the crop top coming. Most people suggested clothes that covered her more, like just because she had a belly roll she should cover it.

She loved that top. It looked great on her. And not that it mattered, but it made her smile that he thought so, too.

Her phone buzzed one more time as she headed out her bedroom door.

Btw nice vibe

I can recommend a better model

No. Heat crept up her neck as she scanned the picture she'd sent. The bright pink vibrator with bunny ears sat perky on her nightstand. It might as well have winked at the camera.

Just some harmless flirting. As long as it didn't follow them to set, there shouldn't be a problem. She bit her lip and fired back,

> A better model?

> Nothing will make me get rid of Chauncy

CHAUNCY??

So much for professional distance.

CHAPTER TEN

JOSH

CHAUNCY??

Don't you dare mock my real best friend

Pls don't tell Libby I said that

Here's the address

HE SNIGGERED. ONLY CASS WOULD NAME HER SEX TOYS LIKE AN elderly duke. Maybe he should get her his preferred model. Then watch to make sure she was using it properly. Hell, he could even step in if she needed help finding the right angle …

Down, boy. You're taking a couple of innocent photos for someone on your crew. Focus.

The dance studio Cass had sent revealed few interior photos in his online search. Hard to tell what he'd be walking into. He skipped over the macro and telephoto lenses, settling on a prime lenses that could handle almost any environment he'd be shooting in. He slung his camera bag across his body, but paused in the doorway.

Digital had its pluses, to be sure. Convenience. Instant gratification. But his high school drama teacher had waxed poetic about the warmth and personality of film. Josh had bought a vintage Pentax K1000 two years later.

It didn't take long to teach himself how to develop his own photos. His mother had grudgingly permitted him to transform his ensuite into a dark room. When he was in his own place, Stephen didn't care if Josh had converted the second bathroom into a dark room, leaving one bathroom for two men.

And making one more reason not to bring women back to their shared space.

The Pentax sat on the dresser of his rental's bedroom. The roll of film had only a handful of shots used. A couple of Brynne draped over a chair, staring into the middle distance as she waited for a scene to be set up. Another of the sun dipping behind the Rockies from his apartment window, a silhouette that would make a perfect outline for the mural he'd probably never paint.

Cass would look great on film. It wouldn't hurt to bring it. And then he could see the light and choose what camera would be best. Maybe a few shots. Just for fun. He didn't have any of his developing equipment here, but he could do that the next time he was home.

Whoever had taken Cass's profile photo had no idea how to play to her strengths. It was even taken at a tilted angle, making the world look drunk around her. She was right: her hair looked amazing, curls bouncing around her ears from the ocean wind. Or maybe the photographer—if he could call them that—had called her name, and she'd turned to look. Whatever they'd said to get her attention had made her laugh. Her sweet smile showed through, even with the blurred image. Everything about her was kinetic colour.

The dance studio was a handful of blocks from his rental, but far enough from set he drove his rental car, if not just for the air conditioning to escape the unseasonable heat of late September. He plugged the address into the car's navigation system, shifting against the unfamiliar seat, and pulled into the parking lot minutes later.

Cass was perched on the concrete benches outside the front doors, wearing the crop top and a self-conscious smile. The short-sleeved top looked brighter in person, a deep cobalt blue, and contrasted beautifully against her alabaster skin.

He couldn't wait to get her in front of his lens.

The early evening breeze blew a curl over her eye as she stood, sliding her hands down the light denim covering her thighs, and she met him at the curb.

"I feel really silly right now," she said.

"Don't."

"Oh, well, in that case." She awkwardly tilted her head to the entrance. "Think I can give you what you need in there?"

His lip half-curled. "Oh, I think you'll give me what I need."

"Oh god, I didn't mean it like that," she moaned, mortified. "I just meant maybe you can get a lucky shot, and this won't be a waste of your time?"

"Are you kidding? I've been looking forward to this all week."

"Really?"

"Really." He stood aside, extending his arm to indicate she should lead the way. "Come on. Might not be as wild as an evening of crochet, but it'll be fun."

She huffed a laugh, guiding him through the lobby, into an expansive studio where the lingering scent of well-worn unitards and cleaning solution permeated the air. The ceilings soared overhead with exposed lights dotting the perimeter of the room, dimmed low. The entire far wall was glass, letting in both the cityscape and the last of the evening light. Glossy black Marley floors reflected her image in distorted ripples as she glided across the room. She looked so comfortable, so at home here, already more relaxed.

He had to hand it to her: she'd picked the perfect backdrop.

"I'm going to feel super weird just posing," she said. "Do you mind if I move around?"

"Perfect."

She plugged her phone into the audio cabinet as he flicked on the studio lights and adjusted the warmth until the soft yellow of a late summer's day surrounded her. He pulled out his Pentax.

"What do you want to listen to?" she asked, scrolling on her phone and biting the bright crimson of her lower lip in thought.

Click, click, click, and her head lifted at the sound.

"Whatever you want."

Her eyes flicked to the lens. "I wasn't ready."

Click. "I was."

Her fingers hesitated over whatever playlist she was on, then hit play, nodding her head and mouthing along to the lyrics. After a few more beats, she lifted her arms overhead, letting her hips roll like liquid thunder. She docked the phone and strutted across the floor in half-time to the music.

"Nice choice," he said, grinning, and switched to his digital camera. Now there was no limit to the number of shots he could take.

"It's my feel-good anthem. Helps me get in the mood."

"In the mood, hmm?" *Click, click, click.*

She huffed a giggle. "Stop it."

"Why would I do that, when watching you blush is so much more fun?"

She knew her angles, that was for sure, playing with the beat and giving him a perfect profile. He dropped to one knee, waiting until she circled past the lights and snapped a series of shots in rapid succession.

The sun dipped behind the skyline, the last of the reflections disappearing from buildings around them, but the lights inside the studio space dazzled off the windows and floors in matte black. An older R&B song he didn't recognize faded in, and her movements slowed to match the new rhythm.

She moved around the space like she owned it. It was fun.

For him, at least. Or maybe engrossing was more like it. Directing her around the space. Getting what he wanted from her, shining through the camera. Seeing the real her again. The woman he watched on set, graceful and confident. Hell, she'd been graceful and confident in his bed. That didn't always translate in front of a camera. And she moved so confidently here. The music, the lights, which room to pick, and he finally clued in. She'd spent time here. Lots of it.

"You dance."

"Used to."

Click, click, click. He'd be able to put together a stop-motion film at the end of this. "What kind of dance?"

Her eyes lit up. "Musical theatre. Ballet. Modern. Even competed in salsa for a few years." She paused. "I almost went to school in California on a dance scholarship."

Click, click, click. "Why didn't you?"

"Because when I got my acceptance letter, they said I needed to lose thirty pounds before the fall semester, and ten more by Christmas."

Josh lowered his camera.

"I tried. I really did, but I was so miserable," she continued. "I kept fainting during rehearsals because I wouldn't eat all day and obsessed over every calorie I put in my mouth. I got help before it got out of control. A lot of my friends didn't."

Why it was a hang-up, he'd never understand. Sizeism and fat phobia ran rampant in the arts. And why? So the Nutcracker performance could have one more sugar plum fairy with an eating disorder? And fuck the artistic directors who said it ruined the look.

"That's super shitty," he said, instead of going on a rant she'd probably heard before from more articulate people.

She slid her hand up the window frame, the last of the evening light washing her features. "Dance had always been my plan, but not after … after that." She shrugged. "I was a skinny kid my whole life. In middle school, all my friends were praying for boobs, and I was praying to get six inches taller. Then puberty hit me like a Mack truck, and I got all this," she said, motioning to her thighs and tits and every other curve.

Click, click, click. "What's your religion?"

"I was raised Catholic, but I'm agnostic?"

"I'm lighting a candle tonight and sending a prayer of thanks to the Virgin Mary for blessing you with that body."

She rewarded him with her musical laugh and kicked back in time to the music, smiling again.

Good. Mission accomplished. And for once, he could stare at her as long as he wanted, even if it was through a camera lens.

"Anyway, I had always sewn all my costumes for dance, so design and wardrobe seemed natural. I love it, and I'm good at it."

She was better than good. She was the best designer he'd ever worked with. *Click, click, click.* "Ever consider teaching?"

"Kids aren't really my jam," she said, then added quickly, "I mean, I love my nieces, and they're fine in small doses, but I'm happy being the fun auntie. And since I got injured a few years ago, I wouldn't have been able to dance professionally, anyway."

"What happened?" As much as he loved directing her movements, she didn't need it here, and he stood back, watching her glide up the staircase in the studio's corner.

"Salsa competition a few years ago. Grady, my partner, slipped and pulled me down with him."

The man in her profile picture with his hands all over her hadn't been her boyfriend, he'd been her dance partner. A partner whose carelessness had ended her career. The jealousy that had simmered in his stomach morphed into outrage on her behalf. "What a piece of shit."

"It could have just as easily been me pulling him down, but the injury never fully healed." She gave him a chagrined look. "You already know my knee isn't great."

Right. The night they'd spent together, she'd balked when he'd pulled her down to ride him. And he'd demanded she get on her knees in front of him. She'd probably been in pain when he was getting the best blowjob of his life.

Who's the piece of shit now?

"It's okay, mostly, but no more heels. Do you have any idea how many shoes I have in my closet that I can't wear anymore?"

He could imagine. A nice pair of four-inch heels, sticking her ass and tits out, getting her mouth closer to his, but she didn't need to be *standing* in them. Flat on her back with her high-heel clad feet slung over his shoulders, his fingers biting into her thighs ...

A burst of photos slashed across his viewfinder before he could release his grip on the button.

Fucking hell. He swallowed, hard. "You should show me sometime," he croaked out.

"Anyway, my back never fully healed, either. I can dance a bit if I'm very careful, but no more competitions for me."

If she's very careful. When she couldn't move in bed with him how she'd wanted, even as she had twined her body around his, wrapped in sweat and bedsheets. And still she'd been holding back. All because of an accident that happened in an instant.

The light outside had faded enough that the room threw shadows around them. He put down his DSLR and picked up his Pentax.

"Put on the dress. Leave your shoes off."

Gotta love a professional who could make quick costume changes. She exited the change room less than a minute later, bare feet silent across the dance floor. The black dress hugged every one of her luscious curves, with those fabulous breasts begging for attention under the crimson scarf wrapped once around her neck.

He ripped his eyes away and dimmed the overheads until the room almost looked black-and-white, with the light from surrounding buildings throwing flashes of colour across her body.

He held out his hand. "I don't want you wearing it."

The gauzy crimson scarf hinted at the barest of shapes through its translucent weave, but it might—just might—work for what he wanted. He wrapped the material tight to his camera lens and peered through the viewfinder.

The room transformed into an ethereal flame. Beams of light illuminated the strands of silk and softened the hard contrast of the dress on her fair skin, the room muting to a glow surrounding her. But still undeniably her, with her huge eyes following his every move.

Perfect.

"Hand against the window. Look outside."

She obeyed, leaning close enough he could capture her reflection, fingertips resting on the pane. God, he loved how she surrendered to his demands without hesitating.

Click, click, click. The mechanical snick of the lens flicked in rapid succession. He beckoned her closer, untying the scarf from his lens and draping it around her neck, letting the end whisper over her arm.

How fucking hot would she look with her wrists bound, arms trapped over her head, like he'd done in his bed with her months ago, closing his teeth over her nipple as she writhed underneath him with choked cries.

"Turn to me." He stepped closer again, leaning over her.

Click, click, click. How much film did he have left?

"Just like that. Yes." He tilted her chin up to him with a finger.

Click, click, click, the viewfinder forgotten.

"Eyes on me."

Her gaze left the buildings across the street and met his, hitting him with the weight of a sledgehammer. It had been months since he'd been this close to her. Her breath hitched, warm on his mouth. The familiar scent of jasmine hit his senses, and he leaned closer to breathe her in.

It would be so easy. So natural. Her fingers trailing over his chest as she parted her lips, inviting him in. She'd be all cinnamon and sweetness. All he had to do was tilt his head down to close the distance between them to taste her again.

Click, click, burrrrr.

The film stuck on the last frame. He sucked in his breath, taking a step back and holding his camera between them like a barrier.

"We're out of film." He strode across the studio to his phone, cranking up the lights as he went, and the dream-like air around them snapped.

Fuck.

Cass turned to look out the window again, body still. "Did you get what you needed?" she whispered.

Not even close. "It'll have to do."

He fiddled with the lens cover longer than necessary, watching her out of the corner of his eye as she unplugged her phone from the sound system, cutting the low tempo song mid-chorus. She ducked back into the change room without another word. Josh slid down the wall onto his haunches, running a hand through his hair.

What the fuck was he thinking? He had one rule. Don't get involved with anyone on set. His life was complicated enough, and he was in no position to pursue anything more than a zero-strings attached fuck buddy.

Which was exactly the kind of relationship she was trying to stay away from.

That was why they were doing this. Because she had feelings for someone else. He dropped his head and hung his camera strap around his neck like a noose.

Cass exited the change room moments later, the crop top hidden under a leather jacket. She adjusted the bag with her dress and scarf in it and held out her phone.

"You still need to update my bio," she said nonchalantly.

He stared down at her profile. Any man who didn't see her beauty shining through, even in this grainy photo, was not only blind, but an idiot. He plugged in a new bio.

A woman of many talents. Maybe I'll show you some. Probably won't sleep with you, but you'll lose sleep over me.

She smiled at what he wrote, looking as if she was weighing what to say next. "Why are you doing this?" she said, finally, her eyes meeting his through the mirror.

Why *was* he doing this? He was busy as all holy hell. It would take him hours to go through the photos and edit them if they even needed that much editing. But she needed help. She deserved better.

And he had wanted to spend time with her. To get her in front of his camera and see what she would look like on film. Even if getting that close to her was playing with fire.

Not that he could tell her any of that.

"Inoculation, remember? No more fuckboys."

"I remember." She gave a weak smile and cast her gaze around the dance space, and the vibrant confidence and energy she'd moved around the room dissipated. "This is the kind of fun I like to have."

"What?"

"My old bio? I said 'I like to have fun'." She motioned between the two of them. "Hanging out with a friend, talking. Listening to music. I like this. This was fun."

That's some dangerous fun, but same.

He smirked to hide the thump under his sternum. "Told you it would be."

SD CREATIVE AND PRODUCTION CHAT

TERRY

Our location for next week fell through.

What the fuck happened?

TERRY

The site flooded.

LIBBY

I can work around water damage or site
hazards but that means an equipment overhaul
- different circuit interrupters, grounding,
everything

TERRY

No dice. It will take weeks to clean.

STEPHEN

this is going to crank scheduling

How much time will we lose? Continuity? This
is our first week of shooting

CASS

Is it the lab scenes?

my friend's fiancé leases a lab in an industrial
park. He might know of something?

STEPHEN

ur brilliant can u send Terry his contact info

CASS

Let me text him

TERRY

Cass's friend came through. Location scout
said it's perfect! We're back on schedule.

September evaporated under them as a polar vortex blasted over
the city and delayed the second unit filming. Nothing they
couldn't reschedule without issue. For all of Brynne's declaring

diva status, the California native had been an absolute champ filming her outdoor shots, gesturing into the frigid temperatures with bare hands at a green screen that would eventually comp in a faster-than-light space vessel to bring her and Dawson to Sirius. Still, neither she nor Dawson argued when it was time to move filming indoors to the lab.

That had been weirdly easy. Cass's friend knew of a vacant space just a couple of doors down from his lab in the industrial park. Would the location scout eventually have found them a space? Probably, but with Cass's help, there was only a one-day delay.

His lucky charm kept bringing luck.

At first Josh had thought the casting director had made an error putting Dawson in the male lead role. The sandy-haired actor looked more like a farmhand than an astrobiologist, all brawny corn-fed sweetness, but he and Cass's friend could have been cousins.

Dawson peppered Alex with questions as he trailed him through the lab, studying how he interacted with equipment, rolling up his sleeves, and aping how he leaned on the counters. Alex went so far as to hand over a few of his pristine lab coats for their wardrobe, insisting he didn't need to be paid.

"Not like I'm going to wear them," he'd said to Cass, who'd returned his easy grin like there was some long standing inside joke.

Josh forced himself to smile along. If Alex was engaged to Cass's friend, he wasn't likely to make a move on her.

No reason to be jealous. Not that he was.

"Cut!"

Josh hunched over the director's monitor. Dawson had inched into Brynne's frame—again—the broad expanse of his loaned lab coat blocking half the shot.

"You getting what you need here, Hoss?" Dawson asked, massive arms crossed over his chest.

Josh bit back a sarcastic comment about him being a scene

stealer wasn't supposed to be taken literally. "I need you to give her space," he gritted out.

Dawson nodded. "I hear you, but these two were lovers, right? Unresolved? He's drawn to her. He can't help but get close to her."

Cass wandered up to adjust Dawson's lapels, her nails dancing over the folds of the wrinkled white jacket, carefully distressed to look like he'd just chased Brynne through a farmer's field and straight into the lab. That scene wouldn't be shot for another month, at least. If the weather cooperated.

She smoothed her hands over his chest, adjusting the number of wrinkles to fit the scene. "You're fiddling again, Big D."

Big D? When the fuck did that start?

"Hands off," she continued, and Dawson dutifully dropped his hands to his sides.

Much better. No hands. Hands-free. If it wasn't her literal job to fix clothes, he'd have personally stapled Dawson's lab coat in place. Or maybe hire Cass another assistant, so they could grope the actors instead.

Especially now, with Dawson giving Cass moon eyes every second the cameras weren't rolling.

Josh forced his attention back to the director's monitor and scrubbed a hand over his chin. Maybe they did need to get the two of them closer. Dawson and Brynne, that is. Fuck *Big D* and Cass getting closer.

He let out a heavy sigh. Not because Dawson was right, but because he hadn't thought of it first.

Everyone pulling in the same direction, he reminded himself. *We're all a part of this.*

"You're right. Get in her space, but wait until she finishes her line so you aren't cutting her out of frame."

Dawson looked surprised at the ease with which Josh agreed and gave a slow smile. "I can do that," he said, and walked back to his mark.

Cass turned an exaggerated shocked face to Josh. "You

haven't yelled at the crew in three whole days. You used your big boy words to talk to Dawson, although he's such a sweetheart"—a foreign twinge pinched his gut—"I'm sure he'd take it in stride. And no one cried during after-work drinks yesterday," she finished, leaning in to press her full lips to his cheek. "I'm so proud of you."

A not-so-foreign twinge tugged his groin, and he pulled back with eyebrows raised. "What happened to being professional?"

"What? I kiss everyone's cheek. Ask around," she said with a wink.

If she was thinking about the dance studio, she didn't show it. Alright, maybe he was overthinking it. Josh gave her a quelling glare and turned his eyes back to the monitor. "I owe you one, Lucky Charms."

"You spent an entire afternoon with me doing an impromptu photo shoot as a favour. I think we can call it even." Cass gave him a curious look. "Where's this 'Lucky Charms' thing coming from?"

The fact that everything just falls into place around you. He brushed past her question. "I have photos for you."

Of the dozens he'd taken, he'd deleted anything straight away with her eyes closed or out of focus, narrowing it down to a short list of twenty shots. Only the photos of her in the jeans and crop top; the photos he'd taken of her in the black dress wouldn't be developed until he got back to his home set up in Vancouver. Those would have to wait.

She was flouncing away from the camera in his favourite photo, arms swinging and peeking back over her shoulder, curls bouncing as she beckoned him to join her with a saucy grin, the blue top swishing up to show just a tease of her belly. She looked devastating. He couldn't imagine who would swipe right on that photo.

Which he now had to add to her profile, because he was lining her up for five more dates over the next few weeks before filming broke for Thanksgiving.

Five more guys who would spend time with this gorgeous woman. Instead of him.

He sucked air between his teeth and held out his hand.

"Homework time."

She surrendered her phone, and he tutted at her on seeing it not on silent. He Airdropped the photos to her phone and uploaded them to her profile.

One with her head tilted back, arms thrown behind her as if she were getting ready to embrace the sky. One where she sat on the steps, chin on her palm, eyes sparkling down at him through the lens.

A woman of many talents. Maybe I'll show you some. Probably not going to sleep with you, but you'll lose sleep over me.

"You haven't been swiping, have you?" he admonished, scrubbing at the bags under his eyes and trying to swipe left on at least a few of the chumps littering her feed. Tinder needed to set up an option to filter out assholes.

But that was the point of all this. Set her up with assholes so she would learn who she shouldn't fall for. Might as well feed her to the wolves.

Fuck that. He couldn't do it.

"Nope. No swiping, sir, that's your job," she confirmed, then tried to grab her phone back as he swiped right on a heavily tattooed twat-nozzle posing in front of a truck. "Hey, he was cute."

Case in point. The dude was good-looking but oozed sketchy vibes. Probably had a pic of himself posing with a fish in his profile somewhere. A definite right swipe.

After a few more left swipes, he passed her phone back. She ignored the messages of her new matches and looked down at the updated photos.

"These look really great," she said softly. "Thank you."

Easy when she was his subject. He scowled into the monitor, trying to focus on the latest replay of Dawson blocking Brynne from view. "Have fun on your dates."

CHAPTER ELEVEN

CASS

Date 6

Alright Lucky Charms, how'd it go

> You might think a date with an actuary would
> be boring, and you'd be right!

Date 7

> reporting in

Who was tonight's sacrificial lamb?

> The only thing we had in common was we
> agreed low waisted jeans should never have
> made a comeback

He's not wrong

> Not enough to base a relationship off of, though

You're not seeing him again, are you? That's
against the rules

> No sir

Date 8

Nice guy, but no. Prob could be friends?

He talked about Pokémon cards the entire time

I appreciate the passion, but not my kink

Back all the way up

What's your kink?

Damn you, autocorrect!

What was that autocorrecting from?

😂 💀

Date 9

Well?

You sent me on a date WITH MY HIGH SCHOOL HISTORY TEACHER!!

That was beyond weird!!

Like weird-weird or kinky-weird?

Don't make me block you

What's your kink?

You'll tell me eventually

Date 10

If this guy was a spice, he would be flour Gluten-free

Are you still on the date?

Unfortunately yes

What has less flavour than vanilla?

Noted, you want spice, I'll change my strategy

I am suddenly very, very nervous

So I make you nervous?

omg

"Ten down, twenty to go." Libby shook her newly fire-engine red hair away from her mouth as she wrapped an extension cord. "Any winners?"

"No, but that's not the point of this. I'm trying to get over someone, not land a new someone, remember?"

The happy sounds of muffled eating and buzz saws filled the crowded set. Libby and Cass stood at the craft services tent for a long overdue lunch, watching Josh and Brynne arguing, as usual. As long as Josh wasn't yelling at anyone besides Brynne, no one worried. Brynne gave as good as she got.

And the sourdough was worth listening to the yelling.

Cass munched on her sandwich, watching them out of the corner of her eye. Josh stood with his arms crossed tight over his chest, biceps straining at the sleeves of the worn black tee shirt. He leaned in, stabbing his finger in the direction of something out of Cass's sightline. Brynne flipped her perfectly blown out chestnut waves over her shoulder to follow where he was pointing and turned back with a knowing smile.

That wasn't a flirty smile, was it? Brynne wasn't a flirty person. Probably just leaning in because it was loud on set.

Cass shivered, searching for something polite to say about the five most recent snooze fests that were supposedly dates she'd gone on in the last two weeks. "Nice guys, but kind of flat."

"Like they were actually nice guys, or the 'I'm a Nice Guy and the chicks who aren't into me are crazy bitches' kind of nice guys?" she asked, making scare quotes to emphasize her point.

"The former. Not incels or anything,"

"So, no love for Team Vanilla?"

"Do I look like I want to be barefoot with an apron on?"

Of the two of them, Libby was the one with her biological clock hammering away. Nothing wrong with dads-in-training, just not for her. The thought of being locked behind a white picket fence with two-point-four kids made Cass die inside.

"Maybe if the apron was the only thing you're wearing, with cut-outs for your tits and the strings tied around your wrists?"

"You're not wrong," Cass muttered. " But I don't think any of those guys would have been into that."

Each date had been … nice. The actuary had a name, she was sure, but she had to look at his coffee cup where the barista had written his name on it four times, and it still hadn't sunk in. She'd gotten wrapped up in Pokémon Go as much as the next person a few years back, but not enough to dedicate her precious days off to it, like date number eight had. Two of the men had been so dull that she wondered if she had fallen asleep with her eyes open. Her high school history teacher—which was the only thing she could ever see him as, even if they'd hit it off—had baby fever so hot she half expected him to whip out a thermometer to check if she was ovulating.

"Mr. Schmidt, I mean Derek—god, that was weird—I swear he was thinking *birthing hips* when he checked out my butt instead of *I want to hit that from behind*. Not that I would with him because all I could think of was how I always fell asleep in his class. I felt like a breeding heifer."

It had been the least sexy date she'd ever been on. Including the tropical fish fiasco.

Libby snickered, then asked, "Have you heard from him again?"

No need to ask who the *him* in question was.

Cass shook her head, eyes down, and crammed her sand-wich into her mouth to prevent her from saying something stupid. It had been almost a month and a half since she'd heard from Nick, which wasn't unusual. They'd always run hot and cold. She was a little relieved. And not as disappointed as she usually was.

"Do you know if he tried to talk to Alex?"

The delicious sourdough went dry in her mouth. When her teeth had pulverized the bread into submission, she swallowed and said, "I don't know. We didn't do much talking."

Which had been her problem with him all along.

"You're smart. You're pretty. You're funny," Libby chided, "so I don't understand why you slept with Nick again."

"Because every time he twitches a finger at me, I can feel the feminism fleeing my body."

And because it had been months since she'd had an orgasm without Chauncy. Maybe Josh was right and she should invest in a stronger model.

Heat surged in her chest. She hadn't let Libby in on any of those details. Nor had she breathed a word to Jill that she'd seen Nick.

Not telling her oldest bestie about flirty exchanges with hot guys? Not telling her newest bestie that her mortal enemy was back in town? When had she started keeping secrets?

Libby pursed her lips. "Why didn't you block him? Addicts need to remove the temptation."

"I'm not addicted."

"Honey," Libby said, exasperated. "You are *jonesing* for a fix."

"I'm going cold turkey."

For real this time? Cass sighed, picking at the last bits of sandwich.

"Or you could lose yourself in a pair of sexy dimples and see if that makes you forget what's-his-nuts?"

"Elizabeth!" Cass huffed. The last thing she needed was to throw herself at Josh. Drowning in that smile had been a one-time ride, even if she'd loved making him laugh and turning his glower into a wicked grin.

The photo shoot had been the most fun she'd had in months. The music, the laughter. The photos he showed her later. Every shot had been beautiful. She had felt beautiful. Seen.

Right up until she was sure he was going to kiss her. His eyes on her lips, leaning in like he couldn't help himself. She could almost feel his mouth on hers, her pulse thudding in her throat, until he shut down without warning.

Pretending for weeks that his rejection hadn't hurt had been exhausting.

Josh still stood huddled with Brynne, their faces serious and quiet now, standing so close to talk over the noise on set.

Cass stared down at her sensible support shoes. "No, I'm not getting involved with anyone on set, especially him."

"Oh come on. The way he looks at you? Dawson would fall over himself to spend five minutes with you."

Cass looked at her blankly. Dawson? He was looking at her in a way? She swivelled her head to look for the towering Tennessean, finding him leaning against a table with his eyes trained on her. He nodded his head, a shy smile spreading dimples to his cheeks.

Oh. Dimples checking her out.

Cass swallowed an unexpected lump of disappointment. The appeal of No Second Dates was not getting hung up on one person, especially now with filming picking up. She managed a smile back and turned to Libby, who was standing up and brushing her dusty hands on her coveralls.

"I'm sticking to the plan. Ten down and twenty to go," Cass said. "Nothing serious, no Nick, and no distractions."

No distractions meant no heartache. From any bearer of sexy dimples.

Costume wasn't needed on set for the last shots of the day, so she pulled her things out of her locker and popped a piece of cinnamon gum to chase the last of her coffee breath away. Josh and Brynne had disappeared. Maybe they were done discussing the scene. Maybe they went somewhere more private.

They were both hot as hell, working closely together. Both were single, as far as she knew. Why wouldn't they? If she started counting on her fingers the number of times she'd been on a production where the director and lead actor hooked up, she'd run out of digits before she was halfway through the list. Cass shut her locker door with a quiet click.

Her phone buzzing in her purse provided a welcome distraction. For a minute.

Suzie. That meant one thing. Cass groaned.

"Hey girl! You free Friday night?"

Cass slumped against the locker. "What do you need, Suz?"

"We just got tickets to that play you were talking about last week and wanted to know if you could watch the girls?"

Musical theatre had been their thing: Suzie, Davie, and Cassie shrieking at their mom to put on her old records to sing along for hours when they were kids.

Why hadn't Suzie invited her instead? Her brother-in-law couldn't care less about musical theatre. His snores would drown out the orchestra by the intermission.

Not that she wouldn't be excited to play with her favourite rugrats, but still … She had planned on going for drinks with some of her old theatre friends. Suzie didn't have the most reliable babysitter, and Cass could always catch her crew next time.

"Of course," Cass said, resigned.

"Oh, you're the best!" Suzie squealed. "They'll be so excited!"

Cass dialled up the brightest smile she could so her sister would hear it in her voice. "Can't wait."

CHAPTER TWELVE

JOSH

THE GRIPS HAD SET UP THE GREEN SCREEN TO BLOCK THE GOLDEN, mid-fall afternoon sun from sneaking through the cracks in the windows. Libby had shouted "Striking!" almost half an hour ago, and the set had lit up like a Christmas tree, if Christmas trees were up at the beginning of November in gutted athletic training facilities that smelled of fresh sawdust, old gym socks, and determination. The sound team had padded the room until it sounded like everyone spoke as if underwater, and a sea of voices murmured through the space.

Everyone was waiting for her. Again.

"Where's Brynne?" Stephen barked at the make-up assistant.

In her trailer, visualizing, if Josh had to guess. She had her process. If they rushed her out, they'd lose more time with shitty takes than if they left her alone to prepare.

That didn't mean they couldn't use this time.

He twisted his lips in thought, his eyes on Cass as she directed her wardrobe assistant. She was at least half a foot shorter than Brynne, but they had the same alabaster skin, and Brynne's hair was only a few shades lighter than Cass's deep chestnut. The lighting would look the same on either of them, and he could stick Cass on an apple box to match her height. Cass would never squeeze into the tailored space suit she'd designed for Brynne's lithe form, but costume was irrelevant in this scene. He wanted to push the shot in tight, anyway.

He motioned to the closest PA. "Bex, get Cass to stand in front of the half console. And ask Libby to come here."

It was damn near perfect. Up on the apple box, Cass was the right height for Libby to catch the shadows that would have obscured Brynne in the same position, and she stood awkwardly on the replica spaceship's bridge while the crew adjusted the light and shadow around her.

Libby crossed her arms over her coveralls. "We need to lower the overheads."

"And add a blue gel," Josh finished. "It's too real, too comfortable right now."

The grips scurried to put the adjustments in place. Josh felt the familiar rush in his gut, and the set disappeared.

Blue tint washed her every curve with an otherworldly luminescence that made her look lit from within. Her hazel eyes looked almost black in the dim light, wide and wondering, with sparks reflected in her irises like constellations. Like she was made from the stars themselves.

"This is what I need," Josh said to Libby, voice low. "She's gorgeous."

Libby slowly turned to look at him. "Is she?"

Human, but only just, almost beyond reach. Ephemeral, barely on this plane. Cass was more than gorgeous. She glowed. She was ethereal.

Josh swallowed and nodded once. "She's perfect."

"Yes, I agree. My best friend is perfect."

He tore his eyes away from the monitor to find Libby studying him.

Fuck.

"She's also sensitive and funny and the kindest person I know."

This was why he kept his mouth shut. "She is all of those things."

"She deserves happiness, and I'm so grateful you are helping her figure out how to stop falling for fuckboys who don't have her best interest at heart. I would hate for her to get hurt again by another insensitive asshole. I mean, neither of us want that, right?"

Josh twisted his lips. "No. We don't."

"So glad we are on the same page." Libby crossed her arms and turned her attention to where Cass fidgeted on the apple box. "And do we think Brynne will look just as gorgeous when she finally gets out of her trailer and into the scene?"

"No. I mean, yes." He scowled at the monitor. "It's Brynne. She'll look fine."

"She always does," Dawson said absently, walking over from where he'd been watching the blocking with his eyes trained on Cass. "I want to get in there with her."

"Not necessary," Josh started, but Dawson was already stepping into position beside her, his usual affable charm erased by his character's angular rigidity.

The blue light transformed Dawson into a Nordic god. Pale and cold beside Cass's otherworldly aura. The two of them looked perfectly matched. Her leaning, now relaxed against the ship's console, and him reflecting her energy back at her. Dawson leaned in to murmur something into her ear, and the smile that lit her face made the lights fade around her. Cass pressed her lips together the way she always did when she was trying not to laugh and turned to raise an eyebrow at Josh.

"You getting what you need here, Hoss?" she called over in a terrible imitation of Dawson's drawl, still fighting her smile, and Dawson broke character to bark a laugh.

"They look really good together," Libby said. "Do we want to block out the scene where Dawson moves in to kiss her?"

"We'll wait for Brynne," Josh said quickly. He shifted his gaze to Brynne's trailer door. Fuck her process. She needed to get her ass out here.

"Are you sure? Could save us some time."

"Positive. It might make Cass uncomfortable,"

Libby sucked in air through her teeth. "Is that what you are worried about?"

The diva in question chose that moment to untomb herself from her trailer. "Are we blocking?"

Fucking finally. Josh clapped his hands together. "Excellent. Great. We're ready. Let's go."

Dawson held out his hand to help Cass down from the apple box, still smiling from whatever he had said to her moments before. Cass adjusted a final wardrobe flaw on Dawson's suit, invisible from where Josh and Libby were stationed, and made her way over.

"Do you know if Dawson's trainer is on set today?" When Libby shrugged, Cass wrinkled her nose, giving him a once over. "He's busting out of his suit. Unless he's planning on launching the ship into space himself, he can probably skip a week or two in the gym."

Josh narrowed his eyes. His lead actor's suit did look snug. There was no reason Dawson's character needed to be built like a brick shithouse, even if he was trying to model Dr. Donovan Rykoff after Dr. Alex Campbell.

"He *is* looking extra beefy," Libby said with a gleeful look at Josh, bumping him with her hip on the way out, leaving to supervise her team.

Since when was his director of lighting the biggest pain in his ass? He ran his fingers through his hair, fighting the urge to flip her off, and ground his teeth together. "Hey Siri. Take a note. Tell Dawson's trainer to lay off the bench press."

Out of the washed blue light, Cass looked human again. She just shrugged. "Don't worry about continuity. It wouldn't be the first time I've made last-minute adjustments like that. Once, I had to lay behind a sheet holding the edges of the actress's dress together during reshoots because she'd had to put on weight for a new role."

Why did she have to bring up laying down and bedclothes in the same sentence? Josh turned his frown to where Dawson and Brynne stood with heads together, their faces tight in concentration, and adopted a teasing tone. "You're a picky woman."

"What do you mean?" she asked in surprise.

"Your most recent slot of dates. You didn't have a lot of nice things to say about them."

Cass's shoulders rose with a deep breath, and she turned to him with her brightest smile. "Oh, those? Those weren't bad, just boring."

"If you ask for spicier matches, you'll get them." Josh forced a benign expression on his face.

"Okay," Cass said, eyes wary. "But not, like, too spicy, right? No sex dungeons or base jumping dates?"

"Unless they post it in their profile, I won't know if they have sex dungeons, will I?"

"Stop it." She huffed out a breath. "Just don't get me murdered."

He felt a shadow cross his face. "That's one of the reasons I matched you with boring guys. Safer."

"I'm not saying I need training wheels," she said. "I hooked up with you, didn't I?"

It was true; she wasn't an ingenue waiting wistfully on a fainting couch for a dashing duke to whisk her away. She got out there and took what she wanted. Just a lot of what she wanted wasn't great for her.

What did that say about him?

They'd worked together for months now, sharing and arguing about ideas. They had exchanged emails in the weeks leading up to the first team meeting. Design. Casting. What would specifically look good with the actors, the overall aesthetic. A thought occurred to him that he should have realized earlier.

"This summer, when we had our first pre-production meeting," he said. "On that video call. You knew it was me."

Cass averted her eyes with a slightly guilty expression.

"Why didn't you say anything?" he asked, and immediately regretted it. Putting her on the spot, when she couldn't get away, was kind of a dick move.

There could be any number of reasons she wouldn't want to bring it up. She'd said herself she thought it might be weird working together after, although that had fortunately not materialized. No weirdness. Only a low-grade burn under his skin whenever they were in the same room.

She turned her eyes to the trailers, as if she was looking for an exit. Fuck, he'd pushed too hard. He opened his mouth to take it back when she spoke.

"I didn't know if there was anything to say. I didn't know if you'd even remember me," she said, not meeting his eyes. "Why bring attention to something that might go unnoticed?"

"You are unforgettable," he said without thinking, surprised by the heat in his voice, and her expression softened.

"That night we were together? It was really special for me. Not like, you know." She made scare quotes with her fingers and adopted a teasing voice. "Best night of my life."

He couldn't help the snort that escaped. "Bet it was up there. Top ten, at least."

It was for him.

"At least," she said softly. She made a show of rooting through her purse, looking like she was buying time to weigh out what she wanted to say. Finally, she said, "I had a lot of fun with you. We made each other laugh—"

"And drove each other a little crazy. I mean, your takes on the end of that thriller? Everyone's entitled to their opinions, just not when they're that wrong."

"Says the man who thinks lens-flariness is next to godliness." She waited for his retort, but he just shrugged, so she continued,

"I hadn't felt that good about myself in so long. And then we'd texted that night …"

A surge of pleasure rushed through his chest. He had hooked up with more than his fair share of partners, but no, that night had been something different for him, too. A lot hotter. A whole lot more laughter. He'd held off on shooting his shot with her for hours, wanting to *talk* with her instead, hear her opinions. Knowing she'd had as good a night as he had felt … like something he hadn't felt in a long time.

"You're really great for my ego, Lucky Charms."

"Why do you keep calling me that?"

He shrugged. "You still haven't answered my question. Why not say something?"

"Just because that night was special for me didn't mean it was for you."

He cleared his throat. "I'm not likely to forget a night like that, either."

Cass looked up and shone a smile on him that sent a flare under his sternum like a warning shot.

He couldn't do this. Not now. They'd fucked, had fun, and called it a night. They'd swapped a couple texts, and she sent him a picture of her tits. That was it. His life was too complicated for this shit.

Josh snapped his attention to the monitors in front of him. "Now you've got homework. Phone," he demanded, hand out.

Her smile faltered. "Oh, right."

He swiped, frowning at the clowns on the screen. Nothing but neck beards, endless flannel, and pick-me-up trucks.

"They need to set an option that filters out fish in profile pictures," he grumbled.

"This is Alberta. That would preclude ninety percent of the men out there. Besides, if they're out fishing, I'll know they have at least one hobby and I'll have some alone time."

"Like quality time with Chauncy?"

"Among other things, and since you've forbidden me from

even kissing anyone, a girl has to take care of herself," she said, the golden flecks in her eyes sparking at him, "and I like to take care of myself."

He knew exactly what he'd be picturing tonight as he did his own self care.

"And on that exceptionally TMI note, I need to fix Dawson's suit again because he can't keep his hands to himself," she said, and scurried over to where the actors stood in position, her hands all over the seams of the Tennessean's costume.

He pulled out his phone. "Hey Siri, take a note. Get Terry to find a budget to hire Cass an extra pair of hands." *So she could keep hers off Dawson.*

His phone pinged before the voice note was complete. Who would be getting through on DND? Cass's hands were occupied on Dawson, Stephen had his head down with Libby, that left …

Shit, it wasn't the studio, was it? Melanie wasn't due on set until next week. He took one look at the text banner, and his stomach clenched.

Fuck, it was never a good time, but today of all days? He ducked into the alley behind the training facility and dialled.

"Vivian. Hi."

"You can't avoid me forever."

The prickle of goosebumps that flashed over his arms was only partly from the afternoon chill. No *hi*, no *how are you?* Not that he could blame her.

"I'm not avoiding you. Did you get my revisions?"

"Yes, and they were unacceptable."

Why was he not surprised? He'd worked on the revisions for a month after their last useless phone call, late into the night, hunched over his laptop and making edits he knew she'd just change her mind about later. He dug his thumb into his temple. "What do you want?"

"You know what I want. Come in and we can talk in person. Sort through the confusion."

That wouldn't help. The confusion wasn't a communication

issue. Not to mention the last time they'd tried to revise the document together while they were in the same room, he'd stormed out in a silent rage. He ground his teeth and willed his voice to be polite. "That's not possible."

"Then let me know when you can," she said crisply, and hung up without another word.

The sun had dipped behind the building, the sky already fading into indigo twilight and any warmth from the fall after-noon long gone. He screwed up his face, pressing his thumbs into his temples.

Every conversation with Vivian ended with him writhing in self-loathing.

Fuck. Well, it wasn't like he had other plans. He could start again tonight. Maybe this round of edits would finally make her happy.

CHAPTER THIRTEEN

CASS

DATE 11

So?

I wouldn't know

he hid behind a cloud of vape smoke so thick I thought I was going to choke to death on a watermelon haze

Date 12

That might have actually been a pitch for an MLM

Ah, an entrepreneur then lol

Date 13

He took me axe throwing

Who still does that?

Lumberjack chic?

My back is killing me

Need a massage? I know how to use my hands

I swear to god...

Date 14

What twisted hybrid of spicy and daddy was this?

I'll be your spicy daddy

Omg

Date 15

You sent me on a date with a gang member!

Drugs or bikes?

What does he ride?

NOT HELPFUL!

Halfway. Fifteen down, fifteen to go.

Fifteen nights given over to guys she didn't know. Each some combination of boring, lame, or just not for her. The prospect of handing over fifteen more nights to fifteen more guys exhausted her.

And what had she learned so far? That there was no middle ground between dudes looking for a wife or a hookup? That she'd rather enjoy her friends or her own company than subject herself to an endless carousel of lacklustre dates that necessitated her plucking her eyebrows?

She didn't need to put herself through fifteen more dates to learn that.

She'd been learning that lesson over and over since her boobs showed up at age sixteen and boys assumed her newly sprouted assets meant she'd put out. Or since the man who she thought she'd been casually seeing had assumed from her sweet face she was looking to become a fifties housewife and dumped her on the spot when he found out she wasn't.

No, thank you.

Cass rooted through her purse to fish out her keys, leaning back against the elevator wall. Her back was on fire. Her feet ached. She knew better than to wear heels. The guy's profile said he was six-foot-one, and after being dwarfed by Dawson on set for months, she didn't feel like dealing with the *wait, how short are you* conversation that was bound to come up. Not like three-inch heels made her artificially achieved five-foot-four that much taller, but apparently she wasn't thinking tonight. And now, with a blister forming, even the thought of walking three flights of stairs to her apartment was daunting.

Her platform loafers would have been better, but they didn't go with the dress she'd wanted to wear. Why she wanted to dress up at all in the first place seemed like a distant memory.

Also, that guy was not six-foot-one. She'd put enough lifts in actors' shoes over the years that she could tell five-ten from six-one at a glance, even if he was wearing combat boots. At least he hadn't tried to lie to her about packing any other hidden inches anywhere else.

Now she had a sore back and sore feet for nothing. At least it wasn't a replay of the awkward cheek mauling she'd endured three nights ago, when her date had thought there would be more tongue involved at the end of the evening.

She dropped her keys into their dish, right between her half-drunk cup of tea from the morning and the dirty dishes from her rushed dinner that night and eased her jacket down her bare arms before draping it over her couch. After a minute of fruitless rooting, she tipped her purse upside down and shook it, letting her phone, wallet, and everything else scatter over her kitchen table. She found her phone and sighed.

Dead, no surprise. She hadn't charged it since yesterday, and the old thing sucked juice like crazy. A debrief with Libby would have to wait. She plugged it in beside her sewing machine, the pieces of a new design waiting to be sewn neatly folded beside her dress form.

How are you going to keep a man if you can't keep a home, Cassidy? Her mother's voice echoed in her head. Her apartment wasn't messy. It just wasn't a pristine showpiece where she was afraid to sip wine on her couch or had use coasters for everything. The mismatched area rugs picked up from estate sales carpeted the floor and collections of her friends' paintings crowded the wall, all boldly patterned and coloured. Even if she did clean, her home was so cluttered that it would never look truly neat. Just how she liked it.

Her phone chirped to life beside her just as she'd lowered herself onto the floor for her back decompression exercises, and a rapid succession of beeps let her know she'd been very, very missed.

Why couldn't you have beeped two seconds ago when I was still standing? Brow creasing, she yanked the charging cord so that the phone fell off the table into her outstretched hand.

Unsurprisingly, three texts from Libby.

> Tonight's date is with the guy with all the ink, right?

> I should get another tattoo

Then, an hour later

> Josh is blowing up my phone. You're not dead are you?

Much more surprisingly, eight texts, two calls, and a voice mail. All from Josh.

No seriously

Beamer or Harley

Okay Lucky Charms. Do you need a rescue?

Lucky Charms?

Cass?

I'm calling you now

Pick up

Where are you?

What the heck? She was in the middle of texting him when an incoming call came through.

"Hey," she answered, massaging her aching calf. "What's the—"

"Thank god," Josh exhaled in a rush. "Where are you?"

"—emergency?" she finished. She flexed her ankles to get the blood flowing to her toes. "I just got home."

"I'm on my way," he said, and hung up without letting her respond.

Bewildered, she stared at the blank screen in her hand, then around her dishevelled apartment. What was that all about? It was after nine, and shooting had been over for hours, and she wasn't needed on set tomorrow. Her insides lurched at the thought that some crisis had sprung up while she was out with the not quite six-foot-one, tatted librarian who ran what he called a literary rebel gang. AKA, a book club for bros learning to dismantle their toxic masculinity. Cool idea, and a fun guy, but he didn't set her heart aflutter. Not like Jo—

Nick. Not like Nick. That's why I'm putting myself through this. She pressed a thumb into the small of her back and looked around the mess flowing unbroken from her kitchen to her living room.

Josh's condo had been pristine. Almost stark in its neatness, all negative space and clean lines. The exact opposite of her happily eclectic home.

Fine. It wasn't eclectic. It was a mess. He was about to see how she lived. In minutes, from the sounds of it. She raced around her living room as fast as her tired feet and sore back would let her, clearing the abandoned piles of mail and discarded clothes.

Don't bother cleaning the bedroom. He's NOT going in there. And why is there underwear on the coffee table? After a beat, she shoved the clothes dropped on her bed into her closet and stashed Chauncy in her bedside table.

No reason. She was just taking advantage of the cleaning frenzy to do a little more.

Her phone buzzed with the announcement Josh was at her door, and she froze with a handful of dirty dishes. Had the man used a wormhole to get here? She dropped the dishes in the sink with a clatter before buzzing him in, kicking the shoes littering her front entry into the closet. There was a strident knock a minute later, and Josh barged through the door.

"How'd you—" she started, but he pinched her chin between his forefinger and thumb and tilted her head back, squinting at her through narrowed eyes, before releasing her with a whoosh of breath.

"You didn't answer when I texted you."

"My phone died."

Josh gritted his teeth, glaring at her sewing machine like it was responsible for draining her phone's battery. "You should charge your phone before you go in case you need to call me. Or someone. Whatever."

"That's what Jill always tells me."

Cass cast a glance at her still-open front door, shifting from foot to tired foot. He looked as good as ever, his hair sticking up in dishevelled spikes, the shadow of his beard coming in dark against his golden skin and outlining the sharp angle of his jaw. He looked down at her with his trademark glower, arms crossed over the chest she knew from experience would be warm and firm and smooth. Her heart pulsed under her breast, and she pressed her hand to still it. "Um, I was going to make tea." Wait, he didn't like tea. "Or coffee." *Don't say it. Don't ask it. Don't do it* ... "Do you want to come in for a bit?"

Shoot.

Josh huffed out a breath through his nostrils as he looked around her mess of an apartment. "No," he said after a beat. "I've got things to do."

Her stomach dropped. "Oh."

"I just wanted to make sure you were home safe," he finished.

She would not be disappointed. Nothing to be disappointed about, after all. To not have a nice, innocent cup of tea or coffee with him. He cared enough to see she was okay. That was kind. Something a friend would do.

It would have to be enough.

She rubbed her hands up her bare arms to wipe away the goosebumps that had sprung up. "You knew that when I called you," she said. "You didn't need to come over."

"I wanted to see for myself."

"Well, you've seen," she said, trying to keep the petulant tone from her voice. "Thanks for checking. I'll see you in a couple days?"

"Yeah," he said, and reached out once more, as if to confirm yes, she was there in one piece. He nodded and disappeared through her door, leaving her without another word.

Her stomach sank for the second time in as many minutes. What else would be so pressing at nine-thirty on a Wednesday night other than meeting a hookup.

Well, good for him.

Fifteen dates down, fifteen to go. Then she'd be over him.

The morning sun hovered below the horizon. The stars had disappeared on the opposite side of the sky, and the nearly full moon slowly slipped behind the mountains like a party balloon losing its buoyancy.

Cass scrubbed at her eyes and stifled a yawn. Call sheets summoned her to set at four a.m. Wasn't as bad as Libby's call time. She and her team had worked through the night.

Brynne, already in position, looked fresh, even from here. None of the gossip about the actress was true. That she was tough to work with. A demanding diva who disappeared for hours to make the crew wait. A few B-words and C-words were dropped.

In fitting sessions, it became apparent Brynne was just exceptionally quiet, extremely introverted, and deeply, deeply self-conscious. The half hour in her trailer to visualize and refusal to watch dailies made more sense. Cass kept their conversations friendly and focussed, and in the short months they'd known each other, Brynne's icy attitude melted.

There was something about having your hands all over someone's boobs for fittings that removed silly things, like personal boundaries and inhibitions.

Dawson, too, had picked up Brynne's loner vibe, and his quiet demeanour complemented her need for restrained energy. The two had become inseparable on set. Which was great, most of the time. Until he had to tackle her as she fled, begging him to stay away from her.

"Hold still, Big D," Cass said with an indulgent grin, tugging gently on the zippers of the oversized parka that wrapped the giant actor.

It was a nervous tic, she'd realized, him fiddling with his

clothes before a particularly stressful scene. He'd tear paper to shreds, bounce a ball off the wall, drum his fingers on any nearby surface. Anything within reach to keep his hands busy was fair game. And if nothing else was available, his clothes bore the brunt of his jitters.

"Sorry, Cassidy," he said, his deep voice tight as he stared into the middle distance.

No surprise why he was so nervous. He was about to race across the snowy field, again, and tackle Brynne into a mattress hidden out of camera line. Brynne had refused to use a stunt double, and the gentle man was terrified of hurting her. Josh had already spoken to him—four times after four takes—and Brynne had reminded him she was made of the tough stuff and could take it, but he'd pulled up short at the last moment every time.

Cass brushed her hands down the front of her own parka, warm even in the crisp November morning. The fields shimmered under a glittery gauze of hoarfrost, and the air sparkled clean and fresh in her nose with every chilly inhale. Stephen had whooped in glee when the forecast had called for the cold snap, and days of shooting were rearranged to take advantage of the bluebird sky and pristine snowy landscapes. That also meant driving the portable trailers with blankets, heaters, and thermoses of coffee outside of city limits into a farmer's field in the middle of nowhere.

Parallel tracks marked Brynne and Dawson's path as they moved the shot out after every take, each one inching closer to the rising sun. It wasn't fresh snow they were running out of. It was time. The sun would be fully up in minutes, and Cass could see Josh glancing over, clearly fretting to get the blue hour light before it disappeared.

Dawson muttered a string of incomprehensible words under his breath, toying with the edge of the jacket's cuffs. Cass caught snatches of "my momma ain't gonna be happy 'bout this" and "I'm gonna hurt her" over and over.

"Ain't nuthin' to be sorry 'bout," she teased, mimicking his broad Southern drawl, and he broke out of his daze to smile down at her.

Josh stomped over to them. "You done?" he asked curtly.

Dawson puffed out his cheeks and stared out at Brynne, silent.

Josh blew on his gloved hands, plumes of white breath escaping between his fingers. "You're not worried about preventing her from reaching her goal. You're just trying to keep her safe. If she gets to that shed, you don't know what'll happen to her."

Dawson nodded and glanced down at Cass making the final adjustments on his jacket. "If he loved her, he wouldn't be chasing her and making her scream."

Cass bit down on her grin and flicked her gaze to Josh, who narrowed his eyes at her, the dimple forming in his cheek.

"Imagine she's about to step into the street and you're the only one who can push her out of the way of oncoming traffic." Cass said with a final tug on his sleeves. She tilted her smile up to him. "She has brothers. She's tough."

Dawson gave her a doubtful look.

"You got this. Now, scoot. Brynne's waiting for you to take her down. Plus, I added padding to her costume. She'll be fine."

He gave a chagrined nod. "Thanks, darlin'," he said, and strode off to his mark.

She pulled her mittens back on as she walked back out of sight lines. Josh glowered as she kicked the snow off her boots and curled up in the chair under the heat lamps. It wasn't *really* cold yet, only minus fifteen, but all the out-of-town crew shivered like they were on the set of *Snowpiercer*.

"Darlin'?" Josh repeated, dimple gone.

If she didn't know better, she would have thought he was jealous. Cass clicked her tongue. "He says that to everyone."

Josh looked unconvinced.

Everyone was in position. On cue, Brynne took off at a sprint, arms and legs pumping and her breath billowing behind her, with Dawson charging after her like a bull. The camera raced ahead of them, lens fixed on Brynne's furious expression, with Dawson gaining on her from behind, a look of brutal determination transforming his kind face. Closer, closer ...

Dawson steamrolled Brynne at full speed, tumbling out of sight and onto the mattress, softer than a kitten batting a cotton ball. Brynne popped up as soon as Josh yelled "Cut!" brushing snow from her hair and pants, and Dawson pulled her into a tight hug.

It was a dick move in the story; Dawson's character blocks Brynne's attempts to discover the truth at every turn, even if it came from a place of concern.

In the book, with the female main character sabotaging the male main character, a whole swath of the fandom had written it off as stereotypical sexist nagging, her chasing him across the fields shrieking like a banshee. In Josh's adaptation, with the gender roles reversed, it framed everything through the patriarchy thwarting a strong woman's ambition.

So much more poignant, topical, and, frankly, fixed a major issue that even the author had admitted over a production phone call.

When the fandom found out their precious Dawson's Dr. Donovan Rykoff, NASA physicist, had been demoted to the love interest of Brynne's Dr. Amelia Andersen, half of them would cheer. The other half would riot.

The set had been locked down for months, with non-disclosure agreements signed by everyone from the producing team to the caterers. Every blog article and podcast contained only wild speculation, with only cast lists and the vaguest of locations to pore over. Cass even stayed tight-lipped with Jill, who followed every fan site and still pumped her for information at every brunch and girls' night. If Jill hadn't learned anything, no one had.

It would be explosive when the word got out.

Josh huddled over the director's monitor, grunting something in approval and his eyes narrowing even farther when Cass came into his field of view.

Ever since he had left her place a few nights ago with barely a *good night*, he'd been not exactly cold, but aloof. Distant compared to the way he'd acted with her previously. He'd speak to her minimally, replying with one-word answers, even as she saw him tracking her with his gaze. If he hadn't been so adamant about setting her up with other people, she'd have thought he was interested in her.

It wasn't that farfetched of a thought, was it? They had insane chemistry that night in Vancouver. But that had been one time. Month ago. She'd just been in town for the weekend. No strings. No expectations. A few spicy texts for a bit of fun. And besides the relentless flirting that she suspected was as natural as breathing for him, he'd never suggested they revisit said insane chemistry. He'd basically said he wanted to avoid it altogether. Avoid *her* altogether.

Besides, the aloofness was probably something else. Not a cold shoulder at all. The shoots had been gruelling the past weeks, lasting well into the small hours of the night, followed by pre-dawn starts the next morning. Maybe his mercurial moods were just from the pressure of the schedule, and nothing at all to do with her.

Why would it?

"That was it. Perfect," Josh said, as Dawson jogged up to view the take, and Cass pulled her shoulders down and turned her sweetest smile to the actor.

"I believe it. I believe him," Cass said, watching the replay, "that he's doing this from a place of love."

"Good. He's misguided, but he loves her," Dawson said, smiling down at her. "That's what I'm going for."

A muscle in Josh's cheek jumped. "Everybody loves a hero."

"Not everyone," Dawson replied, stamping his feet.

Josh reached out and pulled Cass out of her chair, tucking her back in close against his front. "You see, the glow?" he said, pointing to the monitor with a gloved hand.

In theory, she saw it. It was right in front of her face, but his breath tickling the shell of her ear stole her attention. "Mm-hmm," was all she could get out and heat crept down her neck and under her downy parka.

Josh's hand slid down the length of her arm to find her mittened hand, closing his fist around it. "These keeping you warm enough?"

I want to taste every inch of you. The last time his lips had been that close to her, he'd been buried deep inside her, his hands claiming her body like he owned it. Cass swayed on her feet, trying not to lean into him.

"I'm not cold." *Anymore.*

He let a disbelieving noise escape his throat. "If we'd got this scene any earlier, it would have been too dark. Whatever you said to Dawson worked."

"What *we* said to Dawson worked." Her willpower broke, and she closed her eyes as she tilted back on her heels.

He inhaled as her weight leaned into him, closing any distance left between them. He smelled warm and fresh, more citrus than sandalwood, his breath on her neck spreading heat across her body. The pace of her heartbeat picked up from a canter to a gallop in her veins.

"Dawson's standing right here," Dawson said, eyes flicking between the two of them.

Josh released her so quickly she stumbled back a pace. "I have what I need. Where's Libby? We can tear down."

Cass watched him retreat to consult with Stephen and Libby, and she was left with the cold swirling around her neck and her heart thumping in her chest. She drew a slow breath through pursed lips, shivering slightly.

This is what he does. Ignore it. Seduction is his neutral gear. A reflex. He probably doesn't even notice he's doing it.

But he could have asked a PA to call for Libby, instead of leaving me here.

"You alright?"

She dragged her eyes away from Josh's back, pushing down the flutters. "Yep," she said, smiling widely. "Good job out there."

"You're looking cold there, darlin'," Dawson said, his breath misting around him. "We need to get some coffee or something in you."

A jet of steam huffed out her nose like a dragon, and she glanced around in false secrecy. "If you promise not to tell anyone, I bring a thermos of hot chocolate to winter shoots. Way better than that stuff from craft services."

She rooted in her bag to bury herself in the distraction. She untwisted the lid from the battered carafe and poured out a stream of the rich chocolate into its serving cup, tendrils of rich steam curling around her fingers.

She always brought enough hot chocolate to share, and if Josh wanted to disappear, he wouldn't get anything sweet from her. "Come on, I'll hook you up."

Dawson took the proffered cap and sipped, ending in a groan. "That warmed me right to my toes," he said, and took another swig. "I have never been so grateful there aren't shirtless scenes in this movie. I would never be able to drink this on one of those superhero diets."

"Don't worry. If you put on two ounces, I'll let out your tailoring again," she teased, taking back the cup, and stashing it back in her bag. Her eyes wandered over to Josh, who watched her through narrowed eyes, his arms crossed over his chest.

God, he looked good when he was glowering, too. She smiled and waved, determined not to let her mind travel down that road.

What the hell was wrong with her?

"I was thinking," Dawson started, "would you—"

"Good job, Big D," Libby interrupted as she walked up. "Josh needs to talk to you about this afternoon. He has thoughts."

Dawson blinked at the interruption. "Oh, sure," he replied, and tossed a quirky smile at Cass as he followed the summons.

Libby pulled Cass away from the crew tearing down the station, to a space as secluded as could be found on a set with a few dozen people milling about. "Anything new on the romance front?"

"No," Cass sighed. "The librarian gangster was the last one, and I don't have anything new planned yet."

"I'm not talking about those Tinder travesties."

"The Tinder travesties?"

"Name of your sex tape," Libby quipped. "No, not that. I'm talking about whatever's going on here."

There was no way Libby had picked up whatever Josh was putting down from across the field.

Had she?

"What else would there be?" she asked, a little too innocently.

"Oh, please," Libby reprimanded. "You have two dudes practically panting over you."

Two? Okay, that she hadn't been expecting. "What do you mean?"

"Don't play coy with me."

"I'm not playing anything!"

Libby gave her an exasperated look. "Josh is practically pissing on you to stake his territory, and Dawson is just waiting for the chance to wife you up."

"First? Ew. Second? He's not," Cass replied with a grimace. "Third? Extremely unlikely. On both counts." She wiped her hands over her cheeks, likely bright red from cold and embarrassment. "Dawson's a sweet guy, that's it. Josh …" *Makes me feel like we could roll around in the snow for an hour and melt this entire field.* "Is Josh. He's like that with everyone."

Libby raised her eyebrows in disbelief. "Um, he's really not. Just you."

That couldn't be right. She'd seen him charming other people on set. Hadn't she?

Or had she? She wracked her brain trying to think of a time she'd seen him touch anyone to direct their attention. Smile at them with those panty-evaporating dimples. Whisper in someone's ear. Or bite someone's ear.

Nothing came to mind. And she sure had a lot of mental footage to consider. She'd been watching him. Intently. For months.

Dammit.

Why am I my own worst enemy?

"It's not fair," Cass whined, with high pitches and everything. If she could do it with anyone, it was her best friend since second grade. "Why does my vagina hate me so much?"

"I don't think your vagina hates you, but I think your brain and vagina need to have a heart to heart."

"Doubtful that'll do any good," she muttered. Why on earth, after everything, would she trust her brain, either? She'd almost take a text from Nick for the distraction. No one ever said she wasn't brilliant at self-sabotage, either.

"Speaking of brains and vaginas, what's going on with you and Stephen? Is this a thing again?"

Normally Libby would launch into a description of all the dirty things she was thinking of doing with the guy she had her eyes on, but her friend gave a guarded smile and shot him a glance. "Maybe. I don't know. I think it might be."

Cass eyed her. Just because the breakup had been amicable, didn't mean Libby hadn't turned into a ghost for months after Stephen had left. She hadn't dated anyone seriously since. "You sure you're ready for that heartbreak again, Libs? They're leaving when we wrap."

She needed to think about that herself. Why get attached when Josh would be packing up and leaving?

"What if it's different this time?" Libby said softly.

Stephen looked up and caught Libby's eyes, and smiled with a warmth Cass hadn't seen from him before.

Oh, it was like that.

The sun spilled like lemonade over the fields, thin and pale. Nothing like the rich gold of high summer, but bright against the brilliant snow, and Cass felt her longest friend slipping away.

"Well," Cass said, pasting on her brightest smile. "Then it's worth a shot."

CHAPTER FOURTEEN

JOSH

Im bored

So get a fucking life?

Ur my life bro

Get your shit

We're going out

THE PAINTS SAT UNOPENED ON THE SPOTLESS DROP SHEET THAT HAD sat in the rental's hallway for months. A notebook filled with dozens of sketches laid open in front of him, each page offering a variation on the mountain range he'd planned. Places he'd lived. Places he'd visited. The North Shore mountains that had dominated the Vancouver skyline and his childhood, smooth and close and verdant, rising from the ocean like Poseidon. The Dandenong Ranges, though he'd only seen them in the Melbourne summer. A version of the Andes, pulled from a decade-old memory, and admittedly not true to life. Here, the Rockies waited in the distance, jagged and wild, grey against the blue sky, a knife blade thrust towards the heavens. He'd have to decide, eventually.

Josh sat cross-legged on the floor, scowling at the empty expanse of wall mocking him. This wasn't going anywhere tonight, and with just over a month left in Calgary, it was barely worth starting now. He tossed the pencil and notebook onto the counter, and Stephen's pounding on the door sounded seconds later.

The bar trying to style itself as a speakeasy had an artificially accelerated patina, all burnished brass, patterned peacock-and-emerald wallpaper, and richly upholstered shell benches. Good vibe, actually, and busy for a Tuesday night. Gusts of cold December air pushed through the doors at his back and under the collar of his warm-up jacket, doing anything but its actual job, and Stephen cut through the crowd with practiced ease.

"This place used to be a country bar when I was in university," he said, sliding into the booth and frowning at the art déco interior. He nudged his bearded chin at a corner with a wine cave glassed off. "Cover bands used to play on a shitty stage right over there."

"You seriously think I'd be sitting here listening to country covers?"

"Aw buddy, you'd do anything for me."

"Fuck off."

Fine. It was better than staring at the blank wall of his rental, with no clue where to start. Either that, or work on Vivian's revisions. No clue where to start there, either.

Lo-Fi vaporwave filtered in through the speakers, matched to the knock-off Tiffany lamps at every table. Josh leaned back, his arm stretched along the booth's backrest, and swirled his elderberry soda in the crystal-cut lowball glass. "We're going to get kicked out of this four-top," he said.

"Nah," Stephen replied, nodding at the server who dropped off his pint of stout. "Friends are coming."

Minutes later, Libby slid in beside Stephen, who greeted her with a smile and a kiss. Libby stripped her puffer jacket and hung it off the hook at the end of the booth. Josh couldn't be sure, but he thought her hand reached down to squeeze Stephen's knee as she settled herself.

That was new. At least one of them had found a way to stay warm this winter. Josh hid his momentary surprise behind a sip of his drink and waved a finger between the two of them. "How long has this been going on?

Stephen took a pull from his beer. "Short version or long version?"

"Nice to see you, too," Libby deadpanned, shaking the snowdrops from the ends of her hair.

Fair. That had been a dick comment. Josh shot a glance at the entrance.

Libby smirked at him. "Don't worry, she's coming."

He whipped his head back like he'd been caught ogling someone's chest and realized that was exactly what he would have done when Cass showed up. He glared at Libby and swigged a larger than anticipated gulp of his drink, the carbonation burning his throat on the way down.

It didn't help that when Cass showed up a few minutes later, his chest clenched like he'd tried to swallow the fist-sized ice cube floating in his glass. Her warm hazel eyes widened when she saw him, and after a beat, hung her own jacket on the booth's hook beside Libby's and took her place next to him. The light wash high-waisted jeans hugged her thighs before they flared over her suede fur-lined boots.

Hell, this woman could even make winter wear look sexy. The simple black ballet top dipped at her shoulders, inviting his eye to trace the contours of her collarbones.

All that skin on display meant she was probably wearing something like that bustier he'd peeled off her that first night. He wondered if it was the same one, and if not, what colour it was, and if it was silky and red and ... *fucking hell*, his dick was straining against the fly of his jeans.

Since he was already uncomfortable, might as well partake in a bit of light self-flagellation. He leaned over and whispered in her ear, "I can't comment on how you look in low-waisted jeans, but you make these ones look fantastic."

Cass pursed her bright red lips at him with a look of feigned reproach. "These hide muffin tops," she said finally.

His hands had been all over those muffin tops and didn't think they needed hiding. "The tops are the best part. I always eat those first."

"Stop it," she said, but he could see her own smile as she looked away.

Libby pulled a pickled asparagus out of the Caesar the server dropped off and waggled it between Josh and Stephen. "So, how long has this been going on?" she asked, parroting his question back to him. "You two lovebirds meet on set?"

"Do you want to tell the story of how we met, darling?" Stephen batted his lashes at Josh.

Josh sighed at the bottom of his drink. He almost wished he'd ordered alcohol. A double. "Nope."

"So sweet. After all these years, he still lets me do the honours," Stephen said, and Josh dodged the fist Stephen aimed to chuck at his chin. "I was working on a film a few years back, and we were getting hosed by one of our contractors. Josh was called in as our legal advisor."

"Legal advisor?" Cass whipped her head around and looked at him like a pair of horns had sprouted out of his temples. "You're …"

"A blood-sucking lawyer," Stephen finished with a wide grin.

Fuck, Stephen loved bringing this up. "Former. I don't practice anymore," Josh said firmly.

Libby leaned forward with her elbows on the table. "I feel like there's a story here."

"It's not that interesting." And not that high on his list of stories to retell.

"You never mentioned this," Cass said, an odd look on her face.

"Don't hold it against me. Anyway, new topic."

"Okay. How's pimping out my best friend coming along?" Libby asked.

Fuck's sake. Not that topic. Josh glared at her. "It's not pimping."

"It's kind of pimping," Stephen said.

"Did Cassie tell you about the baby daddy fiasco?" Libby asked innocently.

She had fucking not. "A what now?"

Stephen lit up. "There's a baby daddy fiasco? I need to hear about this."

"Date fourteen," Cass sighed. "This guy had all these names tatted up his arm. It turns out he has five kids from four different mamas. My guess is that he had the names tattooed, so he didn't forget them like some absent-parent version of *Memento*. I don't know if he was specifically looking for baby mama number five, but he dropped a lot of hints on how virile he was and how many women fell over him." Cass shuddered as she sipped her cocktail. "He licked my face at the end of the night."

"What the fuck?" Josh jerked. The baby mama drama she'd told him. The face licking and the potential baby mama recruitment had been left out.

"Ah. This was spicy daddy," Stephen said, nodding sagely.

Fuck that. If anyone was, he was her spicy daddy. Not that he wanted her to call him daddy. Well, maybe … He shifted in his seat. "You knew about this?" Josh directed his anger between Libby and Stephen equally. "Can we get back to the face licking?"

"No," the trio replied in unison.

Cass gave him a bemused look. "Have you not had to deal with a weird date before?"

"Not ones where my dates were mauling me."

"Besides," Libby said, thumbing a bit of foam from Stephen's moustache, "before you find your prince, you need to lick a few frogs. Or vice versa."

"I don't think that's how that expression goes, but I'm willing to play along," Stephen offered, and Libby grinned wickedly back.

"No more talk of licking," Josh said.

Cass asked. "I can fend off a little—"

"Assault?" Josh snapped.

She was such a gentle thing, way too trusting. That was her problem. She let people walk all over her. The thought of someone touching her when she didn't want to be thronged through his brain.

Not just someone touching her when she didn't want it—the thought of someone touching her who wasn't *him*.

"That's it." He crossed his arms and set his jaw. "No more dates."

"Or maybe just not dates with assholes," Libby said.

"I'm only halfway through. And besides, I've dealt with worse," Cass said, and that did not make him feel even a little bit better. But if she wanted to keep going, it was her choice. At least he could make sure whoever she saw passed a higher bar than what he'd set.

"Fine," Josh snapped. "You don't want boring. You don't want freaky. What do you want?"

Cass shrugged and took a sip of her drink. "None of these guys are around longer than one date anyway, so what does it matter?"

It matters if your lips end up on someone else.

And where the fuck was this coming from? He didn't get jealous. Ever. Jealous meant he thought she was his, and no one else's. The last thing he needed was to examine why. What he needed was to put distance between them.

By sticking with the stupid plan of sending her out with other guys.

He glowered at her and held out his hand. "Phone."

He swiped. And swiped. *Left, left, left.* What a bunch of clowns. The ones who weren't assholes were just wholesome chocolate chip cookies that would bore Cass to tears. Or put their hands on her. Whether or not she wanted it. Worse, how could he tell the difference?

Fuck. He sank lower in his seat and swiped left again.

"You literally let him do this," Libby said, amazed. "I thought you were exaggerating."

"What can I say? I'm a sucker for punishment." Cass peered nervously over his shoulder, and her flowery scent enveloped him. His gut clenched at the thought of Face Licker close enough to get a noseful of her distracting fragrance. "You have to swipe right on at least a few of these guys," she said.

"I thought the point of all this was fuckboy exposure therapy," Stephen said. "Just swipe right on guys like you."

A litany of ways to make Stephen regret opening his trap crossed Josh's mind. Throw a wrench in scheduling. Or cancel a caterer.

Shit, no. Nothing that would affect filming. They were too close to the end for that. Only weeks away. He pictured himself getting on the plane, alone, and his gut twisted.

"Lord knows I don't have the best track record," Cass murmured. "And any time you meet someone new is a chance, right? People take a chance like this all the time."

"Or maybe this has been a terrible idea from the start, and you should just spend time with people that actually care about you," Libby snapped, shooting daggers at Josh.

Like he was in a position to do anything about that.

Gritting his teeth, he forced himself to swipe right on a few dudes who at least didn't look like mouth breathers, or like they belonged on a government watch list. Each swipe bragged *It's a Match!* and Josh repressed the urge to undo the matches with the firefighter, the architect, and the financial consultant with great hair.

"Here," he said, passing her phone back. "At least a few fuckboys."

Cass took her phone back and swiped through her matches

with a resigned determination. "A couple of these guys seem okay," she said, voice trailing off.

Fuck. He knew he shouldn't have matched the firefighter.

"Shit, you got terrible taste in men, dude." Stephen leaned against the bench, his arm wrapped around Libby and grinning. "Are you trying to make Cassie suffer or is that your natural state with women?"

That smirk was coming off his best friend's maw if it took sandpaper. If they kept ragging on his swiping, he might take it personally. The point was to get Cass exposed to a bunch of different guys to help her get over that fucker who kept jerking her around. He hadn't been making bad matches for her. Not on purpose.

Had he?

He turned to Cass. "This is your cue to say, 'Of course, Josh doesn't make me suffer.'"

"Of course, Josh doesn't make me suffer," Cass recited dutifully.

"Except when he tries to make her be someone's new mommy," Libby finished.

No wonder Libby and Stephen got along so well: they both got off on grinding his gears. "None of these dudes look like they want to make babies on date one."

And no face licking. Or any other kind of licking. Although, if that was what they wanted, Josh couldn't blame them. Cass tasted like sin and candy.

"No date two, so shouldn't be an issue," Cass said wanly.

"Not like you're going to be mortgage shopping with these guys, anyway, so who cares if they have kids." Libby shrugged a shoulder. "With some of these winners Josh keeps setting you up with, they might have kids running around they don't know about."

"Happened to a friend of mine in uni," Stephen said. "His ex contacted him when his daughter was four years old. She's a good kid, but he never planned on being a dad."

"One of the few privileges of being a woman is that we know exactly how many children we have," Libby said. "What do you think, Josh? You got any kidlets running around Vancouver?"

"No kids." Josh pierced her with a quelling glare she deflected with an easy smirk. Stephen shifted his eyes from his beer to Libby.

"Unless you're a monk, you can't be sure," Libby pressed.

"Trust me." A monk, he was not, but his vasectomy a few years back made damn sure there were no random Grahams scampering about. He threw a sidelong look at Cass. "Besides, kids aren't really my jam."

Cass dipped her head and huffed a quiet laugh through her nose. "No family?"

"My sister lives in the boonies," Josh cut in, giving Stephen a look.

"Port Moody is hardly the boonies," Stephen said.

"But our schedules didn't let us see each other much," Josh finished. "My parents move wherever my mom's latest flip is, as long as it's west of Cambie, and I have grandparents in West Van. My mom's family is still all back in Australia."

Partial truths were still truths.

"Happiness is a large, close-knit family in another city," Cass said. "Otherwise, they guilt you into babysitting every chance they get."

"You can say no to that sometimes, you know," Libby said, and Cass squirmed.

"I don't know," Stephen said. "It can be nice to be close to family."

Josh could dispute some of that sentiment.

The silent ride back to the rental was short enough the car didn't have the chance to warm up before Stephen was pulling up in front of their building. As soon as Josh stepped out of the vehi-

cle, cold speared his sinuses like he had snorted crushed pepper-
mint candies. He jammed his freezing hands deeper into his
pockets and Stephen stamped his feet, waiting for the elevator to
arrive.

"What's going on with you and Cass?"

Josh shrugged his jacket up his neck and stared at the elevator's numbers flicking down. "Not sure what you mean."

Stephen levelled a flat look. "Don't give me that bullshit. I
know you're the king of casual, and I don't know why she's
doing this to herself, but whatever you're putting her through
isn't making her happy."

Josh glared at him. "What would you know about what
makes her happy?" he asked sharply.

"Chill, dude. I've known Cass a long-ass time. Way back
from when Libby and I were together."

Fine, that might have come off a bit defensive. What he'd
been defending himself against, he wasn't sure. Josh brushed a
melting snowflake from his sleeve and said nothing.

"Cass is one of the most optimistic people I've met," Stephen
continued, unperturbed. "Whatever she's going through right
now is not the Cass I knew."

An odd pang spiked his gut. Was he jealous that Stephen had
known Cass longer than him? Maybe. Or was he guilty he was
making her lose her spark?

"Nothing is going on between us," Josh said finally.

Stephen shifted his weight from one foot to the other. "Cass
doesn't do anything halfway. She loves with all her heart, every
time. No matter how many bruised edges it gives her."

And here he was, tossing her to the wolves over and over,
with the hopes she'd get bruised enough it would turn into a
scar.

Fuck.

Josh steered the subject to something that wouldn't make him
engage in self-reflection. "So, you and Libby have history?"

"Yeah. I hoped she might be on the crew."

"When did you and Libby become a thing? Long version."

Stephen leaned against the elevator's mirrored back as the doors slid shut, smiling. "She was the first girl I ever kissed. First girlfriend. First everything. We were together all through high school, all the way through university. We broke up when I moved to Vancouver." Stephen stared at the buttons lighting up as the floors ascended. "I thought she would come with me."

"And now you're back in town and picking right up where you left off."

"I don't know, man. A lot has changed." Stephen scrubbed his hand over his beard and sucked the air through his teeth. "Some things are the same."

Maybe the Cass that Stephen had known had changed in that time, too. Maybe it was this piece of shit Nick bringing her down. Or maybe it was him bringing out the worst in her.

"We've got a break in shooting for almost two weeks over Christmas," Josh said, switching topics. "Is Libby coming to Vancouver?"

Stephen looked cagey. "Actually, I'm sticking around. As much as I'd love to keep imposing on you, I've got a whole-ass apartment to myself here. Her folks are having us over for dinner on Christmas Eve, and Libby's coming to my family's place for Christmas and New Year's."

All the bitching Stephen had done for years about being glad to get out of Calgary winters, he didn't have to shovel rain, blah blah blah. Now his friend was passing up a free trip back home? Maybe it wasn't home for him anymore. Maybe it never was.

It was for Josh, still. At least, he had a condo there. How many people in their mid-thirties could say they owned property outright in downtown Vancouver? And he had friends, or people who called themselves his friends. Work he loved, since he'd gotten out of his father's firm and shredded every tie he'd ever owned. But he couldn't pick up and move to the other side of the world in a heartbeat to chase something different. Even if he wanted to, he was still tied to Vancouver a little while longer. For how much longer remained to be seen.

Stephen looked like he was filtering through the contents of Josh's brain faster than he could. "Why don't you stick around?" he suggested. "Give yourself a break here and not worry about everything back home for a couple weeks. I bet Cass would love the excuse to get away from her family for a bit."

Tempting. No expectations, no guilt, and sure it would be a polar vortex, but he might be able to find an excuse to spend some time with her. Josh felt the corner of his mouth turn up.

"You know," Stephen's voice broke into Josh's thoughts, "you actually smile when Cass is around."

But that was part of the problem. He had obligations, guilt-laden or not. And Cass was a distraction from getting that sorted. A distraction from his work. A distraction that took up way too much of his thoughts. When he'd pulled her against him that morning of the sunrise shoot, her softness against his chest, he had to will himself not to slide his arm around her waist and bury his nose in her hair.

He'd cursed every layer of clothes between them. When she'd leaned back, her ass against his thighs felt like a better fit than the gloves that were in the way of him feeling her skin on his. He didn't know if they'd stood like that for an hour or a second before Dawson had broken the spell. However long it had been, it hadn't been enough.

Josh wiped his face clear.

"She and I hooked up. Once. End of story," Josh bit off.

It was a shit thing to say, but he needed Stephen off his back. Josh rolled his shoulders under his jacket and waited for the doors to open.

Besides, he had things to do back home, and avoiding them wouldn't help.

Lord knew he'd tried.

CHAPTER FIFTEEN

CASS

DATE 16

Tonight's the finance bro yeah?

He tried to pick a fight with the bartender to show me how alpha he is

did he beat him up with his giant dick?

Like a baby's arm

you didn't, did you?

You aren't slut shaming me are you?

you can do whatever you want

But did you?

Josh has unsent a message

I didn't sleep with him

Josh has unsent a message

Date 17

So this guy tells me we're going to that gallery opening I was telling you about, then when we meet he drags me out to this outdoor rink

That's a risky play

It was -20 C

I don't skate

He didn't even ask

Then he got grumpy when I wouldn't go on the ice

like it was my fault he didn't check with me beforehand

You okay? Need me to come get you?

No, I'm home, thanks

I thought this batch of guys was supposed to be decent

You call me if you need me

Date 18

Want to know one of the many reasons I'm glad I don't work in an office?

Hit me

Office parties

My date tricked me into going to his

Sneaky little shit

Then he ignored me for an hour while he chatted up a coworker

I think he just brought me to be arm candy to make her jealous

You do make beautiful arm candy

Not now, please

Date 19

Tonight's the firefighter, right?

Burny McHotpants?

He a douche too?

He's a peach! Chat tmr xoxo

what

Cass juggled her phone and mocha in one hand and pinned the swatches under the arm that her purse didn't occupy with the other. The lineup at Rosso that morning had stretched out the door, and there were more than a few people on the roads who could use winter driving lessons. According to her call sheet, she was only five minutes late, but between Terry, Stephen, and Josh, at least one of them would be pissed.

Maybe Dawson would be a doll and run interference again.

The parking lot looked like a group of drunks decided to play bumper cars in a skating rink. Cass made a wild guess as to where the lot's parking lines were and angled her pick up close to her usual spot. Filming wasn't rolling for another three hours, but the set bustled with action. Terry gave a quick wave as they rushed by, and unsurprisingly, Brynne was nowhere to be seen, but Stephen smiled as he jogged past with a crisp, "Morning!"

So far, so good.

The makeup artist applied a final dust of powder over Dawson's perfect cheekbones and holstered her brush as she stepped back. "All done, D."

"Thanks, Amy," he said with a polite grin to the artist, who swooned in reply. Dawson let Cass brush some loose powder from his lapel, his eyes fixed somewhere between her chin and her nose, and she wondered if she'd forgotten to put on lipstick.

"Might want to lay low for a bit," he said, smiling. "Josh is on the warpath."

And that answered that question.

But it was possible, likely even, that he was stressed about the shots for today. Libby had worked some electrical mastery that fortunately didn't blow any fuses. At least literally. So much light blasted the set that the resulting heat forced them to turn the building's furnace off for the day. Libby and Josh had argued for hours over how to get the look; Josh wanting to correct in post and Libby insisting she could get it bright enough with practical effects.

Josh would be antsy until they had a few takes. In the meantime, he'd be growly. Which meant any number of poor PAs might be chewed up over a misplaced pen. And if he was cranky she was late, well, better to get that over with before his bluster turned into a hurricane.

"When isn't he on the warpath?" Cass said conspiratorially. She lifted onto her toes, hand braced on Dawson's thick forearm for balance, to scan the crowded set.

As usual, she didn't need to search long. That, and Josh's bellow thundered across the room, his eyes already locked on her.

"I'll go check on him. Make sure he's not terrorizing the caterer or anything."

"Are you sure you want to do that?" the makeup artist asked. "He's extra murdery today."

Cass clicked her tongue. "He's not so bad."

"With you, maybe."

None of the other directors she'd worked with had cared if she was a couple minutes late, as long as it didn't scrunch shooting. Every director had, however, been a control freak on some level. Timeliness was obviously one of Josh's triggers.

Next time, set your alarm clock earlier, she thought, crossing the set. Josh tore his eyes away from her, scowling at an innocent tablet in his hand.

Even from her height disadvantage, she could see the screen was black, and she rolled her lips inwards to ward off the smile that would just provoke him further.

Actually, that might be fun.

She bumped his thigh with her hip as she caught up to him, turning her sweetest smile on full blast.

"Good morning, sunshine," she said in her most sugary voice. "I checked the weather forecast this morning. I didn't think the snow would turn to rain so quickly."

"What?" he asked, studiously avoiding her face.

"Maybe all the clouds are just in here, raining all over you."

A short gruff left his throat, and while he didn't smile, the line between his eyebrows faded a touch. She scooted into his eyeline again. "I'm so sorry I didn't get in earlier."

"Late night?" he bit out.

Oh, he was in a right state. He couldn't be that mad at her for being five minutes late. And how did that man look so good with such a foul expression on his face? Cass tilted her head. "Later than I planned, honestly. It was fun."

A muscle in his cheek jumped, and the line between his brows deepened again.

Cass continued, determined to be undeterred by his moodiness. "Definitely a player, but he was so sweet, in his own way. He's not looking for anything serious, but I swear he is my friend's type through and through, so I texted her to join us. I stuck around for a bit, but I got a text from her this morning, and they shut the coffee shop down. They're meeting up again tomorrow."

Cass could almost see the sparks fly when her friend had arrived. Unorthodox, maybe, but since she wasn't looking at scoring with Burny McHotpants, who was ridiculously good looking with his bright blue eyes and calendar-ready physique, why not try to hook him up with a friend? Cass had snuck away after a bit to let the two of them get to know each other. She wasn't entirely convinced they'd noticed her leave.

It wasn't clear from the barrage of texts her friend had sent that morning, extolling his virtues, physical and otherwise, if they'd gotten naked last night. If they hadn't, Cass was willing to set a very short countdown clock to the event. And if history was any predictor, Cass could set a timer on the save-the-date invitations.

Not interested in anything serious, my perfectly round tush. My track record is flawless.

Josh narrowed his eyes at her. "So, your good time wasn't because you were playing with his hose?"

"Ew!" Cass hid a snort behind her hand. "No! We both liked the same music and watching them was adorable. Seriously, you should have seen them. They were picking out china patterns by the second cup."

"Oh." Josh twisted his mouth, shoulders releasing down his back. "Good. I mean, for your friend. That's too bad. For you."

"At least one of us is on their way to Mr. Right and not just Mr. Right Now."

"Is that what you want?"

Cass studied her fingernails. "I want someone who respects me. Who is honest with me."

"Jesus, Charms. The bar really is in hell."

The air huffed from her lungs. That was the understatement of the century. Every crappy ex-boyfriend had lowered the bar a little further. Years of unmet needs eroded her standards until the bare minimum felt like a grand gesture.

What did she want, really?

It wasn't a ring, or a minivan, or a house in the burbs. Josh wasn't letting her touch anyone, so it wasn't like she was getting laid. Heck, it was more than just getting over what's-his-nuts.

Actually, Nick hadn't crossed her mind in weeks. That was progress. But it wasn't what she *wanted*.

It was how Stephen had spent days tracking down a rare vinyl Libby wanted. Or how Alex had painted their bedroom Jill's favourite colour because he thought it would make her happy. How all the men Cass had dated took what she said she wanted from them and gave it to someone else.

"Just once, I want someone to make an effort." She blinked hard and turned a brittle smile to him. "Do you think I'm asking too much?"

An emotion she couldn't identify hid behind the shadow that crossed his face. "I don't think you're asking for enough."

Filming was running late. As usual. Josh had demanded extra takes. Also as usual. Craft services had cleared the last of dinner hours ago, and so now not only did her feet hurt, her stomach could be heard rumbling across the set.

Cass braced her hands on the railing to relieve the pressure on her back. Even with the late night, Brynne and Dawson looked as fresh as they had at the start of the day. Like her thinking of him drew his attention, Dawson caught her eye from across the room, and she smiled back.

She had to give it to him; the man was a pro. He'd been on his feet twice as long as her and hadn't complained once.

She added a few side twists, flexing her bad knee to keep up the range of motion. Surely, they had to be done soon, and she could go home and turn on show tunes and do some sewing.

Cass hadn't checked the time since dinner, and she pulled out her phone to check, her stomach bottoming out at the message notification on her screen.

> hey cass
>
> Been a few months since I've seen that beautiful face of yours. Wyd tonight?

Cass shoved her phone into her pocket so hard she thought the seams would rip and skittered across the set as fast as her sore feet would take her.

"I need you to take my phone."

Libby finished repositioning a light and turned to her friend. "Huh?" she asked eloquently.

"I just got a text from Nick."

"What?" Libby screeched. "Why haven't you blocked him yet?"

"I don't know! Reasons!" Cass said, waving her hands in wild circles. "What if he ran into trouble and I was the only person he could call?"

"That is a Nick problem, not a Cass problem."

"Libs, this isn't helpful."

"You want helpful? Nick can get fucked." Libby gave her a flat look. "But not by you."

"Can you just take it?"

"And do what, exactly?" Libby demanded. "Hold it above your head so you can't reach it?"

Cass groaned. It was explosive every time they got together. Even if they didn't talk much, their physical chemistry was off the charts. Hot and sweaty and just as devastating as the stick of dynamite that would blow up her emotions the next morning. She could practically feel his heavy gaze on her and her thighs rubbed together in anticipation.

Only one other person had ever gotten her blood moving like that.

If she and Nick were dynamite, then she and Josh were atomic.

Or had been.

Now Josh was too busy focussing on getting Brynne in frame to notice Cass. Why would he notice her, anyway? He'd said he wanted to keep it strictly professional, and he'd all but outright rejected her more than once. Backing away at their photo shoot. In the farmer's field, with the dawn rising around them. When he'd checked on her after her date, leaving the second she suggested he stay.

Did she need another rejection to hammer the message home?

Apparently, she did, if she was rereading Nick's text.

Cass buried her face in her hands. "What am I doing? I'm so stupid."

"You are not stupid. You have a brain that is as big as your heart, but your heart and libido form an unholy alliance that overrides your brain every time."

"The orgasms aren't worth it." She peeked from between her fingers. "Are they?"

"Now you sound stupid. Just say no."

Cass wrung her hands together, partially to prevent her from reaching into her pocket and texting Nick back. "It's not that simple!"

"No, it's literally that simple." Libby gave Cass a pitying look. "I'm not putting your phone in time-out, and clearly you don't seem able to just ignore him. What about setting up a date tonight? Give yourself plausible deniability that you can't meet him?"

Cass blew out a breath. "Perfect. Yes. That'll work."

She opened Tinder. Josh hadn't swiped right on as many people last time, and only three new people matched her. She'd swapped a first message with each of them a couple days ago, just a quick *hi* with varying inane openers in reply, but she hadn't opened the app since.

A reply sat in her inbox from each of them, and she quickly sent each of them a message.

> Hey! Short notice but want to grab cocktails tonight at 9?

Saved. The cute architect was responding already. Cass hovered by Libby until his response popped up.

> I've got nothing better to do. Send me the name and I'll meet you there

Relief blanketed her, and she hammered out the name of the lounge with a *see you tonight!*

"Crisis averted," Cass said. "Going for overpriced drinks with Leo the architect. No Nick. Nick-free zone."

At least tonight was covered. Cass pecked out a decline to Nick, wincing as she typed *another time* instead of the *eat a bag of dicks* she should have replied with.

She should have just said she was in Cuba until next summer and hoped he'd forget about her. While he ate a bag of dicks.

"I hate seeing you like this," Libby said, shaking her head. "You're a grown-ass woman. You are confusing the excitement and attention he gives you with something real, and you're letting yourself get hurt over and over."

"Can you just celebrate with me that I didn't cave to Nick, for the first time ever, and I'm going to go out with Leo tonight and have a perfectly boring time?"

Libby swooped down for a hug. "Oh, you're right. I'm proud of you."

"Who knows?" Cass said. "Maybe he'll be a proper player and I'll be able to practice my resistance skills."

Date 20

finally hapened

What? You don't sound murdered

He ditchd me

Im just sitting here chuggnig wine like I meant to be heer by myslef

Funny thing is I woudl be having great time if id planned that way

just fleel pahtetic

I can think of a thousand words to describe you, and pathetic would never come up

Tour sweat

tour sweat

your sweet

Are you drunk?

alerb

Where are you?

I wnat to aloen

I'm coming to get you

CHAPTER SIXTEEN

JOSH

Josh fidgeted with his inbox open while waiting for the telltale buzz of his phone that didn't come.

Cass hadn't replied after her last text. Maybe her phone died again. Maybe some shithead had already zeroed in on the vulnerable woman, alone, who couldn't fend off his advances.

It didn't matter if she wanted to be alone. The last thing he'd planned on doing at ten p.m. on a Tuesday was head downtown for a rescue, but if she was as blitzed as her texts made it sound, he wasn't chancing her getting home alone.

If he could find her.

He swore under his breath, scrolling down the text thread with Libby that was littered with details on generators and wattage and gel filters.

> Do you know where Cass is tonight?

Yeah, why?

> Because she got stood up

Dammit

Architect Leo

Piece of shit

He wasn't sure if Libby was calling the architect a piece of shit for standing Cass up, or him for matching them for the date. Both were probably true.

I'll make sure she gets home safe if you can let me know where she is

I'll come with

I've got her

A pin to a nearby address landed in his messages, followed by a demand to keep her posted a second later. Josh shrugged into his jacket and braced himself for the cold.

Fucking fuck. He should have unmatched the architect, too.

The cocktail bar looked like it had been edgy thirty years ago. It glittered with dated chrome fixtures, faux wood panelling, and the brittle chatter of middle-aged divorcees desperate for a hookup. Canned hotel jazz wafted out of hidden speakers, the entire ambiance aggressively trying to convince patrons it was cool and that there was no need to leave in search of a trendier location. By the scant number occupying tables, patrons had either gaslit themselves into buying the vibe of the bar, or already gone home, either with a conquest or solo.

Josh's eyes scraped over to where Cass teetered on a bar stool, its scooped back the only thing preventing her from toppling over. A middle-aged man in a well-cut suit sat on the stool beside her, his hand resting on the back of her chair and shoving a drink toward her.

Asshole. Trying to take advantage of a drunk woman. Called it. Josh cut into the narrow space between Cass's stool and the guy leaning into her.

"She doesn't want to talk to you," Josh said, yanking the dude's chair back so that he stumbled onto his loafers.

"Whoa, friend." The shorter man tugged the lapels of his jacket straight. "Are you Josh?"

"I'm her boyfriend, shitknob." He stepped in, putting his body between them. Just to drive the point home, he reached his arm around Cass's sloping shoulders. "Now, fuck off."

Cass looked up for the first time with bleary eyes. "Oh, Josh!" Even through her slurring, her wine-stained mouth stretched into a soft smile, and the way she said his name, with comfort and trust, sent a rush through his stomach.

A sliver of his worry eased. If she was still smiling, she might not be so drunk that she would turn into a weepy mess. He hoped.

Cass leaned into him, and he refocused his attention on staring down the suit and away from the curve of her breast grazing his torso.

"Thought I was going to be alone tonight," she hummed against his arm.

"Not if you don't want to be." Josh slid onto the bar stool beside her, rubbing a hand down her back and continuing to glare at the unwelcome interloper. "Sorry I'm late, beautiful."

"This is my friend Omar. He said he'd ..." Cass blinked at him. "Where'd your date go?"

"He left," Omar replied. "You're better company, anyway."

Well, shit. This Omar guy comforted her while she cried into her mojito, and his date ditched him for doing a good deed.

Apparently wankers bailing on people was the theme of the night.

Josh gritted his teeth. "I'm sorry I told you to fuck off."

"Don't mention it," he said, getting up to leave. "Can you get her home? And try to get her to drink a glass of water."

Cass left Omar with a series of sloppy hugs and demands to hang out soon before he could finally break free. She turned back to Josh, elbow propped on the sticky bar. "What are you doing here?"

"Rescuing a damsel in distress."

Cass giggled. "Does that make you my knight-in-shining armour?"

Far from it. "Do you remember texting me?"

"I did?" Cass peered down at her phone and swayed dangerously in her seat, the smile fading from her lips. "It's dead, anyway. At least I can't read his texts anymore."

Texts from whom? And why did that make her sound relieved and dejected at the same time? Josh turned his anger to the bartender, who was likely responsible for over serving her. "How many has she had?"

The skinny man scrubbed a palm over the nape of his neck and had the decency to look guilty. "A couple too many."

Obviously. Josh propped his arms under Cass's. "Come on, let's get you out of here."

"I haven't finished my wine!" she protested.

Her morning would be bad enough without adding more alcohol to the mix. Josh reached over the bar and dumped the last of the wine into the sink. "All done. I'm bringing you home."

A light dust of snow had accumulated on his rental car. Josh maneuvered Cass into the passenger's seat and wiped the windshield with his arm, swearing as flakes snuck down the collar of his jacket. He dropped into the driver's seat and texted Stephen.

> Yo what time are call sheets tomorrow?

> Libs wants to know if you got Cass yet

> With her now

> She's in for a rough morning but she's fine

> We roll at 11. Might want to get here for 9 in case Brynne wants to meet before Friday's scenes.

Shit. That's right. Brynne had mentioned she had ideas about the scenes they were filming in a few days. Nine a.m. wouldn't be a problem for him. He wasn't the one whose head would feel like a bag of rusty hammers in a glass factory tomorrow.

When's Cass on set?

Noon

Josh chewed the inside of his cheek and shifted his gaze down to the borderline comatose woman beside him. Noon would come a lot earlier than she wanted.

Even like this, she looked adorably dishevelled. Her curls had frizzed with the melting snow, and her lipstick must have worn off on the rims of who knew how many glasses. At least her lipstick hadn't worn off on Leo. Josh swallowed the guilt that he was still hung up on her kissing other people when she was swaying in his passenger seat.

He reached over Cass's pliant form to buckle her in and enveloped her freezing hands in his. "Why didn't you call me? I would have come for you," he whispered.

"Didn't want to bother you." She leaned into him, face smushed against his collar. "You smell so good," she said in a breathy voice.

He snorted to cover the lurch under his ribs. "Okay, Lucky Charms. You are going to have a rough morning."

"It's already rough."

"What happened tonight?" he murmured into her hair.

Her breathing fell into a quiet pattern. Melancholy misted around her in a miasma, dulling her shine and putting her in shadow. "I wasn't stood up. The guy showed. Stuck around for a few minutes, ordered a drink, and said he had a call he had to make. Then he didn't come back. He sent me a DM and said I seemed nice, but he usually was into women who were different physically. He said it looked like I had cankles."

Josh stopped himself from rearing back. What the actual fuck? Cass was a voluptuous woman, and her profile picture had put every curve joyously on display. How that asshole thought he was meeting someone different made no sense.

He shut down the image of putting his lips to those ankles, slung over his shoulders as he'd buried himself in her. "That asshat doesn't know what he missed out on."

Tonight was his fault. Every single night she'd spent with a dickhead had been his fault. Sending out his sensitive Cass to be chewed up and spit out in the name of fuckboy exposure therapy. He ran a hand down her sleeve, wishing he could brush away the hurt, and tucked her head under his chin.

Cass sighed. "Why did he have to say that? He could have just used his inside voice and I would never be the wiser."

Josh clenched his jaw. Fuck that guy. If he'd have been there with her, he'd have rearranged that asshole's teeth.

If he'd have been there with her, she wouldn't be meeting up with the asshole and getting her self-esteem dunked on in the first place. Fuck. He thumbed the car's start button. "Time to get you home."

"Why am I never enough?"

The words floated to him, and his heart clenched in his chest. He thought back to what he'd so callously said months ago. *Ever think you just make them want more?* He'd almost been right.

"Maybe you make them realize they want more, because you show them what more could look like."

He stroked her arm, her head resting on his shoulder. Everything about her was so feminine. The fleshiness of her body, how it fit so perfectly against his that night they spent together. Even here in the car, her every curve soft against his angles as she sprawled over the console. Her melodic voice, so gentle and kind, even when he was being an asshole to everyone around them. The way she smelled, sweet and flowery and utterly intoxicating.

He breathed deeply and closed his eyes. "You make them realize they want to be better men. They're just not smart enough to figure that out until you're gone."

"That's a nice thought," she murmured after a moment, and sniffed.

The more he got to know her, the more he thought he might have found the answer. People realized who they were, what they wanted, but only after the ship had sailed. Leaving Cass waiting on the docks, watching someone embark on a new adventure that she prepared them for.

"You know the worst part? I could have had a good time tonight if I hadn't tried to meet this guy," Cass slurred against his shoulder. "I set this date up at the last minute to make an excuse to not go out with Nick."

Josh jerked on the brakes a little too hard as his insides curdled. "Nick texted again?"

"Right on time. Just when I start to feel like he might have forgotten about me, he texts me this afternoon." Cass tipped against him. "'Just when I thought I was out, they pull me back in!'" she quoted with a mirthless giggle. "I asked Libby to hide my phone, but she wouldn't. I panicked and messaged three Tinder guys. Should have just gone with the devil I knew instead of the devil I didn't."

So, this fuckknob, that he had swiped for her, was the one who had made her feel like this. Josh didn't know if he or the other dude was the bigger asshole.

No, he did know. Leo, who was blinder than he was stupid. *But I'm right behind in second place.*

"You're not about to cry on me, are you?" he asked, tense.

"Nope. You don't make me cry. You don't make me suffer, remember?"

Don't I, though?

"I wish I could have just gone out with you. I like you, and I think you like me, but you have other more important things going on and well, here we are," she rambled, hand waving in circles and nearly turning on the windshield wipers.

The words cut. She was right. On both counts. He did like her. A lot more than he was comfortable admitting. This sending her out with a parade of assholes to forget another asshole … it seemed reasonable at the time. Now it just flamed a possessive streak he didn't know he had.

But she was also right that he couldn't be with her. He didn't commit to one person for a lot of reasons, and his attention needing to be focused on this film was only one of them. For the first time he could remember in years, he wanted to rearrange those priorities, but he was miles away from being able to do that.

Instead, he snatched her hand out of the air and tucked it back into his. "But you didn't call Nick. That's progress."

"If I would have called Nick, tomorrow still would have sucked, but at least tonight would have been fun. Someone would have told me I was beautiful." Cass turned an imploring look at him with unfocussed eyes. "Can you please tell me I'm beautiful? I really need that right now."

Cass was beyond beautiful. She was charming, sweet, and did impossible things to his brain. She lit up the room whenever she entered and brought the best out in everyone around her. Even him. She was soft and gorgeous and had a laugh that cleansed his soul. She was brilliant and beautiful and …

"You are a vision," he whispered into her hair, pulling her out of his car and onto the snowy sidewalk. "Come on. We're home."

Cass dropped her keys twice up the steps to her apartment and leaned on him all the way up the short elevator ride, then forgotten her keys were already in her hand by the time they were down the hall. Josh unlocked the door, left her keys on the only bare spot on the kitchen counter, and maneuvered her into a chair half-buried under clothes. Even this sauced, she moved with a fluid grace that made her descent into the chair look choreographed to a silent song instead of a drunken stumble.

He zipped her out of her jacket, then knelt at her feet, tugging off her boots one at a time. He circled his thumb over the curve of her ankle. "You are going to be in a world of hurt tomorrow."

Cass giggled, head lolling to the side. "Maybe you can kiss it better."

Oh, shit. Worse than weepy drunk was horny drunk.

In this light, this close, her hazel eyes looked like the golden hour, flecked with green jewels across a stormy sea. Cass transfixed him with her stare, reaching out with light fingertips to caress the angle of his jaw. "I liked kissing you. Did you like kissing me?"

Josh's insides melted. Yeah, he did. Her lips had felt so good on his that night. The feel of her body yielding under the pressure of his mouth, how she'd responded to his every claim, wherever he deigned to taste.

Don't think about how you wished you'd gone down on her that night to taste her everywhere, asshole.

He eased her away from him as gently as he could. He gathered her hands from around his neck and cradled them in his own, holding them against his chest. She'd suffered enough rejection tonight, but he tilted his head up, away from her perfect mouth, and planted his lips chastely on her forehead. "I could write sonnets about kissing you," he said, stroking her cheek, "but you are in no shape for that right now."

With any luck, horny drunk would be replaced with sleepy drunk.

"Sonnets are pretty," she agreed. She retrieved a hand to poke a finger into his chest with faux ferocity. "Okay, Sexy Dimples, you need to write me a sonnet."

There was a first time for everything. Josh swallowed his laugh. He'd take giggly drunk. "I hope for your sake that you don't remember any of this tomorrow." Then he'd be off the hook for writing sonnets, too.

Cass blinked down at her bare feet. "Where'd my boots go?"

CHAPTER SEVENTEEN

CASS

A RAILROAD SPIKE HAD LODGED ITSELF BEHIND HER EYES. RIGHT through the middle of her skull to cleave her brain in two. Someone had replaced her insides with poison, each heartbeat sending corrosive blood to erode her thinky bits. A faint, rancid odour seeped into her nostrils, and she vaguely became aware that it was her breath causing the offence. And the noise. The silence was so loud she almost heard her will to live wither away.

There was only one explanation: she was dying.

Her darkened room tilted as she tried to open her eyes, and she decided that was a terrible idea.

I'm staying in bed for the rest of my life.

No, she wasn't.

Cass made it in time to empty her stomach contents neatly into the toilet. She wiped her mouth and rested her forehead on the closed lid, the cold porcelain transferring a faint bit of relief to her pounding brain. Her whimpering breath echoed in the room, and she was glad that her pristine bathroom was her one exception to her aversion to cleaning.

She was never drinking again.

Cass groped in the dark for her toothpaste and knocked a

few bottles to the floor in a clatter. She winced at the noise scraping her ears and gave a silent prayer of thanks that nothing broke. The bright mint chased the rancour from her nose, and she willed herself not to gag as she scrubbed the demons from her mouth. Her shower beckoned her, but the thought of standing any longer sent a fresh wave of nausea through her guts.

Okay, stomach, she thought, hands propped up on her sink. *Let's go back to bed until the room stops spinning.*

She shuffled across the short hall and eased herself back into her bed, where a glass of water and two ibuprofen sat on her nightstand.

"How many drinks did you have?"

If she wasn't so wrecked, she would have yelped. Josh leaned against her dresser, arms crossed and dimples on full display.

Cass tried to think back, but the poison flooding her system hijacked any possibility of calculating the total. Besides, the exact number didn't matter. The answer was too many. Way too many. She winced. "I don't know. Three?"

"That was you on three drinks?"

"Shh, you're breathing too loud," she moaned. "I just had my glass of wine, then drank the rest of what's-his-face's drink, then a girl beside me said I looked like I needed a shot of whiskey."

It was the whiskey's fault. Or maybe the gin she'd ordered after. Her dad always said gin was the drink for when you wanted to be tough. Or maybe it was the Merlot she'd ordered after the gin because it turned out she didn't want to be tough, after all. She swallowed a heave. "Maybe it was more than three drinks."

Cass palmed the pills and took a delicate sip of water. Oh, ambrosia. She took another sip and leaned back against her headboard. If she lived, she was having a serious discussion with Past Cassie about her choices.

"If you get plastered like that on the reg, you should really have Gatorade on hand."

"This," she said between sips, "is not a regular practice of mine."

Josh pushed off the dresser and took the empty glass from her hands, returning a moment later with the glass refilled. He sat on the edge of her bed, leaning back against the footboard with one hand behind his head. The gentle dip sent a recoil through her belly, and she groaned.

"Thank you, that's really … wait." The night had blurred together after the bartender had set the fifth drink in front of her. She remembered texting Josh, sometime between the whiskey and before the gin. She also remembered saying she wanted to be alone. Drunk Cass wasn't usually Frisky Cass, but sometimes, when she was with someone she was attracted to, her lax filters would let more embarrassments through as her drink count increased. And try as she might to keep her attraction for Josh under control, he was a pro at ruffling the edges she'd tried so hard to pin down.

Now he was sitting on her bed. In the dark. At an unknown time of day or night. With those dimples out in full force, like he knew a secret he wouldn't tell her quite yet.

She swallowed. "Why are you in my apartment?"

"I brought you home."

"Um, thank you."

"You were very drunk," he said, smiling. "And very cute."

"Oh, no."

"You told me I smelled really good."

"Ah …"

"Then you told me to stay out of your room until you hid your vibrator."

"Oh my god."

His teeth looked lethal behind his lips pulled wide. If she was sober, she would have had a hard time deciding if she wanted to kiss or smack those dimples right off his face. "Josh, we didn't, did we?"

Josh pressed a hand to his chest. "You don't remember?"

If the floor didn't open up, she was ripping up the carpet and burrowing under it until spring. "Josh …"

"We did not."

Thank god. "I, um … I didn't get handsy, did I?" Cass blessed the darkness that hid her flaming cheeks. It didn't matter. Josh knew her well enough that he'd know she was blushing, anyway. "I can get a little touchy when I'm drunk, and I'm really sorry if I did—"

"Charms," he cut in, "you didn't do anything that made me uncomfortable."

She nodded carefully, her hangover grinding like gravel between her ears. At least she'd held onto one last shred of dignity last night. Until she spammed Josh in a pathetic texts.

And he still came to her.

She squinted at him through the gloom. His thick hair was purposefully mussed, as usual, and his tee shirt snugged across his biceps, a different shirt than she'd seen him wearing on set that day. Yesterday? Cass took another sip of water. "What time is it?" she rasped out.

"Late. You've been passed out for a few hours. I was just sticking around to make sure you didn't choke on your own vomit or anything."

A wave of mortification washed over her. On the rare times she had too much to drink, she always said something she regretted later. Any lingering attraction he might have had likely evaporated with whatever foolish things she'd said last night. Not like that was a factor.

He'd picked her up, made sure she got home safely, and made sure she stayed that way. He was just being nice.

And tomorrow was a huge day. No, *today* would be huge. For which they both needed sleep.

She wiped at the smudge of mascara that likely sat under her eyes. She hadn't even washed her face last night. She was still wearing her … no, she wasn't. The sweater she'd worn yesterday —the ones she'd chosen for the way its emerald tones brought out the green flecks in her hazel eyes—hung over the back of her slipper chair. Her pants haphazardly kicked to the corner of her room. Now all she had on was a cheeky pair of sleep shorts, no bra, and a strappy tank top that displayed the clear outline of her nipples.

"Can you do me a favour?" she asked, pulling her covers up over her chest. "When I ask how I got changed last night, would you please tell me I did it all by myself?"

Her bed rustled with his repressed laughter. "For the most part. Although you did ask me to help."

"Oh."

"You were quite adamant," he said, his teeth gleaming in the dark. "You very nearly persuaded me."

If her hangover didn't kill her, embarrassment would.

"I declined, although I've never been so interested in a team project before."

Thank god he was making a joke of it. Yes, he'd seen her naked before. No, that didn't mean he wanted to see her naked again. It didn't matter what Libby thought. Josh had made it perfectly clear that he wasn't interested. No distractions with her, or anyone else, as far as she could tell. Cass couldn't blame him. She tried to remember if he'd been seen with or talked about anyone since coming to Calgary, but her mind buzzed too hard for coherent thought to form. Plus, thinking about him with other people turned her stomach in a completely different way than the hangover she would deal with tomorrow.

He rocked to his feet and the bed's recoil sent a combination of dizziness and regret swirling through her. "Now that I know you aren't going to asphyxiate in your sleep, I'm going home. Think you'll need a wake-up call tomorrow?"

"No, my shame will wake me at regular intervals in the night," she muttered. "Besides, I'm pretty sure my phone is dead."

"Nope. Full charge. Plugged it in for you when we got home."

"Oh. Thanks." She entered an alarm that would give her just enough time to shower, caffeinate, and slink onto set on time. "You didn't have to do that."

He stopped in the doorway. "I wanted to."

Even through her current state, she felt better.

As long as she didn't move.

Nobody asked questions when she rolled onto set, with a whole six minutes to spare, wearing her biggest, darkest sunglasses and a toque to hide the noise-reducing ear plugs she had popped in. Cass had slept most of the night, waking once for more water and to put on socks. Now when she moved her head too quickly, she felt like she was only *near* the brink of death, rather than right on it. To make up for the agony everywhere else in her body, she donned her favourite slouchy cashmere sweater she'd thrifted when she'd filmed on site in Dublin, and the wool paper bag pants that draped like a dream.

Warm, comfortable, and it didn't look like she was dragging her tush out of bed hungover after being jilted by a douchey architect.

Or whatever.

Ten years ago, she'd have cartwheeled into work after a binge like last night and gone out again the following night. Now, she had to remember to pack extra meds and electrolytes to make it to lunch.

Being north of thirty sucked.

Libby stormed across the sound stage, hand flexing around a pair of clamps sticking out of her cargo pocket. "Do I need to kill that asshole from last night? I'll do it. No questions asked. Won't even ask you to help me bury the body." She squeezed the clamps menacingly for effect once more.

Cass managed a grim chuckle, then took a swig of her ginger

tea. "Have I told you yet today how much I love you? I'll fill you in later, but right now I'd like to wallow in mortification."

"I had plans to go out with Stephen tonight, but I can bail on him, and we can eat chocolate and watch reruns of Gossip Girl."

"Maybe, but don't cancel on him yet. You'll need more details to fill me in on Stibby 2.0 later."

Libby looked nauseated, but that could have been the last of the alcohol seeping out of Cass's pores just as much as the offensive moniker. "We are not calling us that."

Cass hugged Libby's waist gently enough not to jostle the contents of her own sensitive stomach. "Would you prefer Elizephen? Didn't think so."

"Seriously, though," Libby said, "last night? Getting blitzed on your own? That's not like you. Why didn't you call me when that fuckwit didn't show up?"

Because you were with Stephen and I don't want you to have to choose who you'll spend time with. Libby's priorities would shift. She had a second chance at the love of her life. Cass wouldn't get between Libby and Stephen making up for lost time.

If it meant dealing with the fallout of a humiliating brush-off alone, so be it.

The guy last night was callous, insensitive, and not worth anymore of her energy. In fact, none of these guys were. She'd been on weird dates, dull dates, and dates that had gone way too long. Dates that made her want to run for the hills, dates that had her wondering if she could play games on her phone under the table, and dates that were better suited for her friends.

Cass faked a smile. "I'm alive, and we'll catch up soon, but for now I need to check Brynne's suit fit."

With one stop on the way.

Brynne and Josh stood in their usual huddle, and a discordant pang of jealousy picked at her. Brynne's head popped up at Cass's approach and she did a little twirl.

Every seam, every pleat, laid exactly as planned. Functional, but futuristic. And it even had a hidden bathroom zip. Brynne had cried in relief when she saw that there was no more being sewn into her suit for fourteen hours at a time and going into dehydration mode.

A furtive beat of pride flowed through her. She'd worked on the design for weeks, landing on Brynne's final outfit first, then modelling Dawson's male version after. It was what finally convinced Melanie and the studio to go with Cass's more restrained vision for wardrobe.

"It's perfect, as usual," Brynne said, and Josh nodded appreciatively at the suit's fit. At least, she hoped it was the fit he was appreciating and not Brynne's lithe body.

Cass closed her eyes behind her sunglasses.

"Yeah, um, great. Can I have a minute with Josh?"

Brynne jumped to her feet, her perfect waves floating like gauze around her. Cass smothered a rogue spike of jealousy. Nothing like standing beside a literal freaking movie star to feel any worse than her hangover already had.

"No problem," she said breezily. "I'll be in my trailer."

Josh didn't watch her leave, and gloated down at Cass, trying to keep his dimples under wraps. It almost worked, only the tiniest of divots showing.

"The dead awaken."

Cass rubbed her eyes. "Dead is right. Awakened, unclear. I expect a recovery sometime in the next two to three business days. At least I'll have an excuse not to go on any dates for a bit."

The shadow of the dimples melted away as his face darkened. "About that—"

"I think I could use some time off. From the dating blitz."

It had occurred to her as soon as the ibuprofen and first sips of caffeine cleared the worst of her fog that morning. She'd wasted time on guys that didn't care for her, and for what? It was hard to say if it worked or not. Sure, she'd met a bunch of jerks, and a few who just weren't right for her, but here she was, a handful of months later, and she'd sure spotted the same lines coming from a few different mouths. They must have studied the same *How to Gaslight Women into Sleeping with You* bible. But this time, Cass had seen it coming, swallowing a shout of *Aha!* like an old-timey detective and filing it away for evidence of their habits.

And darn if a lot of those one-liners didn't sound a lot like Nick.

Honestly, she'd heard a few of those lines coming from Josh's mouth that first day they met, but she wouldn't let herself feel foolish for falling for it then. She'd wanted him so much and she had nearly chipped an incisor tugging his zipper down with her teeth as soon as they'd gotten to his place.

So much for keeping their perfect night as a pristine memory.

Nick's text had sent her into a panic. Full fluttering hands, scampering in a circle of panic. It seemed so stupid now. But really, had she felt the usual tightening in her chest at seeing his name? Or thought maybe this was the time he declared he wanted her for real? Or thought about how good in bed they'd used to be?

Cass pulled up with a start. She was thinking in the past tense. How good they *used* to be; not how good they *were*. And no. The usual flutters of excitement and hope hadn't clouded her judgement, her fear that his text might stir those feelings had sent her into a frenzy yesterday.

Did the No Second Dates fiasco actually work?

"Nick texted. I answered, but I didn't sleep with him. That's a win, right?"

A fleeting look crossed his features that Cass couldn't identify. "I'd say that's a win."

"Who knows, maybe I didn't need thirty dates to get over him after all. I got it done in twenty."

"Aren't you an overachiever?" he said with a wry grin.

Sure, that was her. Aiming for the stars. She had nothing near a full smile in her, and rolling her eyes might make her nauseated again, so she just quirked her lips at him. Let him interpret that as he liked.

"Then project No Second Dates is over. Congratulations. You're over fuckboys." His arms flexed as he tightened them across his chest, and asked, "This isn't because you found someone that you want to start seeing regularly, is it?"

"The opposite, actually. I'm thinking I can't really be trusted to make good decisions about men right now." Or ever. Or at least until filming was over. The one person she couldn't stop thinking about, right in front of her, had no interest. She wasn't going to subject herself to any more agony if she could help it. Besides, there was that whole inconvenience of a province separating them. Cass would have snorted if it wouldn't have upset her delicate stomach.

"I think I asked a guy to write me sonnets last night, and that is not an embarrassment I'll forget anytime soon."

"Oof, so no memory loss?"

"No, I remember everything." Every single cutting remark from the jerk who had seen her photo and thought her interesting enough to spend a couple of hours with. Who had known what she looked like, and still decided to show up and insult her. Every embarrassing gaff she'd uttered to Josh, who had to deal with a drunken, horny mess and fend off her advances. Humiliating. Cass shrugged her shoulders. "And if I did ask you to write me Shakespearean poetry, you're off the hook."

"That guy was a dick," Josh said softly. "He doesn't know what he's missing."

And you do, but that's not enough. Cass squeezed her eyes shut. "On that note, since Brynne is good, I'm going to check on Dawson and make sure he hasn't picked his suit apart yet." She almost hoped he had, to give her something to do with her hands and focus her concentration. "This is a win for you, too. No more homework, no more swiping for me. One less distraction."

"Right. No more distractions." Josh nodded, his expression giving no hint of what was going on behind his eyes.

Libby was too good at her job. The set's lights were amped so brightly for the day's scenes that Cass was tempted to put her sunglasses back on. Terry and Stephen criss-crossed the set, scattering PAs and grips in their wake. Brynne hadn't gone back to her trailer after all. She was planted in a chair with one leg thrown over the wooden arm, her arms wrapped tightly around her elbows and head tipped back pursing her mouth at whatever Dawson was saying. Dawson looked up at Cass's arrival and broke out into a grin, dropping his hands from where he had been fussing with his suit. Again.

Brynne shot him a look and got up. "Suit check."

Cass tracked Brynne's exit, heading in the opposite direction of where her trailer lay, and turned her focus back to Dawson. For once, the suit check wasn't needed. Dawson's fitting last week took care of the slight mislay of a couple seams, and the matte fabric held up to even his incessant fiddling.

"You're good, Big D," Cass said, flattening out a few non-existent creases, more out of habit than necessity. She patted down his expansive chest and smiled up at him. "Looking forward to getting home for Christmas?"

The big man rolled his head from side to side. "It's not as warm as LA, but Tennessee won't be colder than a—" he cut himself off with a chagrined shrug. "It'll be good to see my folks, see my horses, but there's a few people I'll miss here," he finished with a small smile.

"I know what you mean," she agreed absently. Josh would be heading back to Vancouver in days. Tomorrow, if they could wrap on time. Barring a snowpocalypse and with Stephen and Terry on the case, they'd wrap. Then it would be two weeks before the crew reconvened to film the scene everyone was nervously waiting for.

The death of Dr. Donovan Rykoff.

Dawson, because he needed to sell Brynne's propulsion into the final act; Brynne, because she would carry the film for its final arc; and Josh, because he would bear the brunt of fandom's ire if the adaptation flopped.

Box office history had shown audiences were far more forgiving of a mediocre male-led film than a female-led one. Brynne had pull, but any female star lower than A+ had fame that came with a target on their back rather than a coat of Teflon. The closer they got to filming the scene, the closer everyone got to the edge.

Cass's eyes landed on Josh in the sea of people. Brynne had found her way back to him, the two of them looking like they were holding back laughter. Cass was familiar enough with the feeling she didn't need to guess what stabbed through her. She rubbed her elbows, arms wrapping over her stomach.

"Do you have any plans for Christmas?" Dawson asked.

"Probably heading to Canmore for a few days, where my family will try to cram seven adults and two children into a cottage." The overstuffed two-bedroom had nearly burst at the seams, even growing up with the five of them; her parents squished into one room and her siblings in the other. Now with her sister's husband and kids stuffed into the nooks and crannies, and her brother's girlfriend joining them, there was a second nearby rental for the overflow, with everyone congregating for presents, pyjamas, and meals. Cass wiped her hands down her wool pants and fidgeted with the waist-tie. "I just need to get there early enough that I don't get relegated to sleeping in the living room with the kids again."

"That sounds right cozy."

"It's the one time a year I don't mind when things close before dinner. All we have is thirty-year-old board games, a fireplace, and a stack of ancient DVDs for entertainment."

He shifted to his other foot. "Speaking of dinner, I'll be getting back in town a few days early. There's this great restaurant in Kensington Bex suggested. Maybe—"

"Dawson?" The PA materialized at his shoulder like her name had conjured her. "Stephen needs you in position."

"One of these days …" he trailed off with a grin. "Catch you later, Cassidy."

Cass stood silently as Dawson loped into position for block-ing. That couldn't have been what it sounded like it was going to be. Could it have been?

Libby had said she was picking up cues, but Cass had brushed her off as ridiculous. Half the people on set—the conti-nent, really—would fizz with excitement at the thought.

That sweet, handsome, about-to-be-famous Dawson James, had been about to ask her out.

CHAPTER EIGHTEEN

JOSH

"Mrs. Westwood wants to see you in her office."

Bex's voice snapped him out of the daydream he'd been reliving all week.

Dawn in the farmer's field. The one where he and Cass were looking into the director's monitor, with her round ass nestled against the tops of his thighs. The scent of her hair enveloping him, the fire in his blood chasing away the chill he'd felt all morning. Then his mouth dropping to her neck, his hands sliding around her bare waist—because in this daydream their clothes had conveniently disappeared, and it was no longer minus fuck-you degrees out—to palm her tits and drive his cock into her dripping pussy …

And once again, he'd missed the last twenty seconds of second unit footage he was supposed to be reviewing.

Shit. This was *exactly* why he stayed away from distractions on set.

He hit pause and refocussed on the screen. The shed scenes should slide seamlessly into the field shoots from last week. If he could concentrate on them long enough to sign off.

"I'll be there in half an hour," he muttered, not bothering to look up at the fidgety PA.

"Um, Mr. Graham, sir, she said now," Bex said, exiting his office door and calling over her shoulder as she left, "And you might want to check your email."

Sure, Melanie, I'll jump! Exactly how high would you like that? Don't mind me, I'm trying to direct a multimillion-dollar movie. Josh tried his best not to glare at Bex's back. He could practically hear Cass's sweet voice in his ear, reminding him the young PA was just doing her job, and had been nothing but incredibly helpful.

He sighed. "Hey Siri, take a note. Make sure Bex gets a good reference," he said into his phone as he pulled up his inbox, already halfway down the hall to Melanie's office before he froze in his tracks.

Who's Dawson's mystery girlfriend in Canada?
Dawson James stays warm in the Great White North
The sweetest man in Hollywood found some sugar in Calgary

Dozens of photos, splashed across all social media platforms. Each post shouted similar interpretations of the cheesy headlines he was looking at now. Big, bold sans serif letters and big, bold full colour pictures. Some taken through a paparazzo's telephoto lens, others with a surreptitious snap on a cellphone. All from set over the course of several weeks.

A grainy photo of Cass tugging on Dawson's suit months ago in the converted athletic facility. A wide shot with their heads together and laughing in the farmer's field with the sunrise glowing behind them, Dawson looking like a previously unknown Hemsworth and Cass all gilded and gorgeous, her red lips a fiery beacon in the snowy morning. One from just yesterday—he recognized her hangover clothes—with Dawson shooting a dopey grin down at her, her hands all over his chest.

Half the pop culture-consuming world would think Cass and Dawson were madly in love.

"What the fresh fuck is this?" Josh demanded, barging into Melanie's office without knocking. Three heads turned to him with wildly different expressions. Melanie sat behind her glass and metal desk in her temporary office with a calculating look on her face. Dawson rocked on his heels in the corner with hands shoved in his pockets. A middle-aged man who looked familiar pecked away at a laptop, face oddly blank.

"That," Melanie said, pointing at the same headlines pulled up on the oversized monitor, "is free publicity."

"I ordered a closed set." Ever since Cass had hinted that Brynne's chilly personality was more shyness and less divaness, he'd closed the set when filming emotional scenes. Without the extra bodies milling around, Brynne's "visualising time" had been cut down to a fraction.

And now there were paps sneaking around when Brynne thought they had privacy. "How the fuck did someone get close enough to get these?"

"They have their ways," the man chirped, his voice overly animated, as if trying to make up for the overzealous administration of Botox halting emotion at his eyebrows. "As long as we don't let Brynne get cast as getting between them. We don't want her looking like a homewrecker."

"Hard for her to look like a homewrecker if there were no homes to wreck," Josh bit out through clenched teeth, swivelling his head to the man striking keys on his laptop like he was playing a piano concerto. "And who are you?"

"Bernie Scott. Promotions," the man said. Ah, that was where he recognized him. Bernie Scott had worked on several projects with Melanie, the latest of which the lead actor had been nabbed for drunk driving. A few unsanctioned photos from a remote film set were probably a welcome, and comparatively sedate, diversion. He hit a few more keys and shut his laptop screen. "It's a bit of a situation."

"It's an opportunity, not a situation," Melanie said, and Bernie's mouth pulled into a semblance of a grin.

The film was getting attention. Like Melanie said. Free publicity. A good publicist could spin anything. Any time the film hit in the news cycle was a win. Josh should be delighted with this.

Even if it meant the fandom would get their hands on every unedited still shot, scouring for Easter eggs Josh had meticulously planned. And Brynne would retreat further into her trailer between takes. And everyone would see photos of Cass cozying up to Dawson with her hands all over him and those wide doe eyes of hers gazing into his.

He wanted to launch the free publicity through the window.

"It would look better if the shots were all of Brynne and Dawson," Bernie said. "It would make people want to see if they look as hot on screen as he and Cassidy do in these photos. But as long as we can get some good photos of her, we can work with this."

Melanie jumped in. "Or we could work the angle that Dawson just has chemistry with everyone. Release the screen test footage?"

Dawson shot her a quelling glance and read over her shoulder. "Has Cassidy seen these?"

"I would assume so," Melanie said in a distracted voice, still scrolling through headlines. "It's trending on socials."

"Since we got a bunch of people in here talkin' 'bout her, seems like a pretty good idea to find out."

Melanie furrowed her brow. "Why does that matter?"

Because she's not his, Josh wanted to growl, but swallowed the words. Terry had hired her a wardrobe assistant. Maybe she needed another one. Then she could focus on the design and look of the movie and not be so hands on. Specifically, hands on Dawson. Unless she wanted to spend all her time touching him. Her hands weren't on Brynne nearly as often. Fuck.

Josh refrained from kicking the foot of the nearest chair.

Melanie waved her hand. "Cat's out of the bag. Best we can do is control the story. Besides, the gossip cycle is short. If we don't move fast, this could all blow over before we even figure out our angle."

"And if she hasn't heard already, she'll get wind of it soon enough," Bernie added.

"In the meantime, let the paps shoot what they will, Dawson and Cass looking chummy—"

"Intimate." Bernie cut in, his eyes sparkling. "Everyone loves an on-set romance."

Fuck on-set romance. Terry was getting a budget increase to hire more set security, along with another wardrobe assistant, as soon as this meeting wrapped.

"Cassidy didn't sign up for this," Dawson said, feet planted. "I'm not putting her in an uncomfortable position."

You have no idea the positions she wants to be in.

Still, it was the first smart thing anyone in this room had said. Unlike Melanie, who seemed hellbent on turning a couple of leaked photos into the next great love story.

"We don't need to make it formal and let the story play out?" Melanie mused, looking at the ceiling as her head wavered back and forth.

Josh felt his heart get sucked through the floor. Suddenly the thought of sending her on dates twenty-one through thirty, even with assholes like the architect, to get her out of this sounded like an easy out.

And then she'd be at the mercy of any number of shitheads. Just so he wouldn't have to see her with Dawson. Not like thinking of her with other men was much better.

Cass had just said she needed a break, both from men and all the drama dating brought. However bad Tinder was, dating in the public eye was worse. At least a few commentators would say something shitty about her, that she'd probably see, and crush her already fragile self-esteem even further. He wiped his hand over his face.

"No."

All the heads in the room turned to him.

"What do you mean, no?" Melanie blinked at him. "Studios pay good money for exposure like this."

Melanie was right. Studios planted leaks like this all the time, hoping to get this kind of interest. And here they were, with fans clamouring for information and media buzzing before they had released a teaser trailer. The hype machine hadn't started, and a few blurry photos had garnered more attention than anything he'd ever worked on. It was exactly what he wanted.

Should want.

What he wanted was Cass as far away from Dawson as possible.

Fuck. Josh prowled around the edges of the room. Melanie hated it when people told her no, especially when it got between her and money. The only time she didn't hate it was when …

"Brynne works better with a closed set." It wasn't a lie. Melanie tripped over herself to make her favourite actor happy, and if this partial truth got Melanie on board, then so be it. "I made a commitment to her. No unsanctioned cameras on set."

The fact that Cass and Dawson wouldn't have an extra reason to get close, posing for pap photos, had nothing to do with it.

Melanie traded a glance with Bernie, who shrugged, face blank, though that could have been the Botox wiping away his emotion. She took a final look at the headlines and sighed. "Fine."

Well, shit. That was easy. "Good, Cass doesn't need that kind of scrutiny," Josh said, then added, "or Brynne."

Dawson nodded slowly his expression unreadable. "Right. Wouldn't want to worry her about being trailed by photographers."

And he didn't need the distraction of wondering if she wanted that.

The last of the crew trickled past his open door and out of the building for the night. The artificially warm lights were thrown off by the wall sconces' LED bulbs flickering along the hallway, and Josh repositioned his monitor to avoid the glare. He eyed the modified storyboards in grim determination.

"There you are!"

He jumped as Cass's bright voice rang out behind him. She stood framed in his doorway, cheeks still rosy from the cold, mittened hands wrapped around a paper to-go cup.

It hadn't been too hard to avoid her, since he was eyeballs deep behind the camera and she had her hands all over Dawson, again, fixing the lab coat that apparently grew wrinkles organically.

At least it wouldn't end up on another gossip rag's landing page.

He grit his teeth and ran a hand through his hair. "A bit late for caffeine, isn't it?"

"Bedtime isn't for hours, and don't police my vices," she said, toying with the lid. "Besides, it's a mocha. Only one shot of espresso."

He crossed his arms and drummed his fingers on his biceps. She looked less than her usual bubbly self, and he doubted it was the lingering hangover from the previous day. Her eyes fixed on him expectantly, and he flicked his gaze back to his screen.

The conversation in Melanie's office had played through his mind all day. They weren't doing anything wrong, really. Cass knew the same amount she did now as she did before, and if she checked her social media, she'd have the same information as everyone else. And it wasn't like *not* knowing would hurt her.

Still, he'd want to know if people were making decisions about him behind his back.

Fuck.

"Do you have anything you want to tell me?" she asked finally.

Josh closed the door behind her and turned on her with the same scowl he'd been wearing all day. She unwound the long-knitted scarf from around her neck, draping it in cozy loops over her arm, and waited.

"What's going on with you and Dawson?" he said.

She blinked at him. "That's what you have to say?"

Yes, because I'm a coward. "Set photos are being leaked," he hedged, stalling.

"I noticed. I had about a hundred people tag me yesterday," she said, and gave a weak thumbs up. "I'm famous."

"They managed to find a lot of photos with you two together."

"Photos of me doing my job, you mean?"

So, she knew. He looked past her shoulder and out to the street beyond. "Let me guess. Dawson?"

Cass sighed. "He told me everything."

Of course the fucking Boy Scout had. It was the right thing to do. Bet he had decided to tell Cass before he'd even left the room, all while Josh had tried to cover his own ass.

"He left that meeting and came straight to tell me about the leaked photos. That the publicist is happier than a five-year-old on Christmas morning, and the fact that everyone wanted to keep me in the dark. Including you." She dropped into the chair across from him and the hurt in her eyes made him look away. "Were you going to tell me?"

The tension he'd been holding in his chest spiked his gut. "Of course I was." *Just as soon as I'd figured out how.*

She raised an eyebrow.

"I was. I wanted to ..." He rolled his shoulders. It didn't matter what he'd wanted anymore. "I just needed to figure out the right way to say it."

"I'm a big girl. You don't need to sugar-coat for me."

Even if she did think she could take it, he'd sent her out to be bruised enough. Josh swallowed a groan. "Our publicist should take over your socials for a while. Lock it down so you don't get harassed—"

"No need. I've set my accounts to private. You should have

seen how many matches I had on Tinder when I logged on this morning to shut down my account. And really, selling me and Dawson as a couple …" she trailed off, peeking up at him.

He thought about the photo with Dawson grinning down at her even more dopily than usual; the caption *Canoodling in Canada* emblazoned across the top. Who the fuck said *canoodle*? These gossip sites needed better copy editors.

And Dawson was an incredible actor, but none of that looked like an act. That man's intentions were declared louder than if he'd tweeted them to his eight hundred thousand followers.

"I bet Dawson would be first in line for that," he said petulantly.

"If I didn't know any better, I'd say you sounded jealous."

We're beyond sounding *jealous, Lucky Charms.* "I wasn't sure if his 'gosh, golly, gee' response was an act or if he really was that concerned."

"D's a sweetheart. Of course he's concerned."

That made it worse. That Dawson had immediately done the right thing out of concern for her, and Josh had sat on the news all day, stewing, like a selfish asshole.

A soft smile traced her lips. "He also said you stood up for Brynne."

It wasn't her I was standing up for. If he couldn't admit it was because he couldn't stand to see Cass in another man's arms, even staged, he wouldn't take credit for the small bit of goodness that had come out of the day. He shrugged.

"Just talk to me, please," she said. She stood to leave and paused by his side to squeeze his arm. "This shouldn't have been a big deal. Respect that I should know these things."

This was the extent of the confrontation? Just a gentle request not to keep her in the dark? Josh raked his fingers through his hair for the thousandth time that day, and fresh guilt churned his stomach.

"Okay."

CHAPTER NINETEEN

CASS

What am I bringing to the cabin? Smores stuff and wine?

SUZIE

Shit, we're out. Hubs and I are bringing the kids to Edmonton to visit his folks this Christmas.

Oh, no prob

Davie?

DAVIE

going to my girlfriend's

Haha

Looks like it's just us mom & dad :)

I get a whole bedroom to myself!

MOM

Oh sweetie we booked a week in Palm Springs when we heard everyone was going to be away this Christmas!

I'm here

We just thought you'd be busy on set

Sure!

Have fun everyone!

Merry Christmas!

CHAPTER TWENTY

JOSH

"DARLING!" HIS MOTHER'S ADENOIDAL VOICE BRASHED OVER FaceTime. "It's been forever! Did your bollocks freeze off yet?"

Josh twisted his mouth to hide his smile. "Still here, last time I checked."

"Your father's upstairs. Hang on. David! Get your arse down here! Josh is on the phone!"

It was fine. Eardrums were overrated.

His father's face crowded into the frame seconds later, forcing his mother to share the screen, and their matching smiles beamed back at him.

"We can't talk long, sweetie," his mother continued in the thick Australian accent that hadn't faded in the almost forty years she'd lived in Canada. If anything, Josh was convinced she hammed it up to charm her clients. "Your father has a client meeting in Burnaby, and I've got a showing in West Van."

A simple thing like an impending statutory national holiday wouldn't derail business as usual.

Despite a reckless youth spent in the southern sun without SPF, his mother's skin remained smooth, her few laugh lines making her look joyous instead of tired, her hair so resolutely black, Josh wasn't entirely sure she wasn't colouring it.

He dreaded the day his mother would tip into old age overnight like his grandparents had. One day, thick heads of black hair and the complexion of teenagers; the next, wispy white fluff held back by full face visors with wrinkles cross-hatching their skin.

His father's age had crept forward in measured steps. The salt-and-pepper in his hair advanced at a stately pace until it turned a fully lustrous white by the time Josh had graduated university. The last time they'd had dinner as a family, he'd noticed his father had begun to stoop, just a little, and for the first time there was the barest thinning on the crown of his head.

Josh's heart squeezed, and he pushed the memory aside. "When are you two retiring?"

"When we run out of houses to sell—" his mother started.

"And contracts to negotiate," his father finished, and they laughed in tandem at the joke they'd told a thousand times, but Josh chilled at the reminder.

He could have retired earlier if I had taken over like we planned.

His father had never said it, not once. Two more years and Josh could have taken over the practice. But they both knew it was true. Right now, his father could be limbering up for his golf game instead of driving across the city to meet with clients days before Christmas.

"What kind of crazy people want to have meetings on December twenty-third?" Josh said.

His father grinned. "Lots of them."

Josh frowned and pulled up the calendar on his laptop balanced on the couch pillow beside him. Filming had wrapped, and after a boozy party last night—where everyone except him and Cass had consumed their weight in alcohol—everyone who wasn't local had scattered back to their homes for the two-week break. Cass had begged off early, and he'd watched her exit the pub with a closed expression and her phone in her hand.

He reminded himself it wasn't his business if she was texting another guy and spent the rest of the night scowling into his tepid kombucha.

People had refreshed flight departure notifications with nervous energy, but everyone had made it out as planned. Everyone needed the break. Including himself. Eight days before filming resumed. Nine, if he included today. He scrolled through the remaining flights back to Vancouver, grimacing at the remaining departure times.

"What's the plan for Christmas?" If he booked now, he could still get the last flight out tomorrow.

His mother glared at his father. "You didn't tell him? You said you were going to tell him!"

A sheepish look was the only reply.

"We're leaving for Oz tomorrow," his mother said, and then looked uncomfortable. "Grace is staying here, but I'm not sure what she's doing."

She knew what his sister was doing. They both did. Which fully precluded Josh from joining her. He bit down on his reply.

"Or we could get you a ticket," his father said, brightening. "It can be your Christmas present."

It was tempting, but that was a lot of travel and crushing jetlag for what would end up being four days of visit. And he'd be on the other side of the world if an issue came up on set.

"Or maybe your sister will change her plans," his mother said about the plans she'd just said she knew nothing about. "I could add her to the call—"

"No." He'd heard the arguments enough to last a lifetime.

His father's voice softened. "Son—"

"When's your flight?" he interrupted.

"Seven a.m."

That was so perfectly his dad. All that money and still flying on a holiday to save the flight fare. Josh snickered despite himself. "You cheap bastard. Think they'll serve turkey on the plane?"

"I hope not," his mother said, the smile held on her mouth

but faded from her eyes. "We'll try not to call you in the middle of the night on Christmas."

Josh signed off the call and stared down at the black screen. Christmas in his family was practically just another day. And if he couldn't spend it with his parents, then spending it alone for the third year was infinitely preferable to the alternative, as much as he'd love to see his sister again. At least, like it used to be.

He sat on the floor and stared at the blank wall that never decided what it wanted to be. His original idea of the mountains, the Rockies or North Shore, never took hold. A passing fancy of a drone's eye view of the confluence of the rivers came and went.

Did it matter if he started the mural now? He could just plan how to paint over the one he had at his condo back home or review the revised schedule for the final shots he'd need to get back to Vancouver for, anyway. So long as he missed the holiday itself.

A blunt pounding rattled his door.

He should have just had an extra key cut.

"Did you get your flights?" Stephen barged his way past Josh and into the kitchen. He stuck his head into the fridge before rifling through the cupboards. "You have no food."

"Please, help yourself."

"Su casa es mi casa."

"I don't think that's how that goes."

"Close enough."

"Jackass."

Stephen liberated a half-empty bag of nori snacks from a drawer and flopped onto the couch. "Well?"

"Not going home."

"Why?" Green flecks coated his teeth. Josh handed him a bottle of water.

Josh dropped beside him. He crossed an ankle over his knee and stole back one of his snacks, its salty crunch crackling in his mouth like a map in the desert. "Parents are heading to Melbourne. Grace is staying in Van, but you know."

"Shit." Stephen tossed the empty bag on the coffee table and swished the water in his mouth in contemplation.

"Yeah." Josh raked his fingers through his hair and bit back a sigh. It wasn't spending the holiday alone that was the problem, per se. It was the fact that every choice he'd made in the past three years made him alone at Christmas. Again.

Stephen brushed seaweed confetti from his pullover onto the coffee table. "I'll ask Libby's family to set another place for dinner tomorrow night."

Josh swept the nori remnants into his hand and dumped them into the sink. "I wouldn't want to impose."

"Her folks are great. They'd be more mad at me for not inviting you if they found out you spent Christmas alone."

"I don't have anything to bring."

"Bring a bottle of wine and your charming self."

"I don't have anything to wear."

"They aren't formal. You could show up in a tutu and they'd be happy."

"It's pretty short notice."

"Cass is going to be there."

What happened to the cabin? Maybe she didn't head out until Christmas morning, and he'd have one more chance to see her before the break. Josh ran his tongue over his teeth. "What time is dinner?" he asked.

"Seven. I'll text you the address."

He couldn't see Stephen's expression with his back to him, but he could hear the triumph in his voice well enough.

Dick.

The house sat at the end of a cul-de-sac, its rusted brick facade pitted with years of weathering. A yellow glow spilled through the open curtains in a stretched square on the front lawn's perfect snow, while multi-coloured lights winked through the branches of the Christmas tree like Morse code.

If he had to hazard a guess, the dots and dashes spelled *here lives a happy family*. He'd lay good money down that there were ugly Christmas sweaters on display. Matching ones.

Josh stepped out of the Uber into a blast of wind that gusted glittery snow up the hem of his jacket and under his sweater.

"Jesus fucking Christ!" he bleated.

The driver snorted, unfazed by the blasphemy, and waved as he drove off.

Fine. Anyone driving on Christmas Eve was either not religious, needed the cash, or needed to stay away from family. Any combination of those reasons, plus the fact that his ride had been blessedly silent, deserved five stars. Josh added the rating and a fat tip at lightning speed and sheathed his hands in his pockets before frostbite set in.

The door flung open as he was finishing his last rap and he dipped forward like he was about to slap a bet on a poker table. A wall of heat and steam curled around him through the open door and Libby yanked him inside.

"Get him in here! I'm not heating the whole province!" a deep voice bellowed from the living room, and Libby slammed the door on the cold.

The house smelled like a pending food coma. Turkey and pumpkin pie and who knew what else wafted in from the kitchen. His salivary glands ached in anticipation. His family had the barest adherence to Christmas traditions, as evidenced by their cavalier approach to holiday planning. His father hadn't ported over any Graham traditions from his side of the family, and his mother's side was far more likely to go surfing than roast turkey in the peak of Melbourne summer.

More than once his father had joked they should just convert to Judaism for all the Westernized Chinese food they'd consumed at Christmas.

Josh suddenly had a visceral craving for mediocre sweet and sour pork.

Libby wrapped him in a sweaty hug, the bells on her festive sweater jingling merrily.

"Glad you could make it," she said.

Josh returned the hug cautiously. "Why are you being nice to me?"

"Because," she said, baring her teeth, "your husband asked me to be."

Stephen popped around the corner and grinned, the bells on his own sweater swaying.

Matching novelty sweaters. Called it.

"Hello, darling. Glad you could make it."

"Yeah, yeah." Josh gave his friend a one-armed hug, peering past his shoulder. "Thanks for the invite. Both of you."

"She's not here yet," she replied smugly.

Josh suppressed a chastising sigh. Of course, he'd want to see the only other person he'd know here. He shoved the wine into Stephen's chest, who cradled the bottles like a linebacker. "Introduce me to the hosts, why don't you?"

Libby's parents welcomed him like a long-lost cousin. Her mother squawked over the turkey, a garish apron cinched under her matronly bosom, cheeks flaming from bending over the oven and her second glass of wine. Her father shoved a beer and a candy cane into Josh's hands, and he wondered absently if it was a Calgary tradition to stir the beer with the candy cane. He left both the full beer and unwrapped candy cane on a coaster by the fire.

With an arm slung around Josh's shoulders, Libby's dad steered him from room to room for the house tour, ending in what was a childhood bedroom. The navy walls sagged with photos and ribbons, with a shrine dedicated to boy bands that was twenty years out of date, posters peeling at the corners. A twin bed with a wrinkled coverlet butted against a melamine bookshelf in the corner that displayed rows of YA books and trophies with dancers frozen mid-twirl on the risers.

If he swapped the dance trophies for basketball and the navy for mauve, he could have been in his sister's room in middle school.

"Here's Libby and Cassie for Halloween in third grade," her father said, gesturing at a framed photo. He squinted, peering over the top of his bifocals. "They'd gone as … I'm not sure what they were that year, but they had fun."

Josh couldn't recognize the costume either, but their blue-painted faces beamed under layers of makeup, buck teeth like Chiclets in their tiny mouths, and he felt his own mouth stretch in response.

"And here they are at the Canadian nationals." The girls wore matching black leotards, tee shirts strategically ripped to look simultaneously badass and age appropriate. Cass had been right. They had to have been all of fifteen years old in this photo. Libby looked like any other teenage girl, but Cass could have passed for a skinny twelve-year-old.

"And here they are, at the eleventh-grade formal."

The two girls stood side by side, flanked by gangly, spotty boys. After a double take, he realized one of the gangly, spotty boys was Stephen, albeit several inches shorter and a hundred pounds lighter. The two photos couldn't have been taken more than a year apart, and while Libby looked identical in both, Cass looked like she'd had one hell of a summer.

She stood with the hunched posture of a girl convinced rounded shoulders would hide her unwelcome new body, making her look even shorter than she was. The boy with his hands respectfully resting on her waist looked stunned, like he had been hit by the same Mack truck that had hit Cass.

"Robbie Johnston," Cass said, appearing at his other side, and his heart thudded against his sternum. The Cass of today stood, if not tall, at least with her back straight. She stepped closer to him, and her sweet scent caressed him, an antidote to the air thick with the promise of dinner. The silky green blouse she wore draped around her shoulders with a complicated twist he couldn't unravel in his mind, falling in a layer of clouds that displayed her collar bones.

He huffed a jet of air through his nostrils to clear his head and forced as much attention as he could muster back to the photos. "I didn't hear you knock."

"That's because I don't knock here."

"When did you ever knock, Cassie?" Libby's father asked and kissed her cheek. "I'm going to see if the girls have put Stephen to work yet."

When the footsteps scuffed down the stairs, Josh leaned over to click the door quietly into place behind him. He swept his eyes up from her shoulders before stalling at her lips. That fiery red. Definitely on theme. "Where's your ugly Christmas sweater?" he demanded.

"I could ask you the same thing," she scoffed, eyeing the black jeans, sans-holes, and the only knit pullover he owned without graphics on it. She toyed with the fine lamb's wool at his throat and flipped the collar to examine the seams. She hummed in approval, her breath smoothing over his skin, the tips of her fingers drawing out a patter of goosebumps that awakened his skin. "Besides, I don't wear acrylic."

I like wearing beautiful things she'd told him the night they met. Whatever her shirt was made of whisked quietly against his chest. Desire flared under his skin like an errant firework. He wondered what beautiful underthings she was wearing tonight. He wanted to drag his fingers under the neckline to find out.

He caught a ripple of the luscious fabric to let it rustle between his fingertips. If he had it his way, he would see that she only wore silk and velvet for the rest of her life.

"But this isn't festive."

"I'm dressed plenty festive enough."

She turned her gaze back to the photo, gesturing to her date with a chagrined tilt of her head.

"That night was the first time I ever kissed a boy. He tried to feel me up when we were slow dancing that night. I mostly remember how sweaty his hands were, and he wore too much cologne."

You smell so good she'd murmured drunkenly against him. She was sober now, and by the way she swayed into him, her opinion hadn't changed. After months of not touching her, being close to her, his blood raged through his veins. His hands still stroked the silky skin at her collarbone, and she didn't pull away.

He forced his voice to rasp past the constriction in his chest. "That better have been the only time he had the chance to put his hands on you."

"He started dating one of the girls in my dance squad the following week. You could say it set my pattern," she said. "The Cassidy St. Claire Story: one bad date that goes nowhere."

"I'd say our date was pretty good."

"And what date would that be?" Her eyebrows raised, half question, half challenge.

"Back in Vancouver. I seem to remember you chatting me up outside a film."

"I chatted you up, hmm?" Her eyes grew heavier with each pass of his fingertips.

"Mm-hmm, and then taking me to several movies." And then back to his place. The front of his jeans tightened, and he longed to press her up against the shelf behind him and knock every single one of those trophies to the floor.

No one could see them. No Melanie, no Bernie. No Brynne or Dawson or any fucking paps. It was written all over her, in her gaze that dropped to his mouth and the pulse that beat at her neck. She was his.

He grabbed her jaw to force her eyes up and felt her throat work against his palm as she swallowed. Her eyes darkened, the hazel irises a thin golden band that threatened to suck him in.

"What are you doing?" she whispered.

Getting just about fucking done keeping his hands to himself. Enough acting like a fucking cuck and sending her out to spend her time with other men. Of holding back and pretending to be indifferent to her effect on him.

She'd imprinted herself everywhere. The way her scent hijacked his senses and crowded everything else out of his mind. A thousand different ways that made him want to rip the world apart and put it back together for her.

He was close enough he could feel her ragged breath on his lips. "I'm sick of watching other men try to give you what you need, and not have a fucking clue what that is."

"And you know what that is?"

He crowded her against the door, tugging the hair at the nape of her neck to tilt her head back. The strain of Christmas carols floating from downstairs did little to muffle the door rattling in its frame. Her breath hushed against his cheek, eyes widening, as he wedged his knee between hers and dipped his mouth to her ear.

"Are you really going to stand there with those fuck-me eyes and your nipples cutting into my chest like diamonds, and tell me I don't know what you need?"

"What do I need?"

The dam of everything he'd held back for months broke, and he crashed his mouth to hers. Her hand wrapped around his bicep, her other under his sweater on the small of his back, and her lips parted like water.

Fuck, she still tasted like cinnamon, sweet and spicy, and her hands snaked up under his arms to close over his shoulder blades. She closed her lips around his tongue and sucked gently, and he wanted to rut into her like an animal. Each urgent whimper she made into his mouth sounded like *yours*. Or maybe it was *more*. He'd take them both.

He slid his hand up the front of her shirt, over the silky skin of her belly, and thrust his thigh against the apex of her legs. Her breath caught, pulling at the air in his lungs, like only enough oxygen existed for one of them. The last of his exhale escaped in a hiss as his hand moved around her ribs and over the swell of her breasts.

Fresh heat washed over him, tight and frantic. There they were, those glorious tips firming under his fingers as he traced their peaks, her back arching to chase his touch. He didn't know what she was wearing under her beautiful clothes, but he wanted his mouth on it before the night was over.

"Fuck, baby, you feel so good," he groaned into her hair. "Take off your shirt."

She shuddered, hips rolling against his thigh. "There are people downstairs."

"And we're up here." He pressed her more firmly against the door, pinching her nipple, swallowing every moan she released against his mouth. "You want this as much as I do. Say it."

"Josh." Her words were feathers brushing over his skin. "Stop."

There was that word he knew she didn't mean, and hard to take seriously when she was grinding her hips against his thigh. "You haven't had enough yet, have you, baby?"

She shook her head, and he smirked against her mouth. That's what he thought.

He peeled the edge of her shirt up, far enough to glimpse the ivory cups covering her tits, the dusky rose of her nipples peeking through the sheer fabric, and he thought his dick would punch through his jeans.

Fucking spectacular.

Running his thumb under the band at her sternum and down her stomach, he dipped his hand below the waistband of her pants. He was so fucking sure whatever she was wearing matched the ivory bra, silky and gorgeous and wet for him already, and he wasn't waiting another second to find out.

"We're not leaving this room until you come."

"Somebody could come in!"

"Then I'll make my filthy little slut come fast."

"But—"

"We're not leaving this room until you come." He drove her against the door with a dull thump and kissed her, breaking away to brush his lips over her ear. "Say it."

Her throat worked, eyes wide and dark, and she whispered, "We're not leaving this room until I come."

"That's my girl." He slid his fingers over her silky skin and into her heat, and licked the hollow of her neck. "Now, can my good girl be quiet?"

Her fist curled into his sweater, eyelids fluttering closed as he circled her clit. She was warm and wet and listened so well, swallowing whimpers and biting down on her lip when he added a second finger to work her G-spot.

"You wish it was my cock inside you, don't you?"

She jerked her head, silent, and dug her nails into his shoulder as he ground the heel of his palm against her. He'd give it to her. Everything she wanted. All her soft parts pressed to all his hard parts, her arms curled around his neck and her bucking hips fuelling the rush that someone could walk in on them at any second.

Just his luck. The first time he'd touched her in months, and he had to rush her orgasm. Next time would be different.

Too soon, her pussy clenched around his fingers. He covered her mouth with his to smother the scream forming in her throat, teasing out her climax until her fluttering muscles stilled and the last choked sounds faded.

He had wrecked her. Hair mussed, lips bruised, and her clothes dishevelled. She wavered on her feet. Her soft panting gasps warmed his cheek as she clung to his shoulders. Gorgeous.

A groan escaped his own throat, stopping himself before he nipped her. Sending her downstairs with bruises down her neck would make for awkward dinner conversation. He sated himself by kissing her instead, withdrawing his hand out from her underwear and sucking on his fingers one by one.

God-fucking-damn, tasting her was worth the wait.

"Mmm," he growled. "That's my girl."

She sagged against the door, and her eyes met his as her head lolled back. "I'm not your girl," she murmured.

"Hard to take that seriously right now, baby." He couldn't help but smirk, feeling his dimples pool as he dragged his nose along her neck. "Why do you feel so good?"

Her lips parted, and she tipped her head back against the door. "Because you know how to make me feel good."

"Only me." His cock asserted its displeasure at still being sheathed, and he pressed his erection against her belly. "Let me make you feel even better. Take off your pants."

For a half second, he thought she was going to do it, but she looked around with a dawning realization of exactly where she was. "Here?" she asked incredulously.

"No, in the hallway. Yes, here."

"I'm not having sex with you in Libby's bedroom!"

"What the hell did we just do?"

"But … naked sex? Not here!"

If location was a problem, he could fix that. "Your bedroom it is. Get your jacket."

Guilt creased her features, and she pinched her eyes shut, palms flat to his chest. "No, I love these people. I'm not leaving dinner for a booty call."

A booty call? His chest twisted. Fuck, he deserved that. Because that was exactly what he was treating her like. And she deserved better.

Besides, next time—and there would be a next time—she was making the first move.

"Okay, beautiful, have it your way." He ignored the insistent throb in his jeans as he dropped a kiss on her forehead. "Let's go downstairs and eat Christmas Eve dinner like I didn't just make you come in front of a poster of the Jonas Brothers."

CHAPTER TWENTY-ONE

CASS

"You might want to clean up before heading down," Josh said, sweeping his gaze over her with a guarded smirk.

For the millionth time in her life, Cass wished for poker straight hair and a poker face to match. Something she could whip up into a bun to look put together at a moment's notice, instead of her curls telegraphing she'd just gotten laid when, well, she'd just gotten laid.

Whether or not her clothes were on.

"Do I look that bad?"

Josh looked completely unruffled, his hair put back in place with a swipe of his fingers and sweater straightened in a second. The flush on his cheeks could easily be blamed on the heat still rising from the kitchen.

The only signs he'd been doing anything other than politely admire Libby's dance trophies was the bulge straining against the front of his pants and a smudge of her lipstick on his mouth.

A sound of dissent left his throat. "You look fucking gorgeous," he said. "But everyone is going to know." He leaned in to tug her shirt back into place, and let his lips whisper over her ear one more time. "But a part of me thinks that's exactly what you want."

The light in the room grew brighter. He was right. The thought of someone catching them, with his hands all over her and her biting back her groans had made it even hotter.

The heat blooming under her ribs wasn't embarrassment.

It was thrill.

His filthy little slut.

Unlocking a new kink had not been on her Christmas Eve bingo card that morning, yet here she was.

The front hall mirror showed she'd rearranged herself as well as she could manage. She waved as she walked briskly past Libby's parents in the kitchen and into the living room. Josh dropped into an armchair by the fireplace, while Libby and Stephen sat cuddled on the couch.

Stephen looked Cass up and down and shot Josh an admonishing glare. "What the fuck, man," he said under his breath, low enough Libby's parents couldn't hear, and Josh returned the look with a bored expression.

The expression Libby wore, however, spoke volumes. *I know that look on your face. Are you sure about this?* And the inevitable, *you are going to get hurt.* Cass swept the looks her best friend was giving her aside.

Because that look *was* on her face. She *wasn't* sure what was happening. And she just hoped she wouldn't get hurt again, but she was willing to take that chance.

Cass glanced around for a place to sit. There was no room to squeeze in with Josh on the armchair. If he had taken the other end of the sectional, she could have sat beside him.

"Here," Stephen said, holding out his arm. She dropped down on Stephen's other side, and Josh stiffened a fraction.

The fire flushed cheeks, and she stared into the flames. She shouldn't like the little possessive streak, especially when there was nothing declared between them to be possessive about.

Whatever game they were playing had rules she couldn't keep up with.

"Dinner will be ready in a few minutes, kids," Libby's father yelled from the kitchen, and the crew dutifully filtered into the kitchen to bring the food out.

"If you don't like someone else handling your woman, then make sure she can sit with you," Libby hissed as she passed Josh.

Cass swatted her butt as she walked by. "I'm not anybody's woman," she muttered under her breath, but didn't miss the side look Stephen shot at a disgruntled-looking Josh.

Maybe Stephen knew something she didn't. Maybe a little jealousy of seeing her go on other dates had awoken something in him. After spending months together on set, working together, getting to know each other, maybe he wanted more.

There was the minor inconvenience of them living in different provinces, but Cass could ignore that for now. She was good at ignoring those types of things.

Like that after the short Christmas break, filming would wrap, and they would go back to living in different cities. She could ignore the fact that despite him pressing his dick against her stomach an hour ago, he'd never said he wanted anything more from her than a furtive romp.

A lot of things were going ignored and unsaid.

Libby wedged Cass between her and her father at the dinner table, across from Josh, presumably where no hands could go rogue under the table.

The sneak. Like putting them on opposite sides of the table would stop her from inching her foot up the inside of his leg.

Knowing her luck, she'd end up playing footsie with Stephen by accident. That, and unless she nearly slid out of her chair, her short little legs wouldn't reach far enough under the table to snuggle her instep any closer than his knee.

As much as it was helpful, she didn't need physical contact to make him squirm.

She passed on the wine but had a second helping of stuffing and sweet potatoes, and still found room for a piece of Libby's father's legendary pumpkin pie. Josh's eyes were fixed on her mouth the entire meal.

She took another bit of the pie, licking the edge of the fork, and a muscle ticked in Josh's jaw.

Maybe he wasn't as detached as he looked.

Libby cracked the back door a quarter inch to release some of the tiny kitchen's heat, and a slice of crisp air snapped across Cass's body. Libby's father had wrangled Stephen and Josh to put away the dining room chairs as her mother bustled back and forth with the leftovers.

"What are you doing?" Libby hissed between the moments they were alone in the kitchen.

"Not having sex in your bedroom," Cass said with a flush up her cheeks. "Even if I really, really wanted to."

"I don't care about that, although you should know I did go down on Stephen in there before you came over. Don't trust those sheets."

"Ew, and thanks for the heads up." Cass stacked the plates in the dishwasher. "You'd think he'd be more relaxed if he just got a beej." Lord knew she felt fantastic.

"He's tense because he's worried about you. *I'm* worried about you."

Cass blew a lock of hair out of her eye and filled the sink, trying to prevent any water from wetting her silky top. She pushed her sleeves up her arms and out of the way of the water before dunking the bowl that had held mashed potatoes. "Well, don't be. I'm fine."

"Don't give me that shit. You're doing the thing."

"What thing?"

"The thing where you fall pussy up for the hot, emotionally unavailable guy."

Cass tried to find fault with any part of what Libby said, but found none. She checked her texts when she heard her phone chime, hoping it would be him. She hung back after shoots to talk about the day, getting lost for hours in their recaps. She'd thrown herself at him after he'd picked her up from her final disastrous date.

He'd shut her down at every turn. And no, he hadn't revealed much about himself. The only personal details she knew, besides what he looked like naked, she'd learned because Stephen had forced it out of him.

Her stomach constricted around the thought, and she shut her mouth while Libby's mother dropped off another load of dishes. "Weren't you the one who cheered me on when I hooked up with him back in Van?" she whispered out of the corner of her mouth.

"Whole-heartedly, but that was when it was a one-night stand to help you get over Nick. Remember the other hot, emotionally unavailable guy who benched you?"

Cass gripped the edge of the sink with soapy hands. Things changed. It was different for Libby and Stephen. What if it was different for her this time?

The kitchen had cooled several degrees with the back door still open. Stephen and Josh filtered into the room, and Cass shivered.

"If you want, I can drive you home," Cass said quietly, and Josh grinned.

After two failed attempts to decline leftovers and goodbyes that lasted ten minutes, Cass and Josh penguin-walked down the sidewalk to her truck.

"Unlock it, unlock it, unlock it," he pleaded, breath misting around him as he stamped his feet by the door with his arms laden with Tupperware. "Sweet holy hell, it's colder than a mother-in-law's kiss out here."

Whatever she had expected, that wasn't it. Cass clicked the door release and let a cackle escape into the night. "Colder than a mother-in-law's kiss? I haven't heard that one before."

"My mother is Australian," he said, jumping into the passenger's side and slamming the door. "I've got a ton of those expressions chambered."

What was this? A personal anecdote, freely given? It was like a fae prince had trusted her with his name. Her heart squeezed between her ribs, and she started the engine.

Josh cuddled a dish on his lap, steam rising from under the loosely wrapped lid. "Would it be weird if I held the Brussels sprouts while we drove? I don't know how you got used to the cold."

"I don't know if you ever get used to it, but it's amazing what you can learn to tolerate," she said, and threw her truck into gear.

The roads late Christmas Eve were empty. Josh was still curled around the dish of leftovers as she pulled up to his rental. The snow crunched under the tires as she slowed, then stopped in the middle of the road. She cut the engine, and they sat listening to the truck ticking and sighing as it cooled in the night.

"What are you doing tomorrow?" she blurted.

Josh turned his head to look at her. The shadows obscured his face, and said nothing.

"I was going to go to my family's, but they made other plans." She rambled, "We can wear comfy pyjamas and watch movies and have hot chocolate, and we even have leftovers, so food is covered. I can pick you up in the morning." She looked down into her hands, folded on her lap. "If you aren't doing anything, I mean."

"Or," he said, running his tongue over his teeth, "I could grab my things and come over now."

Josh in her apartment. In her bedroom. After what just happened at Libby's. And still not knowing where she stood. Cass gripped the steering wheel with her gloved hands and stared out into the empty street.

"I'm not having sex with you," she said stoically.

His shoulders caved with repressed laughter. "I said nothing about sex, despite you leaving me with the worst case of blue balls I've had since I was seventeen—"

"Don't blame me! I didn't shove my hands down your pants."

"If you had, I wouldn't have stopped you," he said. "And I don't remember you having any objections."

And that is exactly why this is a bad idea, she thought. *On both counts.*

"I have way too much turkey in me to think about making a move on you tonight," he continued. "I'm being selfish. I'm thinking about saving myself from being outside again. Plus, it's still early. We can watch a movie tonight."

"You'd have to sleep on the couch."

"Sounds cold. There's more than enough room in your bed for both of us."

Cass nibbled the corner of her lip, her eyebrows drawn together. "Not big enough for sex."

"Every bed is big enough for sex, but see my previous statement. Too full to make a move. We can do facials instead."

"Josh!"

"Honestly, Lucky Charms," he tsked. "I don't know where your mind is, but I'm assuming you have weird clay masks or some shit?"

Of course she did. She nodded.

"Movies. Face masks. Enough room between us for the Holy Spirit."

"Promise?"

She wasn't sure if she was asking him to assure her he wouldn't try to sleep with her that night, or if she really could dollop her bright green kelp revitalizing concoction all over his perfect skin. She also wasn't sure which promise she wanted him to break.

"If I don't come over now, we'll both wake up Christmas morning alone, and that would be sad," he said, and his cheeks dimpled around his pout.

He was goading her. She knew better. Every tease and innuendo tipping way over the line into territory he promised not to cross.

Despite being full on turkey and stuffing and everything else, she was eating up everything he served her.

Having him over at night felt more dangerous than morning. She squeezed her eyes shut. "Okay, grab your stuff."

"I'll only be a minute." He reached for the handle and turned back to her. "You'll wait for me?"

Cass felt like she was dancing to a song she didn't know the steps to, all the while being maneuvered onto the floor by a partner who absolutely did.

She swallowed hard and nodded. "I'll wait right here.

CHAPTER TWENTY-TWO

JOSH

"Make yourself at home."

Josh lined up his runners beside Cass's fur-trimmed boots and stepped into the slippers he pulled out of his overnight bag. She strolled through the galley kitchen, shedding accessories like a cherry tree losing its petals in the rain. Purse dropped on the counter, followed by her keys. Jacket draped over the chair. Lights flicked on as she floated into the living room, unwinding the eggplant and pumpkin plaid scarf to sling it over the arm of the couch.

He draped his jacket over top of hers and followed.

The clutter hadn't changed since he'd left after bringing her home after that asshole had stood her up a few weeks ago. A string of lights added around an ailing tropical plant was the only festive touch, with a couple of near-empty rolls of Christmas paper beside piles of bright fleece fabric on a table.

"A few years ago I sewed fleecy beanies for the crew as a wrap gift, and now Terry has it as a standing request, and I've never been able to say no to them. And I forgot to not spoil my nieces again this year," she explained, shuffling the fabric and rolls of paper to another random pile on a different surface.

Not exactly a paragon of tidiness. He hid a smile.

She brushed her hands on her thighs, sending a soft ripple over the fabric. "Does your sister have kids?"

"Nope."

Grace had been counting on being fun auntie to his hypothetical kids before she'd had her own. One more disappointment he'd laid on his family. He didn't even know if she was still dating that squarehead he'd met once two years ago. Probably. Seemed like a nice guy. He wondered if he'd get an invite to the wedding.

He rummaged in his overnight bag. "I have something for you."

"You got me a present?" She took the box with a surprised smile. "Thank you."

The cobalt silk scarf lifted from its wrappings like mist. Cass followed it unfurling with a soft expression, her fingertips caressing the delicate weave. He took one end and wrapped it once around her neck, adjusting its drape against her skin.

Good. The blue looked exactly like the shirt she'd worn the day they took photos. "There's more."

She pulled out a sachet. "Luxury Himalayan rose and geranium bath soak?"

"You said you liked nice, girly things. Figured this was as nice and girly as it got."

Perhaps also more appropriate than the vibrator he'd mentioned to her months ago when she'd accidentally sent him the picture of Chauncy on her nightstand. He wondered when her birthday was and remembered he'd probably be back in Vancouver before it rolled around. He shoved the thought down.

She stood on her toes to wrap her arms around his neck. "You remembered. Thank you."

He let himself pull her into his embrace. She felt so good in his arms. Soft, warm, and pliant. Like she was meant to be there. She sighed a breath against his neck, and he stroked his hand down her spine.

"If you keep pressing your tits into me like this," he whispered into her hair, "You're going to make me hard again."

"Josh—"

"I promised not to make a move on you. I never promised not to tease you." He let his hand slide down her back to the curve of her hip and squeezed. "Your virtue is safe with me."

It wasn't a lie. Sex would never be the last thing on his mind with Cass near, but he was far too full of gravy and turkey to contemplate doing anything more vigorous than a movie marathon.

"Oh my god, you are the worst," she said, pushing him away with a laugh. "I have something for you, too." She ruffled through the piles of fabric and pulled out an oversized hat, midnight-black, complete with ear flaps and attached scarf.

He tugged it on and wrapped the scarf around his neck, the fleece instantly smothering the lingering chill from the outdoors. If there was such a thing as a perfectly fitted hat, he was wearing it.

"I just figured, since you're always cold …"

"I love it. Thank you." He'd wear it every one of the remaining days before he went home.

She nodded, rocking on her heels, and glancing at her bedroom. "I'm going to jammy up. Two shakes and I'll be right out. You can wait until I'm done and get changed in my room or get changed out here."

Jammy up? Fucking adorable. He smiled as he watched her disappear into the bedroom.

"You remember I've seen you naked, right?" he called after her. She stuck her head back out the bedroom door to blow him a raspberry. He stripped his jeans and sweater, pulling on a change of clothes and groaning in relief as his distended belly was freed from his jeans.

Thank god for elastic waistbands.

The sounds of closet doors opening and dresser drawers closing knocked through her closed bedroom door, so he wandered over to the wall covered in paintings. Barely an inch of wall was visible between the twenty-odd pieces. A few framed, most on stretched canvas. Some of them were very good. Deliberate, measured. Others were random bursts of colour and texture. No skill, but fun nonetheless. All done by different people, from the looks of them, but on a theme he couldn't place. Bold colours he'd have never chosen, but bright and joyous.

"What do you think?"

Cass spoke from just behind him, and he crossed his arms over his chest without turning. He thought they made him feel optimistic. Oddly happy. About what, he wasn't sure. "I think I want to know this story," he said after a moment.

"Libby and my birthdays are a week apart, and when we turned thirty a couple years ago, we surprised each other with a whole day each. She always wanted to try archery, so I sewed her a complete Merida princess dress, and I wore a bear costume. I asked the armourer on the TV show we were working on to give her archery lessons."

Josh huffed a laugh through his nose. Cass would have looked like a teddy bear. "Did she forgive you for making her wear a dress?"

"She'll never admit it, but she loved it, though she was thinking more of Katniss energy than Merida."

That sounded like Cass. Thoughtful and giving. Able to see past the surface to the unspoken thing someone wanted. "That's not your story, though."

He felt her rock beside him. "Libby had all our friends paint how I made them feel. She had an instructor give everyone a quick lesson. Then we all went to a movie, because there is a whole expression around watching paint dry,"—he loved that he could hear the smile in her voice—" and then we packed up the paintings, came here to hang them, and played all my favourite songs on Guitar Hero for the rest of the night. It was awesome. I still remember who painted each one. That one was Libby," she said, pointing. "This one was, well, you don't know any of these people, so it doesn't matter."

"Who did that one?" he asked, pointing at one in the bottom corner. While the other paintings made him want to smile, this one made his chest feel empty. This one looked undone. Like someone lost interest halfway through.

"Oh. Just a guy I was seeing at the time. I'd finally convinced him to come out with my friends." Her voice hollowed, and she shifted beside him. "He started dating a friend of mine he met that night. They got married last year. I was one of her bridesmaids."

Jesus. She hadn't been kidding when she said her track record was flawless.

"Why do you keep it up?"

"A reminder that even though one person didn't love me, I still had a room full of people who did."

"That—" he started, turning to her, and shook his head, "is not what you're wearing."

She glanced down in confusion. "Why?"

Frolicking kittens in Christmas hats festooned the matching two-piece set, but the fabric clung to her lush thighs. Never mind that the top buttoned right to her collarbones, completely hiding her cleavage. Knowing what was under it was worse than being able to see it. Almost. He wanted to stroke the material to see if it was as soft as it looked.

He rubbed a hand over his eyes. It was physically impossible for him to not want to take this woman's clothes off. "It's too cute."

"So?"

"It's not even a one piece. It's easy access."

"Access to what?"

He raised an eyebrow.

"I thought you were full!"

"I'm also not dead."

"Erg! These are the most coverage pyjamas I have!" she said, crossing her arms. He half-expected her to stomp her foot, and he twisted his mouth to hide his grin. "And they are Portuguese flannel," she continued, unfazed. "Do you know how cozy this is?"

"You should take them off and let me try them on. I'll let you know."

"Do you want me to drive you back home?" she threatened. "I'll do it."

"No, I just thought if you were serious about me keeping my hands to myself, you'd have worn a muumuu or something."

"Are you really making a 'you should watch what you wear' argument with me?" she asked, pursing her lips to hide the smile trying to break through.

Josh motioned to his clothes. "I know how hard it is for you to not ravage me, so I dressed accordingly."

"What, like you are going to stand there in your grey sweat-pants and fleecy hoodie and not look like you purposefully didn't pick that, so I'd want to snuggle you?"

Nailed it. Enough women had told him about their obses-sions with men in sweatpants. "So, you want to snuggle me?" he said, smile widening.

"You promised to behave tonight!"

That's right, Lucky Charms. Let those good intentions fly right out the window. If she came onto him, excellent. If she didn't, he'd still get what he wanted. Time with her. Whether or not their clothes were on.

Win-win.

"I'm not above telling you what you want to hear to get close to you. Plus, it's very cold outside. You wouldn't really send me home, would you?"

She covered her face with her hands. "Let's watch a movie."

She knelt in front of the cabinet under the television, one leg tucked under her, the other extended to the side, and flipped through cases. Her thighs spread like butter as they flattened against each other, and he reminded himself he was too full to think of anything other than laying still and digesting.

"Mind if I pick?" she asked, flicking through the dozens of DVDs and Blu-rays stacked in uneven rows.

"No streaming?"

"You never know when your favourite will disappear."

True. "You pick. Just no extended Lord of the Rings marathon."

"That's tomorrow."

She selected a disc, hit play, and settled back on the couch against him. At least she wasn't putting up the pretense of space. He wrapped his arm around her shoulders. She smelled like flowers and dish soap, and she mellowed into the angles of his torso. Something creaked loose in his chest.

The title flashed across the screen, and he felt himself smile. "*The Mummy*?"

"Mm-hmm."

"It's cheesy."

"It's a perfect representation of the action-adventure fantasy genre with a romantic subplot."

"That's specific."

"Not only is it an underrated costume masterpiece, Brendan Fraser and Oded Fehr were my sexual awakenings."

It didn't escape his notice that Dawson, while not a physical dead ringer, had all the hero vibes as the lead actor on screen. It also hadn't slipped his notice that Dawson had sidled up to Cass with that charming leading man energy on more than one occasion, and he didn't think it had anything to do with the photo ops. He forced his grip on her waist to remain loose.

"Fine. I always get a semi seeing Rachel Weisz in that librarian get up."

"Same," she said with a grin, and Josh tipped his head back with a snort.

He didn't get the chance to tease her anymore. She detailed every genius costuming choice and every design flaw. Each anachronistic set piece was highlighted, followed by a break-down on why they still worked. When she wasn't reciting the lines with the actors, Josh pointed out every continuity error while silently wishing he'd had this budget.

If he didn't fuck up *Sirius Darker*, maybe one day he would. No one would trust him with a big budget if he couldn't handle a small one. Weeks left and he would be stuck with what they had done. No chance to make it better.

Who was he kidding? It was going to flop.

"I can feel you tensing up," Cass said through a yawn. "Don't worry. They make it out of the temple."

"It's not that," he said. "It's …"

It was everyone counting on him to pull this off. It was the thought that if he fucked this up, none of these people would ever work with him again. It was the fact that they had two weeks of filming left and he was running out of time.

He chewed the words, bitter in his mouth. "We're behind schedule. We're probably going over budget. I knew we shouldn't have moved filming the end scenes to next week."

He braced himself for Cass to tell him not to worry about it, to think positive, but instead she said, "Sure, we're behind, but I think you made the right choice to delay filming the scenes."

"You do?"

"Dawson and Brynne didn't have the rapport yet to sell the moment, and you saw that. You made the decision."

He'd made the decision because she'd pointed out the answer to him.

"Now they trust each other," she continued. "It'll be incredi-ble. And we might go over budget, but Terry will keep it under control, and Stephen has a death grip on the schedule. You've got a good team."

The credits were rolling up the screen, the triumphant music ushering the characters into the sunset. Josh forced a breath out his nose. "I'm used to doing all that myself."

"This is different. You know that. No captain would be

expected to steer a cruise ship by themself." She sat up and stretched, the hem of her shirt lifting. His fingers twitched to run along the exposed seam of her belly, but he kept his hands to himself as promised, and listened.

"The projects you worked on in the past were tiny. You could do everything then, but even then, you said you weren't happy with the result when you did it all. Your team trusts you. Everyone is doing amazing work. Both Dawson and Brynne are talented, but the performances you are getting from them are next level. People will notice, and it's because you are focusing on what you're brilliant at, not the other details."

Cass was kind, but she wasn't a bullshitter. Some of the turmoil in his stomach released. "Do you think so?"

"I know so. I see it every day."

He clenched his hands. When he'd dropped out of his father's law practice, his parents put on a show of support. Confusion, but support. His grandparents told him he was bringing shame on the family. And other people's reactions ranged from disbelief to dismay to disgust. He'd been a good lawyer. Detailed. Consistent. He put in the hours. But he never would have been an *excellent* lawyer, not like his father, because every hour he had sat behind that desk had felt like one hour closer to death.

Every elective in high school and university he'd taken had been in performance and film. He'd figured out every argument. A background in the arts would make him look well-rounded, and law school would look favourably on his application. Drama classes would make him a better public speaker.

At least, that's what he told his grandparents. Not like his father's contract law practice would have him in front of a judge and jury.

He had tried to forget the rush he felt making short films between his law lectures on contracts and ethics. He'd even tried to specialize in entertainment law, to see if that would be enough to satisfy him. It hadn't been.

Now he'd been in film and television full time for a handful of years, and here he was, already filming his dream project. He was an imposter.

But every time he felt like he was out of his depth, Cass helped him breathe again.

Getting used to that was out of the question.

"What's going on in that head of yours?" Cass had leaned back on the opposite end of the couch, arms wrapped around her knees and the sleep retreating from her eyes.

"I'm wondering why you are sitting all the way over there. Do you want to watch another movie or go to bed?"

Cass looked like she was going to say something, then stopped with a closed smile. "Let's watch another one. You pick."

The chirp of his phone woke him, and he squinted into the darkness. The DVD logo bounced around the edges of the television. Josh peeled his head off the back of the couch and looked at Cass crashed on the other side, their legs tangled together in the middle.

He pulled his feet back, working out the stiffness from the awkward position, and reached for his phone.

Sure enough, through a slew of other texts that didn't crack the Do Not Disturb filter, a message from his mother showed at the top of the screen.

Merry Christmas!

Oh shit sorry it's late there

Call us later love you!

He checked the time. Middle of the afternoon in Melbourne. He knew she'd forget the time difference. It had been Christmas for a few hours in this time zone. Who knew when they'd fallen asleep through *Gremlins*.

A yawn split his face as he tapped out a reply.

> Merry Christmas. I'll ask Santa not to be woken up at 2 AM next year

> Go surfing for me and don't get eaten by a shark. Love you both <3

He hit send with a silent chuckle and read through the other messages, replying to a few as he went. A cousin. Friends. Skipped the messages from friends-with-benefits. And one message he must have slept through.

> Merry Christmas

> You should be here with us

Fuck. Trust his sister to drop a perfectly timed guilt bomb. He ran a hand through his hair and scowled.

> Merry Christmas Gracie. You should come visit. I'd love to see you

Josh hit send and turned his ringer off. Cass slept soundly against the armrest, sunk low into the cushions. He could just make out the rise and fall of her chest under the blanket, pulled up to her chin, and his heart squeezed in his chest.

This was absolutely out of the question.

He gently shook her shoulder.

"Hey, baby."

Nothing.

He knelt beside her, squeezing her arm. "Cass, it's late."

She didn't stir.

All the tension that Stephen had been giving him shit for was washed away. Her face looked peaceful, and he let himself thumb the soft skin along her neck. He leaned forward to whisper against her cheek. "Charms, come to bed with me."

His arms were halfway under her sleeping form to carry her, when she murmured a quiet "umph" without opening her eyes, like she was trying to prevent the awake from sneaking in. She swung her feet off the couch and grabbed his hand to sleepwalk to the bedroom, feeling her way through the room with hands out like a blind man.

His eyes adjusted to the dark, and he climbed into bed after her, not letting go of her hand.

It had been years since he slept in the same bed as a woman without having sex first. He tried to tell himself he couldn't remember when that would have been, but that was a lie, and something close to guilt wracked him again.

Cass curled on her side facing him, already asleep, her free arm tucked under her pillow and top leg bent towards him. The profile of her body looked like a mountain range, all curved valleys and lush darkness in the night.

He stared at the open door, where the couch waited a few steps away. Probably still warm from the hours they'd sat close. There was a blanket out there, and the couch wasn't that small.

But she'd pulled him into her bedroom. And hell, if he didn't want to be with her tonight.

Every night.

The renegade thought took root in his mind, and he hissed a quiet breath.

Fucking hell.

The mattress divotted under his weight as he eased in beside her. He pushed a rogue lock of hair back from her cheek, pulled the covers up to her shoulders, and pinned his other hand under his arm for safe keeping.

"Merry Christmas, Lucky Charms," he whispered.

CHAPTER TWENTY-THREE

CASS

HALF-CONSCIOUS, CASS WOKE TO A BARRAGE OF MIXED SIGNALS. Only the faintest grey-blue light trickled into the room, even with the curtains pulled wide, and crystalline flakes glittered on the other side of the glass. Her usually noisy street was quiet with the Christmas lull, making it seem like the outside world had disappeared.

It would have been a dreamy way to wake up if she wasn't being strangled.

She yanked down the hem of her top from around her throat until she could take a full breath and kicked away the blankets where they had tangled in knots with her pyjama pants.

That's why I don't usually wear these to bed. She peeled open an eye. *Why did I wear these to bed?*

Pyjamas. Because she wanted to dance with fire and let him spend the night.

No. More than let. Wanted.

The space beside her was empty, but warm. Before she could sit up, she heard the toilet flush and taps run, followed by footsteps hurrying down the hall into her room.

Whether he'd stripped his hoodie before or after he fell asleep, she didn't know. Goosebumps flecked his arms and chest, the smooth plain of his torso disappearing below the waistband of his sweats slung low on his hips. He was shaking his hair out of his eyes, and his scowl morphed into a half-grin as he saw her.

Definitely dancing with fire. She rolled to her back to stare at the ceiling and remove his abs out of her eyeline.

"Jesus, my nipples could cut glass." He dove back into bed and pulled the duvet up to his eyebrows. "Thank god you're awake. I didn't want to rifle through your shit. I need coffee."

"Are you always this demanding in the morning?"

His voice came muffled from below the covers. "I'm demanding all the time. Besides, you owe me."

"For what?"

"I'm sure there's something. I need coffee to remember what that is."

Cass felt the corners of her mouth curve up. "How long have you been awake?"

"Two minutes."

Add caffeine addiction to the slim treasure chest of knowledge she knew about him. "Okay, coffee is on its way. How do you take it?"

"Black as my soul."

Cass puttered around her kitchen, cleaning up the more obvious messes while the coffee brewed.

A few messages had come in. A rambling voice note from Libby and Stephen. A trio of texts from Jill. A *Merry Christmas* from Raina, with a picture of her beaming kids unwrapping the presents Cass had given them.

Nothing from her sister or brother, but they could still be busy with the kids and sleeping, respectively. An off-centre selfie from her parents with the caption, *wish you were here!*

If that was true, you would have invited me.

As the final drips sputtered from the filter, Josh shuffled out of the bedroom, wrestling with his hoodie, and plopped in front of her stack of movies.

"One soul-black coffee." She handed him the cup and curled her fingers around her own, doctored heavily with hazelnut syrup and a splash of cream.

"I love LOTR marathons as much as the next nerd, but I'm guessing you've got something better than that."

On second thought, maybe she wasn't missing out on the California sun. Cass nodded, one leg tucked under her, her bad knee extended to rest on the coffee table. "I'm open to suggestion."

Josh flipped through the movies stacked on end. He sat cross-legged, curled over the selection before him. Every so often he'd pause, take a case out to smirk at the cover, either shaking his head and replacing it, or stacking it off to the side. The hem of his oversized hoodie rode up enough to display the dimples at the base of his spine, and the overwhelming desire to kneel behind him and slide her hands over them danced across her mind.

Sexy Dimples. He had to have done it on purpose.

He grabbed two DVDs off his short-listed stack of over a dozen, hiding them behind his back. "Let's start with these. Left or right?"

She tapped his right arm, and he brandished an early seventies French film with a flourish. She clapped her hands. "Oh, excellent! Subs, not dubs?"

"Obviously."

"Left or right." Josh kneeled in front of her, hands behind his back again.

Cass reclined against the cushions they'd dragged onto the floor and tapped her lips in exaggerated concentration. "Left."

"My left or your left?"

She pressed her lips together, utterly failing to prevent herself from smiling, and nudged his left arm.

"Wait." He twisted over his shoulder and switched his hands. "Perfect."

"We're just on the second movie, and you're cheating already!"

"Are you going to put up a fight about it?"

Cass huffed. "No. That's one of my favourite movies of the last ten years."

"Me, too," he said, putting it into the DVD player. He sat beside her and held out his arm. "Are you hungry yet?"

She settled into the crook of his arm and let the scent of his sleep and the citrusy sandalwood that always clung to him wash over her.

"I'm starting to get hungry, but let's watch this first."

"Right or left?"

Josh chewed his mishmash of leftovers and gestured with his fork. "Wheft," he said around a bite of mashed potatoes.

"Ooh!" Cass wiggled as she switched out the movies and hit play. She sunk into the couch, settling her plate back on her lap. "Historical costume design isn't always my favourite, but what they did with this." She kissed her fingertips. "Sublime."

He wobbled his head as he chewed. "It's alright," he said finally.

"And to think I let this Philistine into my apartment," she muttered under her breath, and Josh snickered. "It's a visual masterpiece telling the story of what it is like to be a teenage girl in the public eye. It should be mandatory viewing for child actors."

"Is that so?"

"Yes. It completely inspired me to draw fan art for *Tideways*."

A garbled choke erupted from Josh's throat. "Hold up," he said, eyes watering as he coughed before he managed to swallow his food. "You know *Tideways*?"

"Yep." She motioned with her chin to her bookshelf in the corner. "Two editions."

Josh hit pause on the movie and turned to look at her fully. "Do you still have your art?"

It had been years since she'd drawn it, but it was some of her favourite conceptual work, and she felt her cheeks warm with pride. She rifled through the desk where her sewing machine sat and passed a stack of loose papers to his outstretched hands.

"The movie adaptation was …" she paused, searching for the right words, shuffling through the colourful pages, "not an artistic choice I would have made. *Tideways* as a gritty western reboot? Please. It's like they didn't bother reading the book. Clearly, it should have been a candy-coloured eye-fest like this," she finished, waving at the movie paused on the screen.

Josh leafed through pages and pages of colour block designs. "I couldn't agree with you more," he murmured.

"Wait. Give me a minute." Cass closed her eyes and let an enormous smile spread across her features. "You just agreed with me." She sighed for dramatic effect. "That was beautiful."

"Don't let it go to your head," he said, and slid the designs back into the folder. "Mind if I borrow these? I want to look at them when the light is better."

Cass glowed. "Your wish is my command."

He rolled his eyes and stashed the portfolio into his overnight back. He resettled himself on the couch beside her, tugging her down beside him. "Noted."

"Left or right?"

She'd vetoed one movie, declaring she didn't want to watch massacres on Christmas day, and tapped on his right shoulder.

"*Pride and Prejudice*? Really?" he asked.

"You're the one who made the short list!"

Josh leaned against her legs, his fingers idly circling her

ankle bone. A shiver raced up her body, but she didn't move away. His usually smooth voice burred low. "I know what women like."

Cass moved to take it out of his hand, her cheeks warming. "Stop it. Let's pick something else."

"Nope, not only is it an underrated cinematographic master-piece," he said, fending off her attempted movie theft and holding the case out of reach, "Keira Knightley and Matthew MacFadyen were my sexual awakenings. Well, at least one of them was."

Tiny, delicate Kiera Knightly with the swan-like neck and fine lips. Nothing at all like her. Cass interlaced her fingers in her lap. "Weren't you a late bloomer?"

Josh's smile didn't dim, but grew softer, and he dipped his head in a show of uncharacteristic shyness. "Actually, I was. I don't think I looked at a girl until I was fifteen."

Another tidbit of knowledge to add to her hoard. The thought of a nervous, awe-struck Josh who didn't know his way around women triggered a surprising rush of affection. Cass pressed her lips together and rested against the blanket fort. "I thought you liked movies with ambiguous endings."

"Sometimes you need a happily ever after."

Cass itched to pick up her phone and dissect that comment with Libby for the next several hours, but Libby was having Christmas with a man who'd said unambiguously that he loved her and didn't want to be away from her again. "Okay, I promise not to recite the whole thing to you."

He turned to her with a shrug. "If you're not reciting it, then I will. From 'I have fought against my better judgment, my fami-ly's expectations, the inferiority of your birth' to 'You have bewitched me body and soul'," he quoted. He hit play and leaned back beside her. "It was so faithful to the source material it didn't do a lot adaptation-wise, but ..."

Cass half listened to him listing why fans and academics alike would have revolted with anything less than a perfect retelling or a full Bridget Jones's Diary-ing of the story, but she felt herself getting lost in his voice.

Being bewitched sounded about right.

A swashbuckling man with an unbuttoned shirt and a prim woman wearing heels in the jungle flickered across her screen.

Ridiculous, and unrealistic, but she loved it.

His arm was draped over her shoulders, fingers tracing leisurely circles over the soft material of her pyjamas. Even early as it was, she fought her eyelids from closing, settling into the easy rhythm of his breath and the beats of the movie she'd seen a hundred times before.

"How'd you meet Nick?"

It was the last question she had been expecting. Cass tipped her head back to look at the ceiling, thinking. "It was a few years ago. My sister needed me to pick up my niece after hockey practice, and he was coaching her team."

Nick had been circling the end of the rink, his back turned as he gave instructions to the kids swarming him. When he'd turned his head and met her eyes, that brilliant smile had sent her hormones storming into a tidy formation. By the time she had realized he smiled at everyone like that, he'd burrowed deep under her skin.

"What do you even see in this guy?"

Libby had asked her the exact same thing, and she was no closer to an answer. "I don't know."

"Come on."

"He was cute—"

"*Was* cute?" Josh jumped on her comment with feigned glee. "Has he been hideously maimed in a fire?"

Cass tsked. "Is cute. He could be really funny in a sarcastic way. Smart." She grinned at him. "He has a nice truck."

Josh gave her a look of pure disgust.

"I'm an Alberta girl," she said with a shrug, and he swatted her thigh. His eyes lingered on the way her leg moved under the light contact, and she saw his throat work.

After a beat, he asked, "Are you in love with him?"

Correction. *This* was the last question she had been expecting.

Once, she might have said yes, or at least maybe. But if Nick texted her right now, she'd have no problem leaving him on read.

A feeling like relief unfurled in her chest. She shook her head. "I don't think I even like him anymore."

Josh kept his attention on the nearly silent screen, but Cass thought she saw a hint of a dimple appear on his cheek.

"Technically, it's not Champagne," she said, pouring the wine into the tumbler as he dealt the cards. "But it's still festive."

Josh covered his glass when she moved to pour some for him. "I'll stick to water. Do you always have champagne on hand?"

"You never know when you might need to celebrate something. Even if it's just …" she trailed off and pursed her lips. "Even if it's just a really great day."

"I'll drink to that," he said, raising his empty glass.

"You don't … do you not drink?"

He shook his head, focussed on stacking the cards, and she frowned at her glass. It was cheap. It would lose the bubbles, but she and Libby could drink it in a couple days. She returned the bottle to the fridge and poured them glasses of sparkling fruit water.

Not Champagne, or even fake champagne, but good. Tart and breezy, it sparkled like starlit snow on her tongue. He took a sip, and she watched his mouth catch the drip that snuck over the edge of his glass.

She tore her eyes away to stare into her glass, watching the bubbles rise and pop. "Can I ask you a question?"

His shoulders tensed a fraction, but he nodded without looking up from the cards.

"Why did you leave law?"

"Oh," he said, tension releasing. "It wasn't for me."

She wondered what he thought she was going to ask. "And you made the right choice?" she asked instead.

"Never once had I thought leaving law was the wrong move for me, but I disappointed a lot of people when I did." He twisted his closed lips. "And don't tell me I could always go back."

"I don't know you that well," Cass said, "but I can't imagine you anywhere other than film. You have too much vision. It's incredible to watch you."

"Same." Josh studied his cards. "I've never worked with anyone like you. Melanie wanted us looking like we were cosplaying the fucking Power Rangers out there, and after seeing your designs, she completely changed direction."

The dim lights would hide the pleased flush creeping up her cheeks, the warm glow flowing under her skin. She discarded, and Josh swiped up her rejected Ace.

Shoot. That's what she got for not paying attention to the game.

"What's your dream?"

She blinked. "My dream?"

"Win an Oscar? Get out of film and become an accountant? What do you want?"

"Everyone wants to win an Oscar," she snickered, "but this is my dream. Right now, working with you on SD—"

"You're saying working with me is a dream come true?" he asked, grinning.

"Honestly? Yes."

He looked stunned, and she shrugged. "Working with creative people to make beautiful films," she said simply. "I'd never heard of SD before we'd met. There's a version of this story that is hard sci-fi or dystopian, and sure, I can see the blockbuster superhero version, but after reading your script, it just felt like you had something to say about their humanity. Same with *Oblivion*."

He opened his mouth, then closed it. "I think you're the first person to say that," he said quietly.

"Oh, please. I bet Stephen did."

"Hearing you say it feels different." He cleared his throat and narrowed his eyes at his cards. "Did your family support you going into costume?"

"My parents told me I could be anything I wanted when I grew up," Cass said wryly. "They forgot to tell me that if anything I wanted wasn't something that earned their attention, then I wouldn't get any of it."

Josh looked up. "What do you mean?"

"Typical middle child. The only thing I was ever good at was dance, and the minute I wasn't going to be the best anymore, it was like they lost interest in me. I was never a great student. My older sister is hyper successful, then she got married to her hyper successful husband and brought home hyper cute grand-kids for our mother to dote on. I was supposed to be the boy our dad always wanted, and when my brother came along, my dad had his favourite. It was just me in the middle, finding ways to make other people happy and trying to get their attention. The only thing I was ever good at in my family was seeing when things were about to go wrong and stopping drama before it started."

Josh let out a chagrined chuckle. "Like how you talked me down when I was—"

"Getting overwhelmed by all the pressure on your shoulders to pull this off?"

"You're doing it again."

"Force of habit." Cass brushed it aside. "You had that vision in your head though, already. That's why you were so fast to accept my suggestions. Why didn't you say anything to Melanie?"

Deep fissures furrowed his brow. "I'm not great at communicating what I need," he bit off eventually, rearranging the cards in his hand. "That's why I've always worked solo."

"You can only get so far on your own." Cass rubbed the frown lines between his eyes away. "And that's why you need people like me around."

"I can think of lots of reasons to keep you around," he said. That sly look she knew so well spread over his face, dimples divotting his cheeks, and he held her gaze as he fanned his cards out between them. "For one, you're an easy mark. Gin."

Cassidy St. Claire, you are a damn fool.

The squeezing in her chest released a charge through her limbs, and she sat rooted to her seat. As Josh counted the points and scratched the point totals on the pad beside him, her heart decided, and left her brain completely out of the conversation.

"I never stood a chance, did I?" she murmured.

"You really didn't," he said, dealing another hand. The heat retreated from his gaze, a practiced look of nonchalance taking the place of the smirk as he studied his cards. "I could stay tonight, too. If you haven't had enough of me yet."

"No, I haven't had enough."

"It'll feel a little funny at first, but you'll get used to it."

"Kinky."

"No squirming."

"I can't help it if you make me squirm."

"Josh ..."

"Okay." He closed his eyes and tilted his face up to hers. "Lay it on me."

Josh sat on the edge of the tub, his flawless skin freshly washed and his hands gripping his knees, held wide to let her stand between them. She'd cranked up the heat when she made him take off the hoodie to prevent smearing mishaps, and the lean planes of his torso glowed in the dimmed bathroom lights. His thick black hair was held back with glittery butterfly clips she'd picked out from the selection on her bathroom counter.

"Breathe in." Cass misted the aromatherapy spritz, more for ambiance than anything else, and scooped a double finger full of the green goop. "Now, relax."

"When did you get so bossy?"

She smoothed the mask over his forehead, down the bridge of nose, along the blade of his cheekbones. Her thumbs worked at the tense muscles of his jaw and smoothed down the column of his throat. His broad shoulders released a fraction, and he took a deep breath as she massaged his temples.

"This is not like other facials I've had," he said, slurring slightly.

"I'll pretend that's not an innuendo—"

"It's an innuendo."

"But either way," Cass said, unfazed, her fingertips pressing along the line of his collarbones, "that doesn't speak well to your other facials. I'm not very good at this."

"Disagree. You are very good at this." His hands inched inwards until his fingers rested on the outside of her knees. "I'm feeling very relaxed. And a little tingly."

Same. "There's eucalyptus in the mask."

"Don't think it's the eucalyptus making me tingly."

Also, same. Cass swallowed and stepped out of range of his hands. "Wait right here."

"For what?"

"For me to get my phone so I can get proof of this moment for blackmail."

"Go ahead." Josh stood and surveyed the results in the mirror. "I look sexy as fuck."

"You are green and slimy. You look like Shrek."

"Shrek is green and slimy and sexy as fuck. Your point?"

How could Josh being smeared in green goop still make her heart rate speed up? A manic giggle escaped her throat and her own drying mask cracked around the edges. "I'll try and keep my hands to myself for the next ten minutes."

"Why fight it?"

She wasn't sure if he was still joking. She didn't think he was. Not with his usual playful smirk tucked away, with something darker behind his eyes. Cass ducked out of the bathroom and circled the living room while fanning her face. Josh trailed after her, fingers wiping at a green smear at the top of his pecs.

"A few more minutes, then dinner?" he asked.

"When are you leaving?" she blurted.

They'd watched movies all day, eaten, and the light of the short winter day had long disappeared from beyond the windows. They hadn't planned an end for the evening. If he stayed, she would tip over into something she couldn't climb out of. If he left, she might be able to claw back a semblance of whatever emotional control she had left.

She knew which she wanted, and she didn't think she could have it.

He slowed, eyes narrowing. "Do you want me to leave?" he asked softly.

"No." And that was the problem. Cass resumed her pacing. "Last night was great and today has been wonderful and I've had so much fun, and I don't want it to end, and it'll suck when it does and I just ..." She dropped her waving hands and turned to face him. "I just want to be ready for it."

A muscle in Josh's jaw clenched, and he said nothing.

And now she was getting clingy. They were just hanging out, no matter what had happened yesterday, or what had been sparking between them for months. At least what had been sparking for her. Whatever games they had been playing. This was already in in territory she couldn't handle. "You know, forget it. I—"

"This is really weird, talking to you with green stuff all over your face. Come with me."

Josh leaned her butt against the bathroom counter, running the water until it turned hot, and steam rose in lazy wisps. "Unless you tell me there is a magic potion to get this shit off, I'm just going to use water."

At her nod, he soaked the washcloth with hot water and wrung it out. He didn't need to be standing as close as he was, gripping her chin to tilt it up with one hand and carefully washing her face clean with the other. Slow, gentle circles. The water beaded over her cheeks and down her throat. His heavy-lidded gaze roamed over her face. The steady strokes from his hands were firm but soothing, and she closed her eyes and let him take over.

"I don't want to go," he said after silent minutes.

"Oh. Okay."

He swiped a final pass with the cloth and then stepped away to scrub at his own face like he was trying to remove a layer of skin.

"I like spending time with you, and you like spending time with me." He paused, raising an eyebrow at her in question, and when she nodded, he continued, "I'm happy to eat more sweet potatoes and play a card game before going home, if that's what you want. But I don't think it is." He swiped the last of the green from his face and dropped the cloth on the counter. His eyes burned dark, and he crowded into her jaw clenching as his breath tickled her lips. "Tell me I'm right."

"Josh, I—"

"I can *feel* your heart pounding. I can see your pulse in your throat, right here," he said, tracing his finger down her neck, and her breath caught in her lungs. "Right now, I want nothing more than to slide my fingers in your pussy and see if you're wet for me already. I think it's been way too fucking long since I've been inside you, but if you've had enough, just say it."

No one had ever accused her of thinking before she acted. A

voice she was sure belonged to Libby whispered at her, *you've done this before, you know where this is going.* But Cass was beyond that. There was no turning back now. Not even if she wanted to.

But as much as it felt dangerous—reckless, even—it felt *different.* Not just a headlong dive into what her heart wanted. Need for him ached between her thighs, hummed between her ribs, and her last chance of turning back fell away.

"I don't think I'll ever have enough of you," she said, and the energy in the room changed in a flash.

Josh surged toward her, his mouth taking her like he was starved. Maybe he was. Last night was a taste, a tease, frantic minutes stolen. Now, he gripped her neck to angle her head back, the edge of the counter cutting into her butt as he pushed against her. His loose lounge pants hid nothing, and she ground herself against his growing bulge, matching his frenzy.

The last twenty-four hours had been a dangerous dance. A test, to see if she could resist. Letting him touch her, inviting him over, even as she swore to herself she wouldn't do exactly what she was doing right now.

She skated her hands along the ridges of his abdomen, down his clenching ass, and dug her fingers into the muscle. The man could have been cut from marble, if marble radiated heat and groaned every time she pressed her lips against the pulse hammering in his throat.

The grip in her hair tightened. "Fuck, Cass, I missed that mouth of yours."

"Then let me put it on you."

She licked the V where his hip met his thigh, and his knuckles whitened where he gripped the counter. His muscles coiled under his skin, warm and firm under her tongue, and she winced as she settled her knees on the hard tiles.

"Wait—"

"No more waiting," she said, spitting into her hand to pump his shaft, but he pulled her back before she could wrap her lips around him.

He leaned over and ripped a towel off the rack. "Knees."

She almost laughed, him thinking of her bad knee with his cock glistening a millimetre from her lips, but she dutifully knelt on the towel. "That's so sweet. I—"

"Nothing sweet about what I want that mouth to do." He let go of the counter and gripped a handful of her hair. "Now, open wide."

No more teasing. He'd already waited a day. She held his gaze as she opened just enough to take the tip, swirling her tongue as he let out a string of curses. Her tongue slid down the underside of his cock until he hit the back of her throat.

A harsh noise ripped from his throat, and his hips jerked forward. "You have no fucking idea how good you feel."

If his spasming thrusts were any indication, she had a pretty good idea. Every time her fingers gripped his base or wandered over his skin, him shivering whenever she found an especially sensitive spot. Submitting to his wants felt like power. Making his breath catch and his words devolve into a string of obscenities felt like music. Finding something he craved, and giving it to him, felt like victory.

With the barest pressure, his thighs opened to grant her access, her fingers sliding down the cleft of his ass and over the tight ring of muscle, air whooshing from his lungs.

I know what you need, too, she thought as she flicked her tongue along his crown, *and if you want it, it's yours.*

"Fucking hell. Just … god, Cass." His hand slammed on the wall over her head as he came, cock jerking against her tongue until he spilled down her throat, his eyes blown dark, fixed on her the entire time.

He pulled her to her feet and crushed her mouth to his. She loved that he didn't mind the taste of himself, wanted to kiss her, like his release was one more sense to share. She leaned into him as he sagged against the wall, spent, as he stroked her back, down her waist, over her hips.

"Do you know what I thought the first time I saw you?"

Cass shook her head.

"That you looked like you were lit from within. You glowed. You were radiant. I thought you were the most beautiful woman I'd ever seen," he said, voice low, and trailed his lips along her neck. "Then I wanted to know what your lips felt like around my cock."

Cass stifled a laugh. "I thought you said you'd been thinking about kissing me."

"That came later." He dipped his thumbs under the band of her pyjamas. "Now, I've been thinking about what you have on underneath these since last night," he said, sliding his hand lower, and stopped, an animalistic gleam in his eyes. "Charms?"

"Yes?" she asked sweetly.

"Have you been sitting on that couch with me for hours with a bare pussy?"

It hadn't been a conscious thought. Even though she had an entire drawer dedicated to matching undergarments that she selected every day, that morning she had just ... decided not to put any on. She swallowed and nodded.

"No more holding out on me." He gripped the nape of her neck and walked her backwards into the dark of her bedroom, kissing her the whole time, until her knees buckled on the edge of her bed, and he toppled on top of her. The weight of his body on hers, solid, warm, the slow rolling of his hips against her sliced through any coherent thought.

He worked her clothes down over her hips, kissing every newly exposed inch of skin, sliding his fingers along her slick folds. "Fuck, I knew you'd be wet for me."

The first swipe of his tongue sent a tremor cruising along every nerve ending, tension pulling dangerously at her seams. He pulled her hips into his face and buried himself between her thighs. Her insides tightened, coiling up her spine, until he pulled away.

The build of her orgasm vanished. "No," she whined. "I was so close—"

"Do you remember yesterday when you rode my thigh until you came, and then made me watch you eat Christmas dinner while I sat there with a hard-on like a fucking joker?"

A needy sound escaped her lips. "What?"

"My cock was throbbing all night, watching you smile and laugh and thinking about what that mouth could be doing. Then you made me wait an entire day for you." He licked the seam of her thighs, and she quivered. "An entire fucking day, Lucky Charms."

Dawning horror washed over her. Feeling him all over her, and now to have it pulled away? "No."

He stood, wiping his mouth on the back of his hand, and smirked down at her. "I think you need to beg."

"Please."

"I'm going to need more than that." He stopped her hands from taking off her shirt.

"I want you. Please."

"What do you want, baby?"

She wanted his hands on her body, his mouth on hers. She wanted him to stay. To tell her he felt the same way she did, that this wasn't round two of a one-night stand. Cass swallowed.

His eyes cut like flint, and he gripped the back of her head, forcing her gaze to him. "Say it."

"I need you. Inside me." She licked her lips, mouth suddenly dry. "Please."

He bit her neck, and her knees turned to sand. "Where are your condoms?"

"I don't have any," she squeaked, her stomach dropping. "Are you telling me you don't?"

His laugh reverberated through the short distance between them. "Of course I do. But I wanted to hear you sound so fucking needy for it."

She was beyond needy for him. If he'd demanded she crawl across the floor to get to him, she'd do it forwards and backwards.

"Don't move," he ordered. Her hands ventured to pick up where he let off, to give herself the relief he was denying her, and he pulled her hands away. "You're only touching yourself if I say you can."

She nodded, her eyes heavy.

"Bend over, put your hands on the bed, and wait for me."

There was no thought of disobeying, and she vibrated in anticipation while he left the room. She heard the foil ripping as he strode down the hall and her insides squeezed. He was behind her in a beat, yanking her hands overhead and wrapping them together.

"I said don't move." He wound the blue silk around her wrists once more and let go to roll on the condom. "You'll take everything I give you."

He gathered the scarf in his hand, pushing her down onto her elbows and swiping his cock along her length, teasing her clit. A fuse lit at her core, licked up her back and unfurled around her heart, and she lurched her hips back to chase the friction.

"Greedy, aren't you," he said. "When I feel you get close, I'm pulling out. You don't come until I let you. Understand?"

He lined himself up and pushed into her. He pulled out, once again rubbing himself through her wetness, and a throaty sigh rushed out from her lungs.

"I told you, baby. Don't move." He curled around her again, caging her in so she couldn't move, hand over her mouth, staying utterly still. Slowly, he pulled out only to thrust back in hard, and she choked on a moan. He slid the hand gripping her hip to stroke just north of her clit, and it took all her focus not to slide herself to chase his fingers. After she stayed still, he swiped his thumb lazily over her, and even as she shook, she bit down on her lip to hold back her cry.

"That's better," he said, and let go of her completely. "Get your vibe."

Cass blinked, stunned. "What?"

"Your vibrator. Get it."

Cass crawled across her bed with the blue silk still binding her hands, feeling his eyes on her ass. She opened her nightstand drawer and held out the bunny, incongruously cheerful.

"Show me how you use it."

Her insides tightened around nothing. For all the years she'd used toys, she'd never shared it with anyone before. She lay back on her bed, flicked it on, and held it to the perfect spot. Instantly, the pressure raced through her lower belly, and she arched her head back against her pillow.

"Do you like what you see?"

"Never seen anything more beautiful than you like this." Josh crawled between her legs, nibbling at her breasts, stroking himself, until he pulled the vibrator away before her orgasm could build. "How'd that feel, baby?"

"Like you're making me suffer," she pouted, and he had the nerve to chuckle against her skin.

"Like you made me suffer yesterday." He plunged into her, hard, and she sucked in a breath as he pulled her legs over his shoulders one at a time. With a sinful smile, he locked her legs against his chest with one arm and pressed the vibrator to the exact spot she'd shown him. Her body jerked, clenching around him, and Josh let out his own strangled curse. "Jesus Christ, I think you were made for me."

A rush swept through her chest, and she closed her eyes. "Yes."

He unmoored her. Hard, measured strokes that bottomed out every time he crashed into her. His skin glistened with his exertion, fevered, slick and hot under her hands. The sound of their breaths and their bodies coming together. Time shattered to a halt, and her orgasm wound until she crashed under him.

"You are a goddess," he said, kissing her ankles, her breasts, her cheeks, as the last of her release swept through her. She gasped as he pulled out, turning her back flush to his chest, and slowly pushed back inside her.

"Josh," she whispered, struggling to stay upright. "I'm—"

"Going to take everything I give you," he finished. "I want you to watch yourself come."

He positioned them in front of her bedroom's floor-length mirror, putting her on full display, bound hands wrapped behind his neck. Once upon a time this would have made her shy, conscious of jiggles and stretch marks. But he made her feel worshipped, and she revelled in him seeing all of her.

One hand snaked around her waist, palming a breast and squeezing her nipple, the other hand bringing the vibrator back to her centre. She cried out, almost in agony, but he resumed his work, and she felt the flutters begin again.

"Look at you. So beautiful," he growled in her ear, until she came one last time, limp and spent. He pushed her face down, burying himself, driving her into the bed until he unravelled over her.

His gasping breaths warmed the nape of her neck, his heart-beat pounding against her back as he let loose a quiet rush of obscenities. Her skin, her hair, her softness. How she smelled spicy and sweet. How he wanted to stay inside her forever.

All too soon, he pushed onto his elbows, withdrawing from her. He ran a hand over her hips, down her thighs and back up, before rolling her onto her back to bury his face in her cleavage.

"Mmphl," he said, and Cass giggled.

"I'd agree, but I have no idea what you said."

"I don't know how I'm supposed to do anything else ever again." He tugged at the scarf, freeing her hands, and the silk fluttered to her bed. His kissed where the scarf had bound her. "Told you I would unwrap you like a present."

She fingered the beautiful silk. "So, that's why you bought this?"

"No, but you inspired me."

She let her fingers sweep over the sharp blade of his cheek-bones, the angle of his jaw, the sweet dimples, and squirmed with pleasure. His fierce attack tamed; the edges worn down. It felt like he was about to purr.

He consumed all her senses, too. Golden. Warm. Citrusy. Salty. Firm. Urgent. She wanted to be consumed by him. Then the dark, sated expression on his face faded, and he leaned in until his lips met hers.

It wasn't their first kiss, his mouth whispering over hers, their tongues tasting each other. But this was different. Softer. Slower. The weight of his body pressed her into the mattress. His teeth tugged at her lower lip, loosening a sigh that he covered with his mouth. Her hands followed the hard muscles coiled on his back, feeling the shiver of his skin match the frenetic butterflies in her chest.

It wasn't their first kiss, but no other kiss had divided her life into Before and After.

He drew back far enough to focus his gaze on her widened eyes, and his Adam's apple bobbed as he swallowed hard. "Be right back, beautiful."

He disappeared from her room before she was fully aware of what was happening. Cass blinked as she heard the water running in the bathroom, and moments later he returned, his sweatpants back on and a warm cloth in his hand.

"Want to finish the movie?" he asked, pulling on his tee shirt, grinning as his head popped out the neck hole. "I could eat more. I'm starving."

What just happened? She thought … there had been something. A moment.

A moment that had already passed. Cass stared at the cloth he held out to her, already cooling.

"Sure."

CHAPTER TWENTY-FOUR

JOSH

FOR THE SECOND MORNING IN A ROW, CASSIDY ST. CLAIRE WAS THE first thing he saw when he opened his eyes, and she was so beautiful he couldn't breathe.

She was a work of art. A Botticellian beauty painted in watercolour, all curves and softness pressed against his hard, lean edges, a secret garden of jasmine and sleepy sweat clouding his thoughts. The personification of plenty, and still, he'd never get enough of her. He wanted to tattoo each tendril of her dark curls onto his chest and permanently imprint her on his body.

He stroked her hair back from her face. "What have you done to me?" he whispered into her temple, like she would answer him in her sleep, and when she didn't, he was left to wrestle with his raging thoughts.

On one side, something had awakened in him. She shone a light and saw him. *Him*, not a version of what was expected. Who challenged him and shared his values and understood what he was about and what he wanted.

On the other side, his brain ordered his heart to stop before it went any further.

The second side was losing. Had lost.

Because he'd fallen in love with her. This beautiful ray of sunshine had claimed his heart.

It was going to end before it began.

It had been a punch to the gut when she had said she was preparing for him to leave. Not because she was wrong, but because she was right. Their time was running out.

Focus on the time you have with her. It was all he could do. He leaned in to kiss the space between her brows and quietly snuck out of bed.

Thin winter sun snuck through the cracks in the curtains, sending pale blue shadows across the cluttered countertops. He shoved aside the feeling that he was invading her cupboards, even though she'd given him explicit instructions to not wake her up for his caffeine fix after showing him where everything was.

Their mugs from yesterday—her extra tall mug with *Aunties let you get away with more* and his hand-painted neon monstrosity —were upside down in the drying rack beside the sink. He snickered as he pulled them out and felt an unexpected pang at *their mugs.* He set the coffee to brew and turned to his phone to flick through the messages that came in overnight.

A handful of group spam texts with the generic *Merry Christmas,* his dad, and ones from old hookups were ignored as he went straight to the creative team group text that had exploded.

STEPHEN

Merry Christmas!

u ready for next week?

Then

We have a problem

hey call me back

dude call me

TERRY

I'm on my way to set.

Recalling the team now.

A bucket of ice water doused his insides, and Josh braced himself as he dialled. "Yo."

Stephen's voice came through a Bluetooth, road noises punctuating the background. "It's not an emergency yet, but we need you on set now."

"What happened?"

"Word is union might strike and we need to wrap before they go out for who knows how long."

How was that not an emergency? It was the day after Christmas. Last time he checked, that was a stat holiday. That meant union wages would be astronomical. If they could get everyone back on set.

Shit. Josh would never ask his crew to cross picket lines. That meant they had to hustle even more than usual to finish principal photography. No delays. No mistakes.

No distractions.

A chill crept over his bare shoulders as he stared at the open bedroom door. "On it."

Stephen continued rapid fire, "Terry has it under control and is working all the coordination. Brynne and Dawson are already on their way back. We'll be ready for prep tonight."

Anxiety needled his chest as Stephen rattled off the remaining instructions. Cass shuffled out of the bedroom with the duvet wrapped around her body and her phone in her hand, holding up the screen and giving a chagrined smile.

Cass yawned widely and rubbed the heel of her palm against her cheekbone. "Want to drive in together?" she asked, gliding over to the counter.

His chest hollowed at the sight of her messy curls and sleepy eyes. They should have had days together before the frenzy of filming picked back up. Space to breathe before the mad rush to the end.

He wanted to bury himself in her. To put his mouth on her smile and steal her breath, the soft sighs she made when he ground his hips against her. To hide with her, here, to order takeout and not leave her apartment until the new year.

He thought they'd have more time.

As soon as filming wrapped, he'd be going home. And she'd be here. Looking heartbreakingly beautiful and over a thousand kilometers away from him.

Josh stared at the fifty-eight second call log, grinding his teeth together as the screen went dark. Less than a minute to change everything. She wasn't due on set until the afternoon. Technically neither was he, but the longer he stayed with her today, the harder it would be to pull away.

"No. I'll go in alone."

"Okay, do you want me to drive you to your place?"

"I'll order an Uber."

The last of her sleep faded from her eyes. "Oh." Cass said in a voice just a breath above a whisper. "Right."

His things were scooped up in minutes. He spent extra time brushing his teeth to stretch out the time before his ride arrived. His dentist would be so pleased. With his pyjamas, slippers, and toiletries shoved in his bag, he hoisted it over his shoulder as he watched the avatar on the Uber tick closer.

The coffee pot gurgled the last sputters into the carafe, and Cass dithered, slightly blocking the front door. "You have time for a cup," she offered.

It wasn't about the ride or coffee. It was written all over her face. Lips parted, eyes wide as she wavered back and forth on her feet. Closer, farther.

He wanted to meet her forwards lean and catch her mouth. To push the duvet from her shoulders and take her on the floor. Now. Put his tongue on her breasts and his hand between her thighs, then drive his cock into her until she choked out his name.

Then curl up with her on her couch. Listen to her recite her favourite fan theories. Leaf through the sketchbook she'd left open on the coffee table. Go to sleep with her and wake up beside her every morning.

There wasn't enough time for any of it.

He tightened his hand on his bag. "I'll grab a coffee on the way. I'm going to wait downstairs."

"Of course." Her voice was sweet as toffee and just as brittle, curls bobbing around her cheeks as she busied herself with her own cup, sloshing creamer onto the counter.

He should go. Walk out that front door now and wait downstairs. Not turn back. He reached for the handle, but his body wouldn't let him go through.

Fuck it.

He grabbed her chin and forced her lips to his. Her mouth opened, and a hush of air escaped that he claimed as his own. He crushed her to his torso, hard, her hands sliding up the back of his shirt as she submitted to his attack. Hard, needy.

She was a drug, his drug, intoxicating, consuming, a craving he couldn't sate. A shot straight into his veins. A guttural noise broke from his throat, and he bit her lip, pinning her to the wall as his heart threatened to beat right out of his chest.

Don't tell her you love her right before you leave her, asshole.

"I'll see you on set later," he said, forehead resting on hers, before dropping his mouth to her neck for a last bite. Right where someone would see it. Keep them the fuck away from her. Not like they would be within a thousand kilometers of each other by the end of the month for it to matter.

She pulled back to look at him with bright eyes, slightly breathless, and nodded. "Later."

He dove in for one more kiss before pulling himself away. "Later," he confirmed.

He didn't get her alone for a week.

CHAPTER TWENTY-FIVE

CASS

Good night, Lucky Charms

Good morning, beautiful

> Sorry I missed your text I was already asleep

> Think I can see you tonight?

I want nothing more than that, but it's going to
be another late one

I just wanted to say good night

Good morning

I remember my bed being more comfortable
than this

Hmmm, missing something?

You

:)

I'll try and find you before you leave set tonight

Good morning, LC

Couldn't find you during breaks in shooting today

Today's been crazy

Dawson had another wardrobe malfunction

I bet he did

What's with the grumpy face?

Sitting across from you and not being able to touch you is killing me

I want to run my tongue over your pussy until you make those sexy little whimpers

I don't whimper!

You do

Every time you come

I'm hard just thinking about it

omg

Can't wait to put you on your hands and knees and fuck you until you're begging for it, then make you suck my cock so you see how good you taste

CAN STEPHEN READ THIS OVER YOUR SHOULDER?

Do you have any idea how gorgeous you are when you get embarrassed?

I want to come on your tits again

I know what we're doing tonight :)

Fuuuuuuck. Can't

Late shoot. Not sure when we'll wrap

I guess Chauncy will keep me company

Send pic

———

Fucking hell

For the love of god don't ask me to delete this

———

I miss seeing your face in the morning

Me too

I have ten minutes

Can I see you?

Can't

On set B all day :(

Good morning

Good night, Lucky Charms

CHAPTER TWENTY-SIX

JOSH

WITH THE TIME CRUNCH TICKING OVER THEIR HEADS LIKE A NUCLEAR countdown, *Sirius Darker* careened to the finish line on greased rails. Everything worked. What didn't work got fixed. And what didn't get fixed was brow-beaten into submission by the crew.

Cass had been right. Waiting until Brynne and Dawson knew each other better made all the difference in the final shots. Brynne wore despair that had half the crew in tears, and Dawson a desperate stoicism that wrecked the other half.

Everyone, from the caterers to the sound techs, sobbed.

Except for Josh. He was ecstatic.

They got it. They fucking got it. It was perfect. Now all that was left was a couple of days to film B-roll, and they were done. They might not even need to do reshoots.

He knew he should be celebrating with Melanie, or Brynne and Dawson. Or any number of other people.

They could all go fuck themselves.

He wanted her voice in his ear. Her soft skin under his hands, against his body. Those hazel eyes looking straight past every barrier he put between them. She was the only one he wanted.

His eyes found her from across the set, smiling at whatever

Dawson was saying to her. He ignored the stab of jealousy that flared up and stepped between them.

"Cass, I need you," he said, and Dawson's smile slipped a fraction as he backed away.

Cass eyed him hungrily, following at a trot as he dragged her away by the hand.

Not a trailer. Too cold. Not wardrobe. Crawling with PAs. Fuck.

His office.

Her fingers were in his hair before he could slam the door shut behind them. The desk's legs screeched across the linoleum as he pushed her into it, scattering a sheaf of paper and knocking a cup of pens to the floor. He wrenched her jacket down her shoulders, seating himself between her thighs, and pulled behind her knees until she fit against him. Her sweet scent floated around him, and he descended on her.

The kiss was punishing. Not for her, but for him. A reminder that he couldn't stay away, no matter how hard he tried. It was lunacy to think he could shut off what he felt for her, and he sucked the sigh that escaped her lips into his lungs like the breath of life.

"Haven't seen you all week," she panted, kissing his throat as she fumbled with the fly of his jeans.

"Talk later." Why did this woman never wear skirts? He yanked her forward and off the desk. "Bend over, Charms."

"Josh, we haven't—"

Fine, a little bit of talking now. He gripped her chin and pinned his thumb over her lips, silencing her. "I haven't been inside you for days. You know what to say if you want me to stop. So unless you've had enough, you're going to open your legs wide and show me how bad that pussy wants it. Right now."

For a half second, he didn't know what she was going to do. If she would take her hands off him and push him away. Then Cass's breath hitched in her throat, and she obeyed, eyes wide and hands splayed on the desk. He worked her pants down and groaned as he swiped his palms over the smooth curves of her hips.

Fuck him. The shimmery red fabric of her thong disappeared between her ass cheeks, and he thumbed it to the side to let his fingers stroke her pussy. He dropped to his knees and parted her folds with his tongue.

Days apart, and it felt like years. She tasted like ambrosia.

"Someone could come in," she said, voice husky, even as she rocked her hips back into his face.

"Any minute now." He bit the crease of her thigh. "They're probably looking for us."

She clenched around his fingers and cried as he removed his tongue from her slick centre. He had to be inside her. Make her come on his cock, not his tongue. He pushed her over the desk until her chest flattened along its top, her ribs heaving as she drew ragged breaths. He fumbled in his pocket one-handed, ripping open a condom package with his teeth. Seconds later, he thrust into her hard enough his eyes rolled back in his head.

Goddamn. How was he going to not have her? To fly home and leave her?

Don't think about that. He curled over her back and thrust into her again.

"You know what would happen if someone came in right now? They'd see you taking every inch of me. They'd know exactly who you belong to."

Me. You belong to me.

He released the grip he had on her hair and wrapped his palm over her mouth, wrenching her upright and spinning her to face the door. He worked his other hand over her clit, feeling where he filled her as she shuddered with his every thrust. She was coming apart around him already, her cries muffled against his palm.

The thought of someone catching them sent her right to the edge. He fucking loved it.

"You'd like that, wouldn't you? Someone watching me fuck you?"

A quick knock on the door made her jerk against him, and a flicker of recognition was gone before it could register. He clutched her closer. "If you make any noise, they'll know we're in here. Then everyone would know how pretty you are when you come for me."

Her breath sucked at his fingers still covering her mouth, and he realized that was exactly what she wanted. For everyone to know what she did to him. The thought nearly made him come.

"I'll do it. I'll fuck you so hard you can't keep quiet." He urged himself deeper, each thrust harder than the last, until a whimper warmed his palm, her knees gave out, and she clenched around his cock like a vice.

The last of his barriers broke. He doubled his grip as he bit down on her neck as he spilled himself into the condom, rocking into her until the rapping on the door stopped.

Cass collapsed against his chest, and he chased his breath, releasing his grip on her mouth to hold her up by her shoulders. Fuck, they were too good together. One hand in her hair, he pulled her head back so he could claim her mouth, the other gripping her hip as he was buried deep in the woman he loved.

Love. How had he ever thought he could pretend otherwise? She was perfect. Gorgeous and playful and creative. Sweet and filthy and everything he never knew he needed. His Lucky Charm. His Cass.

Fuck what he was supposed to do. He'd do whatever it took to keep her with him. He just had to figure out how.

CHAPTER TWENTY-SEVEN

CASS

"Fuck, Cass." He inhaled deeply, his nose buried in her hair, before sighing it out with a groan. "I missed you."

Her shirt was rucked up over her boobs, her bra half pulled off, and pants stuck around her upper thighs in Josh's frenzied rush to disrobe her. The room's heating shut off, and the dull hum cut out abruptly, leaving the sound of their jagged breath. She leaned back against his chest, his heartbeat still hammering, and she let out a breathy giggle. "You've seen me every day this week."

One week on opposite sides of the set, barely enough time to trade glances. One time, she passed behind him while he talked to the crew, close enough to trail her fingertips over his back, and he stopped speaking midsentence. She thought her hand would catch fire.

Her hair tangled in crazy coils where his cheek had pressed into the side of her head as he'd thrust against her. She shuffled her shirt down and tried to reposition her bra to do its job again.

Josh swatted at her hands and took a handful of her boob in a nearly gentle grip. "Don't put them away yet. Let me look at you a minute longer," he murmured, and she could feel his smile pressing against her hair.

"The pictures I sent weren't enough? I thought you liked them!"

"I fucking loved them, but nothing compares to having my hands on you."

"As much as I agree, you have no idea how uncomfortable it is to have your boobs half hanging out of a bra," she chided, squirming pleasantly against him until he released her with a petulant groan.

With a final squeeze, he eased himself from her, dropping a kiss on her neck. Her butt found the edge of the desk behind her, the laminate finish cool against her skin. She shimmied her pants up, her underwear a mess after being pushed aside instead of removed.

Not like she had wanted him to take the time. The stolen quickie was so much hotter than a sedate and methodical removal of clothing. All of said clothing now hopelessly dishevelled. At least the day was almost over, and she could go home to shower. Maybe he'd come with her. Her heart fluttered as she adjusted her shirt.

Josh turned away to pull off the condom and wrapped it in tissue, tossing it in the bin. With a quick zip of his fly and a hand through his hair, he looked perfectly put-back together.

Honestly. She scanned the room for a reflective surface. "Do I look okay?"

He ran his tongue over his teeth and gave her a wicked grin that popped his dimples. "You look like I just fucked you over a desk, Lucky Charms."

Well, that was just ducky. She clicked her tongue, hiding her grin. "Will you help me straighten up? Not all of us have well-behaved hair like you."

"I like that your hair isn't perfectly behaved. Almost as badly behaved as you, naughty girl," he said, coiling a strand around his fingers. His smile grew more wicked, and he left a sucking kiss on her neck hard enough to leave a mark before she could push him away. "The minute you leave, everyone is going to know exactly what we were doing in here."

Screwing each other's brains out as soon as we had the chance. All while the crew was probably looking for them—him—for any number of things to wrap filming. Only time would take care of her swollen lips and flushed cheeks, but as soon as they stepped out of his office, her post-orgasm glow would be broadcast across the set. Heat flooded her body. "I can't believe we just did that."

"I can. I've been thinking about this all week." He sat on the edge of the desk, where he'd bent her over minutes ago, and tugged at her until she was back in his embrace. With the frenzy of sex behind them, he trailed soft kisses over her jaw and slid his hands up the back of her shirt. "Let's stay here a few minutes longer. Let people forget they saw us come in here."

Maybe he didn't want people to know they'd been together. They weren't together. Not in that way.

Or were they? After spending Christmas together, all the messages they had sent in the week since, perhaps he wanted to see if long distance would work? Now, with his hands all over her and the bulge in his pants pressing against her hip, they existed in a limbo where nothing was said and nothing was defined.

"Josh," she said, tilting her head to give him better access to her neck. "We should talk."

"We really should." He slid his hand down her back and squeezed her butt. "Later."

God, he'd never let her escape. But why escape, when the man she had fallen in love with was telling her how much he wanted her, and how beautiful she was? When the first chance he had, he spent time with her, and no one else.

Her thighs still throbbed with the feel of him, but she would take as much of him as she could.

"Promise we'll talk later?"

He licked her pulse point. "Promise."

Later, she thought, and opened her mouth to his and let herself fall into his kiss.

A quick succession of knocks broke the air, and the door burst open.

So much for no one finding out, she thought with a sheepish giggle, but Josh froze against her.

A tiny woman Cass didn't recognize stood open-mouthed, hand still on the doorknob. She wasn't part of the crew. Her pants and a blazer were from a designer that Cass never would have been able to afford, her black hair hanging in a crisp curtain to her collarbones. Her oval face had a pinched look that was oddly blank.

Cass wasn't surprised at her confusion—the set was massive —but she was surprised to see the strange woman milling about on premises. Josh had ordered a closed set for their final scenes after they'd caught paparazzi sneaking in again weeks ago.

But this woman didn't look like a paparazzo. She looked like money. Maybe she was an out-of-town producer that Melanie had invited for the last day of shooting. Cass tried to disentangle herself to smooth a rogue curl out of her eyes, but Josh locked his arms around her. For all his dirty talk of having people walk in on them, he seemed much less cool with the reality of it actually happening than she was.

At least all their clothes were in the right spots. Mostly.

Cass gave the woman a grin and tried unsuccessfully to squirm out of Josh's grip. "Um, this is awkward."

"It certainly is," the woman replied in a tight voice.

"Are you lost?" Cass squirmed again. "Looking for someone?"

The woman closed her mouth with a snap, then gave a brisk nod. "Yes," she said, not taking her eyes off Josh. "My husband."

"Oh, sure," Cass said, and tried to step back again. Josh still hadn't released her, and she clicked her tongue at him with a smile. "If you let me go, I can help her find him."

"Actually," the woman said, her pallor rapidly being replaced by a flush racing up her neck, "I just did."

———

It didn't sink in. Not at first. The word rattled around her brain. A key to figuring out something important, like a cipher to a code.

Cass took a step back, fighting against the cage of Josh's arms. Something dark opened up in front of her as it registered. Then, the tumblers of a lock fell into place, the door opened, and her heart broke free from her chest to shatter at her feet.

Her *husband*.

Josh was married.

She'd known him for months and he'd never said. All the times they had been together. As coworkers. As friends.

As lovers. A rush filled her ears and she made herself breathe so she didn't collapse, and the realization sunk in.

Why would he have said anything? He'd never intended for her to be anything more than casual. They lived in different cities. There was no reason to assume they'd ever see each other again once the film wrapped.

Because he'd be going home to his wife.

"Cass." His voice wasn't even a whisper. "It's not what it looks like."

She stared blankly at the floor, as if she could see the broken pieces of her heart scattered there. The warmth of where his chest had pressed against her back still lingered. One hand covering her cries as he'd driven himself inside her, his other hand working where they joined as she came apart underneath him. Minutes ago.

Her centre still ached from him being inside her, and Cass was face-to-face with his wife.

"A PA said she'd thought I could find you here," the woman said, speaking directly to Josh like Cass was a piece of furniture.

Her voice sounded like it was coming from across an ocean. Cass didn't know if her voice sounded far away because the woman was in shock, or if she was. "No one answered the first time I knocked."

As he whispered in her ear that they were too good together, his wife was knocking on the other side of the door. She'd whimpered against him just days ago, promising him all week no one else would touch her. That she was his. Only his. He could have all of her.

And now his wife was looking at her, with his hand still up the back of her shirt, her lipstick staining his mouth, the scent of their sex in the air.

"Oh," Cass whispered. "I didn't know. I'm so sorry. Please forgive me."

Each of her muted footfalls felt like they would sink into the floor, like wading through a bog. Cass fought through the murk and picked up her stride, hoping the air would dry her tears before they fell. She couldn't get the image out of her mind. His wife—his *wife*—looking at him with dawning horror, her dark eyes widening as she registered the scene in front of her.

She didn't know where to go. She looked blindly around the set. Bex running, Terry smiling. Stephen and Dawson huddling in front of the director's screen. Stephen's head popped up, brows knitting together in confusion, eyes darting from her to the footsteps coming down the hall behind her.

Had Stephen known? Of course he would have. They were best friends. And he hadn't said anything to her. A spear of betrayal sliced through her core. All she could hope was that she wouldn't stumble and bring any attention to herself.

She heard the squeak of his sneakers behind her before his fingers circled her wrist.

"Cass." His voice, more than his touch, halted her flight, and his words spilled out in a low rush. "I can explain."

Her feet stalled under her, breaths still coming in shallow gasps. She wanted to believe whatever he'd say, whatever honeyed words would flow from his mouth. But he'd just left his wife standing on the other side of the building. The wife he'd kept from her for the months they'd known each other.

Or thought she'd known him.

And what was there to explain? He was married. That was all the explanation needed.

"Please don't touch me."

"This isn't what it looks like."

"Isn't it? Because it sure looks like I just met your wife." A choked laugh erupted from her throat that threatened to turn into a sob, and she pressed her lips together and turned away.

"It's not like that. I didn't want to tell you because—"

"Then I wouldn't sleep with you."

Guilt flickered across his features. "That's not it," he said in a low, urgent voice.

She gulped a sharp breath and struggled to free her arm from his grasp. "I don't know you at all. I thought … I don't know what I thought. What else haven't you told me?"

He pressed his lips together, and what was left of her heart ripped at the seams.

"Cass," he tried again, his hand still securely on her wrist, "you need to listen to me."

Anything he said would be the things he'd think she wanted to hear. "Actually, I don't think I do."

"Give me a chance—"

"Enough."

Josh stalled, and dropped his hand to his side.

Her eyes burned, and the empty ache in her chest crowded her throat. She couldn't listen to this. Not now. Not from someone who didn't respect her enough to tell her something so important.

Cass wiped her hands over dry cheeks and stared at the rigging over his shoulder, avoiding his eyes.

"I need time to think. Please leave me alone."

He didn't follow her as she walked away.

Libby poured another inch of the flat faux Champagne into the plastic tumbler. An empty bottle of cheap red blend sat beside the remains of a carton of ice cream, upturned in the kitchen sink.

Sirius Darker had wrapped. The proudest she'd ever been of her work, and instead of joining in celebrations with the crew, she'd slunk out at the end of the day without a word. Like she was the one who had done something wrong. Libby had stayed with the crew a short while, showing up less than an hour later at Cass's door with sugar, alcohol, and a shoulder she was prepared to get wet.

Ice cream and wine. The perfect pairing for heartache. A terrible pairing for gastrointestinal distress. The ice cream was already curdling in her stomach as Cass swigged from the bottle.

Josh had blown up her phone the minute she'd left set. He'd buzzed her apartment from downstairs minutes after Libby had arrived. He hadn't tried to sneak up, or at least he'd been unsuccessful, and the buzzing had stopped after an hour.

"You know," Cass slurred, "last time I got this drunk, it was after that jerk who bailed after five minutes on that stupid date. Josh was the first person I called."

He'd said she was beautiful. He'd said he'd write sonnets about kissing her.

He'd said a lot of things. But not that he was married.

She was so stupid.

Libby's brows threaded together. "Why didn't you call me instead that night?"

"You were with Stephen." Cass shrugged weakly. "I didn't want to take you from him. You have other priorities, and I need to get used to you not always being there for me."

"I would have come to get you. Just because Stephen and I are together again doesn't mean you aren't important to me."

But that's what happened. Friends partnered off. Weekly brunches became monthly. Girls' nights out became fewer and further between. Libby's biological clock was ticking like a time bomb, and Stephen was more than ready to put a baby in her. Soon, there would be even less Libby to go around.

It didn't matter anymore.

Libby tugged the bottle out of Cass's arms and put it out of reach. She chewed her lip and said in a low voice. "As much as it pains me to say this, Stephen thinks you should talk to him."

Cass whipped her head up and the room caught up a half second later. Her stomach roiled, and it wasn't entirely from the wine. "Stephen knew. And he didn't say anything. Why should I listen to him? Or Josh, for that matter? So he can tell me about his wedding day?" A fresh wave of pain washed over her, and she pressed her hand to her mouth to stifle a sob.

"I don't think he did know. Stephen didn't tell me much. Just that you should hear Josh out. Stephen wouldn't do anything to purposefully hurt you, and not only because he knows I'd disembowel him if he did."

"What can he possibly say that will make this better?"

"I don't know if it will make anything better, but I know you love him, and you deserve answers, if not peace."

The spot in her chest ached. She wanted nothing more to believe him. And Libby, who took a lot more convincing than she did, was saying she should listen.

She didn't know if she was a sucker for punishment or a hopeless romantic. If her track record was anything to go by, this wasn't going to go well. With a tired resignation, she pulled out her phone.

Okay, I'll listen

"We've been separated for almost three years."

Against her better judgement, she agreed to meet him. Somewhere public. Coffee. Before he had to meet with producers and Melanie, and who knew who else, to start on post-production. In one week, Cass wouldn't need to be at those meetings anymore. Her job would be done. There'd be no reason to see him anymore.

One coffee. She could give him fifteen minutes today.

Thirty, tops.

Still can't say no.

The midmorning sun diffused through the low overcast and gauzy curtains to cover the busy café with a grey tinge. The chair's uneven wooden legs struck the floor like a tap dancer as she shifted from side to side. She swirled the contents of her oversized mug, unable to convince herself to take a sip.

Josh sat across from her, eyes bloodshot and smudged purple, his wet jacket slung over the back of his chair. He hadn't touched his coffee, his posture mirroring hers, hunched over as if to position himself closer to her. A few stray drops of melted snow hung in his hair like jewels, and she wanted to run her fingers through the jet strands. Even now, he looked devastatingly handsome.

Operative word: *devastating*. She tore her eyes away and stared into her untouched mocha.

"I haven't lived with her—hell, I've barely been in the same room with her—in all that time. Ask Stephen. I'm trying to get a divorce, but she keeps dragging it out. In every way, except on paper, that marriage has been over for a long time."

Cass tipped her mug from side to side. "Do you know how many women have been told that same story by a married man?"

He gripped the back of his head and tilted back, the golden glow of his skin rendered wan in the flickering lights overhead. "What do you want to know? I'll tell you anything."

Cass's gut squeezed up into her throat and she steeled herself.

Words. They are just words. Believe what he shows you, not what he tells you.

"Do you want to know about my family?" he asked. "My parents are deliriously in love after almost forty years together and my grandparents never forgave my dad for marrying someone they didn't approve of. My sister barely talks to me anymore because my ex is her best friend, and she still hasn't forgiven me for leaving her. We were only married thirteen months before I left."

"You're still married," Cass whispered, lifting her head to meet his eyes, and his face twisted with guilt.

"I don't want to be. We didn't know anything about each other before we … before. We were too young. She had a crush on her best friend's older brother and I knew she was the type of woman that would make my grandparents happy. I was right. They loved her.

"They were disappointed that I'd majored in film in university but were fine once I was in law. I tried to convince myself that I only did all that because it would make me a better orator if I'd specialized in litigation. Even then, I knew I was kidding myself."

She couldn't imagine him doing anything other than what he was doing. She could almost picture him, dead-eyed behind a computer screen, going through the motions of whatever lawyers did, instead of alive and vibrant on set. Full of life and radiating energy, whether he was swearing at himself or agonizing over camera placement. His eyes ablaze when they got the shot exactly right. Like yesterday, when they'd nailed the final scene. Then dragged her away to put his stamp all over her.

And minutes later, meeting his wife. The smile wilted on her face before it bloomed.

She forced her voice to stay level. "Why did you leave?"

His fingers flexed against the mug, the cords in his neck standing out. "Law is a punishing profession. Self-destruction is the norm.

Drinking. Drugs. Half the guys would do lines of coke in the bathroom at lunch. You had to if you wanted to keep up. It wasn't even a secret. Then I'd get home and drink to shut down. Every morning, I told myself I just needed to get through the next day. Then the next. Every day, I went through the motions." He took a deep breath. "Then on our first anniversary, she said it was time to have kids.

"Until then, I felt like I could numb myself and push through. But I couldn't do that. I left and got so drunk that night the bartender had to dig through my pockets to find my business cards and called my firm. The admin assistant had to track down Vivian to pick me up. She thought I was having a last hurrah and celebrating before we started trying for a baby. Really, what I was trying to do was convince myself I could do one more thing that was expected of me.

"I couldn't tell her what I wanted, or what I didn't want. She thought she was marrying the fantasy of the best friend's big brother, and I thought I was fixing my father's mistake of not marrying a nice girl who didn't swear at the family dinner table. Then I couldn't do any of it anymore. I couldn't stand the thought of taking over my father's law practice. I couldn't give Vivian what she wanted. Everything else fell apart around me."

The damp breeze that flowed over her every time the coffee shop's door opened left a chill that sunk into her bones. She sloshed the lukewarm contents up the sides of the cup, debating whether to ask another question she didn't know if she'd believe the answer to. "Why aren't you divorced yet?"

"She won't sign. I keep trying to negotiate the terms, but ..." he said after a moment, and Cass was even more sure he was feeding her a line.

"You're a lawyer. Why didn't you have a prenup?"

"I have asked myself that question a thousand times." He shrugged uncomfortably. "Her family was adamantly against it. We didn't have assets yet. I wasn't thinking."

The way he'd held her close when Vivian had walked into

the room. He wouldn't let her go. Like he had wanted Vivian to see them embracing. Like it would get him what he'd finally wanted. A horrible thought tried to take root.

"Did you …" She paused to swallow the bile that rose in her throat. "Did you want her to see us together? Did you plan that, so she would finally sign?"

"No! I mean, yes. I didn't plan anything. I didn't not want her to see us. I didn't want her to … fuck." Josh flexed his hands. "I had no idea she was in town. We've had completely separate lives for years. I told her I wanted to move on."

"And did you ever tell her when you did?"

He shifted in his chair. "It seemed unnecessarily cruel."

"And this isn't?" she asked, disbelief gilding her voice.

"Cass …"

"I never asked you for anything. But I expected honesty from you. I thought you were my friend, at least. I thought you cared for me."

"I do care for you." He clenched his fist and pressed it into his jaw like he could knock himself out in slow motion.

She held up her hand. All the time they'd been together. All the times he could have said that he felt anything for her. She'd never been anything more than a place to bury his dick while he was in town.

"Baby—"

A sharp stab of laughter sliced her throat. That was it. She was just some nameless hookup he could call *baby* and let his dimples and charm and sweet words erase all the anguish he put her through. She'd let her idiot heart trick her into thinking this time was different. That *he* was different.

If it didn't hurt so much, it would have been funny. Cass tilted her head back and blinked rapidly at the ceiling.

"I'm so stupid," she said in a hollow voice, her breath scratching her lungs like sandpaper. "I never learn."

Josh's brows knit together. "No, Charms." He reached out for her hands, and she snatched them away to secure them under her crossed arms.

The crazy part was that his story made sense. It fit who he was. The person who she had worked side by side with for months. A laugh escaped her in a surprised titter, and she smiled at him with bright eyes. "I believe you. I have no reason to, but I believe you."

Josh's face cleared. "Oh, thank god. Cass—"

"But it doesn't matter," she finished. "You lied to me."

The words slid between them like a barrier.

"I never lied," he insisted. "Not to you. Not once."

"Lied by omission, then."

"Cass—"

"How dare you?" She felt her eyes brimming and stretched them wide so the tears wouldn't fall. "You knew exactly what you were doing. Making me hope that you wanted me that way, after everything you watched me go through. You knew I was trying to get over someone who treated me like this. You said you would help me, then you went and did the same thing as the rest of them."

"I didn't—"

"But you did." She might as well have handed him the rule book for how well he maneuvered her. For the first time, anger flared in her chest. "Are you the final boss? If I can get over the ultimate player, then I finally win the game?"

"No, I—" Josh bit off his words and curled his hands into fists. "I never played you."

"Could have fooled me. Oh, wait. You did."

"No, Cass …"

"Looks like I still can't spot them until it's too late. Maybe I really did need all thirty dates to learn. I should pick that back up."

"Don't do this," he whispered.

"Am I allowed to swipe for myself yet, or are you still in charge of my love life?"

His face contorted in anguish as he pressed his lips together. God, even now she wanted to take his face in her hands, to kiss away the pain in his eyes, and she choked back a twinge in her throat.

"No, you're right." She pulled her phone out of her purse. "I've graduated to doing that for myself. What do you think? I bet I can knock out a few dates this week if I start swiping right now—"

"I love you." His hand pinned hers to the table. "I love you."

The words doused the anger that had flared in her, and she wished she didn't want to believe another lie. To let the words wrap around her like a caress.

He's only telling me what I need to hear to get me to stay. No matter how much I want to hear it. She bit down on her bottom lip to stop it from trembling.

"Of course, you're saying this now," she said when she hoped her voice would be steady. "How am I supposed to believe you? You're saying you love me, but you've done nothing to show me. You don't respect me. You've hidden yourself completely from me."

"That's not what ..." he stalled and held her gaze. "I didn't think this would happen. I didn't think *you* would happen. You're always there. When I wake up. When I close my eyes. You're *all* I think about."

Words. Anyone could say words. Even when the words were perfect. "That's not enough for me."

All the months they had been together, getting closer, dancing around the feeling been building between them. Months fooling herself into thinking this was something more than every other pathetic so-called relationship she'd put herself through.

Cass shrugged, and the edges of her vision blurred. "I love you, too. I can't help it. I don't even know you and I still love you. But if you really loved me, you wouldn't be treating me like I'm just another hookup."

"You're not. You are everything. All that matters to me."

"You are married. So many times you could have told me. All that time we were together over Christmas. Everything we talked about and this never came up? Back when those paparazzi photos of me and Dawson were coming out, you said you would tell me things that I should know about. You didn't think I should know about this?"

"I ... tell me what to do. I'll do it. Anything," he pleaded. "What do I need to do?"

She dug the heels of her palms into her eye sockets. "I'm not doing that emotional labour for you. You need to figure that out. But right now, being this close to you hurts too much. So please, I'm asking you to leave me alone."

Cass pushed back from the table with shaking hands and didn't look back. Everything ached. Exhaustion over having to walk away from yet another man who couldn't love her how she needed pressed on her lungs. The jagged edges of what remained of her heart scraped inside her breastbone, a thousand cuts carving her from the inside out.

But it hurt less than being lied to.

And one day, it might hurt even less.

And one day, if she was really lucky, she might not feel anything at all.

CHAPTER TWENTY-EIGHT

JOSH

"No shit, she's not talking to you," Stephen said, yanking his luggage from the carousel. "I wouldn't if I were her, either."

Josh swiped through the messages coming in after turning off airplane mode. Ping after ping, but nothing from her. Why would that change now? She hadn't texted him in weeks. He swallowed the hollowness that had taken up residence in his chest and ordered a taxi.

With how everything had been going, he wouldn't be surprised if the cab was rear-ended on the way to Melanie's office. That asshole Murphy needed to change his law.

A trailer of props scheduled to return to Vancouver was stuck due to union negotiations. A master hard drive with ten minutes of final footage was gone. Just, gone. Two grips had come down with food poisoning after an incorrectly labelled tray of sandwiches was left out for three days. At least they were merely projectile vomiting and not anaphylactic. The crew had given him a berth wide enough to maneuver a tanker, partially due to the fact that Josh's preferred communication style had reverted to reaching triple decibels.

None of that mattered.

Cass had been the last to enter a room and the first to leave, head tucked, her lyrical laughter gone silent. He gave her as much space as he could, only asking her questions about the film, and only when he couldn't ask through someone else. She replied, but nothing more than the barest possible answer with her eyeline somewhere over his shoulder. Once, a fleeting second, she met his eyes, and the hurt painted across her features in bold strokes carved his soul out.

"Cass," he had pleaded when he finally broke. "It's been days. Please talk to me."

She'd kept her eyes on the samples she carefully returned to their racks. "What has changed?" Her voice was a whisper. From a desire to be discreet, or that he'd caused her to lose her voice, he didn't want to know the answer. He gripped the sleeves of his jacket to keep himself from reaching for her and watched her fade from the room.

Every night he had sat in his rental, watching the calendar flick over to the day he'd leave. Watching his phone for a call or text from Cass that never came.

Now, this.

The retired rail executive's sprawling corner office Melanie took over the week after she became Mrs. Westwood held the original mid-century modern decor intact. It also held Josh's favourite view in the entire world. Overlooking Stanley Park, with the viridian tips of the Lion's Gate Bridge just visible over the towering cedars, and the North Shore Mountains disappearing into the low overcast.

He didn't see any of it, storming the perimeter of the office and ignoring Brynne and Dawson's faces on screens.

"How did cameras keep getting on my set?"

A slew of new pap photos flickered across the office's largest monitor: Cass and Dawson everywhere. Cass and Dawson huddling at craft services, grinning over sandwiches. Cass and Dawson laughing outside his trailer, her hands all over his chest, as usual. Cass and Dawson walking across the set, his hand on the small of her back.

Why the fuck were they by his trailer? Was it just a fitting correction? Josh had barely stomached watching Cass with her hands on Dawson to adjust his costume. Why did Dawson have his hand on her? She hadn't said if anything had happened between them. She'd said she didn't think of Dawson that way, in so many words. Or maybe she hadn't told him everything …

No. It was him who didn't tell her everything. She'd been honest with him from the start, opening her heart to him from day one. All the while he'd kept himself from her.

He'd fucked up. Now he was paying for it.

Melanie lounged behind her burnished teak desk with her heels kicked up on the unused writing blotter. "Stop being such a diva," she said blithely, stirring her drink in lazy circles. "You can lock it down as tight as you want, but it always gets out."

He hoped her paper straw dissolved in whatever fancy coffee she'd ordered.

"So, we're not going to control leaks?" Brynne asked.

Melanie peered at her calendar. "No, but we can control the story with any new photos that get out."

Who gave a shit if they controlled leaks now? There was nothing to control. Filming was done. No more chances for opportunistic paps to sneak on set. He was home. Back to his empty condo and list of fuck buddies he had no interest in seeing and an estranged wife he couldn't convince to end their marriage.

"Might not even be an issue. Reshoots will only take a week, max."

Wait. Josh stopped pacing. "What the fuck is wrong with my movie that it needs reshoots?"

"We lost a master file with fifteen minutes of footage. We can't just ask the audience to imagine what that might look like."

Ten minutes of footage, he thought. Saying that out loud wouldn't win him any points at the moment. He clamped his lips shut.

"Plus, test audience responded well to your adaptations, but the female demographic is clamouring for a shirtless scene." Melanie turned to Dawson, whose face sunk. "You can thank every superhero movie ever for setting that standard."

"Didn't know I was signing up for a superhero movie," he mumbled, but put down the doughnut he was eating with a resigned sigh. Brynne looked a combination of sympathetic and gleeful.

Josh swivelled his head from Melanie to Dawson. "We know this is bullshit, right?"

"Yep. You can dry your tears with all the money we'll make from this when it's out."

Fuck. "My movies don't need reshoots," he said stubbornly.

"It's our movie." Melanie stared him down. "And our movie needs reshoots."

A prickle ran over his chest. She was right. He flopped into a nearby chair and glared at the floor. They were going back to Calgary. Because they needed to fix the movie he'd poured everything into. The one that he loved, and the one he'd fucked up.

And he would be close to Cass and not able to touch her.

The phone was going for a trip, whether it was through the window or Melanie's calculating face. Or better yet, Dawson's, so Cass wouldn't have anything to admire. Instead, he said, "I'll pack a bag."

"Great." Melanie clapped her hands. "I want to see those photos you took of Brynne back in October. Second unit wants to see if we can use those for the behind-the-scenes featurette. Terry and Stephen are working on reshoot schedules now."

His chest squeezed. The roll of film still sat in the camera, undeveloped. Brynne's few pictures at the start of the roll. And the remaining shots of Cass at the dance studio.

"Yeah," he said, voice cracking. "I'll send those over."

The tight space of his home darkroom held the familiar, sweet acetic reek of developing chemicals, lit only by the single red bulb glowing overhead. Josh poured the developing solution over the roll, sealed the container, and set the timer. He leaned against his bathroom sink and waited.

When the timer dinged, he took the next step. And the next. Each stage a meditation before the anticipation of seeing the final result. To see if the photos he'd taken were blurry or sharp, framed well or trash. He stared at the container like he could see the film developing through the opaque sides.

Cass had glowed in the dance studio that night. The light had cradled her, shading over her in soft waves to roll over her body in a luminescent caress, glinting off her eyes like fireworks.

No wonder she always looked good. He hadn't known then she'd sewn everything he'd ever seen her wear. How her clothes hugged her thighs, the strip of belly that always showed. Every detail carefully considered. She brought that skill to her work. He'd been mesmerized watching her rip apart samples until each bias was perfect, each cut exact.

The timer dinged. Dump, pour. Every drop cleanly back into the container. Repeat. Wait.

The woman who would roll in ten minutes late, not worried about the rust on her truck. The woman who left her kitchen in a mess. Who wore Portuguese flannel jammies and smeared fancy green goop all over his face just to see him look ridiculous. Who believed in him, who put up with his shit. Who'd shared her secrets with him, her vulnerabilities. A book she'd held open, letting him read every chapter.

The timer dinged. He turned the developer case over. Agitate, dump, wait.

While she'd held her heart out to him, he'd held his own shut. Closed himself off, guarding the ugly parts of himself while she'd let him see every imperfect part of her.

No wonder she didn't believe he loved her. He hadn't shown her.

His eyes prickled, and he caught himself from wiping his chemical-covered hand over his wet cheek. He stripped his gloves, cleaned his equipment, and set his timer.

The circles under his eyes had darkened in the weeks since she walked away from him. Since he'd made her walk away. He sagged on his couch and dragged his eyes to the mural. A dark jungle, painted over months, hundreds of hours, a place to lose himself and mediate, to let ideas come to life in the verdant forest. But all he could see was Cass. Pressing her against the wall. Her hair, wild on the pillow beside him. Her sweet cinnamon taste when he slipped his tongue into her mouth. Her laughter floating like treble notes through the air, the sweet vibrations imprinting themselves on his psyche.

The memory of what she felt like crowded against him. Soft and warm, the curves of her body fitting against him. Jasmine and sweet sweat. He tossed an arm over his eyes and let himself wallow in the tightness in his chest.

The timer's buzz jolted him awake. He pressed the heels of his hands into his eye sockets, forcing his feet into his make-shift darkroom.

The first set of negatives were perfectly in focus. At least he hadn't lost his touch with photography. The two of the six photos he'd snapped of Brynne months ago when they were positioning the boom mics could go straight into a magazine. They'd be perfect in the behind-the-scenes featurette Stephen was filming. Melanie would be thrilled.

He moved over to the shots of Cass and had to put down the photos to breathe through the crush of his chest. Gripping the edges of the sink until his fingers whitened, he blew out air through pursed lips. He swallowed and picked up the focus finder again.

She was magic. The blur around her, kinetic and free. Candid shots he'd snapped before she was ready, three shots in succession. In the last one, her gaze seared into the lens like she could see him now. The scarf he'd thrown over the lens muted the light around her, caressing her movements. Her eyes wide, smile open, inviting him to drink deeply of her. How her lips were parting, like a question was ready to spring forth.

Do you want me the same way I want you?

If he'd let himself that day, she would have kissed him. He could have had her all this time. Instead he tried to throw her at other men to convince himself he didn't want her. Or didn't need her.

In a lifetime of mistakes, this was the biggest he'd made. And they'd lost all that time together. Time he might never get back.

He unclenched his fist, releasing the negatives so as not to destroy them. He'd destroyed enough in the last months. Mistreating delicate things and leaving scars, visible or not.

He closed the darkroom door and sat on his favourite spot on the floor, a handful of steps back from the mural. The usual dream he could fall into staring into its depths was gone. Now it was just paint on a wall. Random splashes of lime and sage, moss and olive, in shapes that didn't matter anymore. Nothing else mattered anymore.

Except her.

The screenplay hadn't been touched since he'd graduated law school. Longer even than *Sirius Darker* had sat unfinished. Josh pulled out Cass's fan art, leafing through her portfolio. Vibrant, kinetic colour danced across the pages. He could see it all, through her eyes.

A layer of dust covered his keyboard. A phone number and *call me Chloe xoxo* scrawled onto the notepad beside it.

Chloe? Oh. Right. The friend of Stephen's cousin who'd stayed at his condo. He crumpled the paper and tossed it in recycling before booting up his desktop.

He opened the document and began writing.

CHAPTER TWENTY-NINE

CASS

CASS INHALED THE CINNAMON-AND-CHOCOLATE SCENTED STEAM from the mocha she clutched in her bare hands. A Chinook, the warm breeze that blew over Calgary on lucky winter days, had brought up the temperatures enough that some of the hardier souls on set wore tee shirts.

Good news for Dawson, whose traveller suit had been bunched around his waist to bare his impressive torso to the elements all day.

Cass reminded herself to bring smelling salts for Bex tomorrow.

She'd been expecting the call. She just didn't think it would come so fast. When Terry scheduled reshoots for the following week, she was needed on set right away. Dawson had cut the few pounds of body fat he had, and his suit needed refitting.

No sense in asking if they were sure they needed her. They would. While her wardrobe assistant was good, it needed to be perfect.

Which meant she'd have to see Josh. A fierce yearning had ripped through her chest, and she had cried at her sewing machine for an hour.

"Looking good, Dawson!" Brynne waved cheerfully after

Josh yelled cut, and Dawson trotted back to where his robe slung over the back of his chair. He shoved his arms through the fluffy sleeves and blew out a breath. Josh glowered into the monitor, avoiding where Dawson wrapped the robe's belt tightly around his torso.

"I hope he's got what he needs," he said, shivering. "I'm nearly hypothermic here."

"Having a single digit body fat percentage doesn't let you hold a lot of heat." Cass hoisted up a smile and held out her mocha. "Want a sip?"

"Cassidy, I haven't had sugar since Mrs. Westwood said I needed to do this stupid shirtless scene and I can't have anything delicious until I'm sure we're done."

Cass withdrew her offer and stared at Josh. His eyes narrowed as he bent over the monitors, jacket riding up his torso at the back, and the dimples at the base of his spine showed up against his golden skin. She couldn't tell from here, but she was positive he would be covered in goosebumps. He hated being cold. His black hair fell in shaggy waves over his ears, and she longed to feel those strands brushing over her cheek.

Her heart bruised itself against her ribs, and she forced her gaze into her lap.

"Sorry, Big D, I don't want to tempt you," she said with a small smile.

Dawson turned his nearly famous baby blue eyes on her, searching her face. "I think that ship has sailed. Your eyes melt me like chocolate and your lips look like strawberries and you smell like flowers …" His voice trailed off into a mortified whisper. "I am so sorry. That was completely uncalled for. I don't suppose you'd blame that on me being really hungry, would you?"

Cass looked up at the big man and tried to ignore the twinge in her chest. Libby said he looked interested. This more than confirmed it. Maybe she should. Maybe trying to date assholes to forget someone didn't work, and what she needed to do was date someone lovely. Here was someone who was nice, sweet, and open about how he felt about her. Anyone would be a fool not to at least see what could happen.

"Do you want to go out with me?" Cass blurted out.

"I don't want to pry," he said, and turned a scrutinizing look at her, "but I didn't think you were exactly available."

She looked over at Josh, who had locked eyes with her from across the set. Her breath lodged in her throat, like a hand squeezing to hold the words in. She was a free woman. Nothing stopping her back from seeing if she could make something work here.

Cass shook her head firmly. "I'm not," she whispered, and cleared her throat. She tore her gaze away from Josh and pressed a thin smile at Dawson. "I mean, I'm not looking to jump into anything serious, but I think you're sweet, and we get along, and," she tried to smile, "maybe we can do something fun?"

His grin lit up his face. "I've been trying to work up the courage to ask you out for months, and then I thought there was something going on with … But if that's not the case, then, I'm honoured if you'll take a chance on me. Next Thursday? I actu-ally have a couple ideas, if you'll let me?"

After the train wreck of the last several months, taking a chance on a sweet guy like Dawson barely seemed like a chance at all.

Steady. Reliable. No surprises.

Cass swallowed and blinked her eyes clear. "It's a date."

If there was a ranking of backyard weddings, Jill and Alex's had to top the list.

The gentle Chinook temperatures extended to the weekend, with their friends and family packing every square foot of their bungalow and spilling onto the back deck. Cass and Libby had sniffled happy tears under a blanket as the couple recited their vows and kissed under the January stars.

It helped her broken heart to know that two people could find happiness in each other.

Even if one half of the happy couple was currently pumping Cass for information.

"Wait. Wait, wait, wait." Jill held up a hand. "You are going on a date with Dawson James? Dr. Rykoff in *Sirius Darker*, that Dawson James?"

"Yep."

"Try and sound excited about it, why don't you?" Omar said, dropping onto the couch beside her. "I'll jump on that train if you aren't interested."

"He's really nice. I'm sure it'll be fun." Cass shrugged and pulled up a genuine smile. "But seriously, how long have you planned this, Mrs. Campbell?"

Jill grinned back with the most relaxed expression Cass had seen on her face since the day she'd announced her engagement. "About a week."

"You sneak," Libby said, elbowing Jill in the ribs. "Wedding planning apps weren't cutting it for you?"

"Couldn't decide on the colour for the tablecloths," Alex cut in, and reached his hand to Jill. "Pardon me, but I need to steal my wife."

Jill glowed as he wrapped a protective arm around her, leading her to say goodbye to departing family, and Cass felt the longing for that easy comfort. Of knowing the person you loved, loved you back. Fiercely. With every fibre of their being.

"It's really special, seeing them together, isn't it?" Omar shifted into Jill's vacated spot beside Cass, watching the newly-weds melt into each other's arms as people congratulated them on their way out. The look of sublime bliss on Alex's face was perfectly mirrored in Jill's.

"It really is," she whispered.

"It's not every day people find love like that."

She thought she had. Once. She didn't know if she ever would again. Cass pressed her hand to the raw ache in her chest. "Have you, Omar?"

"Yes."

"What happened?"

"I wasn't ready for it, and I let it go."

Cass followed his gaze to a skinny man in a cowboy hat she didn't recognize, hugging Jill and shaking hands with Alex. Cass pulled her eyes away. "What did you do?"

"I've spent the last decade trying to find someone else to fill his space in my heart."

"Did it work?"

"No," he said. "None of them were him."

"I'm taking a page from Brynne's book and putting a no-topless clause in all my future contracts. I am never doing that to myself again."

Powder-like snowflakes lazed down from the inky sky and melted on the pavement. All three locations Dawson had planned for them to tour at the annual hot chocolate festival were within walking distance, and a short drive from the wearable technology fashion event planned for after.

It couldn't have fit her better if she'd planned it herself.

Dawson sipped his second hot chocolate, his jacket collar open to the early evening cold. He steered Cass around the open guitar case of a busker singing an old country song and dropped in a few bills as he passed.

Cass blew into her drink to make the honey flavoured marshmallows swirl in a tiny whirlpool and took a sip of her chili-spiced hot chocolate. The night she and Josh had met, cherry blossoms and rain flowed along the Vancouver streets. The city's lights reflected off every surface. He'd dragged her under an

awning to kiss her as they waited for the car to bring them back
to his condo.

Thinking about him isn't going to help.

Cass stared into her cup. "No shirtless scenes? You'll disappoint a whole bunch of fans."

"Some, maybe. But if I worried about trying to please everyone, I'd never get out of bed in the morning."

Whether it was the sky-blue parka that nearly matched his
eyes or the fleece beanie he wore—Cass had given one to
everyone on the cast and crew—the cold seemed to eddy around
him. No shiver made his shoulders tense or his teeth chatter.

Josh would have spent half the time grousing about the cold,
and the other half threatening to put his hands down her shirt to
warm up his hands.

If she closed her eyes, she could picture him smiling as he did
it in front of everyone on the sidewalk, too, telling her to say the
word if she wanted him to stop.

Stop.

"I don't know why I'm trying to talk you out of it." She
tipped her head to the side and stopped herself from licking a
rogue drop from the corner of her mouth, and wiped the last bit
away with her glove. "It's good job security. More costumes to
design and all."

"You get to design more costumes, and I get to wear them?
Win-win," he said with a lop-sided smile.

A gaggle of twenty-something women circled back to ogle
him again and he tugged the beanie down lower over his brows
until they passed. He tossed the cup into the recycling bin and
glanced down at her hands, both occupied with her now-empty
cup. He crossed and uncrossed his arms, fiddling with the
zippers on his parka.

"I have never seen someone so fiddly as you," Cass said,
draining the last sips of her hot chocolate. "I know we're off set
and all, but it's killing me not to fix this."

"You ever think I messed around with things so you'd come over to talk to me?"

"Tsk. Stop it."

He shrugged and smiled at her. "I'm just a bit nervous."

"Why would you be nervous?"

"Trying to decide if it's too early in the night to try to kiss you."

Josh had said something similar the first night they met. *Testing the waters*, he'd said, then dove in for a heady kiss that made her forget to breathe. All the kisses after, stolen behind closed doors, tasting, hands claiming each other.

A buzz rustled in her stomach, and she tried to tell herself it was because Dawson James, the handsome, polite, heartthrob standing in front of her, wanted to kiss her.

She leaned up onto the tips of her toes. "Only one way to find out."

Their mouths met. The night air breezed cold as traffic hummed around her ears. He smelled nice. Like Ivory soap and melting snow, and his hands on the small of her back were steady and warm. The last of his minty hot chocolate still clung to his lips, an odd contrast with the chili spice of her own.

Interesting combination. Not unpleasant. She pulled away to settle back on her heels, and opened her eyes. Dawson drew a jagged breath, and she turned the corners of her mouth up.

"That was really nice."

"Yeah, it was." He smiled at her wistfully. "But you deserve more than nice."

Josh had sat her in her chair after coming to get her from another bad date, taking her boots off with gentle care, laughing as she'd drunkenly tried to get a kiss from him. A kiss that would have curled her toes, stolen her breath, and made her forget her own name. Something far more than nice.

He said he could write sonnets about kissing her.

It had been one thing trying to forget Nick with a bunch of throwaway dates with guys she'd never see again. It was another thing completely to try to move on from Josh by asking this sweet, genuine man, who she knew liked her. When she knew she didn't feel the same way.

"I'm sorry," she whispered. She stared down at the toes of her boots. "It was selfish of me to ask you to come out tonight."

He took a fortifying breath and stared out over the crowd flowing around them. "Don't be sorry, darlin'. I'm glad you did. I feel like tonight answered some questions for both of us."

"What would those be?"

A corner of his mouth quirked up. "I think you have some unfinished business with a certain surly director."

"He's not that surly." Except when a shot didn't go right, or when someone was late on set. Or when he thought she was interested in someone else. Her heart lurched, and she sniffed. "Usually."

Dawson thumbed away a tear before it could freeze on her cheek. "Not with you."

She took his hand and squeezed. "What other questions did we answer tonight?"

"I wanted to know for some time now what it would be like to kiss you," he said. "Even if it was just once."

If she was smart, lucky, sensible, or any combination of those, falling in love with Dawson James would have been the easiest thing in the world. Cass fiddled with the zipper on his parka one last time. "You are going to make someone really happy one day."

"I hope you're right."

"Friends?"

"Friends," he confirmed, and tucked her gloved hand under his arm to turn them down the street. "Come on, I got a fashion show to get you to in ten minutes, and I don't want to miss the electric Lego dresses."

Cass covered her giggle in her free hand and smiled her first real smile in days. "Me, either."

It could hardly be called a mobile phone if it had to be connected to a power outlet at all times. When her next pay cheque came in, she was getting an upgrade.

Cass dropped her keys on her kitchen counter and plugged in her dead phone. She dug her thumbs into the small of her back as she checked the time on her microwave.

Almost eleven. Enough time to ice her knee before bed. Before she could settle on the couch with a cold compress, her phone buzzed on her counter.

The five notifications that popped up should have tipped her off something was going on. One from her sister, asking her to babysit next week, one from her brother to borrow her truck, and three from Libby.

> Call me

> Call me

> Before you look at anything else

Cass scrunched her brow.

> What's the emergency?

> Nothing! Just wanted to see how was your date with D? You home? Are you alone?

"Okay, weirdo," Cass said, holding out her phone while searching for her earbuds. "I'm home. I'm alone. What's up?"

Libby's face filled the screen. "I don't suppose you fell madly in love with Dawson over sippy cups of hot chocolate and electrified fashion, did you?" she asked in an inordinately hopeful voice.

Cass heaved a sigh. "No. We kissed, and he's so sweet, but we're just friends."

"Well, shit."

"My thoughts exactly."

"No, I mean ..." Libby trailed off, lips pursed. "Have you been online at all tonight?"

"Nope, too busy having the most platonic date of my life. But no face licking or vape clouds or monologues on tropical fish, though, so honestly the best date I've had in the last year."

If she didn't count the time she and Josh had spent holed up in her apartment, eating Christmas leftovers and laughing over old movies and smearing each other with beauty products. Winding themselves around each other in bed for hours, waking up in the middle of the night with his hand curled around hers.

The missing headphones were lodged between her couch pillows. She fished them out and worked at the tangles one-handed.

A long pause followed, and Cass used the silence to plug in her earbuds. By the time Libby spoke again, her voice was directly in Cass's ears.

"A few gossip sites posted photos of you and D kissing from tonight."

That was fast. Cass let out a weak chuckle. "I saw a few starstruck girls ogling him, but I didn't know we were still trending. No jealous tirades against me for taking him off the market this time, are there?"

"I need to warn you about something, and I think maybe it's best that you hear it from me. Some photos of Josh popped up, too." Libby cleared her throat. "With Brynne."

Cass's heart lurched into her throat. "What do you mean?"

"It's probably nothing. Like, really nothing. The shots are grainy, but ..." Libby pressed her lips together.

"I can't really assume anything if I have no idea what you're talking about." Cass's voice sounded brittle to her own ears.

"Josh and Brynne. There's photos of them hugging, then going into her trailer. The captions said they didn't come out for a while."

The room greyed and pressed down on her. It shouldn't be a surprise. The two had never been anything more than professional on set—fighting, if anything. But Brynne was a stunning woman, and Josh was, well, Josh. Gorgeous and creative and irresistible.

But even if it was something …

"You're probably right. It's probably nothing."

If she said it with a firm enough voice, she might believe it.

Either way, it didn't matter. She'd ignored Josh's every attempt to talk to her. Left him on read with every text. Deleted every voicemail without listening to it. "But what Josh does, and who he does it with, is up to him."

Cass clicked off the call and plugged it into her search bar. Libby was right. It was the first thing that showed up when she searched *Sirius Darker movie*. The talking head videos popped up first, speculating over what was happening behind closed doors. Then, grainy, low-res shots of the Josh and Brynne embracing on set, another with him following her into her trailer, both taken just days before filming had wrapped.

She shut down the feed. It didn't look like anything. Josh had given Libby the same one-arm hug when her brilliant lighting made a particularly tricky night shot work. And Josh almost always went behind closed doors for serious conversations. It was probably that.

But what if it wasn't?

She knew what it felt like to be pulled behind closed doors with him. Not knowing if it was going to be a quiet discussion about a scene or if he would pin her against the wall with his hand working between her thighs. His arms would steal around her, his soft stubble rasping against her temple as he whispered something sweet, filthy—or both—in her ear. How he would fight with her about a movie, longer than its runtime, just to keep her talking.

Stop torturing yourself. He is married. He hid that from you. For months.

Cass swiped her cheeks. No more.

Her phone buzzed again and her already low heart sunk further. The list of people who would text her this late was short.

The man must have a sixth sense for when she was vulnerable. Or her hormones sent a signal into the sky that alerted him when she was easy pickings. Or maybe it was men in general. She half expected a text to show up from some other guy who had ghosted her months ago.

How ironic. She'd been the one doing all the ghosting for the last several months. Maybe this was cosmic payback. She wearily bent her head over her phone.

are you dating dawson james??

How do you know about Dawson?

So you are??

you were tagged in a video

Kissing, it looked like

And that was his cue to circle up and see if he still had her on his carousel of numbers to call when he needed a hookup. Dole out a compliment or two to keep her on the bench.

Her fingers hovered over the keys as she debated whether to respond. She didn't owe him anything. And if she replied, she might not be able to say no.

No random guys to message and hide behind tonight. Only her and her battered willpower. She bit her lip and tilted her head back to stare at the ceiling.

D and I are just friends

Not sad to hear that ;)

You looked beautiful as usual

Wyd now?

Wallowing in my terrible luck with men. So many of the guys she'd gone on dates with as part of project No Second Dates had been losers. Just as many had been fine. Nice on their own, but no compatibility. Steak and ice cream. Orange juice and tooth-paste. Wine and oatmeal.

Even her and Dawson. Sounded good in theory, but it didn't quite work.

Be strong. You can do this. Say no.

> It's late. I'm almost in bed

> please

> I'd really like to see you

She sunk back on her couch and adjusted the ice pack over her knee. The phone screen dimmed to black. She should leave him on read. Ghost him the way he'd ghosted her months ago.

But they had history. It had been fun. Usually. When she got together with Nick, there were no surprises.

> okay

CHAPTER THIRTY

JOSH

STEPHEN MUNCHED ON THE BOWL OF CHEERIOS CRADLED IN HIS hands. His usually wolfish beard was trimmed, his feet on the floor instead of perched on Josh's pristine coffee table. His bedroom door was thrown open, the bed made and his clothes not littering the floor for once. Even from another province, Libby's influence was rubbing off on Stephen.

That influence had never rubbed off on Cass, though. Her bedroom was probably still a glorious disaster. The scarf hanging off the bedpost, a shirt draped over her slipper chair. Her bedside table a collection of half-drunk cups of water and four different shades of red lipstick. The faint scent of jasmine on her pillow and cinnamon in the air.

A room he'd never see again. Josh swallowed against the pressure in his throat.

Stephen shuffled to the dishwasher and put his dirty dishes in. "Did you see them?"

Josh didn't look up from his screen. Post-production on *Sirius Darker* had wrapped. The publicity tour would start in a matter of weeks. Fewer, if Melanie got her way. If she wanted the film out in time for this year's Oscar buzz, she'd find a way to make it happen. Once the film was in front of audiences, it was for them to decide.

"See what?" His voice came out gravelly with disuse and fatigue. Maybe if he played stupid, Stephen would shut the hell up and leave him alone.

Another all-nighter writing, and every blink scraped the inside of his eyelids like sandpaper. But the words that had refused to exit his brain for years had flowed through his fingers and onto the word doc like wine, rich and bold and full of complexity.

Tideways was done.

Plus, burying himself in work gave him the excuse not to think about her. Except that she'd been with him the whole time. The portfolio of art he'd borrowed from Cass sat propped up on the corner of his workstation. Each sketch a shot of sunshine straight to his soul.

"If you hadn't been buried in that screenplay since last week, I'd call out your bullshit." Stephen leaned back against the kitchen counter and crossed his arms. "The photos."

Nope, not getting away with ignoring it. Josh ground his molars together and avoided his friend's pointed stare.

Of course he had seen them. The google alert he'd set for *Sirius Darker* had pinged him last night.

And we thought D'awwwson was over! Our favourite cutie from Cookeville, TN was seen locking lips with an unknown brunette at the YYC Hot Chocolate Festival last night. They were last seen cozying up to each other on set months ago, but we all thought things had fizzled over Christmas. Looks like they are still going hot (and sweet!) even with production wrapped!

Josh glowered at his screen. "He's not even from Cookeville," he muttered. "They just picked that because of the alliteration."

"That's what you're taking from this?"

"Why the fuck do I put up with you again?"

"My good looks and raw sex appeal."

Awesome. He scrubbed a hand over his own less than meticulously maintained stubble. "Tell me, oh wise one. What exactly am I supposed to take from this?"

Stephen sighed. "Libby talked to her. It was just one date. They're friends. That's all."

That much was obvious. The photos couldn't have looked more chaste if they were posing for a tutorial on How to Kiss Like a Virgin. Dawson might as well have had his hands in his pockets for all the touching he was doing.

Even if Dawson had succeeded in behaving like a gentleman, Josh had never managed to hold onto any control around her. To be that close to her, smell her, with her eyes flashing up at him. To dive his hands into her hair and drag her face up to his and steal her breath as he lost his own, pressing his hips against hers until the friction between them incinerated their clothes off their bodies and they lost themselves in each other for hours.

No. After seeing those photos, it was clear nothing was going on between Dawson and Cass. Still. Another man knew what her lips tasted like. And he couldn't do a damn thing about it.

"What Cass does is not my business," he said flatly.

"For fuck's sake." Stephen crossed the few steps from the tiny kitchen and back into the living area, yanking the wireless keyboard out from under Josh's hands "I've watched you act like a prickly bastard for years, having temper tantrums when you can't use your words like a big boy. "

If his so-called friend didn't shut his trap, Josh would rip the keyboard out of his hands and snap it across his knee. "I don't have temper—"

"All the time, my dude. You are the most confrontation-phobic person I've ever met. I always thought you acted like a dick because you didn't like people—"

"I don't like people."

"But I think it's because you don't want people getting close.

And for some ungodly reason, Cass was able to get past your bullshit, but now you're making both of you suffer because you can't figure your shit out."

Fuck. Stephen was right. Wrapping himself in barbed wire had worked. If people didn't get close, they couldn't get hurt. If they couldn't get hurt, he couldn't disappoint them. Everyone he was close to got hurt or disappointed. His grandparents, his sister, Vivian.

Cass, most of all. She hadn't done anything wrong except fall in love with the wrong man.

Josh dropped his head into his hands. "I don't know what to do," he whispered.

"Yeah, you do. Let her in."

And show her every embarrassing, ugly part of himself? Fear spider-walked over his skin, and he wanted to shrink his head below the collar of his tee. "How?"

"You're coming to me for advice about women?"

Not women. Cass. "Just shows you how low I've stooped."

"You know her. You'll figure it out." Stephen dropped to the couch and his voice grew softer. "Since we're being all open and shit, I need to tell you something. I'm moving back to Calgary."

Josh's sleep-deprived brain spun in his skull as he turned to look at his best friend. "What?"

"Come on, you can't be surprised. I've been crashing on your couch for a year."

"You never slept on my couch—"

"You know what I mean." Stephen clasped his hands, elbows on his knees. "This isn't home. And I don't want to be away from Libby again. We want to have a family, buy a house. Terry has a lead on a permanent gig for me."

"Well, shit. That's awesome."

Stephen was wrong. It was a surprise. Not the moving back to Calgary part. His best friend looked happier and healthier than Josh had ever seen him. What was surprising was that Josh envied him.

When people had said they were getting married for the past few years, he'd scoffed. Silently, because he wasn't that much of an asshole, but he'd gritted out congratulations while internally recoiling at the thought of a lifetime with the same person. Even standing at the alter with Vivian, he'd never thought about the implications of what a lifetime meant.

But with Cass …

Going to bed with her, waking up with her in his arms. Telling her some filthy joke to get her musical laugh trilling through the air, then her matching his energy. Bringing each other's visions to life. Going from production to production, wherever the story took them. Vancouver, Calgary, fucking Antarctica.

It didn't matter where, as long as they were together. Who needed a permanent address when a person was home?

Let her in. If that's what it took, he'd find a way. Not having her wasn't an option.

He wiped a hand down his face and turned back to the paparazzi photos.

It wasn't a mystery where these had come from. Calgary wasn't exactly a hotbed for paps skulking in bushes, ready to ambush celebrities who'd made the rash decision to go grocery shopping without makeup. Everyone would have thought filming had wrapped. No, this was deliberate.

Dawson was too much of a boy scout to say anything. Brynne hated attention. And Cass …

Cass didn't have a malicious bone in her body.

But there was one person who had something to gain from this being in the news.

Melanie's fingers steepled under her chin, eyes narrowed and elbows resting on her desk. It couldn't have been comfortable with the sharp ends of her manicured nails cutting into her skin. But it looked good.

At the end of the day, that's what it always was about. What looked good.

All he could do was hope he looked as half as composed as his boss. Even if it felt like his guts were going to invert themselves onto the imported Persian rug under his feet.

Josh leaned forward in his chair, squaring his shoulders. "We agreed. No PR stunts."

"It wasn't a stunt. It was a strategy."

"A strategy that no one agreed to."

His stomach twisted in knots. His entire life, he'd avoided confrontations like this. The only way he'd lasted in law as long as he had was by snorting courage and drinking numbness.

And here he was, sober as a—well, sober as a judge—telling the woman who held his career in her hands that he wouldn't accept it.

An exasperated expression crossed her face. "Scandal works. You think I wanted to show my tits on live streaming?"

"But you made that choice for yourself. Now your choices are affecting our film," he said, throwing her words back at her.

"It might be our film, but it's my money."

"And it's my team." Josh tossed the printouts of photos onto her desk. Dawson and Cass. Him and Brynne. "No one agreed to this."

Melanie gave a contemptuous shake of her head. "No one agrees to this. Once you reach a certain level of fame, you're under a microscope. I love my husband, but you don't think every headline that speculates when he's trading me in for Mrs. Westwood Number Six doesn't hurt? And you don't think Brynne will be roasted every time she leaves the house with a zit? Do you think Dawson will get a choice if he's on some random 'Southern Gentlemen I Want to Bang' top ten list?" A rough scoff escaped her throat. "It's never ending, and if I've learned anything in this industry, it's that you have to grow a thick skin if you want to get anywhere."

"You're right. The outside world is a piece of shit. We can't control what happens outside these walls. But we can do everything we can to give people a safe space within them." He willed his voice to remain level. "I promised Brynne a closed set. She was in tears when the photos of us showed up online. It took me hours to convince her to come out of her trailer. You made her feel unsafe, and you made me break my word."

Cass had taught him that. To take care of his team. Even if that meant putting himself between his team and the threat. Fuck, like Dawson had, stepping between him and the grips. To stand up for the people who didn't have the power.

For the first time, Melanie looked unsure. "She'll get over it."

"Maybe. And what about Dawson? He was in the room when agreed to let the story die. Now he knows you'll go back on your promise the minute it's convenient. And Cass—" he said, and his voice cracked. *Fuck.* So much for being stone cold and in control. He cleared his throat. "We didn't even ask what she wanted."

If this worked, he'd spend the rest of his life making it up to her.

"There's a difference between fighting for an advantage and using people to reach it." Josh drew a breath, heart hammering. "And I won't work with someone who doesn't understand that."

One manicured finger tapped against her lips, eyes narrowing. After a long minute, Melanie spun her chair to face the picture window, the mountains obscured by the low-lying clouds. "Shit."

Josh gripped his knees. Was that a *now-I-have-to-fire-you* "shit" or an *I-hate-being-wrong* "shit"?

Say something more eloquent than um. "What's it going to be, Westy?"

Where the fuck is this coming from? Guess the fear of confrontation Band-Aid was ripped all the way off.

Melanie jerked her head around. The hard set of her eyes hadn't softened, but a wry smile fought to take over her cool expression. "I suppose that's better than what I've been called by other people."

"Other people are dicks. That's not how I talk to the people I work with."

Anymore.

She drummed her nails on the desk. "You and I are going to disagree on a lot of things. A *lot* of things," she emphasized. "I will make decisions you won't like. But I promise that you, and anyone involved, will know about it. And I won't ask anyone to do anything I wouldn't do."

A jet of air huffed out of his nose.

"I meant," she said with a grin, "nothing they aren't comfortable with."

As far as apologies went, it wasn't perfect. Far from it, but relief washed over him. He crossed his arms, tucking his hands under his biceps to hide the shaking. "I can work with that."

"That's great, but if we aren't leveraging soul-sucking gossip sites which, for the record"—she held up a finger—"give cheap publicity, what are we doing instead?"

Being ballsy had worked so far. Josh coughed. "I have a crew ready to put my idea together. Give me a month and a budget and I'll get our film the attention you're looking for."

"Alright." She shook her head, chuckling. "What do you have in mind?"

That wasn't so bad.

One gut-churning conversation down, one to go.

CHAPTER THIRTY-ONE

CASS

For once, Cass would arrive on time. Her morning errands took half the time she'd planned. She knew what to wear without looking in her closet. There was an open parking spot right in front of the coffee shop that she didn't even have to parallel park to get into.

It was like the universe wanted her to see him.

A muddle of voices and acoustic guitar washed over her when she opened the door, letting the bitter, flowery scent of fresh roasted coffee flow past her and into the snowy afternoon. Thin grey slush collected between the cracks of the exposed concrete floor, and she scuffed her feet on the entrance rug to add to the mess. She unwrapped her blue silk scarf from around her shoulders and scanned the busy café.

It didn't take her long to find him. His brilliant smile widened when she entered, and he stood from the end of a communal table to fold her into a leather-and-musk infused half hug.

Hot, dark hair, and a where-did-my-panties-go smile. I really do have a type. Cass stifled a laugh and leaned into his chest a second longer, inhaling the memory of all the nights she gone to sleep with that scent on her skin.

Almost every one of those nights, she'd still ended up sleeping alone.

"What's so funny?" Nick asked, his voice rumbling against her cheek.

"I'm just thinking about patterns." She disengaged from his embrace to sit opposite him, inching her chair a centimetre away from the couple sitting beside them.

He looked great, but then again, he always did. A man in well-tailored clothes had always been a weakness of hers. Today, a long camel trench was layered over a thick cream cable-knit sweater and windowpane wool pants. It was mid-afternoon, and his beard was already showing up against his olive skin. She'd only ever seen it either freshly shaven or several hours older.

"Your hair looks good like that," she said. It was longer than she had ever seen before, just starting to curl around his ears. If she took one of the thick locks between her fingers, it would have the lightest feel of the styling cream she'd seen on his bathroom counter. She folded her hands in front of her. "It suits you."

"Thought I should try something new."

Isn't that interesting timing? She twiddled with the end of her scarf. "I'm surprised you agreed to meet me during the day."

He cocked a brow at her with a curious look on his face. "All the better to see that beautiful face of yours," he said, lip half-curled in a teasing grin.

"Then why do you only text me at night?"

One of the people sitting beside her choked into their coffee. If Nick didn't look so surprised, Cass would have sworn he had the audacity to look offended.

"Uh, do you want a coffee?" he stammered, breaking the silence. "They have an excellent in-house roasted Sulawesi blend."

She wasn't surprised he didn't remember that she didn't drink dark roast. "No, thank you. You said you wanted to see me?"

"I did. I wanted to see you." The brilliance of his smile faded a tick as he shifted in his seat. He reached across the table, thumb rubbing over the tips of her fingers, and she swallowed a chuckle that he was finally—almost—holding her hand.

"Life has been crazy. Really crazy. I had to go back to Montreal for a while."

Like cell phones don't work there? she thought, but stayed silent.

He continued, "And I think I'm staying this time. And now that I'm back, I want to see you. I missed you."

"What did you miss about me, Nick?"

The smile faded another watt. "You. The time we spend together. We don't do enough of that." He stared down at his thumb brushing hers. For all the places his hands had been on her body, he'd almost never touched her in public before. "Have you ever wondered what it would be like to see where things would go between us?"

A quiet huff escaped her lips. Cass withdrew her hands and tucked them under her arms. "Only after every time you didn't call me back after we'd hooked up," she said, and this time, he had the decency to look guilty. "Why now?"

"When I saw those photos last night of you out with another man, I realized I'd be a goddamn fool to let someone else be where I should be."

"Never once have you ever made me feel like you wanted to be with me."

"I-I'm sorry if you feel that way."

"But not for acting in a way that made me feel that way? That's not an apology."

A hint of remorse flickered in his eyes. Finally. She'd spent hours staring into those eyes. Rich, espresso brown, with lashes so thick and curly she'd once been tempted to ask if he curled them. She'd bet anything he didn't know the colour of her eyes.

"But we keep coming back together. We have something here," he tried again. "Don't you think we should give it a shot?"

"Maybe."

"Maybe?" he said, sitting up straighter. "Does that—"

"What's my best friend's name?"

Nick hoisted up his smile a fraction. "What?"

"I've been friends with her since elementary school," Cass prompted. "I talk about her all the time. What's her name?"

"Um ..."

"What am I allergic to?"

He pressed his lips together.

"What kind of movies do I like?"

"Cass ..."

"Your best friend is Alex. *Was* Alex, before whatever went down," she said. "You don't have any allergies, but I know you're lactose intolerant, even though you refuse to admit it. I don't know what kind of movies you like, because you never asked me to see any with you. I love movies."

"I didn't—"

"No. You didn't."

He knew how to make her come. He knew the sounds she made when he put his mouth on her. He knew she answered his texts, even after a year of silence.

And what did she know?

That none of that was good enough anymore.

"You never took the time to get to know me. You only ever texted me when you wanted to get laid."

"That's not ..." *True*, she could see on the tip of his tongue, but he said, "If that's what you think, I'm sorry—"

"That's still not an apology."

"Then let me fix that."

"I think that time has passed."

A lost look sat in the place of his usual smile. The couple sitting beside them had gone quiet, each looking down into their respective coffees with fascinated expressions.

It was kind of nice to have witnesses to hear her say goodbye to Nick.

He pushed the still-full cup away, sloshing the presumably

excellent in-house roasted Sulawesi blend onto the wooden table, all traces of bravado vanished. "What are you saying?"

"I don't think it's a good idea for us to see each other again."

"You don't mean that. I've been a mess for a couple years, and you saw the worst of that, but I've changed. We could be so good together if you give us a chance."

"You've had so many chances." Cass tipped her head to the side to shake a loose curl from her eyes. Dry, no traces of tears, her heart beating a sedate cadence. "There was a time I would have loved to hear you say that, but you treated me like something you could ignore until it was convenient. I'm worth more than being someone's second choice, and I don't want to ever have to guess if I am again."

Nick's eyes searched the room, like someone in the coffee shop would hold up a sign with the correct response to help him change her mind. When no epiphany dawned, he blew out a breath. "I didn't think this would go this way," he said finally.

"I know." Cass pushed back from the table and felt the weight of the attention of the people around her. "If you text me again, I'm not responding."

For once, he didn't smile. "That's not the first time you've said that."

"But it will be the last." She reached over to squeeze his arm. "If you've changed, I'm glad. Really. And I hope the next person you claim to care about gets a better version of you than what you gave me. Goodbye, Nick."

The winter air pinked her cheeks when she stepped outside. In her still-warm truck, she blocked his number and deleted their text thread.

If there had been any pictures of the two of them, she would have deleted those, too, but they had never made any memories outside the bedroom worth capturing. Even those memories had lost their shine.

Cass was finally over Nicholas Martin. For real, this time.

A physical connection was one thing, but that had been the

only thing they'd ever had. No emotion. No shared creative vision.

Josh said he would help her get over him. If only she'd known he would break her heart to do it.

She looked through the coffee shop's windows. Nick was bent over his phone with a hand covering his mouth. There would be no more responding. No more late-night texts. No more wondering if she'd hear from him. She half expected to feel her fingers revolting and undo the changes, but the only thing she felt was relief.

Her own phone buzzed in her hand, and she half wondered if she'd blocked him wrong. Then it buzzed again, and again. She grinned at her favourite, no-chill, triple-texting friend's stream of consciousness messaging.

> Are we still meeting?

> It was 3 right?

> Everything okay?

> > On my way :)

Better late than never. Cass threw her truck into gear and drove to spill the beans.

Jill clutched her elbows across her torso and trapped her bouncing foot around her ankle. If she wrapped herself any further, she'd be airtight.

They sat alone in the living room, Jill curled up on one end with her giant pit bull glued to her side, and Cass on the other side with relief chasing the guilt from her stomach.

"When did he get back in town?"

"The fall."

Jill's head popped up in surprise. "Why didn't you tell me?"

So many reasons. She didn't want to upset her friend. She didn't want to admit she couldn't control herself around someone her friend hated. "I didn't want you to think I was weak for going back to him." Cass ducked her head. "And now that it's been so long, I don't want you to think I'm a bad friend, even though I am, and I should have told you as soon as he was in town and—"

"I don't think you're a bad friend. Or weak." Jill huffed a thin laugh. "I know how hard it can be getting away from someone. You could have trusted me."

"I know. It was never like what you went through with your ex—"

"And let's be grateful for that," Jill finished. "But now, I'm just glad you figured it out."

Cass nodded. It took years, wasted time, a date with a sweetheart, and one broken heart, but she got there.

Jill focussed her attention on scritching her dog's floppy ears. "Have you talked to him?"

She didn't need to ask which *him* Jill meant. Cass shook her head. It had been over a month since the last time he'd tried to contact her. The one message she received for a follow up on post-production had come through Stephen. He hadn't mentioned Josh at all.

"I think he's let me go," she said softly. She tipped her head back, hoping the tears would slide neatly back into their ducts and leave her cheeks dry. "He knew what I needed and couldn't give it to me. I'm not going to settle for less anymore."

Jill's lip wobbled. "I'm so glad," she said in a wavering voice and leaned over for a hug. "You deserve to be a priority."

Cass squeezed her eyes shut and wrapped her arms around her friend. "I really do."

CHAPTER THIRTY-TWO

JOSH

THE WOMAN HE HAD MARRIED BUSTLED THROUGH THE KITCHEN THEY had shared for less than thirteen months. Cupboard doors swooshed open and snicked closed in the search of a missing tea sachet, the soft soles of her house slippers and frilly apron a stark contrast to her couture blazer. Holt Renfrew, if he had to guess.

The blazer, not the apron.

She'd never worn an apron before. Maybe it was an escalation of her desire to keep an immaculate space. Maybe it was an attempt to woo him with her profound domesticity. He wondered if she knew neither option was going over the way she intended.

"Mom brought back a whole case when she got back from Hong Kong last month," she said, going back to the first cupboard she'd opened. The box sat directly in her sightline, eyes passing over it twice more before her hand shot out to pull two sachets from the box. "You'll love it."

Probably not. They'd never liked the same tea. She knew that. Or had, at one time. Now was not the time to bring that up again.

"Thank you," he said, and took a tiny sip out of politeness.

Even when they lived together, they had always been unfailingly polite with each other. Voices level, tone civilized. Even the night he had moved out, Vivian had sat at this table with her hands folded, mouth open and silent tears streaming down her face.

For the first time in years, he leaned into the memory instead of shutting it out.

The clanking of her spoon against her teacup filled the room. Perfect 4/4 time. He could have set a metronome to it.

"You didn't bring anything with you," she said, eyes on her cup.

"No." No sense in bringing the divorce documents. Not today. "I just wanted to talk."

"About what?"

He hated how hopeful her voice sounded.

"About you." The words stuck behind his gritted teeth, and he forced his jaw to unclench. "What do you want, Viv?"

"Like something to go with the tea?" She jumped to her feet. "I have—"

"No. What do you *want*?"

Her breath escaped in a quick *ha*. She dropped to her chair, inching her hand across the table to him. The faintly cloying scent of her perfume wafted across the table. "I want you."

Anything he said would hurt. It was why he'd avoided it so long. From hurting her. "You don't want me. You want the idea of me."

"That's not true," she rushed in. "I want us to have our life back. We can pick up where we left off. You just needed to get that"—she twitched her head over her shoulder, like the life he had been living on his own the past three years was a longer than anticipated trip to the grocery store, like seeing him embracing Cass was an awkward elevator ride in close quarters —"out of your system." She slipped her fingers under his. "It's all I ever wanted."

He didn't avoid her gaze. "Tell me what that is."

"It's ..." She stalled. "Us. Having our life together."

There it was. Hours in therapy together and years apart, and still they talked past each other. Josh left his hand where it was but didn't return her squeeze.

"We want different lives. You want a life that I can't give you," he said softly. "You want kids and a house in the burbs and to have dinner parties with the neighbours. You want summer vacations in Europe and Christmas vacations in Hawaii. You want a husband with a regular job to make all that happen. Tell me I'm wrong."

"We can do all those things," she said, the tips of her fine brows drawing up, and the pleading in her voice cut his heart.

"That is perfect. For you. But I don't want that." Josh blew out a breath and plowed ahead. "I tried to be that for you, but every minute I was behind a desk, billing hours, sucking up to asshole clients, I wanted to die. When I was assigned to work with Stephen on that film that needed the contract renegotiated, I felt myself come alive for the first time in years."

"I can make you feel alive."

Josh closed his eyes. The least he could do was give her patience. "Why did you come to Calgary?"

"Grace said you sounded lonely," Vivian whispered. "I thought that if I came to you, you'd finally see how much you missed me."

If she wasn't bringing up the fact that he'd had his hands on another woman, she was doing it on purpose.

Josh didn't know if this was cruel or not. "I wasn't lonely. I was with Cass."

A flush of colour rose up her neck and cheeks, and her chest rose and fell like the fault line of an earthquake in the aftershocks.

"None of this is your fault, Vivi. I changed, and I'm not changing back. I'm sorry. I'm sorry that I didn't know myself better before we got married. I'm sorry that I acted shamefully in your family's eyes. But most of all, I'm sorry that I hurt you, and

I'm sorry I can't love you the way you deserve. And I'm so, so sorry I was too chickenshit to say all this years ago. But now, please, I'm begging you, let me go."

The facade of her control slid away, and the edges of her face crumpled. "I don't know how," she said, voice wobbling, and Josh's guilt tore a hole in his chest.

"Yes, you do."

Vivian stared down at where her fingers grasped at his, the gesture unreturned. "You never looked at me the way you look at her," she whispered.

He hadn't. He thought he might have, early in their dating, when she went with him to movies and the theatre, before she admitted sitting that long made her bored and restless. Not that he had tried to enjoy her passions, either.

Not in their engagement photos, styled to look like they had been caught frolicking in a park he'd never been to, reclining on a picnic blanket they'd bought for the occasion, her giant engagement ring the focal point in every shot. Not in the formal wedding photos he could see from where he sat, on the meticulously curated gallery wall in the living room, still up years later.

"You are a special woman, and you are going to make someone a wonderful wife and mother. I want that for you, but that won't be with me." He withdrew his hands from hers, cupping the tea he wouldn't drink in the home that was never really his. "And until you let me go, you won't be able to find the life you deserve."

A resigned stillness replaced the hope in her eyes, shining with tears that didn't fall. Her mouth wavered at the corners, but her voice held firm. "I suppose there's nothing left to say."

"Say that again?"

"Doesn't have to be much. A few hours."

"I think this is a great idea." Stephen rubbed a hand over the back of his hair to flatten the unruly edges. "I've got a list for you."

Brynne nodded from her end of the Zoom call, and Terry nodded beside him. Everyone was nodding.

All it took for everyone to agree was to make Cass the topic of conversation.

"Think Mrs. Westwood will be okay with this?" Terry asked. "It's going to cost us."

"I've got her full backing."

"Let me get this straight," Dawson said, staring through the laptop screen in disbelief. "You want me to record a video about how wonderful I think she is, so that you can try and win her back?"

"It's not so I can win her back." Not only that. Josh furrowed his brow and pressed on. "It's a featurette on the importance of costume design and the mood of *Sirius Darker*. If it wasn't for Cass, you two would have looked like late nineties superheroes in yellow spandex or some shit."

"For which I am eternally grateful," Brynne said.

"I want everyone to know how important she is to this movie." Josh continued, "How wonderful everyone thinks she is. How brilliant and talented and kind and—"

"We get it," Brynne cut in, but she smiled.

Josh shot her a quelling glare, and her grin widened in response. "How we couldn't have done this without her," he finished. "It'll make her really happy."

Dawson leaned away from the screen and ran a hand through the blond locks he was already growing out for his next movie. "Alright, for Cassidy, then."

Josh gave a curt nod. Everyone else he knew would be a slam dunk. Getting Big D on board was the second biggest hurdle.

The biggest hurdle glared at him from across the table. "You hurt her again, I'll cut off your dick and put it in a jar on my mantle," Libby said.

Dawson put his hand up. "If it comes to a duel, I'm Libby's second."

"Third," Stephen said.

"Fourth," Terry piped up.

Josh nodded grimly. He wouldn't have it any other way. "Noted. Now, I need help getting her interview portions done without her suspecting …"

CHAPTER THIRTY-THREE

CASS

CASS CHECKED FOR NOTIFICATIONS ON HER PHONE AND WINCED. There weren't any.

It had been years since she'd gone this long without hearing about a new gig. Terry should have been leaving their usual text bricks trying to cajole her into a new project by now. Their last message was a simple *thanks!* for filming the featurette. Nothing from Karl, or her wardrobe crew. Even Libby was being weird since she'd filmed her lines.

At least filming the featurette had paid well.

In Every Universe. That's what it was called on IMDb. It had to be a *Sirius Darker* tie-in.

She wondered when she'd be brave enough to watch it.

A strident buzz jerked her head upright, and she scrambled for her phone. Her shoulders slumped. A delivery person peered into the fishbowl lens of her building's front door camera.

"Package for Ms. St. Claire," the courier droned, handing her a thick envelope that was definitely not the fabric she had ordered weeks ago.

"That's me." She scrawled her signature with the stubby stylus across the electronic screen and accepted the thick manilla envelope. She turned the package over, and her heart jolted in her throat as she read the sender.

Josh Graham.

He had been radio silent since she'd left him. No texts. No calls. No surreptitious messages via Stephen hinting to text him first.

What would he have sent her? The drawings she'd made of *Tideways* he'd borrowed from her months ago? Hardly worth a signed delivery. The envelope was far thicker than the small sheaf of papers she'd lent him. Then, she caught the envelope's heading.

From the offices of Davis, Johnstone, and Mohammad Family Law.

Just as she was sliding a knife under the seal, her phone buzzed again with a new text. She glanced at the screen and dropped the package to the floor.

Have you opened it yet?

How had he ... Electronic delivery signature. He received automatic notification she'd signed.

Cass picked up the envelope from the floor, the first pages peeking out from the open top. She slid the pages out of the legal envelope and pressed a hand over her mouth.

Emblazoned across the top in a formal serif font was a legal heading from the Supreme Court of British Columbia, and halfway down the page, in bold letters ...

Certificate of Divorce. With signatures of Josh Graham and Vivian Long, side by side. Dated yesterday.

Blood rushed in her ears, and she pursed her lips to slow her breathing. Cass drew a shaking breath, unsure on what to feel. Of how to feel. She sunk onto her couch.

Yes

> You are the first person I've told

> I wanted you to be the first to know

Cass scrolled down to *Josh Sexy Dimples* and hit the FaceTime call.

Declined.

> Not yet, baby

> I'm sorry I kept the parts of myself I didn't love hidden

> When I was fifteen, I was such a nerd I was beat up by someone in band

> I was grounded for buying a bag of weed that turned out to be stale oregano

> I didn't lose my virginity until I was 22

> When I was 8 I fell into a lake in the winter and nearly got hypothermia. I've hated being cold ever since.

> I had a goth phase

A photo followed, and Cass choked on a laugh. His skinny arms stuck out of a black tee shirt, and a shag of dark hair side-swept over one heavily kohl-lined eye. Besides the size of the arms and lack of eyeliner, his aesthetic hadn't changed much.

> I guess I didn't really leave all the goth phase behind.

A splash hit her phone screen, and she scrubbed a hand over her cheek to catch the next teardrop.

> Get ready

> Libby's coming to get you

On cue, a hard knock sounded at her door, and a key slid into her lock a second later. Libby busted open her door with a pained look between ecstatic and murderous on her face.

"Let's go."

***

Cass stared out the window of the passenger seat. The last of the thin afternoon sun glinted gold off the half melted ice coating the street. A jolt kicked through the seat back, and she turned a raised eyebrow behind her.

"Sorry," Stephen muttered, trying to shift his stocky legs. "It's a tight fit."

Libby grinned into the rearview and angled her giant pick up into the tight spot between two cars. "I'd apologize for sticking you back there, but my passenger princess gets first dibs on riding shotgun."

"Good to know where I stand," he said. Libby twisted in her seat to pat his knee.

"What is happening?" Cass demanded for the fourth time.

"Priorities."

A *Closed for Private Event* placard was propped in front of the tiny independent theatre's box office. Bex waved from the front door, pointing urgently at her watch.

"Are we late for something?" Cass asked, feeling the start of a smile bloom.

"They'll wait. You're the main event."

Everyone from the crew was there, and before she could say hi, they were shoving her butt into a seat and a bag of popcorn into her hands.

"What's—"

"Shh!" Terry scolded from the seat behind her.

The curtains parted, the screen flickered to life, and Cass's breath lodged in her chest.

Brynne sat in a director's chair, long legs crossed, with a wand-like microphone clasped delicately between her fingers.

Josh sat at an angle, wearing a tight black tee shirt and a scowl. Her favourite scowl. The one that telegraphed him talking about something personal. And now he was about to do it in front of a literal audience.

Cass tilted her face to Libby, who made a twirling motion with her finger to indicate she should look back at the screen.

"So," the towering projection of Brynne said, face drawn in overly serious lines, "*Sirius Darker* has been a passion project of yours for some time."

An obvious silence was edited short. Then, "Yes."

"You need to do better than that." Brynne's smile was already threatening to break through. For such an incredible actor, she was going to make a terrible SNL host.

A muscle jumped in Josh's cheek, and he huffed out his nose. "I am a fan of the book," he said mechanically.

Brynne tipped the microphone closer to Josh. "Pretend you're talking to Cass."

"Fine." He recrossed his arms and looked into the camera. "I read the book for the first time when I was thirteen years old. Every part drew me in. The characters, the message. Every time I reread it I get something new. Even back then, I saw shadows in my mind of the film it should be. Nothing bright, just—" he closed his eyes and tilted his face to the ceiling, searching for the words "—raw sketches. I started to write an adaptation when I was in university, but never finished."

"But you got there eventually," Brynne said. "What changed?"

"You could say I met a wave of inspiration." The corner of Josh's mouth twisted up. "Also, Stephen told Melanie Westwood that I was working on a draft. If it wasn't for him, none of this might have happened."

Cass turned her eyes to Stephen, who smiled and squeezed her hand.

"This inspiration led to one of the most frenetic weeks of my life," he continued. "A piece of work I had started a decade prior and mostly ignored for the better part of a year was suddenly finished in a week. And I knew exactly where it came from."

"And where was that?" Brynne pressed, waving the mic around like it was a sparkler.

"I met Cassidy St. Claire, and she changed my life."

The faded screen blurred in front of her eyes, and Libby passed her a tissue already in her hand.

Cass turned to her best friend. "You knew about this?" she asked thickly.

"Shh. You'll miss the good part."

His scowl had melted. "From the moment I laid eyes on her, I couldn't get enough of her. She is bright and generous and has a way of getting through to me that no one else does—"

"Like when you are screaming at the grips on set?"

"Hey, I stopped yelling after—"

"After Cass told you to stop being a—" The last word was bleeped, but Josh shrugged.

"She was nicer about it than that, but yeah." He paused. "She was so dedicated. She didn't have to, but she read the book, and when she read my script, it was like she could see inside my head. She dug into internet archives and found fan art I had drawn years ago. And made it better. She knew my vision and made it better. She makes everything better."

"What is happening?" Cass asked again, but she thought she was starting to know. She stood and twisted around to scan the few occupied seats in the theatre.

He stood in the doorway, arms crossed and face tight. The Josh on the screen was still talking, but Cass felt her feet moving until she stood in front of the man in real life.

"I'm trying to show you how much I love you, but you're not watching," he said, a nervous smile creeping up the corner of his mouth. "Will you watch?"

On-screen Brynne was walking through wardrobe with

Cass's assistant. The shot cut to Dawson, saying he'd never felt more comfortable away from home, that he had been able to sink into the role because he felt like he inhabited the skin that Cass had created for him ...

"What is this?"

"Melanie was looking for an on-set love story, and it was us the whole time. I wanted to show you," he said. "And if you like it, I want to release it as a special feature."

"Josh—"

"I started an adaptation of *Tideways* years ago," he blurted out. "I could never finish it. But when you showed me your designs, it came to life. You made me see what it could be. I finished it. All because of you."

"But—" The screen flickered behind her, an image of Cass's interview now dominating the screen, her own voice narrating the design journey. The shot jump-cut to a still image.

Again, it was her. Her open smile and wide eyes shone from the screen, lights from the dance studio gilding every curve. She looked so free, happy.

She looked like she was in love.

Josh's voice narrated the image, conveniently leaving out that it was for the dating profile he was crafting for her, instead pointing out her dance background, her injury.

He'd remembered. Everything.

"So," he asked, nervously, "do you like it?"

On screen, the camera switched to the field shoot. Both of them bundled in parkas, washed in the winter sun. He tugged her against him, wrapping her close. Her eyes fluttered closed, and he dipped his nose into her hair, his mittened hand gripping her waist. The steam rising from their breath made it look like they were incinerating.

Cass felt her cheeks redden. "Where did that come from?" she mumbled.

"Turns out the paps got more photos than just you and Big D."

The movie switched to a split-screen, Karl and Stephen howling on one side, trying to narrate a shot of Josh not-so-subtly inching closer to Cass during a break in filming on the other.

"I'm free, and if you'll have me, I'm yours. No secrets. Nothing hidden. I am so sorry I wasn't open with you. But I want you to know me, and I want to spend as long as it takes to know everything about you."

"Josh—"

"And I don't fucking care about distance. We'll find a way. I just don't want to be apart from you anymore. And if you'll be with me now, I am never letting you go again."

The man who had hidden himself, held himself in check, wasn't standing in front of her. The look on his face was open, clear, and begging for her answer.

The tight grip that had held her heart for months released. "Say it."

Josh tipped his head back and yelled into the theatre. "I love Cassidy St. Claire, and I need everyone to know it!"

A whoop went up from her friends surrounding her. She traced the angle of his jaw that would clench whenever he was stressed. She ran her fingers over the ridge of his brow that would crease when he argued with someone and would soften when he saw her. Over the spot on his cheeks she knew would turn into divots any second.

A face she already knew so well, and still so much more to learn.

She curled a fist into his shirt to pull him closer. "You're not bad either, Sexy Dimples."

"You need to do better than that," he said. He sealed the length of his body to hers, winding his hand into her hair to tug her head back and force her eyes to meet his, narrowed with a hungry gleam. "Say it."

"I love you." Cass giggled. "I'm yours."

He dipped his forehead to hers, eyes closed, thumbs swiping

over her cheeks. "Excellent," he breathed. "Now let's go sit down and finish watching how beautiful you are. Back row. So I can put my hand up your shirt."

"And then?" she asked, smiling so hard her cheeks hurt.

"And then we get the fuck out of here, and we do whatever you want, as long as it's together."

EPILOGUE

THE INTERVIEWER PACED THE SOUND STAGE, FIDDLING WITH THE microphone clipped to her shirt. Everything looked in order. Thank god the production crew remembered to set up the low-slung director's chairs instead of the standard, tall size.

The clause was highlighted in the contract. *Do not make her climb anything. Bad knee. We all heard what happened last time this detail was forgotten.*

He'd gone on the warpath before she'd talked him down, and still he'd cut the interview after three minutes.

She sneaked a glance at the open door. Nothing.

"Are they on set yet?" she asked the PA.

"They're just getting out of makeup."

Cool. Great. She smoothed her hair and lapped the stage again, jumping when the producer's voice buzzed in her earpiece.

"They're on their way."

"Thanks," she croaked.

She'd interviewed loads of famous people before. But not the creative team behind her favourite movie of all time.

A lyrical laugh sounded from down the hall, and moments later, a short woman waltzed through the doorway, followed closely by a man wearing head-to-toe black, their hands tucked together. He was leaning over to whisper in her ear, a grin just visible, and a fresh peel of laughter rang across the stage. The woman turned a bright smile to the interviewer, and the grin on the man faded into a polite nod.

The interviewer blew out a breath. This was it. She was interviewing Josh Graham and Cassidy St. Claire.

She strode up to them, holding out her hand like a lifeline, her smile splitting her cheeks. "Ms. St. Claire! Mr. Graham! I'm a huge fan of yours! I can't believe I get to talk with you today!"

So much for being cool.

"The pleasure is ours," the woman said, grasping her outstretched hand between her own. "And please, call me Cass."

"Mr. Graham is fine," he said, giving his own brief shake, and Cass elbowed him. The famous dimples creased his cheeks as he smiled down at Cass's exasperated eye roll. "You can call me Josh. Always love to meet a fan."

Whoa. She'd shaken hands with Josh Graham and Cassidy St. Claire. And that's why he had been voted Sexiest Man Behind the Camera. The interviewer felt a warm glow rush through her at the sight of their exchanged glances, and she clasped her hands in front of her.

Get it together. Fangirling could come later.

She motioned for them to take their seats, Josh lending Cass a hand to settle in the low chair, before angling his chair closer to hers. The interviewer took her place, tested microphone levels, and turned her attention to the couple who, along with several others on the crew, were up for a slew of awards.

"Can I ask you about *SD*?" she blurted. "If you don't mind?"

"Of course," Josh said. He absently reached over the chair's arms to grasp Cass's hand, interlacing his fingers into her. "What would you like to know?"

Sirius Darker had captivated her from the moment she saw it. She picked up the book the next day, a second-hand paperback with an original cracked cover, then broke down and picked up another with an original movie poster cover. Then she made her brother see it with her, then her boyfriend, then her mom. When she got home tonight, she'd watch it again, to celebrate meeting the director and costume designer.

She'd seen it so many times she could recite the plot from seven different angles without a script.

"Sirius, the brightest star in the night sky, darkens with no warning. Scientists across the globe race to determine the cause. It shouldn't run out of fuel for a billion years. No black holes. Nothing makes sense. Until Dr. Amelia Andersen discovers an alien species has built a Dyson sphere around the star to harness its energy, the hyper-massive infrastructure blocking the star's light. She convinces the governing bodies on earth to send her into space to investigate. Little does she know her former lover, Dr. Rykoff, has been thwarting her attempts at winning the bid to take the journey, much like the movie *Contact*. But unlike *Contact*, not only does she convince her partner of her findings, and why it should be her and not the robot-led mission he fights for, he joins her on the trip to space and sacrifices himself to repair the ship so she can make contact with the alien race and return home."

"So I've been told," he said, looking more amused than bored with her rambling.

The interviewer clasped her hands in her lap. "It's about fighting for what you believe in, even when everyone is against you. It's about doing the right thing, even when it's scary. It's about admitting you're wrong, and standing beside the person you love, and accepting forgiveness even after betrayal."

"That about sums it up," Josh said, grinning at her. *Oh my god. Josh Graham is grinning at me.* He continued, "I should have hired you to write my pitch letters."

Cass clucked her tongue and shook her head. "I doubt she was even born when *Sirius Darker* came out."

"I was alive," the interviewer insisted.

Sirius Darker had hit theatres a month before her third birthday.

"What did you want to ask about it?" Cass said.

The interview shifted to the front edge of her chair. "How did you know? The book is so campy. I've seen original storyboards with crazy special effects written into the margins. How did you know to strip the film back?"

Josh tilted his head at Cass, and an entire silent conversation passed between the two. "You tell it this time," he said.

"Because even with giant methane-breathing aliens and faster-than-light spaceships, it was a human story first. We didn't want to hide that under a layer of polyurethane for our actors to be piled under." Cass wobbled her head. "Plus, it saved us a ton of money on the budget."

"Westy still says saving that million dollars funded her next project," Josh joked.

Perfect segue into what they were here to discuss. "Not like budget is an issue for you anymore," the interviewer pressed on, setting up the audience for the few people unfamiliar with the story. "*Sonnets* continues to be the darling of the awards season, having swept the Golden Globes and taking home the prestigious Palme d'Or at Cannes. You're up for your fourth Oscar nomination for Best Director, the film loosely based on how you two met. It's the first original screenplay you've received a nomination for, having won for Best Adapted Screenplay twice previously, for *Sirius Darker* and *Undertow*, the sequel to *Tideways*. If you win for *Sonnets*, it'll be your second Oscar for Best Director, and if buzz is any indication, you're the front-runner for the award."

Josh shrugged.

The interviewer turned to Cass. "You and Mr. Graham have worked together on every project since *Sirius Darker* erupted into the zeitgeist almost twenty-six years ago, having famously met on set."

Cass pressed her lips together to stifle another giggle, and

Josh shot her a wicked smile, running his tongue over his canines. "Something like that," he said.

"You're up for Best Costume Design for *Sonnets*, your fifth nomination. Every film you costume has been drastically different. Your last film had bright palettes and a high-concept approach to design, while this film is muted."

"At least until the midpoint," Cass agreed.

The interviewer steeled herself. The film's dramatic shift had been criticized as reductive by some; lauded as evocative by others. "At the midpoint, the film overblows into colour, almost hypersaturated. Why did you make that choice?"

The couple exchanged another look. "We debated this a long time," Cass said. "It's not the most subtle choice we could've made …"

"But we decided we didn't want subtle," he finished. "I spent the first half of my life asleep. Then I met Cass, and she made the world come alive for me. The colour, the brightness. It's all her."

If the interviewer had known she'd get teary today, she would have worn waterproof mascara.

Josh brushed his silver hair back from his eyes. "I was an unknown hack when I submitted my first film to a festival—"

"*Oblivion* was great!" Cass insisted and turned to the interviewer. "If you can find a copy anywhere, you should watch—"

"The remake, when I finally got my hands on a decent costume designer," he cut back in, and Cass clicked her tongue. "As I was saying, if I hadn't submitted that film, we never would have met. Taking that chance was the luckiest moment of my life. This film captures what that time felt like."

The interviewer cleared her throat, muting the PA's sniffling in her earpiece. "And what made this the right time to make this film?"

Cass smiled as he squeezed her hand. "A long time ago, he promised me sonnets."

ACKNOWLEDGMENTS

When I sat down to write A Better Proposal, I had no idea that Cass would demand her own story, or that Josh would be her match. So many people helped bring them to life. Whether or not our conversations ended up on the page, this book shows hundreds of hours of love and care.

Firstly, to the entire cast and creative team of The Mummy 1999. My love for this movie runs true and deep for a million reasons, not in the least because it was one of the first movies my husband and I saw in theatres together. We fell in love right alongside Rick and Evie.

Beta readers are unsung heroes, so let me sing. To the Beta Late Than Never crew—Ivy, Marlee, Cece, Karlie, and Mimi. Your energy, kindness, and support helped make this story what it is today - extra scenes and all. Riya and Luna, you may have come into the group later, but sharing ideas with you has been everything. You are all funny, gorgeous, brilliant women. Kelsey, same. I live for your commentary! Denise, it brings me so much joy to share this with you early again. Thank you!!

To my street team! Thank you for your hyping and sharing and unhinged DMs when you were reading ahead of everyone else. A, Annie, Beckie & Jamie, Harp, Hrishika, Iesha, Maéva, and Tru - I am so grateful!!

The Literary Poutine Posse. Thank you to this group of baddies who hype each other up and share everything from arcane indie publishing info to cowboy thirst traps.

My editor, Kelsey Holts, who was thorough and clever with

her work. This book wouldn't be what it is without you, and I'm sorry for all the corrections I missed.

Writing this book, I learned more about film, law, and the Calgary arts scene than I could ever fit within these pages. Jocelyn, thank you for all your insight into Young Canadians, theatre, and the scarcity of nude unitards. Rob, thanks for talking stories within stories, science fiction, and filming timelines. I can smell the sawdust from here. Kat, you solved plot holes I didn't know needed solving with our costume and wardrobe conversations. For legal reasons, everything Robin told me about law is for creative purposes only and does not reflect her or any one person's experience in the profession ... specifically.

Mom, thank you for everything. Please don't read this one.

Mr. Douglas, who listened to me talk about these two for almost two years and is still overprotective of Cass. I told you she'd be fine. Your love and encouragement is everything. I love you.

ALSO BY ELLORY DOUGLAS

NOVELS

A Bluebird Sky

A Better Proposal - book 1

A Better Engagement - book 1.5

A Sure Thing - book 3

SHORT STORIES

The Hand-Off - find it in Love Between the Lines

The Mer-Mate: an aquatic monster romance

ABOUT THE AUTHOR

Ellory loves cinnamon roll book boyfriends, everything pink, and summer evenings on the patio with her husband and a glass of wine. She lives, works, and writes swoony contemporary romance in and about Calgary, Canada. You can usually find her outside, even when it's -30 C.

instagram.com/authorellorydouglas

goodreads.com/ellorydouglas

www.ingramcontent.com/pod-product-compliance
Lightning Source LLC
Chambersburg PA
CBHW051317250626
47155CB00007B/2363